facing us

facing us

NICCI HARRIS

also by nicci harris

The Kids of The District

Facing Us

Our Thing

Cosa Nostra

Her Way

His Pretty Little Burden

His Pretty Little Queen

Their Broken Legend

ISBN ebook: 978-0-646-81963-1

ISBN print: 978-0-646-81116-1

Edited by Writing Evolution. @writingevolution. www.writingevolution.co.uk

Internal graphics by Nicci Harris

Cover design by Nicci Harris

Nicci illustration holding kindle by @lamdin.designs

dedication

For my best friend.
You big weirdo.
Trim your beard.
You look like a hobo.

facing us

song list

Kids of the District
Facing Us
The Prequel

1. Ophelia—The Lumineers
2. Seize the Day – Avenged Sevenhold
3. Burn For You – John Farnham
4. Firework – Katy Perrry
5. Penny Lane – The Beatles
6. Only You – Joshua Radin
7. Someone Else's Life – Joshua Radin
8. Sex on Fire – Kings of Leon
9. My Immortal – Evanescence
10. Heartbeats – Jose Gonzalez
11. A Thousand Years – Christina Perri
12. Scars – Allison Iraheta
13. A Little's Enough – Angels & Airwaves
14. Paper Walls – Yellowcard
15. Shadows and Regrets – Yellowcard

16. Fighting – Yellowcard

17. Stay Alive – Jose Gonzalez

18. Lay Me Down – Sam Smith, John Legend

19. A Little Too Much – Shawn Mendes

20. Someone To You – Banners

21. Breathe Me – Sia

22. A Whiter Shade of Pale – Procol Harum

23. Wildflowers – Tom Petty

24. Tonight, Tonight – The Smashing Pumpkins

25. Warrior – Demi Lovato

26. This City – Sam Fischer

27. Knockin' On Heaven's Door – Bob Dylan

28. Fade Into You – Mazzy Star

Go to Spotify to listen.

Facing Us

"i inhale

—*courage and exhale fear."*

one: blesk

Blesk

CRADLED in the warmth of my bed, surrounded by the smell of daisies, peaches, and home, I'm almost content. *Almost.* The bed dips, and I recognise that feeling even from somewhere between slumber and wake. Rolling away from his presence, my body curls to the side. I hug my *Buffy the Vampire Slayer* pillow, slowly drifting back to incoherence, hoping the feel of him beside me is merely a dream. Slipping back into the nothingness sleep usually brings, I breathe heavier and relax into an exhale. But then I feel movement between my legs and his breath spilling down on me —hard, fast, and hot.

My eyes snap open.

Usually, I wake up with him on top of me, but today he's manoeuvring to push inside me from behind. My fingers claw frantically at the comforter.

Comforter —*what an ironic name.*

A moan of discomfort escapes me, and I attempt to recoil by squeezing my thighs together, squeezing my eyes together, but it's an attempt to no avail.

"Thank you," he groans into my ear, adding more pressure. Pressure as he pries my thighs apart with his hands. Pressure on my spine as he envelops my small frame. Pressure from his sharp thrusts inside me.

A sudden bump brings me back to consciousness, and lights and horns inundate me... I must have drifted off.

Swallowing down memories of the past, I focus on my future. A brighter one. For most of the morning, I've sat in the back of a taxi, resisting the urge to jump out. Leaving the District after two decades is going to be a huge change. So much has happened here. In many ways, I should be glad. It's an area apart from the rest of the country, with both a beating heart and sharp claws. As I watch the landscape change from urban to rural, I'm reminded of how isolated the District really is.

Three years ago, my brother left to get his bachelor's in Commerce many miles from the District. Since then, I've basically been an only child. I haven't seen him for months and haven't lived within walking distance of him for years. My brother is four years my senior, and though we are like chalk and cheese now, for most of my childhood, we were inseparable. My father says that from the moment I came into my brother's life, Erik was undeniably smitten, extremely overprotective, and accepting of all responsibility for his new little sister. But I've changed so much since he's been gone. A lot has changed.

As the taxi driver pulls up alongside my new university campus, I blink with nervous tension out the window at the beautiful deep red brick walls, and hustle and bustle of students arriving. After I snap myself out of that state of awe, I pay the fare, then drop my baggage and guitar case off at the campus reception. Even though I know I should make my way to my room, I seek out the library instead.

I've spent an enormous amount of time in libraries, favouring the company of the characters in print to those in the real world. I have travelled with Huck and Tom, fought in wars, learnt from Atticus Finch, and have fallen in love with the likes of Angel Clare and Romeo Montague.

As I approach the library, I am once again awe struck. It is an impressive piece of architecture, stretching ten stories high. When I move inside, I can see all the way to the top. The stacks spiral to its peak, and it takes my breath away. It smells like leather and dust; I absolutely love it.

My dad texts me just as I slump down onto one of the many multicoloured bean bags scattered across the first floor.

> Dad: You only have six of your nine lives left, Kitten. Remember that and let Erik take care of you. Don't be stubborn. He wants to be there for you, so just let him.

I am now my little family's only surviving female member. My mother died a few years ago after a long fight against cancer. She wasn't my mother for my whole life; I'm adopted. However, no one else has ever come close to fitting the bill. With her long, wavy, chocolate-brown hair and her big, kind, brown eyes, she'd resembled an Arabian princess to me.

"How'd I know I'd find you here?" I hear my brother Erik call out from a distant stack. His voice carries through the library and, much to my embarrassment, turns many scowling faces.

I raise my finger, pressing it against my lips. "*Shhhh...*" I whisper as he approaches. "I'm not sure if you've ever been in one of these before, but you're supposed to be quiet." I force a smile as he sits down by my side. We stare at each other for a few moments and I narrow my eyes as I take him all in.

Erik has a casual confidence to him. He's self-assured and forthright and has always been much more interesting than I am. He's really tall —or at least it feels that way to me. He fulfils the Australian stereotype to a T with his sandy-blond hair, sun-kissed skin, and the athletic physique of a man who spends his afternoons at the gym.

He grins at me. "How was the drive?"

I slouch with a sigh. "Non-eventful."

"Miss me?"

"I was miserable," I mumble. Then I grin at him and add, "So it was just like having you at home."

"Oh, very funny." He clears his throat, looking almost disappointed by my joke. "Dad good?"

"Yep, he's fine," I say.

What next? Is he going to ask me about the weather?

"It's been fucking hot, hey?"

I snort.

He rolls his eyes. "Trust you to find your way into the lamest part of the university." Erik takes Jack Kerouac's *On The Road* from my hand and tosses it onto a random shelf. I make a mental note to return it to its rightful place. An awkward silence hangs between us. It's been so long since I've seen him.

Desperate to say something to end the insufferable quiet, I say, "Have you seen the size of this library?"

"Oh, no, never, Bebe. Not once in the three years I've been

going here." He grins at me through parted lips that display his near perfect teeth.

You know I hate being called that.

"Sarcasm is the weakest form of humour," I mention.

"It's also the most popular."

"Well, it's amazing in here," I state very matter-of-factly. "And a brain is wasted on you."

Erik erupts into laughter, and the air in my chest slowly eases out.

Thank God.

"Well I suppose I'm lucky girls don't like me for my brain. Ain't that right?"

"Well, maybe they would, if you actually--"

He interjects with a silly snoring sound. "*And* now I'm bored. You're late for an afternoon of orienting yourself with university life." As Erik stands, he offers me his hand "Up."

"Huh?"

"Your orientation, Blesk."

"A few more minutes?" I plead.

The university is overwhelming, and although my actual reason for being here excites me, the renowned student life-style has the opposite effect.

"No one puts Bebe in the corner," he mocks.

I loathe that reference.

"Erik, please don't say that in front of people," I beg, frowning up at him.

"Get up, Blesk." His smile tightens and he waves his arm insistently. I stare at his outstretched hand, willing myself to take it.

Well, I suppose I can't hide in here all day.

I place my palm in his, and he helps me to my feet.

After flattening my skirt down my thighs and tossing my

blonde hair to one side, I peer at him sheepishly. "Do I look okay?"

He scoffs. "You know you're pretty." Then he pauses to look me over. "Everyone with eyes thinks that, Blesk."

Sighing, I scoop my satchel up and swing it over my shoulder. "Okay. Let's do this"

"Your hair is getting so long, Goldilocks." He flicks a rogue strand off my face.

"Don't call me that," I grumble, stepping behind him to exit through the sliding doors.

He chuckles. "Grumpy."

"I'm not. Sorry." That dream has me in a funk. I fidget with a few frayed fibres on my shirt's hem. "I'm just nervous."

Turning to face me, he rubs my shoulders with his big hands. "Don't be silly. You'll be fine. I'm like a god in this place."

And so modest.

He spins on his heels and wanders towards the outskirts of the orientation festival.

Rolling my eyes, I chase after him, trying to appear as though I belong. "Only in this place? You're slipping."

Erik ignores my comment, and as we pass other students, he either offers them a charming smile of recognition or a flirtatious wink. "I see nothing has changed," I mutter.

"Like I said" –he grins at me– "I'm like a god here."

THERE ARE hundreds of students moving around the oval. But the sun is blazing in a cloudless sky, which, to my delight, means I can wear my sunglasses and hide my anxiety behind them. A stage at the front is surrounded by small stalls, which appear to be run by students advertising an assortment of extracurricular activities. The student guild. Sporting groups. Debating.

Socialites scurry around me. It's colourful and noisy. Most of the girls I pass are wearing jeans and sneakers, making me feel even more uncomfortable in my skirt and wedges. I wish that there were uniforms.

I wish I didn't wish that there were uniforms.

I tense when Erik places his hand on the small of my back. He can be so overbearing and domineering, but I know his sole interest is in keeping me safe. Keeping me near. Close... I know this. Still, his possessiveness makes my stomach stir. Like, maybe things haven't changed for him. Maybe I'm still someone who needs protecting. Maybe -

My thoughts are interrupted when he suddenly guides me to one side. My breath hitches as we approach a group of smiling faces, all of which are eagerly looking at me.

"Hey, dickhead!" A young man laughs as he and Erik share a strong handshake. "Is this Blesk?" He turns his keen eyes towards me.

Erik chuckles at the greeting. "Yes, this is my little sister Blesk."

"Hi, B. I'm Jaxon," he says, extending his hand for me to shake. "Heard a lot about you. You don't mind if I call you B do you?"

"Yes, she does," Erik chimes in.

"No, no, I don't," I reply, shaking his hand. Shaking hands is *weird*. "I may not answer to it though."

They all laugh.

Was that funny?

"So this is the famous younger Bellamy, ay?" Jaxon tucks his hands into his pockets. "You never told me your sister was hot, Erik."

Erik stiffens. "Jaxon, jeez dude, she's my little sister! Show some respect! You got it?"

I squirm. Couldn't he have waited until I was gone to say that?

Jaxon is a stocky guy. One of those high protein, CrossFit types. He stands with his biceps protruding at his sides, as if he's posing for a bodybuilding magazine. With short dusty-brown hair, deep-grey eyes, and a sharply defined jawline, he'd be attractive if he wasn't such a jock.

"Now I'm not saying this just to piss you off, but she just got 50% hotter to me." He smirks as he rakes his eyes down my body.

Wow, I'm standing right here.

A pretty blonde holds out her hand for me to take.

Another handshake.

O...kay, so I'm a hand-shaker now.

"Sorry about them; they're Neanderthals," she says. "I'm Pembie." She's model-level attractive. Taller than me, slightly slimmer, leggy, and with dark-brown eyes not unlike mine. Her clearly expensive jeans fit her perfectly and her makeup is glamorously applied by an evidently talented hand. From the look of her brows, I would say she isn't a natural blonde like me; however, she pulls it off. I can't help but feel a little intimidated despite her friendly introduction.

"Hi," I say, returning her pleasantries as the boys bark among themselves. "I'm Blesk."

Her attention is suddenly redirected to the stage, and she punches Jaxon hard before telling him to hush. "Konnor's up next. Shut up!"

Still wincing from her jab, Jaxon gently shoves her back. Going by the scowl that transforms her face, his gesture doesn't appear to be graciously received.

Erik leans in next to my ear. "Our friend is doing a

speech. *God* only knows how he got the gig. I think his parents either paid the lecturers off or he's fucking them for grades."

"Why would you say that?"

While obviously wary of eavesdropping, Erik mutters quietly, "Because he's a full-blown functional alcoholic. Pretty much everyone knows it, but no one talks about it."

"There he is!" Pembie points enthusiastically at a guy striding onto the stage. The oval erupts in whistles and hoots.

Air floods my lungs and my breath catches when he turns to face the engaged crowd. He's undeniably gorgeous. And while I can't make out his eye colour or the exact shade of brown his hair is, I can tell he's strong by the way his shoulders and chest fill his shirt.

"Slater! Yewww," Jaxon yells, cupping his mouth with both hands.

"Konnor!" Pembie claps and screams through her enormous beaming smile.

"Hey, everyone, I'm Konnor Slater," he begins. His husky voice makes me feel a little lightheaded. I shuffle my feet nervously while my eyes stay anchored on the stage. "Education is not an option. It is not a right. It is the foundation of human existence. Education is not for the young, the clever, or the articulate. It's for everyone. It's not for a term, a semester, or a year. Education is forever."

Although the crowd gave him a big rowdy welcome, they are all now silent, a clear show of respect for his words, specifically, and his presence, in general.

Konnor continues, "I would love to stand up here and tell you that you have the option to embrace or ignore education, that you are privileged enough to choose, but in my opinion there is only one choice. Education is in everything you do.

It's in the way you dress, in the way you move. It produces greatness and it tears it down. It is the backbone of every inspiration. But, most importantly, it enables.

"It enables us to be anything we want to be. I know for a fact that intelligence is not the foundation of success." He pauses momentarily. "I'm standing up here, aren't I?" He chuckles at his own expense, invoking laughter and applause from the audience. "It is not money or family. It has nothing to do with your past. All that matters is right now! The decision you make to move forward. The decisions you make for your future. The past is just that —it's passed."

Pacing the stage with the microphone clutched in his hand, Konnor glances around the crowd. "Education will change your world; it will open it up and brighten it. Count yourself lucky every day and teach everyone around you — enable them. Enable them to teach you. Thank you." He begins to walk off stage, but then he stops to yell out, "Watch me leave, ladies."

And he's a show pony too...

I let out a big breath I hadn't realised I was holding and then attempt to tame what feels like a ridiculously wide grin. Looking around, I realise that having watched him interact so seamlessly with hundreds of people in such a compelling way hasn't only made me admire him; it's made every other girl around me admire him too. They are all flushed and restless.

Konnor Slater.

The crowd applauds as he descends from the stage. Pembie claps so hard, I swear she is going to bruise her palms. Craning her neck to find him in the crowd, she giddily moves towards him.

"He was really good," I say to Erik as I watch Konnor

envelop Pembie in his arms. They look wonderful together. She obviously idolises him.

Erik scoffs. "Yeah, he knows it too."

"Like you can talk, Mr Centre Stage." I smirk.

"God" –he points both thumbs at his chest– "remember?" He laughs and then his attention is redirected to an attractive young girl sitting on the grass in front of us. He winks at her.

I snap my fingers at him to draw his attention back to me. "I could never stand up there and do that," I say.

Looking at me, he shrugs. "What? Yeah right. You *sing* in public, Blesk."

I shake my head fiercely. "That's *totally* different. I don't even look up, and I don't interact. I just pretend no one's around."

His eyes crinkle as he grins at me. I'm immediately suspicious. "And on that topic," he says, grabbing a slip of paper out of his back pocket. "I got you a job."

My jaw drops. "Come again?" I take the slip from his hand and read the typed text, mouthing it as I go.

Grill Bar O Campus, Tuesday & Fridays, 7:00 p.m. Marcus Donnelly 0407789659.

I peer up at him questioningly. "What, like waitressing?"

He turns his nose up. "No way. It's a gig. They want you to play a few sets, two nights a week. Marcus listened to 'Hero Boy' on my phone and loved it."

Not that song, Erik.

I get lightheaded for a moment. "I don't want to play here," I say, trying not to sound ungrateful. "I have to see these people every day."

I can usually lose myself in the music enough to forget about the audience. What differs greatly in this situation is that I will see my audience in class, at the coffee shop, in my dorm, everywhere. I can't pretend they don't exist.

"Whoa, you have officially lost all colour in your face," Erik mocks. He cups my cheeks and directs my nervous gaze to him. "Pretend it's just me out there."

"What are you two talking about?" Jaxon asks, moving closer to us.

Erik lowers his hands and wraps one protectively around my shoulders, squeezing gently. "Blesk's gonna sing at The Grill a few nights a week." He sounds eager and filled with pride. All I feel is nausea.

Jaxon chuckles at my forced smile. "You look shit scared."

I clear my throat. "No, I'll be fine. I just, I ummm, I'm *really* thirsty," I stammer. Whirling away from his scrutiny, I trip over my own feet. Erik catches me by the elbow, steadying me. Jaxon cracks up.

"I'm fine." I rub my face, trying to hide my discomfort, but to no avail. "Seriously, I'm fine." Jaxon positions himself at my side and looks at me with what I believe is pity.

"Are you going to do it?" Erik asks. "I can call Marcus right now and tell him no. I can make something up, like, you're a big bebe and don't want to sing in public." He and Jaxon both chuckle.

Why does he insist on making me feel small on purpose? Using that stupid word to describe me when he knows I can't stand it?

"No, don't. I'll do it," I say, presenting a more believable smile.

"What do you play?" Jaxon asks, folding his arms across his chest.

Yes, Jaxon, I can see your muscles.

I slide the strap of my bag across my shoulder. "Just an acoustic guitar."

As the wind increases, my skirt shimmies up in the breeze. I use one hand to hold my skirt down and the other to keep my hair out of my face. Jaxon notices my discomfort and grins. My brows furrow. I tilt my head at him as he takes a nice, long, noticeable look at my thighs while my skirt swishes around them.

"Don't be humble, Blesk. She writes her own stuff, sings, and plays. She's unreal," Erik boasts.

Jaxon smirks and cocks a brow suggestively. "Can't wait to see you up there."

I refuse to acknowledge his double entendre. "Thanks."

AFTER WE COLLECT my suitcase and guitar from the administration office, we make our way to my dormintory —my new home.

Eeek.

As we approach the front steps, the sun starts to set behind low lying clouds and the chill of the hour nips at my skin. I peer down at my small, unimpressively small, baggage. It only has my essential possessions. I don't really do clutter. Or trinkets. Or posters. They're a waste of time, space, and money and often only remind me that I'm not normal. That my life has been anything but. It is much more like *Buffy The Vampire Slayer* than *Dawson's Creek*.

Once we pass the peculiar gargoyles that guard the steps at my dorm's entrance, I'm surprised by how modern the rest of the building is. The hallways are lit around the clock, and it's a female-only dormitory, which sets Erik at ease.

I approach room seventy-three, but then suddenly freeze at its door. This will be my home for the next year.

I'm excited!

I'm crazy scared!

Universities see brilliance, innovation, and creative genius stream through them in the thousands every year. This room has probably been the keeper of an incredible mind. I drop my baggage on the floor and stand in front of the door, mystified by its presence. I wouldn't be surprised if it needs a secret password.

It'll be a part of my life now but more importantly, for a little while, I'll be a part of its.

"You gonna go in?" Erik asks, eyeing me questioningly.

I sigh. "Yes, it's just …" I spin to look at him. "This is my home for the next year, and I want to really take it all in."

He snorts. "Weirdo."

I take an exaggerated, deep breath. After savouring the moment for a little longer, I then slide my key into the hole and twist it until it clicks. The door swings open. I pick up my things and step into the room slowly.

"Hi!" a girl yells, jumping up from her seated position on the room's central rug. "Hi, I'm Elise."

She yanks my guitar case from my hand, carries it over to a bed, and drops it on the mattress. I like that she doesn't try to shake my hand; we're already past formalities.

"This is your bed. I've been waiting for you all day. Did you go to orientation? How old are you? I've been so nervous to meet you. I really hope we can be friends. I really hope we get along. It'll make this year so much easier. Sorry. I don't mean to come on so strong."

I freeze, wide-eyed and a little overwhelmed by her peppiness. "Umm, hi. I'm Blesk," I finally manage.

"What kind of name is that? Is it religious or something,

like bless?" she asks straightway with way too much eager-ness, jiggling in place.

Erik strides in. "Whoa, slow down, kid; she just got here. How much coffee have you had?" He chuckles.

Her beam drops as she stares at Erik, who's now looking smug. "Hi," she murmurs with a gulp. "Just one coffee."

He gives her a slightly patronising glance. "I didn't actu-ally need an answer to that. It was rhetorical. But, no, her name is not religious; it's just her name. She's twenty-one and yes, we just left orientation. Calm down, kid."

My mouth is still open, mumbling an answer to one or maybe all of her questions, before I realise that Erik has just addressed them.

I can answer for myself, Erik.

"Sorry." I walk over to Elise, who looks like she's just taken a punch. "I'm Blesk Bellamy, and it's really nice to meet you."

I glare at Erik, flashing him a firm look of disapproval. She watches Erik as he peers around the space with scrutiny.

Elise is small and petite in every way. If Pippi Long-stocking and Edward Scissorhands had a daughter, she would look like Elise. Beady blue eyes peer through brown horn-rimmed glasses, and the sweetness of her freckles contradict the attitude of her black eyeliner and mismatched nail polish. She's quite striking.

The room is smaller than I'd expected, but it has nearly everything I could possibly need, so no complaints here — two beds, two desks, and two walk-in wardrobes. Elise's side already has her personal touches influencing the space. She displays, in one fashion or another, a lot of traditional girl-trends. Katy Perry. Lady Gaga. Ryan Gosling.

I sigh as I study my undecorated side of the room. I hope

she won't be disappointed by my lack of self-defining acces-
sories. I'm just not that kind of girl.

She leans closer to me and whispers, "Is that your
boyfriend?"

"No, that's my brother."

"Ah." She crosses her legs in front of her, maybe waiting
for Erik to leave her room.

Our room?

Erik stops and looks at me. "Right, you okay, beautiful?"

I glance at Elise, unsettled by Erik's endearment. "Yes,
yes I am," I say, and I actually mean it.

Erik flashes Elise a smile and leans in to peck me on the
cheek. "First night away from home. Are you sure you don't
wanna sleep on a mattress in my dorm? My roommate will
be at his girlfriend's."

A sickening flutter fills my stomach. "Yes, I'm sure."

"What if you, ya know" –he lowers his voice to barely a
whisper– "have a bad dream?"

"I'll be fine," I say as convincingly as I can.

Will you really, Blesk?

He nods. "Okay, Bebe." He turns to Elise and his grin
widens with mischief. "Call her Bebe; it drives her cra—"

"Time to leave, Erik," I cut in, placing both hands on his
chest and pushing him until he's just outside the doorway.

He chuckles at me sweetly. "Alrighty. I have classes all
day tomorrow, but I'll pick you up from here at six fifteen to
take you to The Grill."

"Yep, okay." I gently shove him again so he knows I'm
ready to close the door.

He stands in place. "Goodnight then."

"Goodnight."

ELISE CAN CERTAINLY TALK; she just rambles, giving information freely without any contemplation for how little she knows me. I begin to unpack my silly little case, removing toiletries, bedding, and clothes, while nodding and gesturing appropriately towards her when warranted.

"I didn't stay for the orientation festival," she says. "It was so packed when I went to look and I was all alone. Everyone already seemed to know each other, so that's when I came to the conclusion that as roommates, we need to stick together. I mean, we are both new and—"

I am going to have trouble keeping up with you, Elise.

Despite accepting a kind of minimalistic existence, I'm still starting to feel melancholic and sad at how easy it is for me to squeeze my entire life into this space on the left side of this room. Taking a bubble-wrapped parcel out, I unwrap it to reveal perhaps my only ornament — a palm-sized metal unicorn, which holds unparalleled sentimental value.

Okay, so I have one trinket.

Staring at its sharp, pointy horn, I run my index finger over the right uplifted front hoof, shivering as I remember the day he'd given it to me. I consciously take a deep breath in before exhaling slowly. The unicorn goes on my bedside table so that I can see it every morning when I wake up.

Elise continues, "*You* don't know many people, and *I* don't know many people. Oh wait... You don't know many people, right?"

I shake my head. "Only Erik."

She grins wider. "Cool. My mum went here. She said her roommate was like family. They even requested to stay together second year when they switched rooms and are still friends today. In her first week at uni—"

"I think," I interrupt, then pause to give her time to halts her mouth's momentum. "I'd love to listen to some music while I unpack. What do you think?"

She brightens and bounces to her feet. "I'll put my Spotify mix on!"

"Sounds great," I agree, watching as she moves with such strange buoyancy around the room.

Elise is like a cartoon character —bouncing instead of walking and beaming with joy instead of offering a simple smile.

I think I like this girl.

While she puts some pop sounding track on, I finish unpacking. Bobbing my head to the music, I grab my hair-brush and pull my —too long —blonde hair up into a high bun. I collect an assortment of products to take to the shower, as well as grab some lounging around clothes: black yoga pants, a mint tee-shirt, and dance flats.

"I'm going to have a shower," I say. "Where's the bathroom?"

She bounds toward me, and I take an instinctive step back, giving her space to join me in the doorway.

"Well, it's the third door on your left," she explains, gesturing with her hands. "But the first two showers are gross, so use the third or fourth. Also, there are only four showers on this whole floor so try to use them off-peak. Ya know, so you get hot water. That's what my mum told me. This was her building too." She takes a big breath. "See, full of useful information."

I offer her a genuinely grateful look. "Thank you. See you soon... *roomy.*" She brightens and I return her smile before wandering down the hallway and into the quiet of the bathroom.

two: konnor

Konnor

I WATCH as she sucks in little breaths through her pink lips and moans softly in her slumber. She is on her stomach, her hair creating a golden crown around her pillow. I like looking at her. Pemberton is a nicer person when she's asleep. The issues start when she opens those lips of hers and they produce words. Her beauty disappears when that poison spits from her, disarming all in its path. I wish I could love her.

I wish she wasn't such a bitch.

I've spent the last hour inside her, and I love the way she feels beneath me and on top of me —anywhere around me, really. I like her name, her brown irises, and her blonde hair. But I don't *love* her. How can I when she doesn't laugh? When she scrutinises everything I do? When she judges everyone around her?

I run my fingers through her golden hair; it reminds me of both a vanishing memory and a promise forever unfinished. She makes a gentle sound of pleasure in response to my touch. Is this the best it can be between us? Will she always be second best? Second to whom though, I'd like to know...

You do know who, Konnor.

It's been at least two hours since I've had a drink, and I'm feeling a lot of nervous tension. Everything is brighter, clearer, harder, and I'm thinking about her fucking hair, so it must be time to top-up. I roll off the mattress and try not to disturb the mean, hot, beautiful woman, snoring sweetly at my side. Sliding my boxers up, I wander sluggishly to the bar fridge in the kitchen.

I'm pleased with the apartment my parents have leased for me this year. It has enough space for Pemberton and I to exist in relative harmony. Although she has her own dorm room on campus, she seems to have almost moved in here. It's pretty swanky. I would have been happy on campus, but my folks had thought that adult accommodation would mean I'd become just that... an adult. This apartment *is* pretty fucking nice though. Pemberton likes nice things and I like being inside her, so we both benefit from this arrangement.

My studio is on the top floor. The views of busy suburban life are entertaining and, at times, beautiful. I have a doorman too, which makes me feel a little like James Bond.

After making myself a drink, I meander into the bathroom, ignoring my reflection as I enter. My clothes come off. The facet comes on, and I step over the shower hob and into the steamy enclosure.

I take a swig of my Jacks on the rocks before placing it on the tiled nib-wall beside me. The combination of my beverage and the water coming down hard and warm on my head revives my senses.

One thing Pemberton and I have in common is our love of daytime naps, or as her Italian family would say, siestas. I sleep a lot. I drink to feel normal. I sleep a lot because I drink to feel normal. Rinse and repeat. Which is why, at 6:30 p.m. on a Tuesday night, I'm just re-joining the waking world, whereas Erik and Jaxon will be at The Grill already, waiting for us.

"Konnor, you have a letter from the dean!" Pemberton's harsh voice startles me.

"Okay, just leave it on the table," I reply, lathering myself up and down.

As I bend down to wash my legs, my calves wince in agony. I need to go back to the gym; rugby practice was harder yesterday than it's been in years.

I've been playing since I was nine. I started not long after seeing my first game. And although I'd barely thrown a ball before that age, the sport had resonated with me and I with it. The outdoors, the contact, the team energy; it was everything I needed.

I finish off my drink and rinse the suds off my body, hoping Pemberton will surprise me by joining me. She won't though. She never does. She can't wear makeup in the shower. In my humble opinion, she looks like a million bucks without makeup, but that just isn't her style.

Why is she going through my mail?

I wander into the kitchen, still dripping wet, but lazily drying myself with a towel. "Where is it?" I ask.

Pemberton is sitting at the dining room table, her long naked legs poking out from underneath it. She's wearing my favourite jersey, and from this angle, I can tell she's not wearing any underwear.

Nice.

My gaze is quickly redirected when I notice the letter open in front of her.

"What the fuck? You opened my mail?" I snap. "When did we get there?"

Her eyes narrow into slits and her beauty vanishes. It happens so often. "Don't talk to me like that!" she hisses. "Do you need another drink or something?"

"Give me that!" I snatch the letter from her hand as she curses at me.

Mr B and Mrs R Slater,

Tuition for Konnor Slater (ID 109678) has been received. Please find enclosed invoice.

We would like to take this opportunity to thank you for your generous contribution to our new sporting complex. Attached for your records are the receipt and official sponsorship certification.

If you have any further queries, please do not hesitate to contact our office at 087654234

Kindest regards,
Dean Kevin Milner

STARING AT THE WORDS, I wonder how much money my parents actually have. They were able to prepay my tuition this year and somehow contribute to the new sporting precinct. Both of my parents are entrepreneurs, so to speak, but I've never been able to decipher whether they are disgustingly wealthy or just strategic fakers.

I quickly flick through the next few sheets, but then fold the letter and all its associated documentation back into the envelope. I don't want to see any monetary figures.

"Pem, it isn't even addressed to me. This is for my parents."

She stands with a huff. Grabbing a drink from the bar, she shoves it in my hand. "Here. This should stop your bitching."

Why the hell am I with her?

For her hair. Her eyes.

"Yes, Pemberton, I am well aware I drink too much. Thank you for enabling me." I scowl at her, but despite the manner with which she presented my drink, I take it anyway. I raise it, giving her a cocky smile. "Thank you!"

Sometimes, I search her perfect brown eyes intently, praying for them to expose some kind of gentleness or purity. They never do.

"What are you wearing?" she snipes, motioning to my naked body.

I wiggle my hips teasingly, my cock slapping my thighs as I do. "My birthday suit."

She rolls her eyes. "No, what are you wearing to the bar?"

I pinch her on the bum as I walk past her. "This," I say, walking into my room.

Pemberton groans at me as if I'm the most inconsiderate man on earth. "Seriously. I want to match!"

"It isn't a wedding, Pem. It's The Grill," I call back to her as I ruffle through my clothes, searching for a pair of jeans or, at the very least, a clean pair of track-pants.

"Do you care about me at all? I want us to look like a couple."

"We are a couple," I yell at her and then mutter under my breath, "A couple of what I dunno."

I can just faintly make out her snide mutters. "*Arsehole*" I think. "*Alcoholic*" perhaps. "*Jerk*."

I find a clean shirt. "White!"

Now shut up.

IT ONLY TOOK me five minutes to get dressed in semi-clean jeans and a shirt —a bloody perfect combo. But now I must wait for her majesty. I drink a few more bourbons as I do. Pemberton eventually makes an appearance, strutting her sexy body around in front of me. The teasing little minx. She's wearing a skin-tight white halter dress that shows off her exceptional thighs and grips her amazing arse. She looks beautiful, and, of course, I tell her as much. She actually smiles at me.

My hair is still damp by the time we leave the apartment. That sends her majesty up the wall, but I'm happily feeling the effects of my previous four bourbons, so I don't care. We make our way into The Grill and search for a familiar face.

"There they are." She gestures toward the lads.

Catching Jax's eyes, I point at her and mouth, "She's driving me crazy."

He nods with a chuckle, knowing quite well that Pemberton can be a real pain. Looking around the group, I notice that Erik is looking particularly off. He's frowning, his lips pinched in a tight line.

I grab a fifty dollar note from my wallet and hand it to Pemberton. "Get me a JD and coke, beautiful?" I kiss her cheek. She's a completely different person in public, almost charming.

Almost.

She ducks off towards the bar, and I go to stand with the lads at one of the rear tables.

The Grill is the best place to drink on campus —well, other than The Basement Lounge. But I can't go there because it can only be accessed by an underground tunnel between the library and the café, and, well —I just can't go down there. I hate small spaces. Whenever I try, my muscles seize up and I often just pass out. I've been this way ever since I can remember.

But The Grill has a good vibe. You can be rowdy or slightly more vocal here than at the other establishments, and our group tends to get that way sometimes.

Marcus, the proprietor, seems to have a lot of time for us, perhaps because we are regulars or maybe because we respect him when so many other drunk students don't. He's a dictator though, a real tough prick. I've had the *daunting* task of comforting many teary new barmaids. Not that I've ever minded. But now my days of perpetual women are over. I'm monogamous and all that.

Jaxon is a solid character. Under his macho façade, he's actually fairly genuine and, dare I say, sensitive. We play rugby together too, and due to the extremely competitive nature of the sport, there is an obligatory level of respect for the boys you share the field with.

Erik, on the other hand, can get under my skin. He's too fake for my liking, too maintained. Like he has shit to hide. He slept with Pembie once, so perhaps my resentment stems from that. Although I can't help but feel like there are more obscurities to him than meets the eye —the dude's kinda irrational and intense. Despite all that though, he's still my buddy.

"Nice speech, Slater, seriously. You're a complete crack

up. 'Watch me leave, ladies'." Jax elbows me in the side. "Ya bloody dickhead."

I chuckle. "Well, I just give the people what they want." Leaning my elbow next to Erik on the table, I ask, "What's the face for, dude?"

He flashes me his attention for a brief moment. "Nah, nothing."

Jax bumps my shoulder with his. "His little sister is playing in a few moments," he mocks with a singsong voice, "and he's *worrriiieddd.*" Jax laughs. I laugh at Jax laughing. "And she's super-hot!" he adds. Erik stiffens and looks a little pissed off, which makes me laugh even more.

Yep, intense.

I'm not sure what happened to all the air or when it got so damn hot or when Pemberton joined us and gave me a drink. All of my attention is stolen by the girl who has just walked on stage. I watch her sit on the main stool inside the roped off area. There's another person beside her, holding a harmonica, but I can't manage to draw my attention away from the girl's face long enough to see what her bandmate looks like...or even decipher their gender. A strange heat radiates in my ears before pulsing almost painfully through my forehead.

Slow down on the JDs, Konnor.

I think the lads are having a chat. I can hear muffled sounds, but nothing really reaches me. Squinting and leaning to the side, I attempt to get a more uninterrupted view of her. She picks up a plain-looking brown guitar. When she places the pick in between her teeth, I feel the need to readjust my stance. She begins to test each string, adjusting the tension. Her concentration and the way she holds the instrument preciously is captivating.

And ... *familiar.*

Her long wavy blonde hair bounces behind her shoulders; a few rogue strands dangle over her breasts... her exceptional breasts.

Shit, how long have I been staring?

I turn my gaze away from her, looking around to confirm that no one has caught me staring. But my eyes become fixed on her again.

I think she has brown eyes; distance makes my view problematic. She has an elegance and purity I don't think I've seen in a long time. Her bare thighs are pressed gently together with the guitar positioned appropriately on her lap. She's wearing a short black dress with white polka dots and pale heels that elongate her beautiful legs. Her cheeks glow a light shade of crimson, making her hesitation visible even from here. She's nervous, and it's the sexiest thing I've ever seen.

Fuck me, she is stunning.

She speaks into the microphone, and I hear Erik hush someone. "Hi, my name is Blesk Bellamy. This song is called *"Hero Boy"*."

Her voice hits me hard; my breath leaves in an instant. Her long, graceful fingers begin to strum the guitar and the melody it inspires is sweet, feminine, and folky. A pained harmonic cadence that thickens the air around me. She begins to sing:

> *You could be the truth; I could be the treason.*
> *I could be the storm; you could be the season.*
> *It's still dark at 3 p.m., dark for no good reason.*
>
> *Let's do all the things we planned to do,*
> *Remember what we wanted to.*

My hero boy.

A nameless hero,
A fameless hero,
For all the wrong reasons hero,
My boy hero. My hero.

You could be the seeker; I could be the sister,
I could be the answer; you could be the asker,
Let's hide our words from the listener,

Let's sing and pretend to dance,
Be young and take a chance,
My hero boy.
Ohhhh strongest boy I have ever seen.

A nameless hero,
A fameless hero,
For all the wrong reasons hero,
My boy hero. My hero.

You could be the hound; I could be the handler,
I could be the trip; you could be the traveller,
Let's run from that faceless predator.

It is finally your turn to be free,
All this time it has been me,
My hero boy.

Ohhhh strongest boy I have ever seen.

And we will run from the clawless fox,
We can unchain and unlock that box,

Let's smash our names with blunt rocks,
'Til they disappear and no one talks.

A nameless hero,
A fameless hero,
For all the wrong reasons hero,
My boy hero. My hero.

A nameless hero,
A fameless hero,
For all the wrong reasons hero,
My boy hero. My hero.

IT WAS *EXTRAORDINARY*, beautiful and raw. Her eyes glisten with emotion towards the end. For some strange reason, so do mine.

She plays several more songs, mostly covers. She rarely looks up, but one of the times she does, our eyes lock together. A stolen moment passes and it seems to never end, and then it does and somehow it's far too abrupt.

The charge in the air subsides once her set ends, and I'm finally able to draw sufficient amounts of air into my lungs. As she squats to pack her guitar into its case, I catch a glimpse of her white knickers. I'm filled with an unexplainable urge to jump up and shield her from everyone gawking.

"White. Virginal." Jax laughs, knocking me with his elbow while watching her intently.

Fuck off, Jax.

"Is that your sister, Erik?" I ask, observing the strange trance he is in. Not unlike the one I was in.

He glances at me. "Yeah," he answers, then wanders in her direction. "I'll go get her."

Pemberton startles me when she puts her hand on my shoulder and kisses my neck.

"Hey, my green-eyed boy. Want to go make out somewhere?" She's acting cute and that usually resonates directly with my groin. Plus, she appears just tipsy enough to do anything I want. Still, I surprise myself when I shake my head in response.

"Nah, Pem," I hear myself say before my brain registers it. "I kinda wanna meet Erik's sister."

What did I just say to my girlfriend?

She scoffs. "I met her already. Dull and boring, trust me. No personality at all."

I furrow my brows. "Be nice. She's Erik's sister." Her eyes widen and I can tell I've struck a nerve. Knowing Pemberton like I do, I'd wager she's jealous.

She clenches her teeth together and talks through them. "Don't use that tone with me. *What?* Over a girl you don't even know?"

Yep, jealous.

I stare at her equally infuriating and gorgeous face. "Pemberton, you need to learn to play nice with other girls."

She tilts her head at me. "Konnor," she whispers in my ear, baiting me. "If you don't come outside right now and cum in my mouth, I'm going to find someone who will..."

Fuck.

———

SINCE PEMBERTON CAN BARELY STAND after a few drinks, convincing her to go to bed once I got her back to her dorm and wore her out, was easy. She snuggled up with the hot water bottle I made her and drifted straight off. I left a glass of water and some Panadol on her bedside table for her post-drinks headache. She looked incredible all cocooned up. Wholesome. No guards up. Just her.

After leaving Pem, I wander to Boe's Kebabs, which is so close to The Grill, I can see its front steps. I'm waiting for me order when I notice Erik's sister sitting alone just outside the bar. My chest tightens and I find myself walking towards her.

"Hey, Slater! Your kebab!" Boe calls out.

I spin around and jog over to grab it from him. "Sorry, Bozo."

"All good. You need me to call you a cab again?"

"Nah, I'm actually all good." My apartment is a thirty-minute walk from campus, a fifteen-minute run, and an hour drunken stumble. The latter seems to be my dominant pace. Tonight, I feel relatively on game though, having spaced my intake like the pro I truly am.

I nod at him in appreciation. "Thanks for this," I say, gesturing to the world's greatest kebab, which is now proudly in my hand. Boe's Kebabs is nothing like a generic chain. He uses only free-range chicken and really takes an unusual amount of care in each kebab's presentation. I have a thing about free-range products. Eggs, chicken, pork. It often makes dining difficult, but it's one thing I won't waver on. No living thing should be caged for its entire life.

Turning back, I walk toward Erik's sister again. I slow as I approach her. Her eyes are downcast and my chest pains instinctively. When I get within a metre of her, she raises her gaze. As her big brown eyes meet mine, my breath hitches.

Crazy beautiful.

To avoid standing idle like an idiot, I run a hand through my hair.

"Hey," I say, lacking my usual charisma. "I'm Erik's mate. You okay?"

Pull yourself together.

Her eyes are wide — dreamy and wide — and encircled by long, arched black lashes.

"Yeah, thank you. I just needed a few moments."

I turn to leave. "Oh, do you want me to go?"

"No," she says so quickly I feel warmth fill my chest. "I'm Blesk."

"Yeah, I know. I'm Konnor."

"Yeah." She smiles faintly. "I know."

I sit down next to her on the step. The streetlamps illuminate us in the darkness. She is elegant and curvy, spectacularly so. She peers at me while her profile is partially hidden behind blinds of golden locks. I'm usually the epitome of a witty conversationalist — I am Konnor Slater — but Blesk has me frozen in a strangely familiar daze.

I take a big breath, then force out the words, "What's wrong?"

She gives me an unconvincing grin as she sheepishly wipes a tear off her cheek. "I just don't like playing that song."

"Which one?" I ask.

She blinks at me, and I watch her swallow her hesitation. "Hero Boy."

"That's an awesome song," I say, trying to console her. I don't know why she's so upset. I don't know why I care why she's so upset, but I feel like it's my responsibility to make her feel better.

Her voice trembles a little as she says, "I don't usually play with other people. I'm a soloist."

"The harmonica sounded great, honestly." Leaning

forward on my knees, I take the opportunity to study her. She's a sad little thing. It sucks to see.

"Yeah, maybe. I just don't want anyone else playing it."

I don't understand, but I feel I should... *somehow.* "Want me to talk to Marcus?"

What are you doing, Konnor? Marcus would kick your arse for interfering.

"No, thank you," she mutters.

Phew.

"Okay," I say. A fucking cat seems to have gotten my tongue or something because I'm just gripping my kebab like a bloody moron. The juice from the tomatoes is making the Turkish wrap soggy; I should just eat it.

Pretty girl... kebab... Pretty girl... kebab.

"Want to go for a walk?" I hear myself ask her.

Girl versus kebab: 1-0.

Her eyes brighten, her sadness slipping slightly. "Yes."

We walk for a while in silence, which I would usually fill with quips and commentary. But this is strangely comfortable. I detour off the footpath quickly to dispose of my now sludgy kebab. A shame. It could have quite possibly been the best kebab ever created.

I know these paths like the back of my hand. I have walked them many times with Pemberton, with Jax, with countless girls. Tonight, though, they seem to have changed. Just like I feel.

Blesk sniffles every now and then. I hate that she's crying. As she uses her fingers to wipe away the stray tears, I have to restrain the urge to raise my hand and brush them away for her. The wind begins to swirl her hair around. She collects it and holds it in her hand, letting it cascade down one shoulder.

Cheer her up, Konnor.

"Ah... Let's do this again," I suggest, turning abruptly to face her.

She matches my stance, frowning at me suspiciously. "O...kay." She pauses. "Do what again?"

"Wait right here."

I spin and walk away from her. Ten steps later, I turn back around. She hasn't moved, but her head is a little higher, her eyes a little wider. I freeze for a moment, taking this sliver of time to study her. Her little black dress hugs her torso and flares out at the waist, making her look both sweet and sexy. Her long curvy legs are exposed as she stands with a feigned confidence. Innocence and nerves bounce around in her eyes. She is extraordinarily beautiful.

Time to act like a complete dickhead and hope no one sees me.

I glance away and casually walk in her direction, adding swagger to my steps. A little giggle leaves her lips and that alone makes the whole performance worth it. That little sound fills my chest, just like her voice had a few hours ago.

I lightly bump into her. "Oh, hey, sorry. I didn't see you there."

Her eyes widen further.

"I'm Konnor. I'm an alcoholic. I like long pointless walks on short paths. I have more hang-ups than a telemarketer, and I hate, hate, *hate*, harmonica players. Don't know why. Just do."

She smiles a little. "I'm Blesk and I don't hate harmonica players."

I shake my head in disbelief. "Really? Huh. Maybe I just haven't met a harmonica player I liked."

"You should get out more. I meet a new harmonica player I like every day."

I laugh. "Are you asking me out?"

Her jaw drops. "What? No."

"Oh, I just thought..." I stare at her, feigning confusion. "You don't have to be shy. I'm pretty sure you just told me I should go out with you. I don't usually do these things, but I will 'cause you're pretty cute."

Her smile grows. I soar.

Her smile... That smile.

"You're so corny, Konnor," she says through that smile.

"I know. Don't tell anyone," I say. "That would totally ruin my street cred."

She bats her lashes at me, and my heart skips a beat. "Your secret's safe with me."

"So, what are you studying?" I ask.

She grins. "Music."

"Cool. What are your electives?" We wander past a spot we'd passed an hour ago. I try not to notice.

Tonight, I wish the campus was bigger.

"I'm doing Child Development 123 and Beginners Education to Music 103," she says. Throughout the past hour, her demeanour has changed; she's smiling more, talking more, and has even laughed. I can't help but be a little proud of myself for that.

"BEM, Beginners Education to Music 103, is one of mine," I state, with more enthusiasm than I should show.

She giggles again; my level of cool dwindles. It's those fucking brown eyes that are doing it.

"What do you mean 'one of mine'?" she asks. Her dress sways across her thighs as she walks, and I can't even pretend to be enigmatic right now because I am desperate for her to give me as much of her precious time as possible.

"I'm a grad student. That's one of my classes, so you may have me as a tutor."

"Really?" She sounds simply chipper; it's a lovely tone for her.

"Yeah, there's a one-in-three chance you'll get me," I announce.

She twirls a lone strand behind her ear. "Will you go easy on me?"

Ah, shit! Is she flirting with me?

I wish I wasn't smiling so much; my cheeks are border-line aching. "If I get you as a student then-" I pause on the 'yes', I'd planned to say. "No..."

She sucks in a short breath, then turns to face me with a grin so wide I can see her tongue poking out between her teeth. It's so cute. "And why not?"

"Because you wouldn't have it any other way."

You are taking a leap of faith here, Konnor.

She's silent for a while, so I press, "Am I right?"

The most unique colour of pink lights up her cheeks. "Yes, well, I don't plan on disappointing you."

I chuckle. "Look, I know your brother pretty well, so I haven't set the bar very high for you. You should be fine."

"Oh, that's thoughtful." Sarcasm laces her voice, and she knocks me playfully with her elbow.

"Custom couching." I laugh smugly. "It's really what sets me apart from all the other graduates."

"I thought it was the long pointless walks around campus with your female students," she teases.

"Ouch." I chuckle, beaming at her cheeky smirk. "That too."

We grin at each other and every part of me feels light.

"Why didn't you go straight from high school to university?" I query. She doesn't look like a schoolie.

Her smile disappears slightly, and I hate that my question has caused that reaction. "My mum was sick. She died a few years ago."

"Damn." I spin and place my hands on both her shoulders so I can search her expression. "I'm so sorry, Blesk."

She shivers and peers down to watch my finger gently stroking her collarbone. Little goosebumps dot her skin. Something inside me shifts and I feel a mixture of discomfort and calm.

Clearing her throat, she raises those lovely eyes to meet mine.

"How long have you and Pembie been together?"

All the air I'd held captive comes rushing out at the mention of my girlfriend. I'd been trying to exist in the now and forget all about the girl I'd just left in her bed. I drop my hands to my sides, but each one mourns Blesk's skin.

I sigh roughly. "Pembie and I are... " I pause to consider the appropriate wording. I don't want to admit that she uses me for my apartment and I use her for her body. "We're not together in the traditional sense. It's still pretty casual. Ya know."

Lame. Very, very, lame Konnor.

Her tongue is visible between her teeth as she beams at me, knowingly.

"I only asked how long you've been together, Konnor." Then she laughs from her belly. I don't care that it's at my expense. In fact, I like it.

"Right, too much information," I chuckle. "About a year, I think."

When we turn the corner, The Grill comes back into sight, but it's overshadowed by Erik's glare. It's dark on the steps at the entrance, but I can still clearly see he's ready to rip me a new one. Aggression rushes from him in waves. He trudges towards us, shaking his head and scowling.

"What the fuck do you think you're doing?" He pulls Blesk towards him by the elbow, jerking her away from me.

She gapes at him as she tries to subtly tug her arm from his grip. "*Erik.*"

"Woah, what's wrong?" I ask, trying to control the caveman inside me. "Let your sister go, mate."

"Stay away from Blesk! She isn't a trophy for you to achieve," he growls.

I look at Blesk to see her reaction to his callous words. God, I hope she knows that's not what this is. She looks a little sad —the sparkle I saw in her expression only a few moments ago has fizzled out. He made her lose it. That has me unnervingly on edge, distractingly so. My eyes drop to where his fingers dig into her skin, and I am overcome with the need to snap them.

"Don't look at her," he hisses. "Look at me."

"*Careful,* Erik!" I warn, fisting my hands at my sides. "Just let Blesk go."

"Don't tell me what to do with Blesk. What would Pembie say about you wandering off with other girls in the dark, hey?"

"You're being a fucking dickhead, Erik. Let your sister go."

He lets her go only to step towards me. "So you fuck Pembie all day and then come after my sister when she goes to bed?" He snarls and shoves me in the chest.

Gasping, Blesk covers her mouth. Her eyes fill with tears. I stare at her, silently asking her what I should do. I want to knock him out. Cold.

She shakes her head slowly, pleadingly. She clearly doesn't like fighting, unlike Pemberton who gets aroused when blokes mash over her. Same blokes. Very different girl. Entirely different situation. I take a few steps backwards, my molars grinding slowly together.

Don't retaliate...

"You've had too much to drink, Erik. Walk home! Don't be an arsehole to your sister."

I'm going to need to blow off some steam before I rip his head off. After a last glance at Blesk, making sure she is comfortable with being left alone with him, I spin and saunter away. All the muscles in my arms twitch with rage. I need to get as far away from him —and her and them together —as possible.

Heat spreads through me, and I growl under my breath.

"Fucking Erik! Fucking Erik!"

The whole event replays in my mind like a goddamn broken record. That hurt look I'd seen in her eyes has me livid. I cross the road and begin to jog home.

Why would he behave like that?

I knew the guy had a problem with me, but his reaction seemed extreme —even for him. When I picture Blesk's sad little face again, I jolt to the side and take my anger out on a trash can. It clangs loudly and rolls across the path, spilling its contents everywhere. I throw my fist into a tree. A hiss rushes through my larynx. The pain hits me like a bullet to the head. Waving my hand, I try to flick the pain away, but my fist is already swelling. As blood trickles down my knuckles, I scowl at the tree. It's fine.

Tree versus Konnor: 1-0.

Despite the pain though, I welcome the distraction. It's better than thinking about Blesk and Erik. Better than letting my mind swarm with regret over leaving her with him. Better than recognising the uncomfortable level of jealousy I feel.

I don't even know her.

Yep, the pain is better than all that.

three: blesk

Blesk

Chapter Song
Katy Perry —Fireworks

AS ELISE'S alarm goes off, playing Katy Perry's
"Firework," my eyes flutter open to the faintly lit dorm room
I now call home. I am inundated with flashes of how last
night ended. Erik pushing Konnor. Konnor walking away
without saying goodbye. Me doing absolutely nothing to
stop either of them.

Erik and I had barely spoken on the walk back to my
dorm, but we hadn't needed too. Erik can deliver a compre-
hensive lecture with just a single look. Konnor and Erik are
friends, and yet, they clearly don't share any mutual respect.
Whether they like each other at all is yet to be seen. The
'Konnor character' described by Erik is not the same Konnor
I'd walked with for over an hour. That Konnor was sweet.
Funny.

Reaching for my phone, I check the time: 9:00 a.m. Luckily, I don't have class until two thirty. There are two missed calls and two messages, all from Erik.

> The first one says: I'm sorry about last night, Blesk. I flipped out when I couldn't find you. I'll talk to you after class today.

And the second:

> Please pick up your phone so I know you're okay.

I'm not ready to forgive Erik for his behaviour. And if my previous actions hold any weight on depicting my future ones, then it's probably best that I stay clear of him until I'm ready. I don't argue with my brother. He has done too much for me and I've put him through too much. Forgiving him really is my only option... But I'm not ready to yet.

Rolling over, Elise clicks her alarm off, then looks at me. I stay gazing at the rug in between our beds, my phone clasped under my chin.

"Hey," she murmurs sleepily. "You okay? You were crying last night. I heard you." Her messy bed hair is adorable in a loose bun, and her eyes look even more blue without her glasses.

I shuffle further under the covers. "Yes, I'm fine."

"Wanna talk about it?" she asks, tucking her hands under her face. "I promise I'm an excellent listener."

I giggle. Given our previous conversations, that statement seems rather funny. "I'm sure you are."

She gives me a sad half-smile. "Is it about a boy?"

It's about two.

I turn to face the foreign white ceiling. I'm silent for too long apparently because she doesn't wait for a reply.

"Well, I'm here if you ever need me," she states adamantly. "Wanna go to the showers together?" She pulls back her pink bed sheets and moves across the room. I watch her collect her toiletries. It's obvious by her downcast face that she wants us to share a *The Perks of Being a Wallflower* kind of relationship, where we mess around, choreograph best friend dances, and gossip about boys. I wish I could give her that.

I wish I wanted that too.

Sitting up in bed, I push my blue cotton blanket down to my thighs and rub my face back to life with both palms. I glance down at my kitten print nightgown, tracing the patterns with my fingertip. I was in such a daze last night that I don't even remember putting it on. My dad always tells me I dress younger than is customary for my age group. My excuse is that I've been denied a fair amount of fashion development, so my defining trend is yet to be established. We didn't have much money growing up, so for a long time, I shopped at second-hand clothing stores. I got quite good at finding gems, really.

Making her way to the doorway, Elise suddenly bends over to pick something up. "Blesk, there's something here for you!"

"What's it say?" I slide off the bed and wander over to her. My cheeks heat up as I read the note over her shoulder.

> Blesk,
> I hope I didn't get you into too much treble.
> Good news is, the bar is so low now,
> Erik just guaranteed you at least a distinction.
> All you have to do is show up, and I'll be
> imp 3

𝄻

"WHY IS trouble spelt like that? And what's that little shape?" Elise asks, handing me both the note and a little black rectangular box. I brighten, my cheeks getting even warmer. As she searches my face, I bite down on my lower lip, attempting to conceal the bizarre grin that is escaping.

"It's a musical reference." I sigh. "That shape is a rest. He's being... *corny*."

She beams at me, mirroring my grin. "*He?*"

"Yes..." I smile. "*He*."

Her lips stretch further as she motions at the box I'm clasping tightly. "What do you think is in there?"

"I don't know," I whisper playfully, raising a brow in anticipation. "Let's find out."

Taking a seat on my bed, I run my index finger over the box's engravings. With Elise silent beside me, I slowly open the box. Inside is a shiny, silver harmonica. I cover my heart with one hand and exhale. This is just so... *sweet*. I murmur under my breath, "Why? Who is this guy?"

"*Wow*," Elise says. "You've been here one day and you're already getting presents from guys. Why did he give you that?"

I relax into a sigh again, breathing out while rolling my shoulders. "So I can learn it," I manage to say. "And play solo." A silly smile stretches across my cheeks. Raising the harmonica to my chest, I hold it firmly against my rapidly beating heart. I almost want to cry, but I don't. There's no way he could know *just* how much this means to me. I need to thank him, especially after the way that last night had ended. This is just too powerful of a gift to not reciprocate.

He doesn't think I'm a trophy.

THE LADY behind the counter at the admissions office doesn't like me, or maybe she doesn't like the world, but either way, her disdain is apparent in the way she glares at me over her glasses.

"I'm not a stalker." I give her a wide-toothed smile. "I just have Mr Slater for a class and I need to find a way to contact him."

"Is. That. Right?" She snickers, scrutinising me from head to toe. "Mr Slater seems to get a fair number of female students needing his *digits*." Her long wiry fingers made air quotes when she said 'digits'.

I bet he doesn't leave them all notes and musical instruments.

She looks at me like I'm a desperate skank.

"Mrs ... ?" Elise cuts in, leaning across the desk as she reads the nametag pinned to the woman's cardigan. "Mckenzie. Mr Slater has Miss Bellamy's wallet. She left it at the bar last night and he found it. She plays there Tuesdays and Fridays. You can check. *He* called her, telling her to pick it up at his place." I elbow her lightly in the stomach in an attempt to stop the lies she is stacking like Jenga blocks. She deflects me without moving her gaze from Mrs Mckenzie. "Mr Slater gave her his address, but she lost it and she doesn't have any way to contact him. She has to say goodbye to her *terminally ill* grandma at the hospital tonight and has no money for a cab. She is her only fam—"

"Alright! God, girls," Mrs Mckenzie snaps, holding up her

hand to stop Elise talking. Her brows knit as she looks down at her computer. As she punches in various keys, she huffs in irritation. She isn't buying Elise's lies, that's for sure.

Sneaking a peek at Elise, I make a little *eeeeek* sound while she gives the word 'composure' a new meaning. She is a proactive little schemer; her level-headedness tells me this is not her first rodeo.

I definitely like this girl.

Mrs Mckenzie looks back up at us and fakes a smile that is more patronising than friendly. "Here you go, girls." She slaps a sheet of paper on the desk and watches as I slide it into my pocket.

"Thank you, Mrs Mckenzie. It's been a real treat spending this time with you." I giggle through a contorted smirk. Her right brow lifts at my sarcasm, and my cheeks begin to burn. I can't believe those snarky words have just come out of *my* mouth.

"Bye." Elise grabs my hand and tugs me swiftly out of the office and around the corridor. We both sprint down the hall, our arms flailing, us buzzing with adrenaline, and laughing. I can't remember the last time I laughed like this. We halt when we reach the quad. Gasping for air between giggles, I clutch my stomach, which is tight with stitches and spasms. To my surprise, it's a delightfully welcome feeling.

"I was trying to be so serious, but you... oh my God." Elise pants while trying to suppress her laughter. "*It's been a real treat,*" she quips, mimicking me. We both slump down onto the grass.

We look up at a blue sky dotted with thin fluffy clouds, some of which are currently hiding the sun's intensity. The wind ruffles the tree limbs around us.

I curl onto one shoulder to peer at her. "You've done that before..."

Still breathing heavily, she smirks. "That's what girl-friends do."

"I guess..." I flash her my most grateful smile. "I guess I've never really had one before."

four: liz

Liz

Sixteen years earlier.

THE GIRL CAN'T STOP her tears this time, no matter how hard she forces her eyes shut, breathes slowly, or wills them away. She can't stop the whimpers from gurgling up her throat, can't stop the heat from coating her tongue. She can't stop her heart from slamming into her ribs and forcing tremors to rack her from her ears to her toes. She won't be able to stop. Not now. Not until her new brother stops screaming. All she can do is shudder silently in her seat and watch her daddy talk to the man outside the car. She hopes her tears and sobs stop before her daddy climbs in beside her.

Her daddy returns and moves into the driver's seat, switching on the ignition and frowning at the road. She sits in fear, staring ahead. Silent. Unwavering. The car cruises slowly through the District, navigating the lamp-lit streets on the way back home. The tires grind into the unsealed front driveway and come to a sudden stop, echoing through the estate. She runs inside the house. He does not follow; he needs to get her new brother out first. The girl rushes into the kitchen, and with her shaky hands, tries to pour her dad a drink. *Ice. Brown drink next. Bit of water.* She repeats this over and over, knowing she always forgets something. *Ice. Brown drink next. Bit of water.* Her hands keep shaking, the ice chinking the glass. Her breath gushes out hard and fast. *Ice. Brown drink next. Bit of water.*

When the flywire slams and his steps boom through the house, she freezes. He bellows her name. Her spine seizes. Out of nowhere, his knuckles connect with her cheek, sending a surge of heat to the back of her eye. *Whack.* Her little body hits the floor with a thud. She withers beneath him; his shadow blackens the ground around her huddled frame. She scoots backwards until the bench hits her spine. A gasp wrestles its way up her throat. His eyes are slits. Hers are wide. She knew this would happen; she knew as soon as the first defiant tear had slipped out.

He leans down and fists her hair. She screeches as she's dragged through the house. Her feet kick the carpet. Garbles of sounds roll up her larynx. Her body gyrates. Her back slides...

The floor creaks below his feet, protesting the anger manifesting through his stomps. She keeps sliding.

"Daddy" –her voice shakes violently– "please."

She presses down on her hair, holding the roots to her fragile scalp, trying to soothe the burn on her skin.

Please, Daddy, stop.

Her heels throb as she keeps slamming them against the

floor, desperately fighting for freedom. Her scalp is raw. She knows crying is pointless. She knows pleading is pointless. She knows nothing can stop him now. She keeps sliding.

"Lizzy, *goddamn it*, I've warned you! Do you think I enjoy this?"

"Daddy," she whimpers. "I'm sorry."

"Tonight, I needed a good girl. Not a bad girl."

The furniture flashes by, each piece blurring together into a stream of wood. She remembers the last time he was this angry; the image of his tight face still churns her stomach.

She hasn't cried in a long time. She has become very good at holding her tears inside, ignoring the stinging behind her eyes and breathing slowly. *Manipulative.* Her daddy once told her, 'Crying is a girl's way of manipulating us'.' She never knew who *us* was. She still doesn't know what *manipulating* means. But she knows deep to her core that she doesn't want to be it.

She slides through the bedroom door, crumpling up the rug as her body is dragged over it. He tugs her up by her hair until she is on her feet. She stumbles once she takes her own weight. Her lower lip trembles.

Daddy, stop.

Her eyes plead with his. She can't help it. His large rough fingers wrap around her throat and the air is squeezed out, hissing through her gaping mouth. Her eyes widen.

A buzzing begins in her head as oxygen leaves her system. He tightens his grasp, crushing, draining, shaking, tighter. The girl's eyes close and she goes limp.

five: blesk

Blesk

AS MY COWBOY boots shuffle through the leaves, my hair swishes around me. I wander the streets, searching for the right apartment building. I have no intention of knocking or going in. I just want to leave a thank you note.

After a half hour, I finally find myself outside of his lobby. And I suddenly have the impulse to run back before anyone sees me. I don't, but I should. The building has one of those grand entrances with a doorman and floor-to-ceiling glazed windows.

It's just a thank you note.

Then I'm leaving. No harm done. No rules broken. No lines crossed.

Wandering inside, I notice the tiled floor is reflective. Cringing at my dishevelled appearance, I barely notice the smiling older man sitting behind a desk.

"Good morning, young lady. Who are you here to see?" He has an odd accent —European laced with an Australian twang. His suit is elegant and he wears it confidently. There is a nametag below his right collar, but I'm too dumbfounded by his presence to read it.

"Umm, I just want to leave something for someone. He won't be home anyway," I say, trying not to fidget.

"What is your name, Miss?" he asks, leaving his desk to approach me. "Are you on the visitors' list?"

"Umm, I'm Blesk Bellamy and...umm." I bite down hard on my lower lip while twiddling my fingers awkwardly around my hair. "I won't be on the list."

Stop fidgeting.

"And who are you here to see?"

I blink at him several times before answering. "Konnor Slater."

"Yes, Miss, he is home. I will call him for you," he states kindly, the corner of his eyes wrinkling.

"Please—" I nearly lunge to stop him from walking towards the desk phone. "I just want to leave him something."

He stops and leans towards me. "Miss Bellamy, he will want to see you. Let me call him?" He nods at me and waits for me to decide.

He will want to see me?

I return his nod.

"Um, okay, thank you," I murmur with a gulp. When he picks up the phone, my heart fills my ears. I hadn't planned on actually *seeing* Konnor. My hair is a mess from the wind, my dress is too short, my face is flushed, and my boots... *oh,* my stupid boots!

"Miss Bellamy?" the man calls out.

I look up from my shoes, grinning nervously. "Yes, sir?"

He chuckles and shakes his head. "Don't call me sir. I'm Adolf."

"Oh, sorry." I walk towards him. "I'm Blesk. Oh, well, I guess you know that already."

Stop babbling.

"He said to go on up. It is apartment 1002. That is level 10. Room 2. Here's a card for the elevator." I take it hesitantly.

"Thank you." I look at the card for a while, motionless. I hear Adolf chuckle, probably at me.

"He said he would usually come to collect you, Miss Bellamy, but-" He peers up in contemplation. "He can't this time."

"That's fine. I wouldn't expect him to," I say. Mustering my resolve, I stride past him and head towards the elevators that are flashing with activity.

I take one to the top floor. When the doors ping open into the hallway, I'm completely flustered. I move quietly, passing various doors until I get to apartment 1002. I stop and stare at it.

Just knock...

I'm positive the masses can walk through doors without a fully comprehensive analysis of what could be behind them and how that could change what is outside of them. I've been on campus for exactly two days, and in that time, I've managed to get in a fight with my brother. Caused a fight between my brother and his friend. And now I'm stalking my possible tutor. Like some kind of crazy lady. All because I went through one door.

As I raise my fist, a quote by Robert Frost rings in my ears: *Before I built a wall, I'd ask to know what I was walling in or walling out.* After a second of hesitation, I knock delicately, secretly hoping that he wont-

The door immediately swings open.

Oh God.

He's shirtless. His bicep flexes beside his head as he dries his wet hair with a towel. My eyes drop to his torso, which is etched with trim muscles. My jaw goes slack.

Close your mouth, Blesk!

Tiny beads of water slide down his chest, and I can't help but watch them trailing through the little tufts of hair that run from his navel to the seam of his jeans. I gulp. My eyes dart up to meet his and my pulse isn't calm at all. It's rapid. Like ... well, *rapids*. Mainly because his eyes are *beautiful*. The most perfect shade of green.

And they're kind too.

"Blesk, sorry about" –he lowers his arm to his side– "not being better presented."

Oh, I like your presentation. High Distinction from me.

My mouth flaps without making a sound; talking and perving simultaneously is surprisingly difficult.

A knowing grin plays on his lips.

"Are you checking me out, Miss Bellamy?"

"Oh my God," I say, mortified. "No. I just wanted to give you this." I hand him the envelope. Actually, I throw it at him.

"Please, come inside." He waves me in.

My feet decide to stroll cautiously into his open floor apartment before I give them permission to.

Furniture designates the different sections. From where I stand, the bedroom area in the far corner is mostly hidden by a large bookcase. There is a door to the right of it, perhaps leading into a bathroom. The lounge area is opposite the front door —and me —because I'm now hesitant to move any further.

The apartment is trendy. Graphic designs and famous street-art posters embellish the exposed brick walls. The kitchen boasts all stainless steel appliances and a large stone countertop. It's cool. It's very...him.

"Wanna drink?" He strides over to the kitchen, where he pours himself a glass of liquor. He pins me with his eyes before looking down to make sure he doesn't over-fill his drink.

"I really didn't want to disturb you. I just wanted to thank you for the harmonica. How did you manage to get it by 9 a.m.?" I ask, taking a step closer to him. His eyes stay glued on me as he throws back a mouthful of his drink.

"You're not disturbing me. What's with the formalities, Blesk? Feeling weird about being here?"

I giggle, and that makes him smile. Two perfect dimples etch onto either side of his lips. Everything about him is oddly comforting, including his dimples.

"Is it that obvious?" I ask.

He manoeuvres around the kitchen bench and stands beside me. "Is it because I might be your tutor or because Erik told you to stay away from me?"

"A bit from column A and a bit from column B," I admit, folding my lip between my teeth and chewing on it nervously.

He laughs loudly. "Well, *fuck* both columns 'cause they don't matter. Erik can get over it. You're not in high school."

"So fraternising with your students is fine here?" I ask. He strolls over to the lounge area and slumps down on the couch. He tilts his head towards the cushion beside him in an obvious get-over-here gesture. He drapes an arm over the backrest and tucks his knee up to one.

His eyes narrow. "Define *fraternising*?"

"You aren't my English teacher, Mr Slater." I smile at him because something about our conversation seems to justify it.

"It's probably frowned upon. But... we're pretty much the same age," he says, watching me intently.

I circle the couch, then sit across from him on the single recliner; a coffee table separates us. The cushion beneath me is hard. This is clearly the kind of fancy furniture that is more for cosmetic purposes than actual use.

He tilts his head. "So did you like it?"

"Yes," I whisper and I can feel my eyes crinkle as I beam at him.

"Good," he exclaims before taking another swig.

"So what do I need to do to get a High Distinction?" I immediately wish I hadn't said that in such a flirtatious way.

His leans forward and grins. "I'll get back to you." His words are slurred. My brows knit as I notice how glossy his eyes are and how his glass sways in his grasp. The brown liquid sloshes up the edges, nearly spilling over, like waves inside a pool.

"Konnor?" I stand up. "Are you drunk?"

"Do I look drunk?" he asks.

I peer down at him and frown. "A little."

He leans back in defeat. "I am, yeah," he admits. "I didn't expect company."

"It's barely noon," I say, walking around the coffee table to sit next to him. He doesn't say anything, just puts his drink down, leans his elbows on his knees and rubs his face with both palms. I know he drinks, but this doesn't seem — what did Erik call it? —*functional.*

"*Blesk...*" he whispers so softly I barely hear it. "I'm sorry. If I knew you were going to be here ..." He winces. "Shit, I'm sorry. Today is a... a bad day for me."

"Why?" I ask.

"I lost someone today."

"I'm sorry, Konnor." My stomach knots up from seeing

him so miserable. I barely know him, but his agony affects me. He releases his face and turns to look at me through bloodshot eyes, which are clearly fighting back tears. The heartache behind them makes me want to cry too.

He chews on the inside of his mouth before saying, "I tried to sober up for you with a shower, but, apparently, that didn't work."

"It's midday on a Wednesday, Konnor." I place my hand on his knee; that gesture of affection should feel awkward — especially for me. But with him, it feels completely natural.

He opens his mouth to say something, but no words come out. Then he shakes his head vigorously as if to physically dislodge his train of thought. "Fucking forget about it, Blesk. Just go home."

My mouth goes slack. "I'm not judging you. It's just... it doesn't feel right leaving you like this."

He grabs his glass, necks its entire content, and then brushes my hand off him. "Seriously, I'm not your fucking responsibility."

Something about what he just said makes my heart beat hard against my ribcage.

He's a mess, but he's right. I should leave.

I stand and stride quickly towards the front door. Coming here was a mistake. I barely even know him.

What was I thinking?

"Blesk... Wait." I hear a piece of furniture slide across the floor, but I don't stop until I have my hand on the handle. He slams his body against the door, blocking my way out. Turning, he dips his head and looks at me through eyes which are at half-mast. "Have I fucked this up?"

"What is *this*?" I murmur, looking sadly at him. I don't *want* to want to stay. As he said, he isn't my responsibility.

But that doesn't stop the feeling sitting in my belly like a boulder.

His brows furrow. "*This,* Blesk." The look of anguish on his face is heartbreaking.

There is a *this.*

Konnor is only inches from me, and his mere proximity is making me dizzy. His eyes watch every movement I make. His gaze follows me when I lick my lips. When I squeeze my eyes shut to fight back the discomfort of his eyes. I swallow hard...

I can still feel his gaze on me. Although there is nothing intimidating about his energy, he still manages to make my heart race. With a strengthening breath, I open my eyes and look up into his hooded green ones. They're so beautiful and so... sad. I press my hand against his cheek, and when he moves into my touch, we both exhale on contact.

How can I feel so comfortable and so nervous all at once?

My whole body responds to the feeling of him against my palm. When he closes his eyes, I stroke his cheekbone.

Finally, his eyes open and focus on me. "Don't leave, Blesk. I'm sorry I'm being a dick."

I give him a little smile. "You're not very corny when you're drunk."

Relaxing against the door, he breathes heavily through a crooked smile. "I'll work on that for you, Miss Bellamy."

six: blesk

Blesk

KONNOR GETS WORSE over the next hour, until he's a wreck. Right now, I'm in a state of chaos. Wanting to leave this person who is practically a stranger. Who has a girlfriend! Who is clearly going through something terrible... *Crap.* I can't just leave him.

After I reluctantly watch him down another three drinks, I manage to convince him to lay down and rest in bed. With his eyes half closed, I prepare myself to leave. But before I can stop myself, I brush my fingers through his hair. A kind of goodbye —you'll be okay.

"Stay," he whispers.

Girlfriend, Blesk. He has a girlfriend.

But I can be his friend. "Okay."

I crawl up onto the bed beside him. We lay on his mattress, facing each other, our knees pressed together. My hair is fanned out around me, and he suddenly reaches for it. Twirling the strands around his fingers, he stares at them in a kind of mystified trance. He's in his own head, barely conscious of me. He's back *there*, with the person he lost. I understand that look.

I can't explain what's happening or why I have this urge to be with him or why I feel liable for him...

He gazes up into my eyes. "The sun... your hair reminds me of the sun."

I stiffen slightly, but then shake off the memories associated with that comparison. "That's really corny, Konnor."

He splutters on a laugh. "Haven't you heard? My new middle name?"

"Konnor 'Corny' Slater." I giggle.

A huge drunken smile engulfs his face. "God, I love it when you make that sound," he says with a pleased sigh. I immediately giggle again, a nervous reaction. And now we are both brandishing goofy grins and neither of us does a thing to hide them.

He's back *here*. With me.

"You're beautiful, you know that," he gushes. "And I'm a dickhead like acting."

I giggle at his backwards sentence. "Yeah." I smile at him. "But this isn't you."

He cocks a brow sceptically. "And how would you know that?"

"I don't know, but I do. You haven't disappointed me yet, Konnor," I say, refusing to fight against whatever force is making it impossible for me to take my eyes off him.

He chuckles. "Well, you mustn't have set the bar very high for me."

I bite my lip and speak through a silly smile. "All you have to do is show up."

A knock breaks through our world, and we both freeze, narrowing our eyes questioningly at each other. My heart skips a beat when his eyes widen in realisation. He jolts up, only to immediately grab his head due to what I can only imagine is a pretty harsh head rush.

"Konnor!" A girl's voice barks through the door. "I don't like waiting."

"Shit!" he mutters, jumping to his feet. He scavenges around the floor for a shirt.

Pembie.

He slides a shirt over his head before turning to look at me, guilt blanketing his expression. I act nonchalant with a quick shrug of my shoulders and a feigned smile.

He isn't buying it.

The discomfort I feel spilling through my veins seems to be reflected in his eyes. I need my head examined. What kind of girl visits a guy she barely knows? Who is involved with someone else and totally drunk?

"Konnor! For God's sake." Pembie bashes harder on the door.

He holds his hand out to me, but I wave him off dismissively. Getting up, I slowly follow him into the living room. I don't want to be touched right now. Konnor half-runs, half-stumbles to the door and unlocks it. As Pembie barges in with a huff, Konnor lowers his head, his eyes meeting his feet. She halts when she sees me standing by the sofa. Folding her arms across her chest, she rocks back on her heals, cocks her head, and scrutinizes me from head to toe.

"What's going on here then?" she hisses.

"Blesk, was... dropping something off." Konnor turns, gesturing towards the envelope on his couch. The backs of my eyes begin to sting with the need to cry. He barely looks at her, but he offers me an apologetic glance. And I wish he hadn't because I don't want him to see me tearing up.

This was a huge mistake.

She glowers at him, her eyes scrolling down his body, clearly disgusted by his appearance. By every crease in his clothes. By his messy hair. "You're drunk."

"Yep." He waves his hand indifferently. "What's new, hey?"

She leers at me before flashing a patronising smile. And I don't like that provocative look —nothing good can come from it. In one smooth movement, she grabs the hem of her shirt and pulls it over her head. She isn't wearing a bra. I'm so shocked that my mouth drops open. I'm frozen in place, staring at her perfectly sculpted torso, muscular abdomen, tan skin, and majestically shaped breasts, which are far too perfect to be real.

She throws the shirt at him. "Well, if you're drunk, *lover,* I'll go on top." She winks at me. "Just the way he likes."

Konnor growls under his breath, rubs his temples, and grimaces. "*Fucksake.*"

She approaches him, her naked toned torso moving seductively. And even though he's shaking his head at her with a scowl fixing his brows together, there is definitely a mixture of anger and lust in his eyes. "What?" she asks him.

"Put your fucking shirt back on," he orders, training his eyes on hers.

Her delicate hand presses to his cheek, and she whispers something in his ear that seems to almost physically hurt him. As his jaw muscles work hard, he stares at me over her shoulder. And I don't know what I expect him to do. For him to push her away? For him to react? He could barely form words a few minutes ago. She's going to seduce him and that's all there is to it. I watch her caress her fingers down his chest and cup his groin tightly. She gazes at me over her shoulder and smirks.

I'm going to be sick.

I need to get out of here.

Without further hesitation, I rush towards the door. My hands are trembling as I reach for the handle.

"Blesk, wait a sec," Konnor says from behind me.

I don't.

Before I know it, I'm literally running towards the elevator. My stomach is twisting into knots. Tears are forcing themselves from my eyes as I repeatedly hit the elevator button. And I don't know why I'm reacting like this because he owes me nothing. Less than nothing. I'm a complete stranger to him. But something about him has me all confused —in a trance. Like I was someone else for a moment. Maybe I had just surrendered to his charm. That'd be just like me. I hit the button harder and harder even though I know it won't make a shred of difference.

It finally opens.

And when I step inside and turn to face his door, the ache in my chest prays to see Konnor standing in the hallway. Alone. Wanting to talk to me. Or dragging Pembie out by her arm. Or —The elevator door closes on an empty hallway.

seven: blesk

Blesk

SITTING in a corner of The Basement Lounge, I lift my legs up and cross them on the vinyl cushion. So as to not appear awkward, I pretend to read the textbook I have open in front of me. What I'm really doing, though, is cursing myself. Over and over. And of course, reliving the last few hours' worth of events. Including dwelling on the idea of Pembie and Konnor and whatever it is they're doing with each other —or to each other —right now.

Not being able to call Erik and knowing literally no one else, I finally text Elise.

'Help'.

Poor Elise —day two of knowing Blesk Bellamy... *yeah,*

nothing is ever peachy. I should warn her now before things gets crazy. Interrupting my thoughts, my phone rings.

"Where are you?" Elise asks through the phone.

I try not to sound sad when I say, "At The Basement Lounge."

The Basement Lounge can only be accessed through an underground tunnel between the library and the bookshop; for some reason, that made me feel safe. Hidden. Booths and couches line the room's perimeter, while standard tables are scattered throughout the middle. The low ceiling appears to be carved from natural rock, and the carpet is fire-engine red.

Strangely, for 1:30 p.m. on a Wednesday, the restaurant is surprisingly busy.

"What. Did... that... A-hole do?" she asks breathlessly. Her voice comes in at different volumes, leading me to believe she's jogging.

"Nothing," I grumble, flipping another page over in my book.

"Lie to Elise not," she pants in a funny Yoda voice.

I chuckle. "His girlfriend showed up and gave us a strip tease."

"What? You're kidding, right?"

"I wish I was," I sigh.

She laughs. "Oh, that sounds interesting. You should have called me. I have, like, a whole jar of ones I've been *dying* to get rid of." Her voice is suddenly muffled by those of passer-bys.

I scoff. "My apologies. How thoughtless of me."

"I hate ones," she says in mock anger. "They're so obnoxious. They are the weakest dollar, but still physically bigger than the twos... Ones are bullies."

This girl is crazy... I love it.

"They are," I agree. "Imagine the attitude of the fifty-cent piece?"

"*Oh,* don't get me started on the fifty... I tell ya." She pauses. "Now, Blesk... you never told me he had a girlfriend."

"Yeah, sort of." I huff. "He said it isn't serious." I smack my forehead with my palm. "I know, I know. I'm an idiot."

"Not you are. Softy you are. Suck boys do."

I chuckle. "You're *soooo* weird."

"I'll be there soon. Order me something vegetarian." Then she hangs up, leaving me anxiously waiting for her arrival.

I'm so glad I have Elise in my life. I have a feeling she's going to keep me sane... and also possibly make me a little insane, but in a good way.

Standing up, I wander over to the bar. I lean on it to look down into the kitchen. While I wait, I recognise someone in another booth. Jaxon. *Oh, no...* I hide my face by leaning on my hand, but just as I do, his eyes pluck up with acknowledgement.

"B!" He waves. Standing up quickly, he struts over to me.

I pretend to look pleased to see him. "Hi, Jaxon, nice to see you again."

"Hey, you answered to B." He laughs. Leaning on the bar beside me, he grins from ear to ear.

"It appears so. Are you guys always drinking? Or do you actually go to classes?" I ask, rolling my eyes.

The bartender literally slides over to us on the slippery floor.

Turning towards him, Jaxon pats my back in the same fashion he might a male friend. I like that. "This is the mini Bellamy, Shawn."

"Is this guy bothering you?" Shawn chuckles.

"I suppose that answers my question," I mutter as the bartender and Jaxon share a meaningful look.

Shawn smiles kindly at me. "Hi, mini-Bellamy, what can I get for you?"

"It's Blesk, and can I please get a haloumi salad and a chicken Caesar? *Annnnnd* two–" I hesitate. "Beers?"

If you can't beat 'em, join 'em.

"Is that a question or do you actually want a beer?" Shawn asks with a grin.

"Yes, Little Creatures Pale, please." I pick the local boutique beer to appear seasoned.

"Come sit with us?" Before I can decline his invitation, Jaxon says to Shawn, "Put that on our table." Jaxon seems like a decent kind of guy today. Maybe I'd judged him wrongly.

"Hey!" I hear a small voice come from behind me.

Before I know it, I'm engulfed in Elise's arms. "Want me to cut him?" she whispers in my ear.

"God, I hope you're joking." I laugh. Wrapping my arms around her in return, I squeeze her tiny body lightly.

She chuckles. "Just a little maiming?"

Jaxon shuffles to our side, seemingly wanting to be noticed. As we release each other, he holds a hand out politely.

Another handshake.

"Hi, I'm Jaxon."

Elise looks at him wide-eyed, and I brush a piece of hair from her alarmed face.

"Hi."

That's it? Just hi?

She is not quite her usual conversationalist when in the company of the more masculine gender. An awkward moment passes quickly when Jaxon realises she is going to leave him hanging and lowers his hand.

Unaffected by her refusal to take his hand, he says, "Come on, girls." He wanders over to his booth, taking a seat. "You two are much nicer to look at than Drake."

"Afraid of boys Elise is!" I whisper in the same tone she'd used with me earlier.

She adjusts her glasses and swallows nervously. "Not all boys, just the ones that look like they've just walked out of a Hugo Boss magazine. So, yeah, all the ones you seem to know."

I wrap my arm around her shoulders and guide her towards Drake and Jaxon's table. I enjoy touching someone I feel nothing but comfort with. Old squeamish thoughts resurface and they remind me of how very few people I have in my life that I feel comfortable touching. Which is why it was so weird I'd felt so comfortable with Konnor...

Shaking that thought away, I say, "It'll be okay. They're just people, like you and me."

"Like *you*, maybe," she mutters softly, gawking at them.

"They don't bite," I whisper.

We slide in opposite Jaxon and his friend —Drake. "Hi, I'm Blesk," I say, holding my hand out — because apparently university students shake hands — for the unfamiliar person to take. "This is Elise." Lovely dark eyes stare at me, and a little grin tugs at my lips when he takes my hand in his.

Boys are okay, I guess.

"Hi, Blesk. I'm Drake." He doesn't let go of my hand. My cheeks start to heat up as we continue to stare at each other and, seriously, Elise is right. Why are they both so handsome? I pull my hand from his grasp. Rubbing my palm on my dress, I watch as he politely offers his attention to Elise. "And, Elise, nice to meet you."

"Drake, like, short for Dracula?" she says with a nervous chuckle. I laugh and so does he. There must never be a dull moment inside Elise's head.

"Sure, why not," he says, flicking his eyes to me and grinning again. His dark hair is pulled neatly back off his face. High cheekbones are separated by a strong nose, and his jaw is lightly dusted with stubble.

"Whoa, don't let Erik catch you two looking at each other like that. He'll have a heart attack." Jaxon laughs.

"Why, whatever do you mean, Jax?" Drake asks without taking his gaze off me.

Our beers suddenly appear and I take that opportunity to redirect my attention. I'm quick to take a sip, thankful for now having something to do with my hands.

We spend the next hour debating, laughing, and getting to know each other. We knock heads over intense topics, purposely, yet diplomatically, getting each other riled up. Apparently, university students live for this kind of stuff. Drake —or Dracula —and I bond over our views on the diaspora in Australia, and how it will further shape future generations. Elise eventually joins in, in prime Elise style, as soon as Jaxon argues that our biggest drain on the environment is the mining industry. She fires off some amazing facts about the damage the cattle industry is doing.

Listening to her rant, fast paced and passionate, I enjoy watching the surprise on the boys' faces. She'd been all sweet and coy at the start, but now she's morphed into this confident, awesomely-weird person.

But despite her compelling case, Jaxon isn't about to give up meat for the environment anytime soon.

As the food arrives, we continue to act like friends — drinking and sharing stories. I suppose that is what we are now. Friends? There is a smile playing on my lips because this is fun and I don't feel the least bit like hiding in the library.

And I'm finally able to get my mind off Konnor. At least for a little while...

eight: konnor

Konnor

THE RIGHT SIDE of my bed is empty. The room is quiet; there is only stillness. I'm alone. I was hoping to see Blesk with her hair spread across my pillow. Like it was yesterday. Like it was five seconds ago when I'd been dreaming of her. Of her body facing mine in a way that emphasised the impeccable concave at her waist. But no.

Flipping onto my back, I stretch my arms above my head in an attempt to loosen my body. Agonising fatigue clutches my abdomen muscles, and I wish I could remember more about yesterday than just her hair and the way her body looked on my bed.

The sun's beams invade my senses. I spin over and squint at the alarm clock that mocks me on my bedside table. 10:00 a.m.

Goddamn it.

I hate that clock.

With a groan, I roll off the bed, hitting the floor with more force than intended. My muscles are clearly not awake yet. I'm glad I don't have practice today. I

Despite my pounding head —the alcoholics constant reminded they need more alcohol because they drank too much alcohol —I attempt my morning push-ups. Exhaling forcefully, I focus on my posture while ignoring images of her *fucking* hair. I keep my elbows tucked close to my body. I engage my core with each dip. My brain growls within my cranium. I keep going, fast and hard. Thinking about yesterday. Thinking about her leaving. Thinking about me doing nothing to stop her. Thinking about her sad face, and how this time it was *my* fault.

I grunt. Trying to maintain a straight back on the decline, I lock everything in place. I pump out four sets of thirty reps before slumping over onto my back and relaxing on an angry sigh. There was something there. Between us. Not just her hair, her eyes, her hands. I lie on my back, staring up at the ceiling, and contemplate how much I've let alcohol do the majority of the heavy lifting for my actions. Yesterday had been an exception. Yesterday was the anniversary of her death.

After I hoist myself to my feet, I shuffle over to the kitchen bench. I flip my laptop open and log in to the university's database. With a mission in my mind and anticipation in my chest, I print off my class list and timetables. I anxiously scan the list for her name. Blesk Bellamy... please, fucking, be, on —I exhale with relief. *Blesk Bellamy.*

At least I know I get one hour a week with her. Right, I need to get my shit together. I've given her the wrong impression of me.

After a shower, I stroll into my dressing room and put on

my most presentable shirt and tie. It isn't until I stand in front of the mirror that I realise I don't know how to tie a tie because I've always had a girl do it for me. I throw the useless slip of fabric to the side. Who needs a tie anyway? It's the twenty-first century.

My brows knit as I stare at the hungover dickhead in the mirror. Who is this guy? How much of that boy is left in him? That boy the deceased little girl had loved for all those years. Is there any of him still in here? All I see now is a drunk, arrogant arsehole. I turn from my own reflection with a scowl and wander towards my desk.

As I pack my bags with today's course material, I spot an envelope with beautiful cursive writing on the front. It reads: *Corny Konnor*. My chest tightens as I reach for it.

Corny Konnor,
Thank you for the gift
You are very #
Now I feel I harmoni -can.
Blesk

A COLOSSAL SMILE stretches across my face and I laugh. She's terrible at puns. I fucking *love* that she's terrible at puns. She must have been happy when she wrote this, excited even. Excited to see me. *And I'd fucked it all up.*

I wish I'd chased after her, but if I remember correctly, even standing had been problematic at that point. We could have stayed lying on my bed, hardly touching all night, and it would have been the best night of my life. I don't care that I barely know her, that she knocks me off my tracks, that Erik wants to kick my arse... I just want to be around her.

ONCE THE ELEVATOR opens onto the ground floor, I stride out, making my way across the lobby to Adolf.

"Looking sharp today, Mr Slater," Adolph says, nodding once with approval.

I raise my hands as I ask, "What were you thinking letting Pemberton up yesterday?"

"Mr Slater, she is on the list," he says, his eyes slowly widening. "She doesn't need to ask."

"Well, *damn it,* take her off."

"Of course, sir!" He wanders over to his desk and lowers his head as he types on his computer.

You're being a dick, Konnor.

"I'm sorry, Adolf. I'm pretty hungover today," I admit, approaching him and smiling graciously.

"It is fine, Mr Slater. Pemberton Wright has now been taken off your authorised guest list." He nods at me kindly.

I'm not sure that I want to know the answer, but the words come out anyway. "Was Blesk okay? Miss Bellamy, I mean, when she came down yesterday?"

Adolf looks regretfully at me, and my heart sinks. "She was crying, sir."

I wish I could punch myself. I wish I could kick the arse of the guy who'd made her cry. Me. "Dammit."

Fuck, Konnor. You're an arsehole.

I pat Adolf on the shoulder and force a smile. "Thank you, Adolf."

As I walk towards the sliding doors, he yells,"Mr Slater!" I spin to face him again. "Would you like me to put Miss Bellamy on the guest list?"

I raise my eyebrows. "Aren't we optimistic?"

A wise sort of smile crosses his face. "Girls don't cry like that for no reason, sir. They only cry when something important happens or someone important does something to them."

I exhale long and slow as a grin softens my lips. "Yes, Adolf, put Miss Bellamy on my list." Because he's right. Girls don't cry like that for no reason, and since those tears had been because of me, it's my responsibility to make sure they never are again.

I begin to stride towards the exit once more, only to halt abruptly and face him. "Hey!" I call out across the lobby. "What did you think of her?"

He smiles and for a moment I see a young man thinking about a girl. "Beautiful, Mr Slater. Inside and out, I would wager."

I couldn't agree more, Adolf.

I WANDER TO CLASS, my bag slung over my shoulder.

Do I pull her aside and chat with her?

Wait until after class?

Am I going to come off as desperate?

I am bloody desperate.

As I round the corner of Block F, I see Blesk sitting with Jax and Drake. My chest tightens. It surprises me how the mere sight of her makes me feel. I love the clothes she wears. Tight black leggings hug her long legs while a white lace shirt flows to just past her arse. I'd like to see that shirt without leggings —or panties. I clear my throat.

Her golden hair is pulled off her face in a high ponytail, which bounces whenever she moves her head. I love how her hair bounces like that. I love that she's wearing flats, not heels. I love that she clearly doesn't wear much makeup. Fuck me, that's a lot of loves.

Blesk is my brand of perfection.

As I near them, my stomach lurches at how closely Drake is sitting next to her. Unable to tame my expression, I glare at him while tightening my jaw. They are almost touching. *Almost.*

I like Drake though. He's a good guy. We've known each other since high school, and when we matriculated here together, we shared a dorm for nearly two years. He's practically family.

I fucking hate Drake right now.

I tense up when she laughs at him...

He's making her laugh.

My knees feel weak when I see that smile wrinkling the corners of her eyes and reddening her cheeks. She sticks her tongue out slightly with each bright expression, and I can hardly handle how that makes me feel. My heart pounds. As she giggles, her head flies back, her shoulders shake, and her ponytail bounces around again. I want to capture this moment forever. So now I find myself smiling, grinning like a bloody moron, at this girl laughing with some other guy. Her happiness makes me happy even though it has nothing to do with me.

My gaze falls straight on Jax. "What up? You're not hassling my students, are you?" I laugh, giving Blesk a charming smile. She blushes slightly and lowers her head evasively. I don't like that. She's blushing... Why is she doing that? Because of me? Because she likes Drake?

"Oh, no, B, do you have this dickhead as your tutor?" Jax rolls his head back, wearing a shit-eating grin. "Well, you are *soooo* lucky I know him. I'll make sure you get off easy."

"I'm sure she won't need any help. Blesk's a smart cookie," Drake says, knocking his elbow into hers. And how the fuck does he even know that? Feeling like I'm in the twilight zone or something —lost, completely baffled as to how everyone is so cliquey —I stand idle like a statue. Now he's staring at her as if they share a secret, and I really hate that.

"Mr Slater knows not to treat me any differently," she says, still avoiding my gaze.

Mr Slater?

"*Mr Slater,*" Jax taunts.

Drake glances at me. "So, *Mr. Slater,* we're still on for tomorrow night, right? I'm gonna kick. Your. Arse."

Friday night is poker night and I usually lose. I completely ignore his comment.

Swallowing hard, I find my voice. "Seriously, Blesk, just call me Konnor, okay?" I dip my head, trying to get her to actually acknowledge me. Her eyes drift everywhere other than to my face, and her smile tightens slightly.

"Slater?" Drake says louder, eager for my attention. Stiffly shifting my gaze to him, I frown. When he wiggles his brows at me, I become well-aware of his intentions. We have known each other far too long to not know when the other is looking to hook up. He juts his chin out at me and nods towards Blesk in a *game on* kind of gesture. I feel like knocking him out. Blesk's not a game. God, we're a competitive bunch of arseholes.

Drake passes Blesk her bag, then tucks a piece of her hair

behind her ear. "See you at six, okay? I'll pick you up outside your dorm."

Why did he have her bag?

What the hell is going on?!

"Okay," she mutters, her cheeks pinkening. He made her flushed. She's blushing because of him.

Barely getting the words out through clenched teeth, I ask Jax, "So how do you all know each other exactly?"

Real subtle.

"We bumped into B at The Basement Lounge yesterday. Had a few bevys."

"Right, well, *B* needs to get to class now," I state very matter-of-factly.

Acting like a dickhead again.

"Right-o, see ya, *Mr Slater*." Jax sniggers as he walks away. Calling back over his shoulder, he adds, "Catch ya soon, B."

Drake starts to meander off, but a few steps later, he turns around and walks straight back to Blesk. He casts me a furtive glance to make sure I'm watching. Then... he kisses her on the cheek. "Later, Blesk."

He kisses her.

Fuck. Drake verse Konnor: 1-0

My cheek muscles dance beneath my skin. I feel my back tighten between my shoulders, and I think I unintentionally growl. Blesk looks stunned. Her eyes had widened when his lips had touched her skin, and now, for the first time today, she's looking straight at me. I open my mouth while our eyes are locked hard on each other. There is so much to say. And I have no idea how to say it. Suddenly interrupted by several noisy students moving around us, I just shake my head. The moment's gone.

He kissed her, but she looked at me.

Her eyes went to me.

She likes me.

I inhale a big breath and then exhale it slowly, channelling my resolve to get through class. I nod at her. Trailing my students into the classroom, I meander to the front and place my bag on the desk.

My heart pounds in my chest, so I shuffle papers around before trying to speak. When I look up and search the room, everyone is pulling chairs out from the stacks and placing them around in front of me. It's a small class, only fifteen students. It's apparent some of them know each other, while some don't know anyone. Blesk is in the latter group.

Whether it's an instinct based on my own personality or not, I'm not sure, but I can pick out the players straight away.

A few of the boys have positioned themselves beside her, and she offers them a shy, girlie half-smile.

I want to tell her that won't help.

I can't exactly blame them for noticing her. She is gorgeous, unassumingly so.

"Right-o," I say as chairs are still being shuffled around. "My friends call me Slater." All eyes are on me now as everyone quickly slides into their chairs. "So you can call me Konnor." I hear a mixture of masculine chortles and sweet giggles.

Time for my ice breaker.

"Firstly." I can't help but chuckle as the next sentence leaves my lips. "Who in this room wants to sleep with someone else in this room?" The girls erupt into fits of giggles while the guys glance awkwardly at each other. "Raise your hand if you want to have sex with someone in this room," I say. No one moves.

"Okay, okay, you don't need to tell me who, but have a good look around and then raise your hand." I wait patiently while they look around at each other, but no one raises their hand. "Does this help?" I ask, raising my own hand. More girlie giggles fill the room.

No, not you.

Most of the boys and a few of the girls raise their hands. Blesk does as well.

Daring... that hand best be for me.

"So about eighty percent of you want to have sex with someone in this room." I pinch my thumb and index finger together, pretending to hold an invisible pin. "Now do me a favour; put a pin in that feeling. I know what first-year university is like. Put a pin in it, at least until after class." They all laugh now, including Blesk.

"I'm a cruisey guy. I am just here to guide you. The idea of this class is to teach you how to teach your passion—*music* —to kids." I pace back and forth in front of them, finding it easier to talk when I'm on the move.

"One of the most important things to remember about this class is that I'm not a music major. You probably know more than I do about general music theory. I'm here to help you work through what your lecturer wants you to know. She teaches." I halt in the centre of the room and smirk. "I'm just a peer with the answers to your tests."

Everyone chuckles again. "This class is more about *teaching* music to students than about music itself." I grab a pile of unit outlines from my desk and hand them to the students in the front row.

"Pass them back. I know some of you will have taken the initiative and printed this out prior. Some of you are lazy and some of you don't have printers. I don't know who fits into which category... yet. But I will soon."

"Konnor?" I hear a guy call out.

I nod at him. "Yep?"

"Do you mark the assignments or does Mrs Kale?"

I laugh. "Are you trying to figure out how much you need to suck up to me?" The guy gazes around the room. While the other students snicker, a low glow touches his cheeks.

"Maybe," he finally admits.

I address the class as if the question had been universal. "Your assignments and tests are all distributed randomly among three grad students, including me and Mrs Kale." I turn my attention back to the student who'd asked the question. "To answer you, possibly. But you'll never know. Neither do I at this point."

For the next twenty minutes, I review the course outline, what is expected, and how the marks are broken up. My students vary in age and demeanour, but most of them seem eager and interested in what I have to say. Teaching is my absolute life. I want them all to succeed.

When I divide the class into four groups, I can't help but put Blesk with the two lads I'd noticed eyeing her. I give them a task; as a team, I ask them to tell me what they want to get out of this class. I promise them I will try to make it happen.

Blesk sits with one voluptuous thigh over the other, the leg on top rocking back and forth. She clicks her pen, studying the paper in front of her. The thickness of her thighs are perfect. Forcing down imagines of my hands gripping that soft skin, I find myself walking over to her. All three students look up at me as I approach.

"Hey," I say, offering my hand for one of the lads to shake. "Konnor."

He takes it with a smug look. "Hi, Konnor. Matt."

I hold my hand out for the other guy. "Konnor."

"Justin." He takes my hand, grinning at me.

"Miss Bellamy," I say, looking straight at her half-startled, half-smiling face. "Do you mind if I pull you away for a moment?"

She bats those long lashes at me for several seconds. "Ah, yes of course."

I wave my hand towards the door. She stands and flattens her shirt-dress down her stomach before proceeding me out of the room.

"Did you just pull rank on me for personal reasons, *Mr Slater*?" she says once I close the door and block us from any prying eyes.

"Blesk, I'm *so* sorry." The words just tumble out.

Her expression falls slightly.

She talks through a tight sad smile. "Konnor, you don't owe me anyth—"

"I told her to leave," I interrupt in a desperate tone I barely recognise. "I told her it's over." She glances away from me; her eyes bounce around the space at her feet as she contemplates my words. "I'm sorry," I repeat. "I just want you to know, that isn't me, not normally. That was a weird day for me and I drank a lot more than I usually do."

"Konnor." Her eyes narrow as she tries to smile genuinely this time. "It's okay, thank you, but it's okay." I put my hand on her waist and move her until her back meets the brick wall. Both cheeks redden instantly. She looks shocked or excited, or perhaps both.

I put both of my palms on the wall next to her head, caging her in front of me.

Leaning in, I stare her straight in the eyes. "Where are you going with Drake tonight?"

Her lips part as she sucks extra air in. As her breasts rise and fall with more need, my eyes dart down to watch them before trailing up to her mouth as she licks her lower lip. I'm overwhelmed with the urge to taste that lip and tongue.

"We're just friends," she finally says, snapping me out of my trance, "going for a drink."

I shake my head with a smirk. "He doesn't want to be *just* friends."

Her chin tucks into her neck slightly, and her eyes peer up at me, so shy, so demure, so *fucking* perfect. "And why does that matter to you? You had a girlfriend up until a few hours ago." She breathes hard as if that sentence had been a challenge to say.

I lean down to brush her ear with my mouth. Her shoulder rolls when my breath hits her neck, and I absolutely love how flustered she is. "It matters, Blesk."

Silence fills the space between us, and it's anything but comfortable. My heart is racing and I can see the flutter of her pulse beneath her skin. I wish there was no space between us at all. I wish my lips were on hers. I wish I could feel her breasts pushed against my chest. I wish I could taste her tongue. I'm only inches from her, but those inches are the difference between me and her... and *us*.

I wonder what she's thinking. Her hands are flat against the wall by her thighs, desperately pushing against the bricks. Her cheeks flush further and the skin on her throat prickles as my breath rushes down her chest. Before I can stop myself, I'm pressing my mouth to her neck. I feel her heart throbbing against my lips, a moan vibrating in her throat, her body pressing into me... *Fuck.* She is just as responsive to me as I am to her.

I force myself away from her. "Fuck." We stare at each other, astonished by what had just happened.

Clearing my throat, I take a few calming breathes and try to ignore a certain appendage, which is now twitching in my pants. "Don't go tonight," I say breathlessly. "Hang out with me instead."

She exhales and her hands flex around the bricks at her side. "Okay."

I lift a brow at her. "Really?"

Her shoulders shake gently as she giggles. "Yes. Really."

"Well, okay then. Ummm. Can you go in first?" I wave her in with a grin. "I need a few minutes."

Her tongue peaks out between her lips and she laughs.

That tongue isn't helping, Blesk.

With the idea of my date with Blesk in my head, I continue the class in a great mood. The hour flashes by. After everyone leaves, I collect all the activity sheets and papers, packing them away for Cathy to review. While I continue completing my menial tasks, I think about Blesk's neck, her soft skin, her physical reaction to my lips on her throat. Her moan. How she rocked into me... *Damn.*

Calm down.

Think of something else...

I pack everything away and lock up just as my phone buzzes inside my pocket. Pulling it out, I swipe to see the message.

> Pemberton: Konnor, I'm sooo sorry please cum and see me. I'm not doing good.

Her spelling is not lost on me. Ordinarily, I'd hightail it over to see her, but I know her games. Pemberton uses sex as a way to command men and for the most part, it works. But she's a damn drama queen. I know if I go over there to check on her, I'll find her downing wine and sobbing relentlessly. Then she'll say or do something to get me riled up and start the kind of fight I can't just walk away from. Blesk's face is the only one I want to see.

I ignore Pemberton's text, drop off the paperwork in Cathy's pigeonhole, and make my way to Blesk's dorm.

I scruff up my hair and untuck my shirt in an attempt to make myself look less formal. The sun is beginning its descent toward the horizon, filling the sky with pinks and oranges. I wonder what Blesk's favourite colour is. I wonder if she like sunsets... Most girls do.

Luckily for me, I catch Drake in the quadrangle. "Dude," I say.

"Slater, so how'd my girl go on her first day?" He smirks, provoking me.

I laugh. "Desperate Drake, it isn't happening. This one's not a game."

He gives me the kind of grin that makes me want to cave his face in with my knuckles. "And what makes you think she wants what you have to offer?"

"She does." I rattle that response out, feeling like crap for talking about her like this. "But it isn't like that."

"Pussy. What about Pemberton?" he asks.

"It's over," I state, expressionless. "That's how much I need you to back off, Drake."

He guffaws. "What does she have —bourbon-flavoured nipples or something?"

Right, because I'm an alcoholic... Very clever, Drake, you bastard.

I'm extremely glad I have better things to do than get into a fight. Had Blesk not put me in a good mood, I might've been inclined to rearrange his smirk. Shaking my head at him, I say, "Just leave this one."

His smirk creeps wider. "Can't guarantee she won't come to me."

"I can *guarantee* she won't," I hiss.

He huffs. "Whoa, you work fast. Can't keep up with you."

I have nothing to say to that. I heave myself away.

"Slate!" He yells at my back. "Konnor! Seriously, what's

going on? Of course I'll back off! Why are you acting like this?"

I don't even know myself.

BLESK IS IN A GIRLS-ONLY DORM, one of the last original dormitories on campus. It's small and only borderline legally sufficient in amenities. Despite all that, I'm glad she is here instead of at the mixed dorms. Having been there myself a few years ago, I know exactly what goes on in them.

I approach room seventy-three. After knocking, I adjust my shirt, run my hands through my hair, and roll my shoulders loose. The door swings open and a set of stern blue eyes hit mine. A petite brunette stares at me in the same fashion as someone who knows all my secrets might and I feel immediately apprehensive.

Her eyes are so wide they almost pop out of her face.

"Hey," I say with a nod.

"Konnor?" She tilts her head. She steps back and measures me up, her eyes scanning every inch of me. I can't help but laugh at that. Holding my arms out to the sides, I grin while I do a little spin.

"All in check?" I ask, gesturing to myself. "Do I pass?"

She brightens. "Blesk," she calls out. "Konnor's here." She waves at me, flapping her wrist awkwardly. "Hi, I'm Elise." I get the impression I make her nervous.

"Elise, pleasure is all mine," I say, slapping on the charm. I stick both hands in my pockets and rock back and forth on my heels, waiting to see Blesk.

A few seconds later, a vision in red steps out from behind Elise. Blesk smiles at me from under a little black side beanie, and my heart stops. Everything about her body says she is one of a kind: the way she holds it, the way she dresses it, and the way she clearly respects it. She has a regal sort of elegance, like a duchess.

Her blonde hair is swept to the side. It dangles down her torso, splaying over her breasts. She twists from side to side, and as she does, the hem of her red dress sways across her knees, making her look too sweet to be real. Even if I could design my perfect girl, Blesk would be superior in every possible way. She isn't going to be happy about getting that dress dirty though, but I can't wait to see it stained.

Little does she know...

Elise stares at me while I stare at Blesk, who is eyeing me from head to heel.

Is she checking me out?

"Blesk is my new best friend, Konnor," Elise says to me, narrowing her eyes. "If you hurt her, I will beat you over the head with your own leg." Not expecting that, I nearly choke on my laughter.

Fair enough.

I grin at her. "Which leg? Because I have a favourite."

She peers down at my legs, pretending to take my question seriously. "Your right one," she says, pointing and smiling with glee.

I tilt my head at her and give her a questioning smile. "Dammit. How did you know?"

Blesk seems different tonight. Comfortable. Confident. I'm in awe of the expression on her face. Did Elise cause that?

"Elise?" I smiler wider at Blesk's new best friend. "Would you like to join us?"

Her eyes widen and she glances at Blesk.

"Oh, yes!" Blesk blurts out, knocking Elise with her elbow. "It'll be fun."

Elise stares down at her clothes and motions towards them. "I just have jeans on."

"Oh, you don't need anything special for where we're going," I say. "But if you need a few moments, I can wait." I turn to Blesk and act like a complete moron again by saying, "I'm a pretty patient guy. I've waited a long time for her."

Are you even still a man, Konnor?

Elise turns to Blesk, who is now blushing from her cheeks to her ears, and says, "I'm not sure whether to say, *'Aww'* or throw up."

"That is *really* corny, Konnor." Blesk giggles. And once again my heart skips a beat.

"So I've been told."

ALL I WANT to do is hold her hand, to thread my fingers through hers, to feel her palm pressed against mine, and to mimic the rhythm of her stride as she walks. But I'm trying to be fair to Elise. Anyone who has managed to put a skip in Blesk's step has my seal of approval.

As we walk into the Arts & Grey Theatre, I hold the door open for both girls. I follow them inside and casually place my hand on Blesk's waist, steering her down the corridor.

The theatre is at the east wing of campus and open every night, which often means it has a non-existent audience. It's really what university is all about; it's run by students, for students. Anything goes. The shows vary from poetry to dancing to singing to hour-long monologues that usually end in at least one performer committing suicide.

And the audience wanting to follow suit.

The whole experience is pretty casual. Mismatched chairs, recliners, couches, and park benches make up the seating arrangement. The stage is barely six metres long and only slightly raised. I'm not an artsy guy. Not really. But I've shared a few electives with some of the art students and with Frank, the theatre manager. He's pretty good value.

The lighting is coordinated by a guy named Jojo, and I have it on good authority that during most performances, he's up on the truss getting stoned. I love this place. I hope Blesk does too.

We approach the front three-seater couch, and I take my place on one end. Blesk slides in next to me, followed closely by Elise. Blesk folds her dress delicately under her as she sits, making me squirm slightly. Resting my arm along the head rest behind her, I then wait for her to set the pace. I hope she moves in close to me.

With little hesitation, she slides her shoulder under my arm. When I pull her in closer, she shuffles over willingly. We are a perfect fit. I peer over to check on Miss Elise, who is closely tucked up beside Blesk and eagerly peering around.

I lean towards them. "This is one of my favourite places to go on campus," I whisper as the lights begin to dim. "You'll see some wild stuff here."

Elise pushes her glasses back onto the arch of her nose, trying to take it all in. "It's funky; I like that."

"Dickhead!" I hear someone say inappropriately loud right before the back of our sofa shakes. I release Blesk. Pulling my arm down to my side, I crane my neck around to see Jax and Drake grinning at us. Bunch of bloody miscreants. I wonder what Blesk said to Drake when she cancelled their plans. His lopsided grin tells me he's not surprised to see us here. He winks at me, letting me know we're all right.

"I thought you'd be here, dickhead." Jax laughs.

I hold my finger up to my lips and shush them. "Sit down and shut up."

When Elise sees them, she squirms with anticipation in her seat. "Dracula!" Elise acknowledges Drake enthusiastically.

So they all know each other.

I must have missed something.

"Hey, *Dracula!*" I mock with a cocky smirk. "Sit down, you ugly blood-sucking bastard."

Drake scoffs at me. "Fuck off. Dracula is a stud."

When I turn to Blesk, I find her peering at me with nervous uncertainty. She flicks her eyes at the boys before glancing down at my arm, the one no longer touching her. I suddenly realise how my instant recoil from her at the sight of the lads might have been interpreted.

I wrap my arm over her shoulders again. My fingers brush the curve at her waist, dipping down to her hip, causing her to wriggle beneath my touch. *Jesus Christ...* I can't help but imagine her wriggling underneath me.

My need to focus on functional processes, like breathing and maintaining an appropriate level of arousal, is imperative right now. The boys jump into the seats surrounding our couch just as Frank walks on stage. He's followed closely by a spotlight that isn't quite in the right spot. Bloody Jojo.

Everyone goes quiet. All my senses begin to channel the feel of the girl beside me. The subtle movements of her body as her chest rises and falls. The feel of her hair brushing the side of my neck. Turning my head slightly, I watch as her eyes dart around the stage in anticipation of something happening.

"How long have you known Elise?" I whisper in her ear.

"As long as I've known you," she whispers back.

I chuckle. Some things just work. Elise and Blesk just work... and so do Blesk and I.

I start to say something else, but I stop just as Frank begins to speak.

"Welcome. Tonight, we are going to show you what live art is all about. When you go to a gallery, the items you view have been constructed, nay, designed, over a period of time. The place of said production is unknown. The state of said producer is also unknown. Its living essence, unknown."

Artsy guys are so dramatic.

Frank continues, "The painting you fell in love with could have been painted under any circumstance, in any mood, during any event. What does it mean to them? Only words. What they tell you it means. So how can it mean so much to you?

"The first step your daughter takes. Your mum is fighting back tears. Your dad stands with his arms outstretched, ready to catch her. Wouldn't it be nice if you could capture a piece of *life*, perfectly *in time* and *in space*? Well, that's the beauty of live art —the piece or experience happens right in front of you. We are bridging the gap between the art and the consumer."

With that, Frank calls a young couple up on stage. He stretches up and pulls a board with a piece of canvas attached to it down towards the floor.

"I'm going to paint them as they are right now. In love."

Jax and Drake splutter out a laugh and I almost follow suit until I notice Blesk and Elise are both wide-eyed and enthralled. These girls are making me soft. Blesk chews on her bottom lip as her attention is glued on Frank. She is completely in love with this.

Frank turns back to the audience. "Watch this."

He positions the couple in front of the canvas, then begins to spray paint around them. It's messier than I'd expected. He coats the canvas, moves the couple as if they were stencils, and starts spraying them again. Within minutes they're completely covered in paint and chuckling happily together.

We watch for fifteen minutes as a blank canvas becomes an abstract piece of artwork. When it's all done and the couple move off stage, Frank slides his work of art behind the curtain.

"That looks like what it felt like to watch," Blesk whispers in my ear. She giggles. "You know what I mean."

And I'm a goner.

Her giggle resonates in my chest. "Yeah, I know what you mean."

"*Oi,* Slater!" Frank yells out into the audience, peering around until his eyes find me. "Nice to see you, buddy. Who's that next to you?"

I acknowledge him with a nod. "A pretty girl, ever seen one before?"

"Cheeky prick. Get up here; it's your turn," he says, dragging a new piece of canvas down. *Fuck, it's nearly three metres long.* I turn to look at Blesk; she's white, completely stunned, like a bunny in headlights. A damn adorable bunny.

"Everyone up!" I say, standing. Elise just blinks at me with her mouth open. Drake and Jax eagerly jump to the challenge, encouraging the girls to join them.

Originally, I'd planned on this being for just Blesk and I, but I'm glad it'll be a group moment. As the lads wait for us, I reach down to grab Blesk, who seems to sink further into the seat.

"Blesk," I say, pulling her into me. "Let's do this?" I nod at her, encouraging her with my playful eyes. "Yeah? You'll have fun, I promise."

My hand moves to the small of her back as I steady her against me. Her breathing quickens. Her eyes close tightly as she takes a big calming breath, and I'm suddenly not sure if I should have done this. She is so shy. I thought that because she sings in public, she'd enjoy this. "You'll regret it if you don't," I whisper. "See, look," I say, pointing to Elise, whose grin stretches from ear to ear as she walks across the stage.

A nervous smile tugs at Blesk's lips. "O...kay," she says in a cute, defeated voice, rolling her eyes at me.

I pick her up before I step onto the stage, causing her to squeal with excitement.

Frank begins to position us in front of the canvas. Blesk remains cradled in my arms. She cuddles my neck. Her nervousness is apparent by the pace of her heart as it beats against me. I rock her back and forth until she relaxes. She giggles slightly and begins to kick her feet. I make sure I have her dress folded across my forearm so no one can catch a glimpse of her knickers. Although I'd love to know what colour they are, whether they're lacy or silk or cotton or boy shorts...

Clearing my throat, I force myself to forget about her underwear. This would be a very bad moment to get a boner. Captured forever. The thought actually makes me laugh.

Once we are all in place, Frank begins to spray us with paint, switching colours, coating us and the canvas, splashing up and down, switching motions and consistencies.

Blesk kicks around, laughing nervously. I wouldn't change this for the world. Jax keeps grabbing Blesk's feet, trying to hold them stationary, but that only makes her giggle and kick more.

I hold Blesk for nearly twenty-five minutes while Frank scurries around us. The whole time, I can't take my eyes off her lips. I want to kiss her. I'm dying to taste her. I want our first kiss captured right now. Despite how much I want to, a strange apprehension stops me.

Once it is all done and we are well and truly coated in paint, Frank puts the canvas away for drying and sealing. When I finally lower Blesk to the ground, I thread my fingers through hers and we leave the theatre hand-in-hand.

If she were any other girl, I'd be inviting her back to my apartment right now. But I don't want to scare her off and having just broken up with my *kinda-girlfriend* last night, it might be seen as a little hasty.

So we approach the girl's dormitories instead, cause I'm a fucking gentleman tonight. Before the girls venture inside, I need to steal a few seconds alone with Blesk. I walk her through the dormitory courtyard and into a softly lit corner. She shivers as the cold wind hits us. Rubbing her shoulders to keep her warm, I struggle not to stare.

She's covered in paint; it's in her hair, on her hands, on her cheek. I grab her hand while looking her straight in the eye, wishing I had something impressive or sweet to say to her. Or something corny. I gently push her back until she is wedged between the wall and me. As she touches the cold bricks, a small gasp leaves her lips.

Goddamn, those lips.

I raise our combined hands and stroke my fingers down her palm. I gaze into her eyes, enjoying how she gazes back. A huge grin draws my lips out, and I press our index fingers together, mimicking a gesture I haven't done in so many years. And I'm not sure why I'm doing it now, but -

Her face falls.

What is that look?

Fear?

Something unexpected and heavy drops in my stomach.

She gasps, retracting her hand from mine so quickly I could have sworn I'd burnt her.

"What is it, Blesk?" I squint at her questioningly. Her face slowly loses all colour. Cheeks hollow. Every part of her appears paralysed, and the look in her eyes... *Fuck, the look in her eyes is freaking me out.*

What did I do?

"What did I do?" I finally say.

Petrified, she stares at me, searching every inch of my face as if she sees something disturbing— my secrets.

"Blesk, what is it? Tell me what I did! Please? You're fucking freaking me out right now."

What the hell is happening?

She looks like she's just seen a ghost.

nine: august 23, 1999

THE DISTRICT DAILY NEWS

NERROCK FAMILY SON and Heir Missing Since Sunday

Police are investigating the disappearance of Deakon Nerrock, age 5, only son and heir to the prominent family's estate.

He was last seen asleep in bed on Saturday night just after midnight by the family's captain of security, Adolf Bauer. At 5:30 a.m. Deakon was found to be missing by his mother Madeline Nerrock.

A 5km radius around the family mansion was searched by volunteers, security, and eight police officers on Sunday. No trace of the boy was found.

"As far as we are aware, no one went in the house, and no-one left—the security system was still engaged when we realised the boy was missing," Mr Bauer said.

More search parties have gone out and several people are being questioned. No suspects have been found.

The police and his family are concerned for his welfare due to his young age and legacy as the only heir to the Nerrock fortune. No demands have been made.

"If anyone knows anything, you will be generously rewarded for your information. And if you took my son, please bring him back to us. We will do anything to have him back," Mrs Nerrock said.

Deakon Nerrock is three feet, five inches tall. He was last seen wearing a batman shirt and black cotton pants. A generous reward is on offer for any information that leads to his discovery.

If you have seen Deakon Nerrock or have any information about his whereabouts, contact Cape Rogan City Police: 08 98263521 or www.mp.crcp.gov.au

ten: blesk

Blesk

"WHERE. ARE. YOU?" Erik screams into the phone. I know he's frantic because each word comes out between gasps. I'm having trouble constructing thoughts, let alone converting them into words. I mumble, and my mouth fills with tears. I can't believe I'm here, again. I can't believe I'm making my brother endure my shadowy past, again.

The last seven hours have been a blur of traffic, of running, of hiding. I'm always hiding from my past. But now I'm walking, covered in splatters of paint, my hair knotted with acrylic as I trek two kilometres through the estate. My feet sink into the undisturbed ground. Water seeps through the soles of my shoes, and the daisies and weeds sponge my landing as I walk to the top of the hill.

The hill I hate.

I squint at the sun. I'd forgotten how bright it is up here.

And yet, still somehow cold. I shiver in the crisp morning air. The beauty of this part of Australia takes my breath away, just like it always has. But I'm not me when I'm on *this* particular hill.

The view from the top fills my chest, as do the waves of daisies that take the ground by storm. I was constantly told back then that daisies are little more than weeds, that they were ploughed into the ground to make way for more important foliage. I never cared; I still don't care. I love daisies.

"I'm home," I manage to say to Erik when I remember I'm on the phone. Those words tighten my throat. I caught a bus. A train. Another bus. I went home. I didn't really think it through. I wheeze for a few seconds as my body forgets how to breathe and how to swallow. There is no response.

"I went home," I whisper again, kneeling on the spot, the spot that marks the entrance to a place only a few people could ever find ... or have ever been to.

"Just stay where you are," Erik says curtly, pain clear in his voice. "I'll be there as soon as I can." I lower the phone from my ear. I'm knotted up with all kinds of delirious feelings. I stare at the space below my feet, a clear patch of grass that leads to a set of stairs.

"Blesk!" he yells.

I raise the handset back in a daze. "Yes?"

"Do *not* go in," he commands before he disconnects.

I hate that Erik is coming back here. I know what seeing this place does to him. Saying goodbye to Liz was one of the hardest days of both of our lives. I was nine years old. Erik was only thirteen. When our parents brought us to this hill, we spent the day picking daisies. Then we laid them by Liz's favourite tree, saying our goodbyes and burying her memory forever.

It was hard, the hardest thing Erik and I have ever done,

but it was a closure I'd needed. Because, the year before that had felt like hell on earth for me. No one could get through to me. I kept having this nightmare. A cloudy memory of before I was adopted.

In this nightmare, I'd be watching television when suddenly I'd see his face. I'd see *his* face, people crying, a mother crying, and then I'd know—know I was ruining his life.

When I was shaken back to the waking world, I'd still be screaming, flooded by the guilt *his* eyes summoned in me.

Erik was often there when I woke screaming. He'd me while I wept, while I tried to remind myself that it was over. That I could let go. He would curl up beside me, smothering me in his arms, rocking me back and forth and hushing me tenderly. His heart would always race. His cheeks were often wet with his own sorrow. My mother couldn't sleep, my father couldn't sleep, my brother wouldn't sleep —I was to blame for their misery.

And that's why I did it.

That's why I had to say goodbye to Liz.

Leaving her behind meant I'd have to leave him behind too and everything he and Liz were together, but I tried —I try still —to forget about him. Because in the end, I needed my new family's suffering to end.

We each wrote a letter to Liz and read them aloud.

We then buried them below the roots of her tree, never planning on coming back, just leaving those words of love with her.

Today though, I broke my promise. I came back. I'd sworn I never would, and I had never intended to. But I didn't come back for Liz. I came back for *him*. And because I didn't know where else to go.

I hold my breath as I brush the leaves off the hatch I'm

sitting on. Standing, I swing it open. It flies back, having been pent-up with over a decade of concealment. Years of dust and eerie darkness are released. Fresh air is sucked in to mingle with its demons.

For a few moments, I only look down the dark hole. I know what walking down these steps will do to me. The numbness has already set in.

But my feet take me forward without my consent. I'm surprised when I need to duck my head as I cross the threshold. It's quiet. The room is windowless. Except for the big barred cage in the corner, it is empty. The deafening silence is suddenly filled with ringing, and it takes me a few moments to realise it's my phone.

Pulling it out, I answer, "Elise?" My own voice sounds foreign.

"Oh. My. God. Blesk! Where are you? Everyone is *so* worried. Jaxon and Konnor have been all over campus looking for you and then when you didn't come home ... It's 6:00 a.m. Where did you sleep last night?"

"On the train." Although I hold the phone pressed tightly to my ear, her voice sounds so distant. It's this box under the ground. It seems to separate everything inside it from everything outside. I take a seat on the fifth step — my favourite one. The concrete is cold on my thighs, but it isn't the literal cold that has me shivering.

"On a train? What do you mean? Where are you?" She sounds panicked.

"Um." I try to snap myself out of my trance. "Konnor was looking for me?"

"Oh my God, Blesk, seriously? Of course he was looking for you. He lost it. You just ran off. He looked for you everywhere, like a mental patient. He got really drunk and ended up knocking himself out when he fell over. Jaxon is with him now. Why didn't you pick up your phone?"

I gasp and cover my mouth, thinking of Konnor passed out on the floor. "I'm sorry." The words are not enough. They never will be.

"Sorry?" Poor Elise sounds so strange and confused. "We don't care. Please just tell me you're safe. When will you be home?"

"Erik is coming to get me."

"Okay. I'll tell Jaxon." Elise pauses for a long time. For a few moments we listen to each other breathing hard. "Blesk?"

"Yes."

"What's going on? You walked away with Konnor and then ran off. Did he do something? Did he hurt you?"

I draw a sharp breath in and release it slowly. "No, Konnor didn't do anything. Maybe one day I'll explain, but not today."

"One day? So it's something bad, hey? Okay, I'm not gonna pressure you to tell me anything. I will be here for you though. Whether you like it or not, you're stuck with me."

"That sounds *really good*, Elise." I know my voice is unconvincing, but I really mean every word.

"I'm small, but I'm scrappy. I'll kick Konnor's arse if he hurt you!"

"It wasn't anything Konnor did."

"When will I see you?"

A small sigh escapes me. "I don't know. Maybe tomorrow?"

"Seriously? Don't shut me out. I know I'm a new friend, but I don't care. I want to be there for you."

"Tomorrow. I promise, tomorrow," I state with more conviction.

Elise sighs and then tries to lighten the mood with her Yoda impression. "Best friend Elise has."

"Best friend Blesk has," I say before hanging up the phone. Alone once more with his memory, I curl up on the step to wait for Erik.

———————

"BLESK?" I hear Erik's voice spill down the stairs. The time that's passed is vague. However, due to the dull ache in my thighs, my stiff back, and the growling of my stomach, it must have been hours.

"Shit, Blesk, I told you not to go in." The scratch of the dirt rubbing between his shoes and the steps grows nearer. Before I can even raise my head from the cold concrete, he has me in his arms.

"I'm okay," I say as I'm pulled protectively against his chest. His hand strokes the back of my head. He smells like home. Warm and nurturing in his movements, he rocks me back and forth. "I'm sorry."

"Shhh. Don't, Blesk, it's fine. I don't understand why you're back here, but it's fine."

Erik squeezes me tighter as I begin to cry.

My shoulders tremble in his embrace. "Thank you."

As my tears fall onto his chest and soak his shirt, he begins to cry too. My heart aches for every bit of sorrow I cause him. He loves me. I'm never going to be worthy of it. No matter how much I give him, I feel like it's not enough to account for all the drama I cause.

Lifting my head, I look up into his eyes. They are reddened with anguish and from a lack of sleep. His cheeks are flushed and wet, like mine.

I'm sorry, Erik.

"I love you." I hold his stare and he holds mine. "I'm sorry to put you through this again."

"Blesk, why are you here?" His brows knit into a serious line.

I look up at him through pools of tears. "It's Konnor."

His arms around my back stiffen unnervingly. Gripping my hips, he pushes me away so that he can inspect my face, scrutinise it even.

"What about Konnor?" The depth of the creases between his furrowed brows and the tightness of his grip on my hips caution me. I subtly try to shake him off, but his fingers are unforgiving. His eyes seem to dilate, filling with nothing but black.

"I know you spent the night with him," he mutters coldly.

"So we went out on a date," I say defiantly.

A callous look tightens his face. "Oh. Right. *A date.*"

"Why are you doing this now?" I ask. "Please don't do this now."

"I hate that guy." He cups my face with his hands. "He's a total dickhead."

I try to pull away from him, but he doesn't let me. "Erik, don't do this now. Not here."

"What did the dickhead do to make you go off the deep end?" His eyes make me squirm. He's always been jealous of other men with me, but I'd thought he might have moved past those feelings of ownership. My heart is filling my ears now, thinking about what those feelings had eventually led him to do. With me. To me.

"Erik, don't," I plead.

He leans in towards my ear. As his breath slides down my neck, I shudder. "Tell me what he did to you, Blesk."

I pull away from him again, but he grabs my arms, pinning me in place. "Let me go. What's gotten into you?"

My breathing feels strained.

"Blesk," he hisses. "I spent last night with Pembie."

I still in his grasp. I can't even begin to imagine what she's been saying to him. "Erik, whatever—"

"Shut up for a second," he snaps. "She was really upset. She told me she found you in his apartment. And that you spent last night with him as well." I try to tug away again, but he moves in closer until I'm pressed against his body and his hands are spanning the back of my head and neck.

As his cheek touches my forehead, he purrs, "Has he been inside you, Blesk?"

My heart all but stops.

Whimpering with panic, I try harder to get away from him, tugging and pulling, but his fingers just twist in my hair and bite at the skin on my neck. "I swear to God, Blesk, if you've let that dickhead inside you, I'm going to lose my shit."

Struggling in his grasp, I desperately fight back tears. And then the begging starts. "Erik, don't talk to me like that. Please. Don't do this."

I gasp when he scoops me up and cradles me against his chest. He walks me down to the bottom of the chamber. "Erik!" I scream at him. "Put me down!"

When my back hits the hard floor, the wind is knocked from me. He covers my mouth with his hand as I try to scream. He drops down on top of me, crushing his body against mine, holding me captive beneath him. I can hardly breathe.

Tears drip down my cheeks. I blink through them, trying to search the eyes of the man above me, trying to find a glimpse of my loving brother.

"*Shhhhh*." The chilling intent in his brown eyes seeps into my soul, stirring my stomach to nausea. "Blesk, I'm not going to hurt you. God, I love you. You know this. I would do anything for you. I have. But I know you won't listen to me unless you feel this again. How good this feels."

My eyes widen further as he uses his hips to force my legs apart, kneading his pelvis into me. The sudden taste and heat of bile fills my throat. I clasp my eyes shut, not wanting to see his face, not wanting to see the chilling look in his eyes.

He nuzzles the crook of my neck and slides his tongue up the column of my throat. As his breath slithers over me, a shudder snakes up my spine. I begin to sob.

"Blesk, see how good this feels. Please don't cry, Bebe." It's hard, but I try to ignore all the places his hands are touching and the disturbing ardency to their movements. My breasts become tender even though his touch is gentle. As he rocks his erection between my thighs, he groans, "God, no one else gets me this hard. Ever..."

My hands scrabble against the floor at my sides, nails digging into the concrete until they hurt. "See, it's you and me. It will *always* be you and me."

He lifts my dress up to my waist, and now the thin pieces of fabric separating us aren't enough. The ridge of his erection is so hard, his pace against me so needy, I feel I may bruise. A deep groan vibrates from him and through my chest. I wish away this moment, trying with absolute desperation to sink into oblivion.

"Don't you remember how good this was? The first time we did this? How close it made us? Best friends. Lovers. I don't want to pretend it didn't happen anymore, Blesk. The thought of Konnor touching you... Fucking hell, it's driven me out of my goddamn mind. I've been going crazy. And I know now that I just need to make you remember." He licks a tear from my cheek. "Please don't cry, Bebe."

I want to cry out, "Stop."

"I'm the only person who's been inside you, right?"

I nod frantically.

"Good."

When he unbuttons his jeans and shifts his weight to pull them down, my mind fades out, leaving him with my body. I can see the old lightbulb hanging loosely from the ceiling, swinging back and forth... or maybe it's me that's swaying.

It's dark down here, but light pours in from the hole above. Although I've spent many hours here, I've never looked at the ceiling from flat on my back before. But my hero boy must have, every night for years. I've never slept here. It has all these cracks running through the concrete like veins through skin. It may give way at any moment.

I don't think that would be a bad thing.

eleven: konnor

Konnor

THEIR WORDS ARE BARELY AUDIBLE. Their voices are barely recognisable. My bloody head. My bloody angry, throbbing, pulsing head. Why didn't I chase a Panadol with a litre of water before going to sleep? Rookie mistake.

I sigh into the covers. Soft and warm. As conscious thoughts slowly seep back in, the uninvited light flickers into my half-masked irises, causing me to squint further. Searching for the time, my pained eyes land on my jackarse of an alarm clock: 6:30 a.m. Which means I have an hour left to sleep. Sleep is *good*... I'm just about to drift off when I hear a girl's voice. Realising that it isn't Pemberton, I jolt up.

Blesk!

Gripping my forehead, I stumble to my feet as fast as I can. I almost trip over the rug on my floor. When I peer down, I'm confused to see I'm fully dressed. What happened last— *Oh, fuck!*

Rushing, I skid from my bedroom to face the terrible world that has seen me inebriated for such a long time. I trip over something and fall to my knees. The tiles under me do not forgive. My brain struggles to engage. My muscles wrestle to react. And my better judgement is caught in a thick fog.

When I look around the place, I am inundated with memories of last night. My apartment is a complete wreck. *Blesk.* Her face fills my mind the way a projector portrays an image on a blank screen. How she felt in my arms, cradled beside my body. The feel of her rapid pulse against my skin. I begin to shudder, hungover and in shock. I need her here, need to touch her, need to know she's alright. I need to see her heart-shaped lips, her long hair, those damn chocolate pools. Two hands grab me and I squint up at Jax as he pulls me to my feet.

"Fucksake." He drags my drunken arse over to the couch and tries to lower me down, but I shake him off.

I shoot up. "Where is she?"

"Mate, she's with Erik. She's fine." He puts his hands on my shoulders, pushing me back down until I'm sitting.

I frown and squint up at him. "I heard her!"

Elise walks over to stand in front of me. "No, Konnor, you heard me."

I rattle my head for a moment. Confusion clouds my mind; it's an unpleasant feeling that is hard to describe. The significance of yesterday is undeniable, although I'm not sure I could articulate what it even was. But she knows things. She responded to my finger on hers. She knows -

"You know where she is? You spoke to her?"

"Yes, she's fine. She'll be home tomorrow," Elise says delicately.

I massage my jaw with my palm, and wince. It feels like it took a punch last night. Which makes me think of -"Where's Drake?"

"He went home, buddy. He has early classes. Just chill out for a while." Jax nods; his pitying expression pisses me off.

"No." I stand, swaying in place. "I need to find Blesk."

Jax puts a hand on my shoulder again. "Konnor, you're not thinking straight—"

"I don't expect you guys to understand!" I snap. "But I need to find her. Now."

They stare at each other, sharing worried looks.

Elise turns towards me and tilts her head. "She said—"

"I don't care what she *fucking* said!" I yell.

Those words were not meant to come out so aggressively. I definitely didn't want to make Elise's smile recoil the way it just has. Jax frowns at me, and I sink to the couch in defeat. I glance up at Elise apologetically, but she's already smiling down at me again.

"Seriously, dude?" Jax shrugs at me. "Don't talk to Elise like that, man."

Fuck.

I shake my head. "I'm sorry, Elise."

She feigns indifference. "Don't be silly; it's fine. I'm glad you care so much about her. I'm sure it has to do with the whole beating you with your own leg threat, so... I'm going to take complete credit." She laughs again, and Jax chuckles. My head still drums. I try to shake the noise away, but it just vibrates louder in between my ears.

"Elise," I say, "what happened? Did she tell you? Was it something that I did? I—"

She cuts in. "She didn't tell me, but she sounded

concerned about you... So I don't think it was something you did."

I look Jax straight in his eyes, almost pleading. "Please, mate, understand, I need to look for her. I'm going with or without you."

"You don't know where she is," he insists.

"She's with her brother, right?" I ask.

Confusion crosses his face. "Yes, she's with Erik."

"Well, Pemberton has Erik's Find My Device password." She'd set it up on his phone when they were sleeping together, and I know this, because she did the same to me. "Let's go get her!"

Elise's face brightens as she turns to look at Jax. "Let's do it, Jaxon."

He blinks at her. "Really?"

"Yes, definitely!" she exclaims with a big cheeky smile.

Jax tilts his head at me and smirks. "Konnor, I don't think Pemberton will help you find Blesk." He shrugs in a dubious manner. "Just saying, buddy."

"How about we tidy up a bit and you go talk to your *ex*?" Elise says.

As if I need reminding she's my ex.

I would do anything for Blesk, even if that means facing Pembie.

THOUGH IT TAKES some cajoling and sweet-talking and reminding her that we were friends before we dated, I finally get the information out of Pemberton.

We hit the road.

Jax drives while Elise sits in the back seat, watching the

world go by. According to Erik's phone, he's on the highway headed north.

I put my feet up on the dash and lean my seat back slightly. I have an old pair of jeans on, and I've pulled my hoodie down over my stinging eyes. Slouching in the seat, I ponder what I'm going to say when I see Blesk.

If I wasn't so hungover, I could potentially form more constructive thoughts, perhaps formulate a game plan of some kind. Elise brought Blesk a change of fresh clothes; she's such a considerate little thing.

"I've never been on a road trip before," Elise says.

I pull back my hoodie and sit up, twisting in the seat to look at her. She has her legs scooped up to the side as she leans on the door and stares out the window.

"Never?" Jax glimpses at her in the rear-view mirror.

"Nope," she confirms.

"What about with your family? Vacations or something?" He keeps both hands on the wheel and a keen eye on the road, but offers her a glance every so often.

"No, my mums both work non-stop. Trying to save the world from scum. I had a nanny for a while, but then I was just sort of on my own. I liked my nanny, though. She was good fun and would paint my nails and stuff. My mums hated that." She chuckles under her breath.

"Mums?" Jax asks as he bumps my arm.

"Mums?" I repeat with a grin.

She giggles. "Boys are pathetic." She shakes her head at our eagerness. "Yes, mums. I have two mums."

"What do your mums do?" Jax asks.

"They're both lawyers. They saw a lot of messed up stuff, a lot of messed up people. It was hard for me to have a life."

"So no road trips with friends, no school-leaver weekend? No summer camps?" Jax asks. "No road trip songs or games? *No road trip junk food?*" He sounds genuinely disgusted and I can't stop myself from laughing at his mock distress. As if never having been on a road trip is one of the worst things he's ever heard.

"Nope, none of the above. Although I don't need road trips to have junk food," she states adamantly

"That sucks, Elise," I add.

"Oh, man, no. This is no good," Jax says in comical disapproval. "Junk food on the road is totally different than junk food at home." He continues to shake his head and frown. "Nope, this will not do at all."

I grin from ear to ear when he pulls into the strip lane and takes an exit off the highway.

I look back at Elise, who is peering at me, confused. "What's he doing?"

"You'll see."

We pull into a petrol station and we both jump out of the car, leaving Elise staring inquisitively through the window at us. We shove each other a little as we strut into the servo. The sliding doors open, and I make my way straight for an iced coffee. Blesk must be hungry, so I grab two and check out the snacks bar. I hover over the meal-replacement congregation and feel immediately disappointed that I have no idea if she is allergic to nuts or if she likes chocolate or if she even drinks coffee.

What do I know about Blesk? She's a musician. Her mum died a few years ago. Her brother's a dickhead. She is the most extraordinary girl I've ever met. She has the sweetest smile and a giggle that makes me want to spend every day of my life making sure it happens over and over again... Is that it? Is that really all I can come up with?

Jax approaches me with his arms full of food, packages crunching within his grasp. He dumps it all on the counter and grabs a couple of magazines from the rack, as well as *The Best of The Beatles.*

As we climb back into the car, Elise beams at us. Jax leans over the seat and hands her the bags. "Right. Now, I know you don't eat much meat?"

Elise looks shocked —so do I —and impressed. I know absolutely nothing about Blesk. "How do you know that?" she asks, searching through the bags.

"We chatted about the agriculture industry at The Basement Lounge, remember?"

"Wow, I can't believe you remember that. I never actually said I was vegetarian. It's kind of a well-established fact that guys don't usually listen to girls like me."

"Girls like you?" I query, unimpressed by her self-deprecating words.

She snorts. "You know."

"No, we don't," Jax states, his brows knitting together in disapproval.

"Well, I don't look like Blesk," she mumbles.

"No, you don't," he repeats. "You look like Elise, and that is exactly how you should look... Anyway, well, I got the usual must-haves: Starbursts, Skittles, Maltesers. I couldn't find any Pez, which is disappointing, but I found these weird Vege-Strip things that look kinda like jerky, but are vegetarian."

Smooth motherfucker.

He starts the car and tries not to look too proud of himself, but I can see the smugness oozing from his eyes. I want to taunt him mercilessly. I chuckle on a cough and he subtly hits me in the stomach. "But I did get us boys real jerky, Pork Crackle, and cheese sausages 'cause it ain't a road trip without 'em. I hope you don't mind?"

I flash a serious expression at Elise, who is flushing pink. "I *am* eating my cheese sausage," I say definitively.

"Oh, of course," she mutters, shoving some lollies into her mouth. "I don't expect you guys to go without."

Jax chucks me a grin. "Good to know." He slides *The Beatles* in the CD slot and we all start singing "Back in the U.S.S.R" at the tops of our lungs in between digging into our assortment of preservative-based goodies.

Australia is a weird country. As we travel north across the plane, the landscape varies from vast reds to flourishing greens. For the first few hours, it's flat and dry, akin to a desert. Hours later, it's green and tropical. Elise researches each town we drive through, relaying some interesting and some not-so-interesting facts.

When we turn down a dirt road and pass a sign that reads "Main Estate", discomfort immediately shifts through me. We pass an old broken-down homestead, which is overrun by vines, but still distinctively stunning. With its large white pillars and original timber frame construction still in good nick, the three-story house looks like a waste of a great family home. It isn't until we come to the end of the dirt-track that we notice Erik's car parked up on top of a hill. A sandy track leads up the hill to its peak and then continues along the top.

"Lucky we brought the Prado and not the Beamer, hey?" Jax says, pulling to a stop at the dead-end. "Should we drive up there? Or walk?"

My pulse suddenly quickens, but I'm not exactly sure why. Something is wrong. My gut knots up and I unconsciously clutch at my stomach. Squinting up at Erik's car, my attention drifts. *All those daisies. Trees. That beaming sun. That sweet smell.*

Ringing fills my ears and I start breathing violently in

response to my heart's frantic beat. This doesn't make sense; it's not like I've been here before.

Words float into my foggy mind.

"IT IS THE DAISIES. *They are my favourite flower. I will bring you a new one every day.*"

"*You don't have to.*"

"*I want to share them with you. They light up the world.*"

"*No, you do that.*"

"WHAT'S UP, man? Slater? What's up? Slater!"

Someone is jerking me back and forth. I meet Jax's eyes. "Huh?"

"Slater, where did you just go?" He looks at me with concern before turning back to Elise.

Elise touches my shoulder and leans forward to catch a better view of my face. "Konnor? Are you okay?"

"Yeah." I nod in a haze of uncertainty. "Sorry. Why wouldn't I be?"

They frown at each other. Elise speaks cautiously while she rubs my arm with her little hand. "You just zoned out."

"Wait here," I say, and before I know what I'm doing, I'm running up the hill. Every muscle in my body is tight and focused wholly on my incline. My feet and arms drive me forward as I grunt under my breath.

Why am I sprinting?

I couldn't move faster if I were being chased.

Running, jumping, and panting, I reach the top of the hill. I'm suddenly drilled by the sun's beams. I raise my forearm to shield my eyes from the invading light. Squinting, I search around the area.

That's when I see it.

I freeze up. My muscles lose all strength, all motion, all density. My head gets lighter and lighter as if inflating with air. The silence around me only makes the sudden thundering in my ears seem louder.

My head swivels around as I try to find something to focus on. But I can still see the hatch and stairs leading down, down into a basement, a dark, dark *fucking basement.* I slam my jaw shut and clench my teeth until they hurt. Some seconds pass, or moments, or an hour. Time has no order right now. It isn't until I hear her small cry that my brain retrieves its senses.

Fucking move, Konnor.

That little weeping sound. My whole body hurts as my pulse runs rampant through my veins. I peer down at my immobile shoes and attempt to lift them, wrestling with the terrifying paralysis. They stay frozen on the grass beneath.

I inhale several quick, fierce breaths.

I hear it again.

A masculine moan.

A feminine sob.

Listening through the beat of my heart, I can't quite make out the words. "Please" I think. "Stop" I think. My whole body throws itself forward and down the stairs as if it were possessed. As soon as I'm officially underground, the air gets so thick, it is hardly breathable.

Erik's lips are on her. His body is pressed against her, his pants around his ankles.

Her eyes are filled with tears...

A bolt of heat strikes my temple, and everything goes pitch-black.

And I'm not sure how I got to them, but now I'm wailing on him. My fists are red and raw. Every punch deforms his face further. I'm straddling him, pinning him to the ground —just like he did to her. Nailing him with every inch of strength I contain.

The *thumps* turn into *cracks*. All I see is red. I'm going to destroy him. I hear grunting, loud, angry grunting, and it takes me a few moments to realise it's coming from me. My fists pummel his face and come away from it wet. When I hit a bone and hear a *crunch*, my hand flies back, spraying blood everywhere.

Suddenly, I can't reach him anymore. I'm being pulled backwards. I'm torn from him, swinging and howling. Erik groans on the floor, spluttering up mouth-loads of blood and bile. I heave wildly.

Elise rushes over and attempts to clear his throat. She checks his pulse, rips his shirt, and presses the material to the gushing cuts on his face.

I can't think straight. I can't feel anything other than the need to inflict pain on him. He was on my girl. My hands are pumping at my waist; anger is clawing at my back.

I jolt towards him and spit on his face. "Leave him to rot!" I growl.

"Shit, Slater!" Jax yells while dragging me back. "Think about the girls, Slate!"

"Konnor."

Her sweet, shaky voice crashes through my haze, snapping me back to the here and now. Snapping me back to what I saw and to what I now know. I shove Jax off and spin like a crazed animal in search of her face, desperation manifesting itself in my every frantic movement. I am covered in sticky blood and dripping in sweat. Every inch of me is twitching with fury and fear, a tangled combination of fight and flight. And even though the whole world is blurry, I can still make out their silhouettes. I focus more sharply until I distinguish her trembling frame. I see her face, that sweet girl, my everything.

My sunshine.

I remember.

We both stand still as statues as the truth we've been feeling since we laid eyes on each other engulfs us. I gulp down a dry knot when I see her beauty in a totally new way. The word gets caught in my throat. I mouth the name first.

Then I yell.

"Liz!"

Her face breaks and floods of tears burst from her eyes as she drops to her knees.

"Oh, God, don't call me that!" she cries.

I rush to her as she lands on the floor. Wrapping my arms tightly around her shuddering body, I hold her with desperation. Pained sounds explode from her.

There is no way I'm ever letting her go. No way I'm ever going to let anyone take her away from me again.

You died.

"You died, you died!" I blubber hysterically, gushing with emotions I hadn't realised a man could express. My tears fall down hard and fast on her like rain. Her little hands clutch at my clothes. Her face buries in my chest. I try to calm down. I try to calm *her* down.

Threading my fingers through her golden hair, I grip it like silk against me, remembering how often I'd wanted to do just that — touch her hair. She is finally in my arms. After all these years, I can touch her. Ever since I saw her at The Grill, a part of me had known it was her. I'd felt it.

Through the haze of my memories, through the daze I'd been in for nearly four years, I'd still known. Though I feel like I don't know much about Blesk, I know everything about Liz.

She loves to read. She loves to twirl. Her smile can light up the whole damn world. When she's nervous, she bites her lip. She would rather skip than walk. She loves white chocolate. Her birthday is the 20th of March. Her favourite colour is the same green as my eyes ...

Liz is my best friend.

This is by far the best moment of my *entire* life. I can't hear anything other than my heart drumming in my head. I'm so overwhelmed. Full of sublime happiness. My mind aches on overdrive, processing and evaluating. She's alive.

The girl I have been in love with for seventeen years is alive.

As she sobs, I rock her back and forth. Pretending it is once again just the two of us, my voice cracks as I whisper to her the last story we wrote.

The story we'd written the day before she died.

"There was once a boy named Deakon. He spent a lot of time away from the sun, but he had shining dreams. One day, he looked in the mirror and reflected in his eyes was a girl. She had golden hair and chocolate eyes.

"Years later, while he was walking past a shop front, he caught the reflection of a girl in the window. Yet, when he turned around, she was gone. She was the same girl reflected in his eyes.

"He dreamed of her, saw her by his side everywhere he went. He spent years travelling, searching and meeting beautiful people and beautiful girls. No matter how far he went, though, or how many people he met or how beautiful they were, they were never as beautiful as the girl in his eyes, the girl in the window, the girl in his dreams.

"One day, they will be together, and she will be by his side, reflected in his eyes, next to him in the window and in his dreams. His dream girl."

twelve: deakon

Deakon

Sixteen years earlier.

THE BOY SPENDS many minutes or hours or days huddled in a bed, crying and moaning for help. He holds himself and rubs his arms, pretending his hands are not his, pretending they are someone else's, someone who cares. He wants to know if he is still alive, a boy, a son, loved...

How do I know if I am alive? he thinks. The boy isn't sure.

When he falls asleep during the day or night, he has no tears left inside him. And when he wakes, salt streams are crusted on his soft young cheeks.

The boy doesn't know what time it is or what seconds, minutes, and hours are. But when the girl brings him meals, he counts them, desperate to know how long he's been away from home. How long he's been in the cage. Soon though, he runs out of numbers. The boy can only count to ten, and he's already done that ten times.

Why have I run out of numbers?

He makes a wish for more numbers because he believes without the numbers to guide his living moments, he might not be alive. Not moving forward.

The numbers never come.

To the boy, that can only mean one thing — he has been in the cage forever. He is lost in the dark, losing himself, losing his name, losing his memories, losing his mind.

The dark starts to swallow his feelings, but in return it gives him new ones —exciting ones.

Now, after lots of tens of meals, the boy believes he has become a dog. Pacing his home, from the bed to the toilet and back again, he ponders this revelation. He squeezes his eyes shut and concentrates, summoning his inner dog. He bares down, trying, trying, changing... And then it happens. He can hear the trees talking and chatting around outside the basement. He can hear the bees gossiping and singing, telling him stories and making him laugh out loud. He can hear everything and everyone; they all talk to him at once.

The boy opens his eyes and stares at the concrete wall, nodding to himself. The darkness has given him strength. His mind is expanding to connect him with the world.

He is evolving. Becoming something else.

When he hears the girl, every step, every step, every step, he rushes to the edge of his cage. The latch swings open. He can hear the chamber breathing, sucking in clean air and releasing the stale. He can hear her heart racing as she slowly descends the steps, each little step measured and cautious.

Yes, he thinks. He has *finally* become a dog.

"I want to be a dog," the boy says as the girl comes down the stairs, carrying a bowl of food. Those six words change him, sate him. The beautiful girl has never uttered a word to him. No matter how many times he's begged for answers.

"A dog has good hearing," he continues. "Very good. A dog can run fast too. And... and they live in cages too. Boys don't live in cages. I think I might be changing into a dog. Do I look like a dog?"

She stares at him, rings of violet blemishing each brown pool. "You could be a dog." She nods slowly. "*Maybe*. Turn around." The boy spins around, his arms sweeping out wide so she can inspect him. She nods again. "Yes, yes, I think you are."

I like her voice.

A spike of excitement hits the boy, and he grips the bars, peering between the gaps at the girl. "If I'm a dog, then this is okay," he says, his tone calm for the first time in minutes or hours or days — he isn't sure which. "This room is good for a dog. The food too."

A small smile tugs at the girl's swollen and bruised lips. "I'd like to be a cat."

"Why a cat?" he asks, scrunching up his nose in disapproval.

"A cat can climb high. Higher than people can reach."

The boy tilts his head in thought as he releases a little sigh. *Yes,* he thinks, *she should be a cat.* "Can I name you?" he asks, a flutter filling his chest at the thought. "The cat you?"

"Yes," she replies, sitting on the fifth step, watching him pace around in contemplation.

"*Ummm?*" The boy hesitates. "What about Sunshine?"

"Okay," she agrees. The boy's lips curve up, his cheeks revealing distinct dimples. She smiles back and askes, "Can I name you?"

"Yeah," the boy says to Sunshine.

"Kon." The girl's sweet voice fills his chest with hope.

"My mum…" her voice falters. "My mum was Irish. Kon means 'dog' in Gaelic."

Unfortunately, the girl isn't turning into a cat. She can't climb out of reach.

But she does go to school for the minutes or hours or days and learns to read, count, write and then tells the boy stories.

She is a girl, and he is her dog. The boy doesn't mind; he likes being hers. Even though his place is in the cage, in the basement, below the daisy-covered ground, he still wakes up with bright eyes. He knows that she will come for him.

thirteen: blesk

Blesk

WHEN I WAKE up in bed with Konnor's arm draped over my waist, his chest pressed against my back, and our legs tangled together, I know everything I have tried to escape has caught up with me.

The room is dim with its iridescent overhead light. The curtains are pulled shut, and the only indication of the hour comes through in honks and horns from the city street below.

I squeeze my eyes together, not wanting to accept the dawn. As I chase slumber, the harrowing look on Konnor's face when he pulled Erik off me comes crashing into my consciousness. I did nothing.

As Konnor beat Erik within an inch of his life, I just stood there, motionless —my mind blank, my mouth dry. I was incapable of pleading with Konnor to stop because part of me didn't want him to.

A bittersweet feeling contracts my heart as I fixate on a framed picture on Konnor's bedside table. It is his high school graduation photo, which features him alongside two attractive girls and a doting father and mother figure. He has siblings. A non-biological family, but it's apparent by their expressions of pride and Konnor's smile that it was never an issue.

He was gorgeous... *is* gorgeous. I wonder how many girls have fallen in love with that smile.

I can feel my eyes stinging. I would be crying right now if I had any tears left inside me. Looking at him as he was, with his dimpled smile and perfect green eyes, I can see he was happy.

And now, I can feel his breath like silk on my neck, and when I shuffle my feet, his arm pulls me in closer to him. I wish he were just Konnor Slater. But when he touched our index fingers together the other day, I realised he wasn't. Not *just* Konnor Slater.

He's the boy whose life I'd ruined, whose life I'd stolen.

On the drive home yesterday, I fell asleep in the car, huddled against Konnor. He was quieter than me for the most part —except for his heavy breathing.

Neither Jaxon nor Elise had spoken nor inquired about what had happened. They will, I'm sure. Oh God, I need to speak to Elise. She must be so confused. Perhaps she hasn't realised what a complete headcase her new best friend is.

When I get close to people, they get hurt. So I usually avoid relationships. Erik taught me a lot about pain and love. My feelings for him have always curdled in the pit of my belly, a messed-up ball of emotion that is both content within my big brother's arms and ashamed of the things I'd let him do to me after dark.

As I think on his actions from yesterday, I wonder whether I actually told him no. I can't remember. Surely, he'd have stopped if I'd said the word... No.

"Blesk?" Konnor murmurs, drawing me back to him. His arm tightens around me. His breath is warming. I want to snuggle against him as if he is just Konnor.

After what I did to him, I've always hoped he would hate me. But I'm not sure he knows about my role in his capture. In those years of torture. That is why I hate Liz and why we buried her. For closure. I was Blesk. I wanted to move on as if she'd never existence, wishing the guilt would disappear with her and with him.

Yet, here *he* is, with his warm chest pressed against my back, his scent all around me, and his face nuzzled in my hair.

He doesn't hate me.

"Blesk?" He moves. When I turn around to peer at him, I find him leaning on his elbow and staring down at me. His chest rises and falls noticeably faster while we gaze at each other. His eyes are sleepy and stunning. "Baby, shit. I thought I'd dreamt yesterday." His expression is tight, but filled with relief. I know mine portrays the opposite.

"Say something, Blesk," he presses, searching my face with those big, wholesome green eyes. The same eyes that had inspired my love of the colour green.

My mouth moves and I want to say, "Hi. Have you had a good life? How was your first day of school? Did you enjoy your high school graduation ball? Did you ever learn to waltz? Were you popular? Was your second kiss as beautiful as your first? How many girls have fallen head-over-heels in love with you? And... I'm sorry." Yet, all I can manage is, "Morning."

"Good morning." He sighs with relief. "Do you like coffee?" He stares at me as if that question has been swirling around in his mind incessantly, and now I can see something like excitement bouncing across his face. "Do you eat bacon?" His voice hits a higher pitch. "Or eggs? I just have to know. I want to know everything. Do you want pancakes? Blesk, I will make you fucking pancakes if you want, or waffles or—"

"Konnor." I hold my hand up to his silly smile and can't help but grin back at him. "I like coffee."

He exhales loudly. "I like coffee too. Coffee it is. How do you like your coffee?"

"Black, no sugar."

When he rolls off the bed and walks towards the kitchen, I jolt up and try to remember how to breathe. Trembling, I shake my head back and forth as if to say 'no' to the universe. No. This is all wrong.

I don't want to be *her*.

I hate her. He should too. And yet, I can't deny him anything. His adorable smile gives me everything, every inch of its truth. His great smell, deep and masculine, makes me hopeless in his presence.

Breathing hard, my eyes bounce around the room until they land on Konnor. He's watching me from the doorway, a cup of coffee in his hand. His brows are level and the excitement that was just in his eyes is gone. When he walks back over and sits down beside me, he says, "Here" –holding the cup out for me to take. "You don't look happy."

"I am," I say. "I'm just... It's a lot."

He sighs. "Yeah... Did you know?"

"No." I shake my head as I take the cup and smell its lovely pungent scent. "No, I mean, sort of. I don't know."

"Same," he says, peering down at the crumpled sheets. I sip my coffee and observe his change in demeanour. It's my fault. He was happy to wake up next to me, whereas I must look uncomfortable and morbid. Guilt hits me. I wish I was nothing but happy to see him. I wish this meant we could start over, be together, have the life we'd spoken about.

"Konnor?" I put my cup on his bedside table.

His eyes bore into mine as he strokes my cheek with his knuckles. "Liz?"

I gasp. "Please, please don't call me that."

He cringes at my tone. "What should I call you?"

"Blesk! Call me Blesk!"

"That isn't your name," he states blankly.

"It is!" I insist, moving away from his gentle caress and scrutinising eyes. "It has been for a long time."

Konnor winces, disappointment distorting his features. "Why don't you want to remember us?"

"I need a shower," I mumble evasively.

His frown pulls his face tighter. He points at a door. "There. What's mine is yours."

Even though I shouldn't stand and walk away from him, I do. I spin on the mattress and pace over to the bathroom, locking it behind me. If I turn back for even a moment and see the pain in his eyes, it will break my heart. When the door clicks shut, I slide down it and cover my face with my hands. My elbows meet my knees, and I cry tearless sobs as silently as I can.

I look down at my stupid red dress. It's still covered in paint from a time before yesterday, from a time when things were simpler. Twenty-four hours. That's all it's taken for everything to change. A small whimper forces its way through my lips as I consider what I've lost: my new life, my brother, and the chance to be with Konnor as just Konnor.

"Blesk?" Konnor's worried voice calls through the door. "Blesk, I'm so sorry." That he just apologised *to me* after everything I've done floods me with guilt. I drop my head backwards against the cold wooden door. Knock. *Stupid.* Knock. *Stupid.*

"I shouldn't have pushed ..." He pauses. "What's that noise?"

I drop my head back one last time and sigh. We both remain silent for several minutes before his deep husky voice permeates the door again. "I don't know what you've gone through. Or what this must be like for you. And after yesterday—" He stops abruptly and hisses through his teeth. "Fucking Erik."

He growls and hits something hard enough for me to feel the vibration. "Just know I'm happy. I couldn't be happier. I thought you'd died. Everyone told me you'd died. But you're here, in my bathroom. It's so much to take in, and I'm so happy, but I'm also scared I'm gonna lose you again. I want to be here for you. I *am* here for you, every day for the rest of your life, *Blesk*. No one will ever hurt you again. Ever." He knocks on the door with his palm or perhaps his head. "Blesk? Look, just take a shower. But then come out and talk to me... *Please.*"

HUDDLED up in the corner of the shower with the steamy water pouring down on me, I consider actually accepting my looming fate — just for a few days. He has been through hell and back. I hold all the answers and memories to his past. Once I tell him everything I did to him, everything I kept him from, he'll let Liz go too.

This might just be his closure.

I can give him that.

Then the both of us will be able to move forward again.

Sitting under the hot spray, I analyse something he said. *"I am here for you, every day for the rest of your life."*

He doesn't know that I can't be what he wants me to be because finding each other is not a blessing; it's a tragedy. We can never be more than friends now; I don't want to be loved as *her*.

I soap myself up and down. Standing under the faucet, I watch as the water rushes down me and the soap disappears beyond the drain. All trace of Erik's mistake, his touch and smell, is sucked into the pipes.

I scrunch-dry my long, thick blonde hair and blanket myself in a towel. When I swing the bathroom door open, Konnor is slumped over on the bed with his face buried in his hands. Noticing the bandages around them, I cringe a little. He raises his head when he hears me, then quickly stands. "Blesk, you okay?" His eyes are bloodshot. I hope he hasn't been crying, but I think he has.

"Yes." My heart thumps hard inside my chest as his eyes rake my towel covered body. A chill rushes through me. My naked legs break out in goose bumps. I like how he's looking at me as if he's worshipping me. But then his eyes dart away and he shifts in place, almost out of discomfort.

That response is another reason why I don't want him to think of me as *her*. He wouldn't have avoided me a few days ago; he would have tried to hold me. But now, not even thirty-six hours later, he turns away from me.

Does he think of me as a sister now?

Did seeing Erik with me spoil me?

"Konnor?" I mutter without moving from the doorway.

He walks away from me and out of sight, not glancing up once. I grimace, get quickly dressed in the clothes Elise brought for me, and then tip toe over to him sitting on the couch.

He shoots up. "You okay?"

"I'm fine! Please stop acting like I'm made of glass."

He shakes his head in confusion. "What?"

"You're treating me differently!"

"Yeah" –he nods– "of course I am. You mean more to me than anyone else in this *damn* world. I am not going to look at you like you are just *another* girl."

"So that is how you looked at me before?"

"No," he exclaims. *"Fuck,* I always looked at you different."

"Then look at me like that again."

He locks his jaw and speaks through gritted teeth. "I *can't.* Not right now. You're my Liz," he gushes.

My brows tighten. "No, I'm not!"

It's taken me years to build some semblance of a life and bury my past, but now he wants to dig it all back up. Before I realise what I'm doing, I rush towards his apartment door. I need to get away from him and process this alone.

He runs after me and slams himself against the door. He slowly turns, his face dipping to mine. "Come on, not again. I'm sorry. I don't know *how* to act. I'm doing the best I can, given the circumstances."

He searches my gaze as I try desperately to avoid his. I know his soft, beautiful eyes will further weaken my resolve. I try to stiffen my lower lip even as trembles begin to rack me. He clasps my jaw, tilting it until my eyes meet his. I can feel my body start to quake with repressed emotions wanting to burst out and be free.

"I'm not acting like this because I don't want you, Blesk,"

he says. "I'm just trying to respect you, babe, and be nice to you. That is *all* this is. After everything that happened yesterday... I have no idea how to act..."

We take a few moments just like we did last time, with his back to the apartment door and my hand on the door handle.

"Blesk. Do you want me to be corny?" He grins and both cheeks display those adorable dimples. "Will that make you smile again?" He forces a chuckle before saying, "You had me at cello!"

A subtle smile betrays my anguish as I squeeze my eyes tightly shut, feeling so confused. I'm completely drained.

"Konnor." My voice shakes. "I just want you to treat me like Blesk. *Please.*"

"Okay ... Blesk." He lets out a heavy sigh. "Can we go back to the couch? Can you stop trying to run away from me?" He combs my hair with his fingers and gives me a feigned cocky grin. "It kinda hurts my ego." A half-smile draws my lips out and I nod, just once. He pulls his fingers through my hair and stares at the strands as if they are the most beautiful creation on earth. His eyes stop on my neck and then trace my long locks as they bounce down over my décolletage. "I remember *you... Blesk.*" He studies my face, shaking his in amazement. "You're a duchess, ya know that? You were always beautiful, but now, you have grown into this *extraordinary* woman. What happened yesterday with-"

I raise my hand and cup his cheek. His jaw tics with barely restrained anger, but he closes his eyes and moves into my caress.

"Konnor?" My voice is weak, overcome by the intensity of what I'm about to ask. "Have you had a good life?"

His eyes flutter open, and they fall softly on my face

again. "I've had an awesome life. And it's about to get better."

AS KONNOR COOKS us bacon and eggs, I can see the unanswered questions filling his eyes. Questions that clearly make him angry and volatile. He'd be terrible at playing poker; his thoughts and feelings are blatant in his expression.

He's softly spoken with me though —cautious — as if I'll detonate at any moment. Perhaps, that's a fair stance he's taken.

Abruptly, he turns the cooker off. He stares at the pan for a few moments before turning to face me. "Are you okay?"

Of course, I'm not. But I'm a lot better off than Erik, who was air lifted to a hospital yesterday. Will the hospital call my dad? Will my dad call me? Because now I can't help but think about whether Erik is in critical condition or if he's even awake or angry or remorseful or-

Forcing those thoughts down, I lie, "Yes."

Shaking his head, he struggles with the next set of words, wincing as if he hates them. "Do you want to go to the doctors? Have a -"

"No! That's not necessary."

Moving towards me, he places his hands on the breakfast bar that separates us. "Please, talk to me. You have to want-"

We both jump at the sound of a phone ringing. Konnor retrieves the cordless handset from its station on the kitchen bench.

"Hello?" He turns to face me and leans on the counter, crossing his ankles in front of him. "I'm okay... Yeah, she's fine... Yeah, you can send her up."

Please don't be Pembie.

He smiles tightly at me. "Thanks, Adolf. "

I stand up, both wanting to avoid an altercation with whoever is on their way up and needing to find out if Erik is awake. "I have to make a few calls."

"To who?" he asks, putting the phone down.

I gulp because I know he won't approve. "The hospital."

"Fuck that!"

"Konnor, he's my brother."

"No, he isn't! Blesk, what the hell? He was..." He growls and strides over to me. My feet shuffle backwards to keep the space between us, but I'm slower than him. When he reaches me, he runs both hands down my arms and grips my hands. His eyes narrow and cut into mine. "Has this happened before?"

Yes.

Ashamed, I glance at my feet. "No, not like that."

When I look back at him again, his eyes have turned into slits. "Like... how?" he demands.

A knock breaks through the tangible intensity around us, and I wave his hands off, needing some space. Konnor can't possibly understand how much I owe Erik for all those nights he listened to me cry and was my only comfort. He saved my life. In more ways than one.

Konnor's eyebrows furrow, and he appears equally as pained as he does livid. Whoever's outside his door knocks again.

"This conversation is not over," he mutters before walking over to unlatch the chain.

Elise bounces in, holding a big paper bag. "Donuts?" She forces a beaming smile, but the worry in her eyes is undeniable.

"Please come in," Konnor jokes as she shoves past him.

She rushes over and we embrace tightly. She rests her head on my shoulder as we revel in the comfort of each other. It is then that I notice she has a backpack on, and I know exactly what's inside it. As we hold each other, I hear Konnor moving across the apartment.

Elise whispers in my ear, "Wanna go outside to talk?"

I open my eyes and find Konnor; the sight of him making my belly flutter. "No, we can talk here."

Elise releases me and waves the bag in her hand. "Donuts?"

"Do you want a drink, Elise?" Konnor asks as he collects a tumbler and a bottle of liquor from the kitchen cabinet.

Elise frowns at him. "It's nine, Konnor."

"Yep, it sure is." Gesturing towards the couch, he adds, "Take a seat." Elise moves to the sofa and sits down, glaring at Konnor as he tilts the glass to his lips. There is a kind of suspiciousness to Elise; she's ready to go rounds with Konnor over what had happened. The tension stirs between them.

"Konnor, what the hell happened yesterday?" Elise asks.

Konnor shifts his feet, murmuring something too low to hear before saying, "Elise, I'm so sorry you had to see that." He lowers his head and shakes it slowly. "I have... I don't know what else to say."

"What happened?" She looks at him questioningly. "Please. I had to take two showers last night. I was completely covered in blood. I deserve to know." Her voice is relatively steady, given the situation, but I can tell she is struggling to remain calm.

Konnor moves to console her, but she puts her hands up. His face falls.

He grips his nape and then drags his fingers through his

hair on a low growl. "Elise... I'm so sorry. I'm not a dangerous guy."

"Really?" she says dubiously. "Yep, okay. I believe you. It's just, you weren't the one holding *Erik's face* together." Konnor winces, then turns to me for support.

My breath lodges in my throat, and my legs give way. I sink onto the couch near her. "Elise..." The words strain on my tongue. Hard to say. Harder to hear, I imagine. Casting Konnor a quick pleading glance, I ask him with my eyes to tell her.

He inhales for courage. "Erik was hurting Blesk."

She flashes her wide-eyed gaze to me. "Hurting you how?"

I don't want to say it. God, no, I don't want to hear it either.

Every part of me wants to rush for the door again and never come back. Konnor is seated beside me before I realise he had even moved. His arms quickly envelop my shoulders. He seems to read me like an open book. "Blesk," he whispers, nuzzling into my hair. "It's okay." I nod and his warmth filters through to me, settling my nerves.

"Guys, what is going on?" Elise asks.

"Erik raped Blesk," he states, squeezing me against him.

Yep, harder to hear.

She sighs. "Damnit. I was hoping there was some other kind of explanation for what I saw." She slides over to me, hugging my waist from the other side so I'm enclosed in a Konnor and Elise sandwich. "You're a psycho, Konnor," she murmurs softly. And then I feel her and Konnor grip each other's arms and rub them affectionately. That small action affects my heart so profoundly.

For a while, we all just cuddle. Their arms hold me between them; my head rests on Konnor's firm chest. The fabric from Konnor's shirt brushes my chin as I peer up at his expression. His eyes are shut, engrossed in the feeling of me in his arms, so I take a few seconds to enjoy the smell and sight of him.

"Konnor?" I whisper. A flutter fills my chest when his lovely green eyes open and find mine staring up at him. "I have something for you."

Before we left the cell yesterday, I found the box we'd hidden in the wall under the stairs thirteen years ago. An old fishing tackle box filled with letters, drawings, stories, songs, and notes from our four years together. While Jaxon called an ambulance for Erik, I gave the box to Elise to keep safe. In case she was tempted to open it, I told her that Konnor and I share a past. That we've known each other since we were five. That's all I told her.

We release each other and Elise grabs the backpack at her feet. She pulls the box out and places it on the coffee table.

Konnor follows her actions, uncertainty in his eyes. Knowing he needs reassurance, I link our fingers and pull him down on the rug so that our legs are crossed in front of us and our knees are touching.

"These are your memories," I say, glancing up at Elise who looks lost, but firm. Konnor watches, stone-faced, as I gently place the box onto his lap, as if its significance could somehow weigh him down and hurt him.

"Should I go?" Elise asks, shifting her legs.

Konnor shakes his head. "No. I think you should stay. You wanted to know. And you're right, I owe you the truth." Exhaling nervously, he reaches for the box and opens it.

My head starts to spin when I see its contents, and our shared memories wash over me in waves. As he touches the multi-coloured pieces of paper with his fingers, I'm over-whelmed with too many feelings at once.

He picks one up. "Should I read it?"

Glancing at Elise again, I say, "Only if you want to."

Unaffected by her presence, he unfolds one and peers at the text; a small smile plays on his lips. My hand flies to my mouth when he begins to read it aloud.

"Deakon: *D is for dream, E is for Everything, A is for Armour, K is for King, O is for Oath, N is for New.*" His face brightens and he chuckles to himself. "Kids, hey?" Strangely enough, I laugh too. "Did you write that or did I?"

"Liz did when she was five," I murmur.

He unfolds another piece of paper. "It's a song."

Konnor reads the words aloud, his voice shaking as he says, "It's called One Day."

The merry-go-round will spin her hair, will swirl like a mill.

The grass gets caught in his socks as he rolls down the hill.

The sunshine stays all night; they'll live in emotional light.

The boy won't let them fight; they'll forever be alright,

One day could be one day away.

One day isn't that far away, but just sure isn't today.

Certainly not this, certainly not now, certainly not this way.

When they dance together, he holds her and never lets go,

When they sing together, he's proud to put
her on show,

The sunshine will warm his morns with her
lips and kisses,

The boy will support her bow, make sure she
never misses,

One day could be one day away.

One day isn't that far away, but just sure
isn't today.

Certainly not this, certainly not now, certainly
not this way.

They will yell from the hill; their voices will
fill the air,

They will promise with their special index-
finger swear,

That one day.

The sunshine will smile, on a new day, that
day, one day.

The new boy will glow, on a new day, that
day, one day.

One day could be one day away.

One day isn't that far away, but just sure
isn't today.

Certainly not this, certainly not now, certainly
not this way.

But maybe one day.

AFTER HE READS the last sentence, he holds the sheet to his heart and shuts his eyes, letting out a sigh. "I thought–" He breathes out fast. "Fuck, that I'd never have this moment. Reassurance that everything that had happened was real. That you *are* real. Your memory started to disappear. I fought to keep it, but I had no one to share it with. It was like I'd made you up. I'd made it all up."

I place my hand on his, allowing the recollection of those memories and a promise never fulfilled to play in my mind.

When he opens his eyes again, they are glistening with emotion. "Wow," he breathes. "There is no way I wrote that song." He looks sad and happy... if an expression can be both. "Blesk, you're a genius... How old were you when you wrote that?"

I glance at Elise, who has glossy eyes despite not truly understanding any of this. "Liz was eight," I mutter, still looking at her.

He puts his hand on my knee and strokes my leg tenderly. "Does it have a melody?"

I nod shyly as a little tear rushes out of the corner of my eye. "Yes."

He smiles at me sweetly as he wipes the tear from my cheek. "Play it for me one day."

"One day." He hands me a folded sheet, but I push it back towards him. "No, they're yours."

"They're ours," he states, gesturing for me to take it.

Sighing, I unwrap the letter with shaky hands. I swallow hard at the sight of a crayon-drawn rainbow cake with six candles. Flipping the page over, I show it to him. "You drew this for her. For her birthday. She didn't get a cake that year." My eyes meet Elise again, thinking she'd be uncomfortable by now, but she doesn't look that way, so I continue, "She didn't get a cake most years."

When I look back at Konnor, his brows are weaved. "Please stop talking about yourself in third person."

"That isn't me anymore, Konnor. I want to be Blesk."

"Well, I feel like him, especially with you here, the way we were together." Reaching over the box, he strokes my hair and runs a finger along my jaw. "I remember some things."

"What do you remember?"

"I remember everything about you. I remember certain days, especially the days you didn't visit me. And I remember the last day. I could never forget that day, Duch."

More guilt slithers up my back. I know *exactly* why he remembers the days I didn't visit.

It was my fault he was forgetting in the first place.

Feeling absorbed in the moment, I almost forget about Elise. I lean back and look up at her. She's a little teary, confused. "I want to tell Elise."

He nods and smiles once before saying, "So do I."

"So do I," Elise says jokingly and slides down onto the floor beside us.

After a few awkward moments of silence, Konnor says, "Blesk and I ... We know each other. Like, from when we were children."

Elise frowns. "*Okay.*"

"I don't remember a lot because I was lied to all the time."

Elise nods as an anxious look fills her face. Pushing to his feet, Konnor goes to pour himself a glass of what looks like bourbon, his hands shaking as he fills it up.

Walking back to us, he sits down and breathes in his courage. Then he pours his courage down his throat in the form of liquor. "Dutch courage," he mutters with a feigned chuckle. Jumping right in, 'cause like what could shock her now, he says, "I was taken from my parents when I was five."

Elise blinks at him. "What do you mean 'taken'."

"Kidnapped. I don't actually remember the night it happened, and I'm not sure if most of the things I do remember are actually my memories or if they are from reading articles or hearing stories from other people. The last few years are a bit clearer. Obviously, I was older. The first few years are nearly completely lost. That place you saw yesterday..." The words get wrapped around his tongue. "I was locked in there for a while."

Elise hesitates on the question, her face now ashen. "How long?"

"A long time." Konnor states. "Four years."

Elise gasps, her hand flying up to smother the sound.

He continues, "My brain was always foggy, is foggy, from the lack of sun, vitamin D... I don't know what it was, but I was sick. I don't remember specifics. Liz..."

He was never sick.

I shudder in response to the name I've fought to forget and *almost* had until recently. He stops talking and stares at me, brushing a rogue blonde tendril off my shoulder. "You okay, Duchess?"

Although that pet name is sweet, I know he's just avoiding calling me Blesk. Well if the alternative is Liz, then Duchess it is. I choke down the huge knot that has slowly been expanding in my throat.

"Yes, I'm okay," I finally say. Elise's anxious eyes bounce between Konnor and me.

With a heavy sigh, Konnor continues, "It was Blesk's biological father who took me. Liz and I were both so young and really only knew what we were told, believing things we shouldn't and imagining things that had never happened.

"I find it hard to separate my fantasies and dreams from reality. Liz was younger than me and used to bring me meals.

She was my maid, my best friend, and then she was my everything. She still is. Even though her father was caught, he never told the police why he'd taken me. The newspapers made claims that it was related to organised crime. That Liz's father was somehow involved and that he'd never speak up or he'd suffer a fate worse than imprisonment. He just pleaded guilty and there was little to no trial at all. After I was found, I was put up for adoption because my biological dad thought it'd be better for me to get a fresh start and my biological mum had died a few years earlier. It was all over The District News for years, so officials decided that a new name and family would probably be for the best."

"Four years," Elise mutters, shaking her head in disbelief. "You're so... normal."

"Yeah right! I'm *really* not. I drink like a fish," he says, glancing at the empty tumbler. "I lose my shit in confined spaces. I struggle with lots of stuff, Elise. I'll tell you, though, I wouldn't be here if it wasn't for my adoptive family. They went through hell with me for those first few years, but they got me a shrink, loved me like their own, and gave me pretty much anything I wanted."

I choke down my tears. I just haven't had time to process this, and hearing it out loud, from Konnor's mouth, is too much. His eyes soften as he looks at me. He touches my cheek and rubs his finger over my lower lip as it trembles. "I won't continue if this is too painful."

"No," I say. "I want her to know. "It's just hard hearing this stuff, Konnor." I sniffle. "I don't know how you talk about it with such—"

Konnor's finger goes to my lips, cutting me off. "Duch, I've spent hours talking about this with my family and my shrink." He blows out a long breath before turning to meet Elise's line of sight.

"She feels differently about this. She always did. But that little girl kept me alive and gave me hope. When you have nothing, what you do have becomes *so much* more precious. Her sweet voice and golden hair that reminded me of the sun. Without her, I would have forgotten what that colour looked like. I called her my sunshine because that is exactly what she was."

fourteen: erik's letter

Erik's Letter

Dear Liz,

Do you remember the first time you cried and I cuddled you? The first time I cradled you in my arms and cried with you? You wouldn't stop apologising. For crying...

I couldn't understand why you were sorry for crying. From then on, I would cry whenever you cried. Because you should know that it is okay. It is okay to cry, Liz. My crying meant you could cry as much as you wanted to. And not be alone.

I'm sorry that wasn't enough. That you still hurt every day. I am sorry I couldn't save you from yourself. I am sorry I wasn't there when you needed me. I am sorry you had to cry alone for so long. You will never ever have to cry alone again.

Erik

fifteen: konnor

Konnor

WHEN HE GETS RILED UP, he usually spits.

"Fuck you, Slater! You missed the last two practices and now you wanna play?" he grumbles, spraying me in the face with saliva. "You're a real piece of work! Ya know that? Mess with my time, and now you show up like nothing happened."

Nodding cheekily, I say through my mouth guard, "Yes, Coach. Sorry, Coach."

"Well, fuck you! Sit on the bench. Maybe I'll bring you in later."

I frown at him. "You need me out there! You can't put David on the wing!" I yell, aggravated and pumping with adrenaline that's completely unrelated to rugby. I gesture disdainfully towards the clumsy tool taking my position on the field.

Couch flips me off. "Fuck *you*, Slater. David is reliable. *He's* been here all week."

What an arsehole.

"Fine!" I saunter over to the bench, slam my body down, and chew on my guard. I glare out at the field, revelling in the smell of freshly mowed grass and the sounds of the lads rumbling. I really need to play; these past two days have drained me emotionally and I need a release from my thoughts.

Blesk and Elise will probably still be asleep. I really wish she had slept in my bed and let me hold her. Goddamn it, I don't want to go another night without her next to me. When I woke up spooning her yesterday, with her perfect curves snug against my body, her feet tangled with mine, the smell of her hair in my face, and our fingers threaded under her cheek, I remembered this whole other side of me. A better side. Her presence was like a breath of fresh air, and I hadn't realised until that moment that I'd been suffocating without her. Then those beautiful wide brown eyes had peered innocently up at me from my pillow... and it had all faded away. I had to do a double-take before realising her face was telling me a silent *goodbye*. It was fleeting and diluted, but I saw it.

And that wasn't the last time I'd seen it either. When she thought she was alone with her thoughts, I watched her from the doorway, watched her face fall and terror fill her expression. She wasn't happy to see me. Air had been squeezed from my lungs and panic had run through me, filling my head with scenarios of losing her, *again*. And then she goes and expresses a desire to check on Erik. Oh fucking Erik! Forcing that down, I focus on the game, wanting just a few hours away from the thought of him and her —together.

Grabbing my jersey, Coach drags me up. "Get on the field,

Slate. If David wasn't such a complete waste of space, you would be benched for weeks." Before I can move, he fists my hair and tilts my head to stare at him. "Don't piss me off today."

"Yes, Coach!"

I jog out to join Jax and the lads on the field. Flexing my neck, cracking my jaw, I jump up and down to limber up. I spend a few moments sizing up the opposing arseholes around me. After a good amount of time on the sidelines, I know who I can dominate. There is one guy I haven't seen for a while on the opposing team, Max Butcher. Last time I saw him, he was playing for The Wedges at Connolly High. We both grew up in the District; however, his mates were never the kind I wanted to associate with.

Max is built like a brick shithouse, but he's also fast like a mother-fucking six-legged cheetah. I will have to keep an eye on him.

I pump the air and stretch, thinking about a million things all at once: Liz, Erik without appendages, my little sister Cassidy, Blesk-

The whistle blows.

Jacob feeds the ball into the scrum. I eyeball the opposing captain, feeling extra twitchy; I just want to run. As soon as Jonno has the ball, my feet start pounding the turf. I think about only a few things now.

The ball. Their defence. The line.

It's like dodgeball, but instead of dodging balls, I am ducking and weaving through incoming brick walls with fucking arms. It is a good thing I'm fast.

Flex has the ball. Panting hard, I push forward, knowing it will come to me upon release. He tosses the ball. I feel the thud of the leather against my chest. The ball is in my hands.

My fists ache momentarily, but now I have only one thing on my mind.

The try line.

My eyes dart around, checking the incoming traffic. I dodge and swerve, jumping over the dickhead too inept to take me down. And now I have a clear run. My feet thunder on the ground.

Giving the crowd a shit-eating-grin, I dive, driving the ball into the grass.

Try, bitches!

———

"WHAT A GAME, hey? Too bad they didn't put me in earlier," I state smugly, pulling gear out from inside my locker. This room smells like bleach. Despite its fundamental purpose, I usually leave feeling like I need another shower. A small scoff escapes Jax. Turning to face him, I say, "What's wrong with you?"

He huffs. "A lot."

I wander over to him and place my hand on his shoulder. "Thank you."

He tenses, his features tightening disapprovingly. "That was fucked up!" He slams his locker shut.

My knuckles tend to agree.

"That layer of fucked up is just the icing on top of a layered cake of fucked up. Trust me," I say.

He lowers his voice. "You gonna tell me what I saw down there?"

Offering him a regretful smile, I shake my head. "It isn't just mine to tell. Can you understand that? I mean, mate, I get it, you deserve to know, but I can't tell you without Blesk's permission."

"You called her a different name and she freaked out," he states.

I take a long exaggerated breath in and blow it out with as much ease as I can muster. "Yeah, because we used to know each other, as kids, and I lost her, but..." I pause and contemplate my next set of words. "Now I've found her. Her name was Liz then."

He shrugs at me. "Is that all you can give me?"

I nod apologetically and pat him on the back. "Yep."

"And Erik?" he queries.

I tighten at the mention of his name. "Erik can go to hell... I promise if you saw what he was doing to her when I got there, you might not have pulled me off."

His face hardened. "I still would have. Even if it was just to stop you from going to jail."

"Just..." I pause. "Trust me? Please."

Jax sighs. "Beer tonight?"

"I have to get Blesk. I have a few things planned, but maybe we will come by the hall after." After every home game, we host a postgame piss-up. We didn't win, but had I been on field for the whole game, I'm sure we would have. Dealing with the hubris of the Preston Retreat University lads tonight will challenge all of our egos, and I have never missed a party; but Blesk is my number one priority.

Whether she likes it or not.

The song she'd written when she was eight, "One Day," has inspired the plan I have for her. By the time the sun drops behind the horizon, Blesk will certainly be madly in love with me. I know about her predisposition to run from complications. I know she is in constant turmoil over what had happened. I am the living embodiment of that tragedy and memory, and with my presence comes pain. I know this. I don't want to cause her any pain. But we are worth the pain, worth the struggle, worth the fight. This is fate... *us* presented on a silver platter. It's worth the effort, dammit!

That little girl loved me, as much as I loved her, and Blesk is retreating due to that familiarity. I won't let her. She needs to remember the love we'd shared, the joy we'd brought each other despite the darkness around us.

That song is about a promise we made to each other, that *one day* we would do all the things we never could, and that is exactly what we are going to do today.

Slinging my sports bag over my shoulders, I make my way across campus. I reach into my jeans pocket and retrieve my phone, wanting to know where Blesk is.

Konnor: *Duchess, where are you at the moment?*

Blesk: *At home.*

Konnor: *Define home?*

Blesk: *You aren't my English teacher, Mr Slater.*

Konnor: *Lol, your dorm or home-home?*

Blesk: *My dorm*

———

TOUSLING my still-damp hair with one hand, I approach the gargoyle-manned steps of her dormitory block. Several girls skip down the chipped concrete hazards as I stride up.

"Konnor!" one of them calls out. I look around and my eyes land on a pretty, petite, blue-eyed girl who I feel I should recognise, but don't.

"Hey?" I search my memory for her name, clicking my fingers as if it's on the tip of my tongue.

Which it isn't.

"Faith. I'm a friend of Cassidy's." She gestures to herself with a sweet smile.

"Right! Faith, hey." My little sister Cassidy has a handful

of friends, yet I still don't recognise this chick. I shove my hands into my pockets and look at her questioningly. "What's up?"

She turns to her girlfriends who have halted a few steps above us and says, "Go ahead, guys. I'll meet you there."

She turns back to me, a little more flushed than I'm comfortable with, and says, "I watched the game today. My brother played nine. Jack Man."

"Right ... yeah. It was a nice win." I acknowledge The Dingoes' accomplishments like the classy fucker I am.

She bats her eyelids at me, causing me to immediately think of Blesk. I glance up towards the entrance, not interested in a flirting session.

"You played really well," she coos. "My brother wouldn't stop talking about you. He said if Max Butcher hadn't been on field, you guys would have won."

"Yeah, Max is pretty aggressive. Well, that's a nice thing for your brother to say, so thanks, Faith. Congratulate him for me, will ya?" I try to be as polite as I can, but I'm feeling increasingly impatient. I want to get away and go up to look at Blesk's incredible brown eyes. "Sorry, but excuse me. I have to meet someone. Nice seeing you." I jog up the steps.

"Konnor!" she yells up to me.

Take a hint...

I roll my eyes and turn back to her with a feigned smile. "Yes, Faith?"

She twists a strand of hair around her finger. "Will you be at the party tonight?"

"Maybe." And with that I continue towards room seventy-three.

Knocking on her door and waiting, I listen intently to the shuffling of feet on the opposite side. The door swings open and Blesk fills the doorway with a subtle grin, looking exceptional in jeans that hug her thighs and waist impeccably, and a black tank-top with butterflies on it. I sigh loudly, taking her all in. Every time I see her, she is more extraordinary. The butterflies are appropriate because that's what she summons within me every time I see her.

"Duchess," I say, taking her hand. "I hope you are free for the rest of the day because I have some things planned."

She angles her head curiously. "And what might they be?"

I immediately cringe because if I tell her, she might object. "An array of various activities."

"Intriguing... And worrying." She giggles.

She just giggled. Fuck, yes.

Her demeanour seems different from yesterday, more resolved. Maybe she just needed some time to absorb everything. Or maybe Elise's presence and support has helped. Either way, she seems visibly more at ease. I would be lying if I said I didn't wish I could make her feel that kind of contentment, but her feeling *that,* despite its origin, is enough for me. I'm thankful to whoever can fill that void for her.

I grin at her. "So is that a, 'Yes, Konnor, I will come with you and engage in said various activities'?"

She chuckles again. Her eyes crinkle in the corners as she smiles sweetly. "Yes."

She's going to be madly in love with me by the end of the day.

"Awesome," I say with way too much eagerness to be cool, but I don't care. "But after, I'd like to meet Jax and the lads at the rugby party. Will you come?"

She hesitates and begins to fidget with her clothes, so I grab her idle hand and pull it to my chest. "It'll be fun. I should go, and I don't want to go without you."

She nods. "O... *kay*," she says in a cute tone. "Did you

win? Because I'd like to go to the party with a winner." Amusement plays on her face.

"*Ohhhh*," I bellow, laughter knocking at my chest. "My apologies, Miss Bellamy! You're going to have to go with a loser." Grinning and shaking my head in awe, I'm again amazed by the woman she has become, the funny, witty woman standing in front of me, smirking.

"Oh," she says, mock disappointment drawing her brows together. "I can't go then."

Cheeky little thing.

"Well, unfortunately, I'm going to have to insist," I say, cocking my head at her. "And pull rank on you."

"What?" She gasps, faking shock. "Mr Slater, this seems like a personal request?"

"Well, *custom coaching*, remember?" I pull her hand and begin to walk down the hall with her.

"Wait ..." she says, tugging back on my hand and parking her heels into the carpet.

I spin. "What?"

"I need a change of clothes for tonight." She grins at me like I should know this.

"You look great," I say. Which gives me another excuse to roll my eyes over her fantastic form, taking in the slope of her breasts, the tiny slither of midriff, and the little gap between her thighs. "Yep, looking good to me."

She smiles, tilting her head at my obvious perusal. "It's a party, Konnor. I need something else to wear."

"Okay, Duch, go grab something else. But don't worry, you'll still be the most beautiful girl at the party."

Now who is the smooth motherfucker?

She beams at me and rushes back into her room. As she bounds off, I watch her jeans stretch around her incredible arse. *Oh,* how I want more than anything to peel them off her, bend her over, and see what that arse looks like pressed to my pelvis. I want her bad; my heart rate, imagination, and cock take every opportunity to remind me of that fact. But if she was half as beautiful, I'd still be just as persistent. That little girl made me feel like I was worth something, long after everyone else had forgotten me. It's a complete bloody bonus that the girl I've been in love with for most of my life is the perfect mixture of classy, sexy, and sweet... an awesome bloody bonus.

Blesk skips out a few moments later with a bag over her shoulder and a sweet grin from ear to ear. I grab the fabric strap of her bag and slide it off her shoulder, watching as it pulls the neck of her shirt down, exposing her soft naked collarbone. I turn and kiss the newly exposed part of skin and then hang her satchel over my shoulder.

The taste of her skin makes every part of me vibrate.

The scent that is exclusively hers, hits me like a wave of pheromones. She freezes and looks into my eyes as if shocked by my lips on her body.

"Sorry," I murmur, holding my hand out for her to take.

"Don't be," she whispers, feeding her fingers through mine. "Just wasn't expecting that."

"Good, 'cause I lied." I stick my tongue out at her. "I'm not sorry."

WHEN I WAS NINE, two days before she died and I lost her, we'd made a promise that has never been realised. We wrote down three things on a piece of paper that we wanted to do together in our new lives. The kind of things children dream about when they have nothing to stimulate or fracture their purest desires.

When you are alone, when you spend hours looking into the black or being afraid of the man who is meant to protect you, your wishes become unique to that of a common child.

My cage had consisted of very narrow, cold metal bars, which were so closely set together that even a finger struggled to move between them. We used to index-finger swear. I would put my finger in between the bars and she would meet mine with hers. That was the only human contact I had for four years.

That's why it took me nearly two years before I could cuddle my new sisters and not feel awkward. However, once I'd felt their warmth, I never took *touch* for granted again. If it were up to me, I would always be touching Blesk, touching Liz.

Promise #1: We will go on a Merry-Go-Round.

The entrance to the park is nothing if not grand with its natural tree pillars that seem skyscraper-high and yellow flags that flap from various limbs. Decades of work has gone into forming the trunk arches that act as a threshold to the maze made of hedges and oak.

Blesk and I walk hand-in-hand towards the labyrinth. Children shoot past us, almost bowling us over, with water pistols and happy, cheeky faces. Other than the accompanying adults, we are the only ones over the age of twelve.

She grins at me and shakes her head like I'm crazy. "Where are we going?"

I point into the labyrinth as children whiz past, getting a mouthful of water from a nearby Water Soaker. "In there."

She laughs. Her smile is so beautiful. My heart feels too tight, too in awe of those lips and the way they curve. "Okay, let's go," she says, tugging me in.

When we hit the first green grass fork, she looks at me

mischievously and says, "Beat you to the centre!" Then she disappears to the right, giggling as she bounces away.

I duck off to the left, jumping over kids as they scoot around my legs. I halt in front of another fork: left or right? I dodge off right and sprint down a weird row of water fountains. Hopscotching over them and around a statue of a goblin, I suddenly reach a complete dead-end. She can't beat me. I shove what looks like a perfectly normal wooden wall in front of me. It opens.

As my feet jog carefully through it, I listen for any sign of Blesk. I hear her voice not too far away, but I'm in a tight hallway of hedges now. Kids sound riotous in this section of the maze, but their sudden absence around me seems eerie. Then I hear a splutter of laughter and I'm running, picking the directions by following the noises. As I corner a grass mound, I come to a screeching stop in front of the merry-go-round. Alone. Silent.

It is as awesome as I remember.

With goblins, unicorns, archers, and centaurs, all of which can be ridden, it is magical. I'm encircled by dark green hedges that are lit up by the colours beaming from the carousel.

The air is crisp and distinct as it blows through the channels and arches; the silence seems to conflict with the vibrancy of the ride.

Feeling a bit of unease, I frown and wrinkle my nose. I dart my eyes around suspiciously; I can't help but notice there is a strange nonattendance of children. The whole carousel is empty, shimmering and waiting. There is only me halted in front of it.

Then, out of nowhere, a kid appears and stares at me.

An abrupt chuckle escapes him. Grinning mischievously, the kid pulls out his gun and squirts me in the face. My jaw drops. The noise of more feet surrounds me, quickly followed by the contents of their pistols. Before I know it, I have a crowd of children running at me, spraying me with water. Blesk appears from behind the carousel as her minions fly out and soak me.

She giggles the kind of giggle that will flash in my mind the moment I take my last breath.

"You got here first, hey?" I yell to her, shaking my wet hair like a dog.

Blesk sticks that tongue out and nods innocently. "Apparently, kids will squirt anyone you ask them to." She walks towards the rear of the carousel. Grabbing a pole twirled with ribbon, she pulls herself up onto the platform. Her leg goes over a unicorn, positioning her on top of it. A big grin pulls her cheeks back. All the kids follow, filling spaces quickly. As the carousel begins to spin, I jump on and move around the objects to find a spot beside her. I sit on the side of a centaur paired with her unicorn and watch her smile at the eager and noisy children. She offers me her attention, and in that moment, she looks so much like Liz that I have to fight the tears threatening to come out.

I mouth, "You're beautiful."

She blushes an exquisite colour of pink and says, "So are you."

Promise #2: We Will Dance Together.

Afterwards, we grab hotdogs from a vendor down by Storm River. I wanted to take Blesk somewhere with a view, where a waiter would pull her seat out and treat her like a lady. But she just wanted a hotdog...

I fucking love that.

With our stomachs full, we stroll hand in hand along the docks. I watch her skip instead of walk, watch the sun flicker through her flowing hair as we head to our next destination.

This is how I want every moment for the rest of her life to be — skipping before walking, laughing without consideration.

As I hear the sound of the local busker, I'm reminded of the first night that I ever felt freedom. One night while I was sleeping, my sisters, Cassidy and Flick, crept into my room and quietly woke me up. All three of us then snuck out through my window. I am the middle child, but at that time had acted like the youngest. Losing four years of development will do that to a kid.

What blew my mind though was the *act* of climbing from the window, that there was a window to escape from, and to me, it was a portal —a way into the world that no one could take from me. I used it often after that night. As often as I could. Not running, chasing, nor escaping anything, but just because... I could.

That night, a friend of Flick's was busking down at the docks. They'd usually only gone together —my new siblings. That night I officially became one of the *Slater* kids... They'd wanted me to be there and experience their harmless, childish rebellion. Flick sauntered down the docks, thinking that as the oldest of us, at the age of fourteen, she was mature and wise. Cassidy jigged with so much energy, dancing here and there, while I played the brother role that they'd cast me in. It felt right. Good.

Their faces filled with the kind of freedom only someone who has been stripped of it could truly appreciate — someone like me. Their hair rushed in the wind as they pulled silly faces, jumped on park benches and pushed each other, acting like exactly what they were — children.

That night is still one of the best nights of my life.

And so today, I'm taking Blesk here. To show her the exact spot I *first* remember feeling true *freedom*. When I spot the entertainer, some bohemian dude playing guitar, I sit and pull Blesk down with me. She shivers, so I wrap my arm around her shoulders, rubbing her affectionately.

As she watches him and respects his talent, I study her face. Blesk is clearly loving this. Her smile is content and sweet, and it makes my heart beat a little faster. I grab her hand and stand, attempting to pull her out in front of the spectators. She tries to park her heels in the ground as she tugs away in gentle protest.

"Trust me," I whisper as I begin to dance with her, and... she lets me. It's a weird rhythm to dance to, but we laugh and I take responsibility for our inadequacies. I lead her, gazing at her as her eyes shuffle through emotions like a deck of cards: nervous, excited, happy, sad, happy again, giddy, and what could be mistaken for love. But if not, I'm surely getting close.

Promise #3: We Will Scream As Loud As We Can.

We watch the sun drop behind the horizon before making our way back to my apartment. While waiting for Blesk to come out of the bathroom, I begin to feel nervous about her meeting the rugby lads.

As I swig on the bourbon in my tumbler, the heat from the alcohol warms my body. I don't have the most valiant reputation when it comes to women, and the last thing I want is some arsehole saying something about my past indiscretions to Blesk. For her sake and mine.

She isn't just Blesk to me. Every time I look into her eyes, I see glimpses of that fragile little girl looking back at me. I wasn't able to protect her then — from her father, from her isolation — and it tore me apart. So now I will be beating the shit out of anyone who does anything less than make her smile. I owe her that.

The door opens, halting my train of thought immediately. The sight of her slides pleasure through me not unlike the liquor in my hand, warming and soothing. She looks bashful as she crosses her feet in front of her while I ogle every inch of her flawless appearance. Her little black dress clings to every curve, treading boldly on the edge of being too short. There are little pink ribbons at the bust line, just to remind any guy who looks at her that she's sweet. Her hair is pinned up loosely, exposing every inch of porcelain skin from her neck to her breasts. I love that part of her body; it's so delicate. Her pulse beats at the base of her throat, and the need to kiss it is overbearing. Her heels are pink, and thin silk ties wrap around her calf.

"Wow... Fuck, Duch. How am I meant to be a gentleman when you look like that?"

She giggles, rolling her shoulder up to hide her blushing cheeks.

"It isn't funny. I'm serious." I jump up, but I'm almost unsure if I should approach her yet. I want to peel the dress off her and watch every inch of her slowly become exposed. Then I want to taste every little dimple, curve, and soft portion of her skin, and then make love to her in those heels. Exhaling steadily, I try to think about something else: my coach, the lady at the coffee shop with the whiskers ...

"Do you want me to change?" She laughs.

"Hell no! I mean yes, I mean... no." I walk over to her and peer down. "You look extraordinary." She leans up and kisses my cheek. Her lips part slightly as they linger on my skin, and when she pulls away, our eyes lock inches from each other. I drop my eyes to watch her lips as she breathes long, deep breaths that summon every part of me.

She pulls away to give us some much needed distance, then bats her lashes at me.

"You're gorgeous, Konnor."

I'm standing like a statue. If I let so much as one muscle

do what it's pulsing to do, her breasts would be pressed against my chest, my tongue would be in her mouth, and I would be swallowing her moans. I shake my head and inhale. I thread my hand through her long fingers and we exit my apartment together. Adolf gives me a gracious smile as we stroll from the rear elevator across the foyer.

"Mr Slater, Miss Bellamy, enjoy your evening." He raises his hat and tilts his chin.

Blesk beams at him. "Thank you, Adolf, and you too."

I love how polite she is.

I wait until we walk past and then turn, gesturing to Blesk's back, I cover my heart with my hand and smile. Adolf nods, mouthing, "Look after her."

THE HALL IS TECHNICALLY off campus, but it's within walking distance from my apartment and most dormitories. By the time we get there, it's already buzzing with the lads. A few of them are obviously already a little pre-partied. They probably started drinking at lunch time, not that I can judge since I take a flask with me almost everywhere I go. Strangely, Blesk doesn't seem to judge me based on my drinking habits —and that is usually the very first thing girls complain about.

We move through the crowd, fingers threaded together, and the first sign of trouble hits me square in the face. Pemberton scowls at us from across the hall with a look that would crush most men. A red halter dress that screams 'give me attention' hugs every curve of her body. Its plunging neckline flashes everything except her nipples. The slit up her leg cuts to the seam of her underwear. She looks hot. But Blesk is hotter; there is no question. Curvier, softer skin, and with a natural glow and an authentic beauty. Pemberton was always too fake, inside and out.

I whisper under my breath, "Why the hell is she even here?"

Blesk's brows pull together. "Because she's in love with you, Konnor."

I nearly cough with laughter. "She doesn't love me. She hates me. I was an accessory."

She rolls her eyes. Sassy Blesk. I like Sassy Blesk. "Sometimes girls don't know how to show you that. She does. *I* can tell. Be nice to her, please." I want to tell Blesk what horrible things Pemberton said about her. Yet, I want more than anything for her to smile, so I never will. Even if it means I'm the bad guy.

"Alright, I'll be nice, Duch," I say running my knuckles down her cheek.

She blinks at me a few times. "Boys just don't get girl cues."

I shrug. "You're kinda enigmas."

The night passes by and Blesk gets along seamlessly with everyone I introduce her to; she is charming and witty. Although her specific variety of perfection attracts an irritating amount of attention from a lot of arseholes in the hall, she stays by my side, and she doesn't pretend to want to be anywhere else. She is rare. Our *togetherness* is rare.

While I take manly gulps of my bourbon on the rocks and listen vaguely to the lads around us chattering, my gaze gets drawn to her. Her long delicate fingers clasp the stem of her white wine glass as she sips her drink modestly. Every time her lips wrap around the rim, tingles run directly to my groin.

Stop staring, Konnor.

I'm slowly slipping into a nice inebriated state. Still, I'm

completely distracted by Blesk, her every graceful movement, her every little smile. It's probably because I'm yet to
kiss her. The anticipation of which is killing me.

"Slater? Slater!"

I get drawn back to the other people around me. "Huh?"

"You and that bloody phasing out thing. Freaks me out,
dude, stop it." Jax grimaces at me. "Yeah, buddy, she's
smoking hot. Stop drooling."

"Get fucked." I playfully shove him. Blesk giggles as we
continue our immature, testosterone-based banter.

She wraps her hand around my forearm as someone from
behind us shouts, "I know that arse!"

Jax's face drops in response to whoever the voice belongs
to, which inundates me with immediate unease. Every
muscle in me tightens when I hear a slap and see Blesk's legs
buckle beneath her slightly. Heat rushes up my spine,
knowing that someone has just slapped her on the arse.

I spin around, seeing nothing but red. "What the fuck?!"

Fucking Max Butcher.

He holds his hands up in a ceasefire kind of motion.
"Whoa, no disrespect Slater, I've had a few too many." He
smirks at me. "You'd know all about that."

I fist my hands at my sides in preparation, but then
notice Blesk smiling with recognition at him. The familiarity
in her eyes unsettles me further. I don't want to think about
him and her or whatever kind of acquaintances they are. Or
why she is smiling at him.

Why is *she smiling at him?*

My face starts to ache as I grind my molars and scowl,
hard.

"Hey, sweetheart, I forgot your name." Max grins at her,
his lips lopsided and arrogant, and presents her with his
hand. "Know that arse, just not the name. My bad." My eyes

go directly to his hand and I watch as she places hers delicately in it. Then his fingers wrap around and enclose hers within them. And maybe it's in my head. Maybe I'm just too drunk, but it seems more sensual than necessary. My eye twitches. If I didn't know any better, I would be throwing my elbow into his jaw right now.

I fantasise about picking up the chair to my right and shattering it over his disrespectful head. The only thing stopping me from teaching him some manners is Blesk. She hates fighting. Any retaliation against Max would definitely end that way, resulting in me bludgeoned and him walking away with a few meagre scratches. That doesn't bother me as much as Blesk having to witness something like that again. Despite that, if he puts his paws on her again, I won't be able to stop myself.

"Blesk. Erik Bellamy's little sister." She shakes his hand and they linger on that gesture far too long. A deep rumble, like a growl, courses through my chest.

His face lights up with recognition. Smirking, he leans back on his heels. "Ah... of course!" He pats me on the arm and I want to break his hand. "Slater, I went to school with her dickhead brother." Looking amused by my expression, he tilts his head to eyeball me and then folds his arms across his chest. "So, I hear you beat the shit out of him?"

Fuck, news travels fast.

Of course, Max is from the District too; we District kids don't have any bloody private lives.

Blesk narrows her eyes at me and shakes her head. It's clear she doesn't want me to join in on this particular male banter. "Not something I'm proud of," I lie.

Palming his jaw until it cracks, he scoffs in disbelief. "Yeah, right." Then he pats me again like a dog, knowing I can't do a *single* thing if I want to keep all my teeth. "Been there, done that. Funny it's over the same girl though." He turns and slowly saunters off.

I turn, lock-jawed, and stare at Blesk with the calmest questioning expression I can muster. Every part of my face is on fire, akin to someone igniting a furnace behind my eyes. *"Funny it's over the same girl though. Funny it's over the same girl though. Funny it's over the same-"* Fuck!

"Blesk? Can you explain, please?" I barely get the words out without yelling.

Her face tightens at my tone. But when she looks at my expression, she smiles softly at me.

"Nothing happened." She giggles. "We kissed a little. Don't let him get to you. Max derives great pleasure from messing with people."

Max is messing with you. I hate the way she says his name.

This jealousy thing is new to me and it's nothing short of irritating. I rub her beautiful arm before turning to walk outside. My legs move faster than normal. To a common observer, I probably appear to be rushing away from a fight. Perhaps I am. The fight is in my head, but still.

He's kissed her. There is this whole side of her life I know nothing about. How many guys has she been with? How many guys have kissed her? My Liz. My girl. She has this whole past that I haven't even contemplated.

Bumming a cigarette off a friend, I find a spot alone. I press the cigarette to my lips and replace carbon dioxide with nicotine. As always, it's disgusting, so I chase the ashy taste with the bourbon that's sloshing around in my glass.

"Hi?"

I tilt my head in the direction of the voice, leaning back on the pillar behind me. It's Faith. Her blonde hair swirls in the wind as she struts towards me provocatively. Her hips swing like a pendulum, and the light from the hall is making her silhouette's movement way too stimulating to a guy who hasn't had sex in over a week. There are three of her right now and all three look... *good.* I try to stabilise myself by gripping the pillar behind me with one hand. "Faith, right?"

"Konnor, what are you doing outside *all alone*?" she purrs.

"Getting drunk. You?" I mumble.

She bats her long lashes at me and coos, "Looking for someone to get drunk with." Faith's eyes sparkle as a slow sexy smile spreads across her face. I could spot that look anywhere. That's the 'fuck me' look.

I am so drunk. I am so horny. Blesk...

I straighten and walk away from her, ignoring her when she calls me back. I am *way* too drunk. I can barely focus on walking straight, let alone anything else. Once I see my duchess, I begin to stumble in her direction. She smiles at first, but soon her expression falters. Rushing over to me, she wraps her arm around my waist and walks me back outside. She helps me down onto the step before positioning herself beside me with a little sigh.

She places her hand on my leg and peers at me. "You okay?"

My elbows meet my knees. Hanging my head between my legs, I focus on breathing. "When did I get so drunk?"

She giggles and rubs my leg. "You've been inhaling drinks since we got here."

"Blesk, Duch, I'm freaking out. About Max. About you. About us."

"I'm twenty-one. I've kissed boys, Konnor."

"How many boys?" I comb my fingers through my hair before rubbing my temples, feeling tightness through my forehead.

I don't want to know... Yes, I do.

She sighs, her warm breath bringing colour to the crisp air. "Ummm, maybe six?"

"But not me," I huff before I can stop the words from coming out. *Fuck.* "I'm *sorry,* Duch. Sometimes I'm an arse-hole when I'm drunk."

Silence settles between us while I stare at the pavement, shuffling the dirt with my sneakers. I'm glad I can't see her face right now; it seems to undo me. If I see even a glimpse of hurt in her eyes because of me, I'll rip my own head off. And I need my head.

Despite my lack of knowing how to use it sometimes.

I look up at her. "Duch?"

Her lips curve up slowly as she asks, "Do you want to kiss me?"

I hold my breath for a second and then release it in a rush. "God, yes!"

She moves her head closer to me and her breath hits my lips. The smell of peaches overwhelms my senses. "Like this?" she whispers. "Now?"

Sitting up, I grab her nape and pull her to me, stopping inches from her mouth. As I brush our lips together, a small gasp escapes her. She waits, letting me take complete control. Our lips barely touch, but her panting matches mine. I want to kiss her. I also want to remember it.

You're too drunk, Konnor.

I watch her line of sight drop to see my hand entwining with hers. I pull her up, staggering a little as I do. She catches me around the waist, laughing. Then we walk —stumble, stagger, jog, whatever you want to call it, towards the middle of the field that surrounds the hall.

It's damn cold, so I pull off my jacket and wrap it around her shoulders, covering the tiny amount of fabric she has over her. As I slump down onto the grass with a loud exhale, I pull her down with me. She leans into me with a sigh.

"I'm not used to feeling jealous," I admit, attempting to explain my behaviour. "If a girl doesn't want me, well, then, whatever." I smirk at her. "Not that it's ever happened."

"So modest," she says with a giggle.

We stare up at the stars sparkling and glistening in the black dome above us. Our breath steams the air and the scent of freshly mowed grass fills my nose. Other than the subtle drumming and murmuring coming from the hall on our side, there is no noise, no presence nor person other than us. We steal a comfortable moment of silence together, listening to the sound of each other breathing.

Her hair is still pinned delicately above her head. When she turns to stare at me, her eyes are heavy-lidded; she may be a little drunk too. The urge to touch her is too strong. Her neck and chest are exposed and covered in goose bumps, and I'm crazy in love with that section of her skin.

Flipping onto my side, I memorise the curves of her torso with my fingers. I trail the beating vein in her neck to the dimple where her collarbone meets her chest. As I stroke over the fleshy mound where the fabric of her dress meets her breasts, she swallows nervously.

I want to tuck my hand into her bra and squeeze, feel her nipple tighten in my palm. She quivers beneath my fingers. I love that I can make her body respond that way. I look up from where my fingers linger on her plump chest to meet her sexy glistening eyes and my breath is squeezed from me.

Fuck.

I want her so bad.

"Thank you," she whispers, smiling coyly. "For today. It was... *perfect.*"

Her words fill my heart. "I want every day to be perfect

for you," I say. "But it isn't over yet." I roll onto my back and twist my face to look at her, focusing my thoughts on our final promise. "Scream."

Her face tightens. "What?"

"*Scream,*" I state. "It's on our list."

She looks at me with wide hesitant eyes and shakes her head over and over. "No way."

I chuckle and turn to the sky before howling loudly at the moon. She slaps me in the stomach and laughs.

"You're so corny." She curls onto her side, watching me watching her.

"Go on, Duch, do it," I press, pulling her legs off the grass so they drape over me.

"*O... kay,*" she mocks in that silly tone I adore. Her hand rests on my chest as she answers my call with a much cuter howl. "How howw howwwwwwl!"

sixteen: liz

Liz

THE GIRL GLARES at her reflection, wondering at what age she will be beautiful. She glances at the photo of her mother stuck to the side of her mirror and then back to herself. Her hair is always a nest woven together like barrels of hay, strands dead on the ends. She narrows her eyes, turning to the side to see if she has developed yet. Nothing. With a sigh, she moves towards the mirror and opens her swollen eye up, flattening the skin around the bruise.

Why can't I be beautiful?

Lately, the girl has felt strange. Different. She wants to look beautiful, and she wants Kon to say she is. Even if she blushes and tells him he's gross... For reasons she can't quite comprehend, she still wants to hear it.

When she is at school, she thinks about him. She thinks about him all the time. The girl knows he can't wait until *he* is allowed to go to school too. He loves the idea of learning. With education, he can be anything he wants to be. Not a dog. Anything he wants. When he was six, he pretended he was a firefighter. When he turned seven, he pretended to be an explorer, discovering things all over the world, like untouched mountains and desert scapes. When he was eight, he pretended to be a sports star running around under the sun on an oval made of green and gold. Now that he is nine, he wants to make sure every kid can learn and be anything they want to be —he wants to be a teacher. The girl wonders what he will want to be next year...

She watches her bunny slippers slide across the floorboards, their floppy ears bouncing with each step. She giggles. She walks into the old kitchen and begins to make dinner. Three bowls first. Pasta. Cheese. Milk. Butter. The girl knows how to make a meal on a budget even though she is only eight. It has been her responsibility to prepare meals since she could reach the stove. Pasta is only fifty cents a bag and will feed four adults. It lasts a few days. She can get cheese and butter for only five dollars; they last a week. Milk is a luxury. The man at the deli gives her the expired stuff for one dollar. She boils it up with the cheese and butter and never has a problem. Her favourite meal is mac and cheese, and it only costs six dollars and fifty cents to make.

Mrs Renalds from two streets over lets the girl take a few cobs of corn during the season from her corn field. Kon loves sweet corn straight from the cob or in mac and cheese. The girl likes making him happy. He is her little secret. She knows something isn't quite right about their situation. It has been four years since he came to be her brother. Her father once told her that Kon is allergic to the sun and that if it ever saw him, it would burn him to a crisp. The boy is safe in the cage, under the ground, away from the rays. She is safe too. And they are together.

She remains silent and inconspicuous as she slides onto the brown futon and flicks the television on, desperately trying not to disturb the man who is passed out on the recliner with a highball clutched in his hand. She presses the mute button and switches the channel to the nightly news, peering at her father every so often to assess his state. He snores loudly. The girl wonders if all men snore. She isn't allowed to watch the news. Her dad says she has a soft heart and the news will corrupt her. She loves the news.

The girl shovels the mac and cheese into her mouth, the sweetness of the corn exploding as she pops the kernels between her molars, and watches the inaudible program.

Suddenly, she is rendered frozen, shell-shocked by the images on the television. The girl all but stops breathing, unsure of what she is looking at. Or why her body wants to break apart. Or who she is looking at. Or who... Then she knows.

His face.

She blinks at the screen. His face. The girl sits up immediately and, without her conscious consent, her fingers rub the volume key until she can hear the voice speaking. A knot rolls down her throat. Her body tightens as she listens. And stares. At Kon's face on the television.

"Nerrock Missing and Beyond is an annual charity event that raises funds to assist with services necessary when a child goes missing, including law assistance and travel," the voice says.

"The boy who inspired this affluent event is none other than the famous Deakon Nerrock, son of Dustin and Madeline Nerrock, who went missing four years ago without a trace. Last year, just after the death of Madeline Nerrock, the charity CEO—"

She still can't move.

His face.

Kon.

Deakon.

Missing.

Why can't I breathe?

She tries to suck air in, but something is stopping her. Realising it's her hand clasped over her mouth, she blinks at her brother's face and slowly unfolds her fingers. Air inflates her lungs in a rush as she gasps at it. Heaves.

He isn't my brother.

Thud.

A rough hand slams into the back of her head. Her neck wrenches forward, her vision dims, and she hits the floor, her face crushed against the carpet.

A metallic taste fills her mouth.

Like a snake suffocating its prey, her father's hand encircles her ankle. The carpet burns her cheeks as she is pulled backwards along it. The girl knows what is happening, but she is too dizzy from his face, from the hit, from the truth, to react.

He isn't my brother.

Moments pass as she lies limp. She is dragged into her father's room. Then she remembers what she heard: the truth about who Kon is and what her father has done. What *she* has done. A gut-curdling scream crawls up her throat. She begins to fight back. With her voice. With her cries. With her clenched fists and kicking legs. For the first time, she fights. For Kon.

seventeen: blesk

Blesk

AFTER THE PARTY LAST NIGHT, we fell asleep talking to each other. He babbled to me about his life, sharing stories of snowboarding trips to Falls Creek, running amuck around the District when he was a teen, camping adventures, Bali holidays, and backpacking around Europe with a mate from New Zealand. I felt a sense of relief knowing he has flourished.

He told me about the significance of the places he'd taken me to yesterday, and all about Cassidy and Flick and how they'd brought him out of his shell.

He shared lessons the wise Ben Slater, his adoptive father, had taught him to help him learn from his past and use it to build strength in himself. He told me his mission is to make me fall in love with him and that I don't stand a chance.

Funny, as if I'm an opponent.

Yesterday, we finished Liz and Deakon's story together. It was the most perfect day of my life. And yet, when we went to sleep and I heard him mumble, "I love you, Liz," as he drifted off, the whole truth of this reality came crashing down on me. He loves Liz. Not me. I don't want to be loved for another person, especially one I hate.

If only he loved Blesk, just Blesk. He looks at me like I'm some kind of mythical creature, but I'm not. I am just plain old Blesk. Blesk, who does more damage than good. When Konnor looks at me, his eyes are unwavering and there is too much pressure in them. He talks like our forever is set in stone. He is too much and so are his expectations of me. I've tried to be who he wants me to be, but I'm not Liz. More than that, I don't want to be. So if being with him means being her, then I just ... can't.

Taking a little time to appreciate him, I watch as he sleeps. His eyes flicker around under his heavy lids, and his incredible mouth twitches every so often. I gently stroke his cheek before running my fingers through his hair. I study its exact shade. It's light brown, the perfect kind of brown that flashes natural highlights in the sun. His cheeks are a little stubbly, but I think I like them this way. I use my finger to smooth out the frown he has fallen asleep with, but that expression quickly forms again. He's a worrier.

Sighing a quiet goodbye, I slide out from the bed and make my way into the kitchen. I find a note pad and begin to write, my mind and heart hurting as they wrestle over this decision.

Dearest Konnor,

Being with you is like living in a dream.
Every moment we are together, I feel like someone
else. You are everything I dreamed you'd be and
then some. And most nights I did dream about
you. Your life is beautiful and warm, just like
you. There is nothing stopping you now from
being everything you want to be. How you have
taken yourself from that poor boy and turned into
this man ... You are a miracle. You're my hero
boy, Konnor!

    If I could be what my parents want me to
be, then perhaps I could be with you. If I
could be what you want me to be, then I could
be with you. But I am none of those things. I
am broken inside and I can barely manage to be
a complete person. You deserve someone who can
flourish with you in your amazing life, with your
amazing friends and family. You don't have to
have tragedy in your world anymore, Konnor. You
are free of it! You got out! I didn't, and I
will destroy all the progress you have made.

    I am not her. Not anymore. It took me
years to break away from her so I could live
the remnants of a normal life, but when I am
with you, she is all around us. She is in every
look you give me. In every smile. You see her.
Not me.

Yesterday was the greatest day of my life,
and nothing will ever change that.
I promise you will thank me one day.
I'm sorry.
XO,
Blesk

AFTER LEAVING the note under his alarm clock, I exit Konnor's apartment building, rushing past Adolf on my way out the sliding doors. Tears stream from under my sunglasses as I stride back towards my campus dormitory. Needing to talk to someone, I call Elise.

"Wally, my sweet, sweet, crazy, Wally, what's up?" she answers with a lot of pep and I love her for that.

Last Saturday night, we spent hours watching chick flicks, including *The Perks of Being a Wallflower.* I told Elise about the significance of that movie, our movie, and our friendship. She loved it. She has been calling me Wally ever since because, according to her, I make silly decisions.

We also talked a lot about Konnor. She said it was a fairy tale romance and that most girls could only ever dream of such a love. And perhaps that's true. Most great romances are a mixed genre —mystery and tragedy.

"I've just ended things with Konnor." Silence. Crickets. I can imagine her face.

She sighs. "Are you being a Wally, Wally?"

I hail a taxi on the other side of the street and hurry over to meet it. Putting my phone momentarily in my pocket, I speak through the driver's window, "St Bernard's Hospital, please." He nods and gestures to the backseat.

"BLESK! DO. NOT. GET. IN. THAT. TAXI!" I hear Elise's strangely articulate yell coming from my handset.

Putting the phone back to my ear, I prepare myself for the impending disapproval. "I need to check on him."

I hear a displeased huff escape from her. "Not without me. I'm walking out now. I have a class at ten and so do you, so we *will* be back by then. What the hell? *Why* would you break things off with Konnor? He adores you!"

"He's too good for me. He doesn't adore me; he adores that little girl. She was pure, whereas I'm damaged goods, trust me. There is no way—"

"I know you feel like it was your fault, but it wasn't. You were a child, Blesk! There is no way it is your fault," she chimes in with a hint of exasperation.

"He's too good for me," I insist. "I am a complete head case. I swear, I'm protecting him. He will realise one day when it's too late that I've been a drain on his life." A sigh filled with pain and regret escapes me. "Just like I was for Er—"

"*Oh my God,* if you say Erik, I swear I will tit punch you."

A small chuckle fills my throat. "Well, I won't say that name then. That sounds painful."

"How did he take it? *Oh God,* I'm not even sure I want to know."

I gulp before I answer her. "I left him a note"– my voice breaks – "while he was asleep." My belly twists. Running has become such a natural response for me. I face-palm myself.

"*Oh. My. God.* I am not judging you, but *oh my God.* He'll be crushed."

My phone beeps with a second call. I peer down at the name flashing intrusively: Konnor. Shame and guilt surge through me.

I raise my phone back to my cheek and breathe out loudly. "Konnor's on the other line."

"Pick it up. Talk to him!" she pleads.

"I can't."

IT IS no wonder people hate hospitals. They intrude on every sense and are filled with people who avoid you when you need them most. The receptionist has a permanent scowl on her face, and my appearance in front of her further etches her annoyance in her features.

"Hi, I'm Blesk Bellamy," I say as sweetly as I can. She doesn't even look at me. Glass separates us and phones ring relentlessly. She picks up a phone, yells into it, slams it down, writes something, picks up another phone, and yells into that one. And so it continues. I glance at my phone: ten missed calls from Konnor. I flick through my texts.

> Konnor: Don't do this Blesk. It's you I want! You! Please call me. Just talk to me about all of this, tell me what you want me to do. I will do it. I will do anything!

> Konnor: Maybe I came on too strong. I will wait as long as you need... just call me. Please don't block me out.

My heart is weak. I focus intently on forcing the absence of feelings.

"I'm here to see Erik Bellamy," I murmur, bobbing my head at the receptionist, trying to gain her attention.

She rolls her eyes and tilts her head towards me before slamming down the phone once again. "Yes, I know. Wait and I'll tell you his room number."

And with that, I sink back into my chair.

"Wally!" I hear a familiar voice call out, instantly filling me with relief.

Elise slides into the chair beside me, wearing hipster jeans and crazy nail polish. "Excuse me, Miss?" She taps on the window that separates us from the hospital staff.

The nurse, or receptionist, or whatever she is, turns to us with a crushing glare and grumbles, "Don't touch the glass! It's room thirty-nine, Karri Ward."

With that, we leave and try to navigate our way through the hospital. When we arrive at Erik's door, I stare at the threshold between me and the beeping and pumping sounds of room thirty-nine.

"Are you going to go in?" Elise asks delicately.

I grip her hand and clear my throat before walking in with steady, cautious steps. When I look at him, I am utterly lost for words. Erik is usually so tall, such a big, prominent man, with such confidence; he is just so tall. Fidgeting with everything —my hair, my clothes, Elise's bag —I move to stand beside his bed. He doesn't look big or tall anymore.

He looks *small.*

When I try to touch his hand, something rubber presses against my palm. I pull away almost instantly. A canula. He also has a horrendous-looking tube jutting out of his throat. I study his face and all the new colours: dark reds and blues from deep bruising, greens and yellows from ones that have started to heal. Tears make their way to my eyes, demanding release.

"Only family is allowed in here," I hear from behind me.

I jump. "Hi," I say. "I'm his sister. Is he okay?"

He peers at me. "Are you family?"

"I just told you. I'm his sister."

He paces around the room, checking the equipment and

making notes on the medical chart in his hand. Then he stops in front of me, scrutinising my expression. I feel fuzzy in this room with the bleeping and the humming.

"Mr Bellamy is in serious, but stable condition. He has already been to theatre." His tone is pointed.

I blink at him in the midst of what has become a deafening silence. I blink again. Time is strangely slow. Or I am slow. Or he is slow.

Elise grips my hand and squeezes. "What happened in theatre?" I hear her say through my fog.

"We had two specialists look over his injuries. Although he's in need of facial reconstruction, our biggest concern was a cerebral haemorrhage. So we placed him in an induced coma and did an MRI. He has swelling and minor bleeding on the brain. Now, he needs time. His jaw was broken and we have wired it shut. We had to give him a tracheotomy so he could breathe easily while under, and he's on IV fluids and is being monitored hourly."

"How long will he be under for?" My voice sounds mousy.

"Probably about two weeks." He narrows his emotionless eyes at me. "He needs plenty of time to heal. This *is* a big deal, girls, and keeping secrets is a bad decision."

What is it they know?

"Okay, we'd like some time alone now," Elise says.

I'm staring at the ground, but I can hear his shoes shuffling as he moves through the door. "Why was he so mean?" I whimper, collapsing into the chair beside my brother.

Elise exhales and moves to stand beside me. "After the helicopter arrived for Erik, so did the police. That's routine, apparently. They knew he'd been attacked, but we said we didn't know anything. I'm not sure they believed us."

As Konnor and I were in shock, we'd stayed away from

the scene. Shaking my head, I peer up at her. "You lied for us?"

"No," she states. "I just decided I wanted to know what happened first. I saw the way you and Konnor broke down. I mean, he called you Liz and you *freaked* out. I knew I wasn't ready to talk about what had happened."

Not knowing what to say, I look at Erik. We both sit quietly beside him for what feels like hours. After a while, I pull my phone out and look over the texts from Konnor.

> Konnor: Answer your phone! Damn it, Duch, you are fucking me up!
>
> Konnor: I'm sorry for swearing at you, Duchess. I'm sorry. I should never do that. Just talk to me.
>
> Konnor: Alright, Blesk, alright, just remember I'm here. If anyone ever hurts you. If you ever need a ride, a cuddle, a bodyguard, a friend, a servant, a wizard, lol. Anything. I'll be there for you.
>
> Konnor: This is not happening. It can't.
>
> Konnor: Just stop fucking running! Seriously, this is bullshit.
>
> Konnor: Sorry again for swearing at you. Please just talk to me.

I press my hand to my heart and count to ten in an attempt to steady my urge to scream from the ache within it. I wish I could take away his pain...

Despite jumping up when the door swings open, my entire body relaxes at the sight of a large, stubbly fifty-year-old man with a solid build and a generous girth, which is the result of his love of wine.

My dad.

"Kitten," he says, stretching his arms to me.

My feet take me to him without my conscious permission. I bury my face in his chest just as my tears begin to fall.

He kisses the top of my head. "Don't cry." His arms tighten protectively around me as he exhales a long, agonising breath.

"Hello," he says to Elise while stroking my hair and resting his cheek on my forehead. "I'm Blesk's dad, Jasper."

I look at the picture on the wall, not quite ready to be released. There is no cuddle in the world that feels as genuine as the ones my dad gives me.

Konnor's are just as amazing.

"Nice to meet you, Mr Bellamy," Elise says nervously.

"No, no, just Jasper is fine," he states, worry painfully evident in his voice.

"Okay. Nice to meet you, Jasper."

"I hear you brought Erik in. What happened?"

The picture stays the same, yet the intensity in the room becomes palpable, thickening and separating us from each other. There is an awkward pause. Poor Elise; this is only her problem by association.

We can't tell him about Konnor; we just can't.

My brain tells me to answer for her, to intercept the question, but when my mouth starts to move, my voice is suddenly held captive by fear.

"I'm not sure, Jasper. I didn't see much," Elise answers uncomfortably.

My dad grasps my shoulders and pulls me away from him, forcing me to look at him. "Blesk? Are you okay, baby girl?" I nod. "Tell me what happened?"

I focus on my breathing and speak delicately while trying to also project a sense of finality in my answer. "Erik got into a fight. You know how he can be."

He arches his brow sceptically. "The doctors seem to think you two know something, kitten."

I shake my head and drop my gaze to the floor, shuffling my feet nervously and fidgeting with my nails. "No."

He lifts my chin, snagging me in his line of sight. Solemn, distraught eyes stare back at me. Losing another member of his family will break him. "Blesk, this is serious. Tell me who did this to your brother."

Every suspicious gesture of his slices at my insides. Hopeless tears trace the contours of my cheek and fall down my trembling lip.

This is all my fault, all my fault.

If I had just stayed away from Konnor, he wouldn't be hurting right now, Liz would still be buried in a closet in my mind, and Erik wouldn't be so small. I can never tell my dad. I can never tell anyone. Not what Erik did to me and not what Konnor did to Erik.

I search my mind for the right thing to say, shuffling various versions of the truth around in my head like puzzle pieces, seeing which bits form a picture with the least consequences.

"I don't know who it was." When the words come out, their deceit strikes sickness into my soul. He looks at me with heavily disappointed eyes. I've never lied to my dad before.

Time rushes by, but I am strangely detached.

Shortly after my father arrival, the police come and ask Elise and me a lot of questions. We feign ignorance, both agreeing that the attacker was a stranger. I get the impression they don't believe us.

They ask my father if he wants to press charges, subsequently opening a case for further investigation. I'm both surprised and relieved when he reluctantly says no. I'm not sure if it was done for me, or because he doesn't want the police poking around Erik's personal life. The police are used to this kind of dissonance from residents of the District; we lost faith in their authority many years ago.

They don't control our area; we know it and they know it.

eighteen: blesk

Blesk

14 days later

IT HAS BEEN NEARLY two weeks since the morning on the hill and the night in Konnor's arms. Since my brother became a stranger. Since Konnor and I reunited. Guilt and uncertainty have always been an ever-present state of being for me and yet, the past few weeks have challenged my resolve the most. Should I forgive Erik? Did I even say no?

I can't remember.

Elise and I lie on our backs with our feet up on the wall, heels pressed against the brick. We stare at the ceiling. The dormitory is quiet at this time of night, not filled with its usual muffled chatter and giggles. We haven't spoken about Erik. I think she's been waiting for me to bring him up.

"My dad called me," I say, turning to face her. "He said

they are considering titrating Lord Voldemort's drugs down. Which means he'll wake up soon."

She smiles for a moment. "I'm so glad you have embraced pop culture." Pushing a stray blonde hair away from my face and tucking it behind my ear, she suddenly displays her 'serious Elise' face. "And what will you do when he wakes up?"

The answer to that question comes with so many strings, most knotted around others. He's my father's only biological child. They both love me —Erik in a way that maybe he shouldn't. That doesn't change the fact that he does, in fact, love me. "He never meant to hurt me, Elise."

She glances around dubiously. "What did he mean to do then?"

"He lost control."

Her expression doesn't hold back any punches as she stares at me. "What? He lost control? You don't just rape your sister because you lose control. There must have been some pent-up anger. Rape is usually about violence. Was he angry at you for-"

"Elise." I hold my hand up to stop her from talking. "It wasn't about violence."

"Okay, well tell me what it was about?"

Churning my stomach is the truth of what I'd let him do. Maybe they'd understand that he wasn't to blame, at least, not any more than me.

I look away from Elise, knowing she wouldn't approve of my thoughts. But when it comes to Erik, my brain becomes an excuse-making machine. It binds issues up so tight that they become a twisted mess in my mind. I know I don't want to have that kind of relationship with him. I also know that I love him. Deeply. Truly. As a brother. As my kind father's only living blood relative. As my confidant. Protector... He just couldn't protect me from himself.

Rolling onto my shoulder, I take a big breathe and look into her concerned eyes. "I'm going to tell you something that you can never repeat."

"Who would I tell? All the guys and girls lining up outside to be my friend?"

I grin at her. "Jaxon?"

"No way," she assures, a pink glow illuminating her cheeks. "Nothing leaves these lips."

Giggling at her, I say, "Really? Nothing?"

"No, I don't talk that much. I'm more of the strong silent type."

I laugh. "*Okay*." My back flattens on the carpet again and I stare up at the ceiling, preparing myself for the disclosure of something I've never spoken aloud before. God, I try not to even think about this confession. "The first night that it happened, I let him."

Pausing for a moment, I feel the bite of tears behind my eyes. Elise slowly turns to face me. Swallowing, I continue, needing it out. "I remember waking up to his fingers tracing my cheek and throat. That wasn't unusual as he was often in my bed with me. Due to my terrible nightmares, I'd usually wake him up. He'd comfort me. It was sweet.

"This night, though, his eyes were rolling lovingly over my face when I woke. His fingers begun to tickle a gentle line down to where my breasts rose and fell. And up until then, I'd taken comfort in his touch. But that night... he changed everything between us.

"He told me I was the most beautiful girl in the world and that he had been feeling things for me that he knew he shouldn't. Wanted to do things to me that he knew were *wrong*." As my voice shakes on the word, Elise touches my cheek. I feel a tear slide down my temple, settling in my ear. I continue, "He said it felt like someone had their fists around his heart, squeezing it to the point of pain. He told me that his love for me corrupted his mind. Then he began to beg me to share one night with him as just a girl and a boy... where we weren't adopted siblings." As I finish that sentence, I realise how many more tears are now streaming down into my hair.

"And you let him?"

I shake my head. "I don't know. I don't remember. I never said *yes*. But I don't think I ever said no either. I just let him touch me until he was done. He kept thanking me, over and over and over again while he moved inside me." I swallow hard. "He thanked me for easing the pain in his chest."

"Oh my God. That's heavy."

I nod, still not looking at her and yet, acutely aware of her eyes on me. "Yeah."

"Why didn't you push him away?"

I shrug. "I stole his parents."

She scoffs. "Come on, Blesk. That's not the reason."

At the time, Erik's and my new parent's love was the most wonderous thing to me. I'd never felt anything quite like it. A family. Protection. They never yelled. They never hit me.

"I was only young and it seemed like a small thing to give him for loving me," I admit. "To be honest, I thought that when he left for college this whole other side of our relationship would change. I don't want that kind of relationship with him. I don't love him like that. And I thought he was finished with me and that we could go back to being siblings. I guess I was wrong. I'm an idiot." This is the first time in my life I've been able to talk about my personal life with a reasonable level of calm.

"No you're not," she says and I finally turn to look at her, already recognising the bullshit in my own words. "You're amazing. But I have to be honest with you 'cause, like, that's my jam. You came from a broken home. He used your vulner-abilities. You don't owe anyone for loving you. There is no price on love."

Searching her big blue eyes, I realise she's right. I knew that. I did. Maybe not at the time. But when he left the District I had a lot more time to think on it —I knew it was wrong. But that fact just hit me square in the face like a sledgehammer. I need to stop the excuses. What he did was wrong. I'm sure he'll wake up and know that too. My chest burns as if I've just sprinted a mile. "Erik knew my innocence was taken from me to support my father's lies." I shake my head. "And then he does even worse and takes another piece. He used me, just like my father did. He touched me as if he owned me."

Elise smiles at me strangely. Maybe she's proud? "He doesn't own you, Blesk."

"*I* own me," I state adamantly. "He made me feel like it was his right. And I'd believed him. I seriously thought I owed him... for *loving* me."

Elise beams at me. "I think my work here is done. Actu-ally, no it isn't." She leans a little closer under the pretence of stroking my shoulder and then her knuckles hit the side of my breast with a thump. I turn wide-eyed to stare at her. "That was a tit punch. Now, let's talk about Konnor."

My stomach stirs at the sound of his name as duelling emotions blend inside me. The constant flow of messages, begging and pleading with me to talk to him, had stopped a week ago. I don't want to analyse what that might mean. Changing the subject, I say, "I think that's enough for one session. I've already had one lecture today that felt like a lobotomy. I don't need another."

"You know Konnor's love doesn't come with a price, right? He just loves you."

"He doesn't love me," I press. "He doesn't know me."

She shrugs. "What is love?"

"It's knowing someone and wanting to be with them anyway."

"*Ah*, so you think that once he gets to know Blesk, he won't want to be with you."

Crap. Maybe? And I struggle to argue with that, so I just retort, "Thank you for that analysis, Freud."

Ignoring my tone, she smiles wider. "You're welcome, Blesk."

I lower my feet from the wall and roll to sit up. "Konnor is perfect with a perfect life. He has all these awesome friends. Every girl wants to be with him... He's a star rugby player, and I'm just a burden. I'm damaged."

She laughs. "Pity party."

"Come on, Elise," I groan. "I actually mean it. I'm emotionally unavailable. I'm messed up. He'll be unhappy with me."

"Okay, that may *all* be true. You are damaged and strange. You say the strangest stuff and make Yoda impersonations all the time; it's just odd." She laughs and then turns serious on a sigh. "But can we get real? Like, real real?"

"If I say no, will you liste-"

"No. So you know what? I reckon I'd rather be odd than normal. And I think you'll make Konnor very happy. You *are* his happiness. Being with you, that is what *makes* him happy... I think he's one of those guys who falls in love once and forever. You've had his heart since he was, like, five."

"He'll get over me. *He will*," I insist, shuffling on the floor as an uncomfortable flutter fills in my stomach; I don't want that to happen at all. Not in the slightest. Actually, the words alone make me want to run to his apartment.

"*Oh, okay.*" She snorts, dubious. "Delusional you are. He dated Pemberton, a blonde-haired, brown-eyed girl just to be closer to you. He's been trying to fill your void since he was nine. Don't you get it, Wally? He's never getting over you. You're scared of letting someone in, I get it."

She may be right.

I blink at her and ask the same question that sits on my tongue every moment of every day. "How is he?"

"Do you want to have this conversation?" She tilts her head at me.

"Yes?" I say unconvincingly.

"Last time, you got upset."

"I want to know." Looking past her at the metal unicorn on my bed side table, I nod, hoping that motion will convince myself more than her. "Yep, I want to know."

"I saw him yesterday with Jaxon. He's..." She hesitates. "Not good, Blesk. He still texts me daily, asking for updates, and he barely leaves his flat. He's drunk all the time. He's a mess." My breath hitches as I try to stop the guilt and shame from clawing at my insides. The thought of my actions causing him that much pain is too much to bear. I hate myself for, once again, being the inflictor of his pain. I continue to stare at my unicorn.

Elise searches my expression before following my gaze to the small trinket. "What is that, Blesk?"

Sighing, I remember the last story I told Elsie. I'd seen him on the television. His parents crying. The cluster of confusion and guilt I'd experienced for helping my father hold him in that cell. "Another story."

"Tell me it."

I smile tightly. "As soon as I had the chance, I called the police, but when they asked me for the address, I couldn't remember. Couldn't see past the images of Kon on the television as they played in my head. I hung up on them. I helped him escape. We were so scared. More scared than ever before. We were running from my father and his dogs through the forest. It was life or death this time. I remember the moon was huge that night, drilling beams of light through the terrain. We had no one to trust but each other — both helpless children with no understanding of why these things happen." Elise moves so that she can wrap an arm around my shoulders. "Lights and voices surrounded us. I turned to Kon so terrified for his life. Not mine. I kinda accepted I might die anyway. My dad would do it. Kon had that" –I motion towards the unicorn– "with him. Apparently, he was clutching it the day he was kidnapped. It was the last remnant of his past life. And he gave it to me." I swallow that feeling down. "As I held it, I knew what I needed to do. I pressed my lips to his and kissed him. Then I ran towards the lights, hoping I could divert my dad's search party away from Kon." I find her eyes, glossy and overwhelmed. "And that's the last time I saw him."

Tears fall from her eyes. "No, Blesk, it's not."

I breathe out fast, realisation knocking on my head. I'd been so wrapped up in not being Liz to really acknowledge who he was —is. To me. I'd lost him too.

He's my Kon.

"Oh my God."

nineteen: konnor

Konnor

BARELY AWAKE, I scroll through my phone and
search for my inbox. This is a new phone and I'm still not
used to the interface, so I struggle in my half slumber to find
what I need. When I do, I reread some of my desperate
messages to Duch.

> Konnor: So, it's been 2 days since you broke
> my heart, Duch. At some point I'm going to
> need someone to save me. I have 5 cans of
> beans, 10 rolls of toilet paper, 5 bottles of
> bourbon, 2 bags of pasta, 6 tomatoes, 2
> onions, 3 cloves of garlic, 5 frozen meals, 5
> batteries, 1 spare light globe, 1 block of
> cheese, so at some point I will run out. Now
> I know you can't just let me starve, right?

Konnor: 4 cans of beans, 9 rolls of toilet paper, 4 bottles of bourbon, 1 bag of pasta, 4 tomatoes, 1 onion, 2 cloves of garlic, 5 frozen meals, 5 batteries, 1 spare light globe, 75% block of cheese.

Konnor: 3 cans of beans, 8 rolls of toilet paper, 3 bottles of bourbon, 1 bag of pasta, 4 tomatoes, 1 onion, 1 clove of garlic, 4 frozen meals, 5 batteries, 0 spare light globes, 50% block of cheese.

Konnor: 2 cans of beans, 8 rolls of toilet paper, 1 bottle of bourbon, 0 bags of pasta, 2 tomatoes, 0 onions, 1 clove of garlic, 4 frozen meals, 3 batteries, 20% block of cheese.

Konnor: 2 cans of beans, 7 rolls of toilet paper, 0 bottles of bourbon, 2 tomatoes, 1 clove of garlic, 2 frozen meals, 3 batteries, 10% block of cheese.

Konnor: 0 cans of beans, 6 rolls of toilet paper, 0 tomatoes, 1 cloves of garlic, 1 frozen meal, 3 batteries, 5% block of cheese.

Konnor: 6 rolls of toilet paper, 1 clove of garlic, 0 frozen meals, 3 batteries, 0% of a block of cheese.

Konnor: Getting hungry… 5 rolls of toilet paper, 0 cloves of garlic…tried garlic wrapped with toilet paper, I wouldn't recommend it, Duch. 3 batteries

I sigh angrily. I bombarded her message box, grief having chopped up my emotions like a damn blender. No reply.

I went insane.

On day seven, my phone had an unfortunate accident when it rammed itself into a hammer.

Hammer verse phone: 1-0

Now it's been fourteen days. The worst fourteen *damn* days of my *damn* life, and in my case, that's quite the statement. It's been fourteen fucked up days since she snuck out of my room after the best day of my damn life, leaving a fucking note under my fucking arsehole of an alarm clock.

Fourteen days since I've eaten a real meal.

Fourteen days since I've gone to campus.

Fourteen fucked up days.

The most frustrating thing about the feeling churning in the pit of my stomach, feeding on my sanity and chewing on every cell inside me, is that it isn't *even fucking real.* No one has hit me. No one has beaten me. I didn't get hit by a road-train. So why do I feel like I've been dragged behind a car for ten miles and then buried and am now slowly suffocating?

Just fucking talk to me!

Goddamn it!

I feel like, without her voice and words, this fictitious pain will never stop. The crippling wound she left that morning is so concentrated, so deep that I need her voice like medicine. But she won't talk to me.

Thirteen years ago, I lost the most important person in my life. But I mourned her every day when I looked at Pemberton. I mourned her annually on the day she'd died. I mourned her every night when I closed my eyes and saw her sweet face. I mourn her still.

Then to find her again and have her *choose* to leave. Words...words to describe that feeling. Pain. Shock. Despair. Shame. Aching. Broken. Shattered. Nothing. Fucked. It feels like someone is ripping any organ, any piece of flesh they can possibly clutch on to, straight from the easiest access point. Little pieces at a time.

My heart leaps into my throat when a message appears

in my inbox. It soon drops back into its black cavity again when I see it's just from Flick.

> Bossy older sister: Missing Cassidy's eighteen birthday is a criminal offence! You're in trouble!

Fuck. Last week, Cassidy drove four hours from the District to personally invite me to her eighteenth birthday party. I know how much she loves me. I feel the same. That day though, she brought Faith with her, who is like a dog with bone —the bone unfortunately being me.

Dropping my phone onto the floor, I close my eyes. My mind won't let me sleep, but goddamn it, I'll try. Suddenly, the door sounds like a damn drum, over and over and over as someone knocks on it.

I make a mental note to get Adolf fired.

"Go away!" I yell, burying my head in the pillow. "Fuck off!"

I keep my eyes shut and grumble, planning on ignoring my visitor in the hopes that they tire and go away. As I roll onto my back, my cock jerks up, running up my navel and demanding some early morning attention. I rub my face with both hands and mumble inelegant words to myself. The sound is so loud, it's as if shots are being fired point-blank behind my eye sockets. Hiding from the drones of life seems better than answering the damn door and being forced to string together coherent thoughts.

Gripping my boner, I drag my palm up and down its length. I imagine that the knocking sound is my bed slamming against the wall as I fuck Blesk hard. Imagine her soft, fleshy thighs wrapping around my hips as I shove her up the mattress with each thrust. I feel her walls grip me, begging me to stay deep inside her.

Oh fuck, *yes.*

My cock contracts. Beads of precum slide over my fingers. As I hiss her name, my muscles start to quiver. I stroke faster, squeeze tighter. Biceps twitching, abdomen clenching, a groan rolls up my throat. *Fuck,* feels so good. So tight. *Blesk...*

"Blesk."

A moan shatters my illusion. "Oh, don't tell me you've forgotten my name, baby. It's Vanessa. Can you get the door?" Her pelvis rubs against my thigh.

Releasing my cock, I turn over to scrutinise the girl beside me.

She looks nothing like Blesk.

I'm not surprised to find a stranger in my bed. As the days passed, each without Duch, I ended up trying to wash her memory away, down the fucking drain. Tried to heal the holes. The holes from all the pieces of flesh that she had ripped from me. I filled them with alcohol, of course. And then... I filled them with girls. Blondes. Faith included.

I attempted to no avail to fuck her memory away —hard carnal fucking. But it didn't work. Because for a few moments, for a few heavenly seconds when I joined the waking world and saw that blonde hair fanned out around me, I would forget... I would forget she'd left. Then... I'd start to mourn her all over again.

Pulling the sheets away, I reveal a tall naked body that's way too skinny. Not a natural curve in sight. Knocks continue to break the silence.

Her eyes scroll over my face and down to my erection. A little grin plays on her lips. "Baby, you wanna play again, let's do it, but get the fucking door first." Her tone and gutter mouth just reinforce how unlike my duchess she is.

I jolt up and pull on a pair of tracky-pants, tucking my erection into the waistband.

When I answer the door, my whole body relaxes at the sight of blue eyes staring at me from the doorway —even though they're narrowed and fiery. I've put a lot of pressure on Elise lately. No matter how I behave, how much it hurts her or would potentially hurt Blesk, Elise comes by every day. She has literally put me to bed, been on the receiving end of my drunken temper, and now she is, well... she's one of my best mates.

And the fact that she even gives me the time of day shows that I haven't lost Blesk —not completely. Elise's presence is like having a little piece of Blesk here with me. I crave her visits.

"What sleazy whore do you have in here this time? It smells like skank!" She walks in as if she owns the place, but I don't even bat an eye. She can do whatever she wants.

"How is she? Is she okay? Is she ready to talk to me?" I ask, sounding desperate as I wipe my drowsy eyes with my palms.

Elise searches the apartment, noticing the clothes on the floor, the messy sheets, and the girl. Spinning to face me, she scowls. "I haven't told her, ya know —*my best friend* —about you and your blonde addiction, but you need to stop it, Konnor. Aren't we trying to get her back? Huh? Isn't that what we're trying to do?"

"I thought *I* was your best friend," I joke, then cover my mouth as I cough.

Revulsion distorts her face. "Have you been smoking again?"

Her scowl makes my knees buckle. *"Maybe...* And yes," I groan.

"Yes, what?" she asks forcefully.

"Yes, we are trying to get her back!" I snap. "But you told me to give her space!"

Avoiding The Grill on Tuesday and Friday nights has been like trying to avoid my own personal variety of meth. I knew she would be there, looking exceptional and singing our song. "I wanna see her already. Can I try?"

But when the half-naked model walks out of my bedroom, I am inundated with shame. As my heart pounds with the side effects of last night's bourbon, I rub my chest.

The not-Blesk scowls. "Did that nerdy little bitch just call me a whore?"

Did she just call Elise a bitch?

I spin to face Vanessa. Heat not associated with my hangover penetrates my temples. "Watch your mouth around my friend!"

An insulted gasp breaks from her pouting lips. "What? She just called me a whore!"

Elise's eyes rake over Vanessa with disgust. Her lips twitch and her face scrunches up. I point to Elise while staring sternly at the girl I just woke up next to. A girl who is as familiar to me as a stranger.

"See that girl?" I wait until she nods before saying, "She is *crazy* important to me, and you aren't. So I'm confused why you're still here. *Oh,* and by the way, that was me telling you to leave."

I point to the door.

IT'S TUESDAY NIGHT. I don't give a fuck; I'm going to see Duch play despite Elise's disapproval. The threat of separated limbs kind of disapproval. She told me not to make an appearance today because she is still working on things with Blesk. Elise says that Duch still needs more time, but I can't go another moment without seeing her. Too many blondes have clouded my memory of her. I need to just take a peek.

Walking into The Grill, I wander over to the bar. While leaning on the 90s Jacks bar-run, I signal Jewels. Jewels has been working here for as long as I can remember. As she approaches, I slam a card down on the bar a little harder than intended. My eyes flicker in response to the sound.

I look at Jewels apologetically. "Sorry, gorgeous. Can I grab a Makers Mark and dry?" There is a very real possibility that she will bat those long lashes at me before flat out refusing me service. She tilts her head, and her eyes don't give me a flicker of 'swooning'.

Damn.

"Slater, you're drunk, and I've known you too long to fall for that shit."

"Jewels, give me a drink. The girl playing tonight is my girl and I can't see her without a drink in my hand. Be a friend?"

She rolls her eyes at me and smirks. "I have no idea what that even means, but okay. You can have three drinks. This is number one. And I'll make sure all the other bar staff know."

"Thank you," I say, clapping my hands together in a prayer-like gesture. "Thank you! You're a goddess. Has Brock told you lately how good you look, Jewels?" I continue sucking up to her as she smirks in my direction. Grabbing a tumbler, she pours my drink. "Well, if he hasn't then... you are looking *good,* Jewels." I lean on the bar and peer around, looking through the crowd for friendly faces. No Jax. No Drake. No one I know.

"Slater!" I hear someone yell. I search the room for the bearer of the voice. As I'm searching for that person, I see Blesk walk out and start to set up.

Fuuuuck...

I knew I shouldn't have come. I knew it was a bad idea to see her on stage. Damn Elise for knowing that too.

Is that the kind of shit Blesk has been wearing this whole time? Maybe she is just my type or maybe she is just perfect, in the purest, truest sense of the word. Like, you look up 'perfect' in the dictionary, but you don't get a picture because it isn't a fucking picture book, but you do get a detailed description of Blesk.

I wish she wasn't wearing that dress. I can't handle how obviously she displays vulnerability. Her legs are completely exposed and I know how good they look when they move. Loose and fleshy, curvy in the most spectacular way. She presses her thighs together as she places the guitar on her lap, tuning it with her long slender fingers. I've seen her. I've seen her, so now I should just leave. But I can't.

I won't.

She removes a black piece of pipe from her case and attaches it to her guitar. Adjusting it, she positions the frame until it sits just in front of her mouth. She pulls something from her bag and lays it on her lap. After running her finger along its length, she places it in the cradle and tightens the screws.

My harmonica.

Maybe that is what she has been doing this whole time.

Thinking of me?

And learning how to play the harmonica.

"Hi, my name is Blesk Bellamy, and this song is called 'Without You'." As her fingers begin to strum the melody, she takes a big breath in. She licks her lips and I can tell she's nervous. A flutter fills my chest, making it hard to breathe. She moves her mouth to the harmonica, and frowns with concentration as she blows through the channels. I can feel her nerves pulsing through me as if they were my own. I glare and hush anyone around me who imposes the slightest disturbance.

She begins to produce a new sound with her lips on my harmonica and her fingers picking the strings. The harmonica's music fills the spaces that aren't filled with words. God only knows how she manages her breathing like that.

It isn't 'till I didn't know,
It isn't really truly alone,
Until you aren't there,
Until I made it unfair.

Fear forever tests time,
Time is tested in the mind,
Mind forever questions time,
Time's worth nothing without you.

Greens don't say go,
Greens stay gold forever,
In between go and slow,
In between like and love.

Fear forever tests time,
Time is tested in the mind,
Mind forever questions time,
Time's worth nothing without you.

Touch isn't worth its dime,
Touch can't be all of mine,
Coins aren't worth the content,
Coins won't spin like mine.

Fear forever tests time,

Time is tested in the mind,
Mind forever questions time,
Time's worth nothing without you.

THE LAST LINE of the chorus fills my chest with hope, which is all I've wanted.

She plays a few covers before ending on my favourite —"Hero Boy". She plays it, and every chord runs the entire length of my veins. I lose my shit, tearing up and falling in love all over again. I love her. I love her. I love Blesk. Listening and admiring this song with a fresh perspective, it seems so obvious now.

Every line takes the listener through our story, from beginning to end. In the basement: '*It's still dark at 3:00 p.m., dark for no good reason*'. Making our promises: '*Let's do all the things we planned to do, remember what we wanted to*'. Running away and changing our names: '*and we will run from the clawless fox, we can unchain and unlock that box, let's smash our names with blunt rocks, 'til they disappear and no one talks*'.

It is all there.

I lean on the bar and struggle to catch my breath, fire burning in my lungs.

Breathe, Konnor.

As I'm trying to hold myself together, struggling to contain all the emotions radiating from me, someone pats me on the shoulder. I turn to acknowledge whoever it is, despite knowing my eyes are red and swollen.

"Hey, man," I say to Drake, wiping my eyes on my sleeve. He diverts his gaze to the ground.

"Fuck, Slate, sort ya self out, will ya?" He squeezes my

shoulder. His voice sounds genuine with worry, and that makes me feel worse because I hate pity.

"Yeah, I know, right? What a pussy," I say with a forced huff. I'd be mocking me mercilessly, if I were him.

"Nah, mate. Pussies are useful. You're more like a... an appendix or something." He chuckles at his own joke. So do I. "How much have you had to drink today?"

"Not enough."

He glares at me dubiously. "I think that's a subjective analysis, mate."

I hold my hand up to signal Jewels to pour me another drink. "I've already been limited. Jewels is looking after me."

Drake nods at the lovely Jewels in appreciation. "She does some things right."

"You'd know," I say, preparing myself for an entertaining interaction between the two of them. They dated for a year. It was a hot and heavy romance. The kind that ends in a train wreck.

Jewels approaches us. "Drake, you still haven't done anything about that thing on your shoulders."

He chuckles. "And you clearly still haven't been to the gym."

She rolls her eyes. "I don't need a gym. Brock keeps me fit enough."

"Funny, looks like you're losing definition. Maybe you should take me back so I can show you how mattress gymnastics should be performed."

A flirtatious smile pulls at her lips. Mirroring her expression, he leans on the bar, edging closer to her.

She smirks. "I've been trying to get that disgusting five seconds out of my mind for the past six months, and I wouldn't want to undo all that effort," she says, before walking off with a slight skip in her step.

Drake grins from ear to ear and calls out, "It took you six months?"

She scoffs and spins to face him. "That kind of trauma takes a while to get over."

As he watches her lean across the bar and serve another person, he says, "She wants me."

I crack up. "You got burned, man." I chuckle, looking around to see the band area empty.

Blesk has completely packed up. She didn't even look out into the crowd once. Now she's gone. Her absence immediately forces the air out of the room, and I begin to panic.

"Does she usually have a drink after her sets?" I ask Drake.

Drake looks at his feet evasively.

"What?" I ask, frowning at him suspiciously.

He takes a weird exaggerated breath in and releases it quickly, pushing the words out at the same time. "She usually has a drink afterwards, dude. Usually someone buys her one or she sits with some people she seems to know."

"Why are you looking so nervous? What aren't you telling me?"

"Nothing. It's just," he starts, talking calmly as if not to startle an animal, "I saw her getting a bit cosy with this guy last Friday."

What the hell does that even mean?

I feel like I'm at a boiling point. Drake notices my expression and continues, "Calm down. I intercepted her, mate. She looked startled to see me, and then I hung out with her the rest of the night."

"*Intercepted?* Intercepted what exactly? Seriously, Drake, you being all vague is making this worse. Did he kiss her? Touch her? What happened?"

"His arm was draped around her shoulder. And they were

close. Like, if I were her boyfriend, it would have been *too* close. I couldn't see much more. When I approached, it was like a bomb went off. They turned into shrapnel."

Calming breaths.

"Point Casanova out to me. Is he here?" I gesture towards the booths. Every muscle in me is distractingly tight and rigid, and the alcohol is stopping rational thought from settling in my mind.

"What are you gonna do?" Drake asks hesitantly.

"Nothing," I say, feigning innocence. "Have a chat. A *nice* chat."

He points and my eyes narrow in recognition.

It's Matt from my Beginners Education to Music 103 class.

Little shit.

I didn't like him from the moment I saw him. Though he's alone, there are two drinks on his table. I'm going to make damn sure one of them is for me. I wander over, ignoring whatever it is Drake is trying to say to me.

Grabbing the drink that is opposite him, I slide down into the chair. "Thanks for the drink."

Yep, I'm going to lose my job.

Shock transforms his face as I swig from Blesk's drink. "K … Konnor," he stutters. "Well, that wasn't for you, but I can grab another one."

I eyeball him warningly. "She likes wine. White."

"What?" He avoids my eyes, pretending he has no idea what I'm talking about. I part my legs, slouch down, and make myself comfortable.

I snort. "Blesk. She likes wine. Not whatever cheap rum is in this."

"It's Captain Morgan, actually, and I really like it." I'm

completely startled when I hear her voice coming from behind me.

I fly up and spin around as she approaches, a little smile faintly visible on her lips. Gravity, time, space, any quantifiable relevance to moments and places, completely cease to exist.

She is so beautiful.

And I'm pretty wasted.

My heart lodges in my throat when she is only a few steps away. She stops and lifts a blonde brow at me, grinning. She sees straight through me.

"Hi, Mr Slater. You aren't dead. I thought you ran out of food."

"I ate the batteries," I murmur as a grin tugs at my lips.

She laughs, and we both beam at each other.

"I'm glad you aren't dead."

"Wouldn't you rather have wine though?" I ask cheekily. "Over rum, I mean. Wine is so delicious and corny and good looking."

She giggles, sticking that gorgeous tongue out. "Wine *is* corny and good looking." She rolls her eyes before continuing. "*And* delicious. But rum is *easy*." Her sly little smile makes my eyelids heavy.

I take her hand. "Oh, now nothing good ever comes easy."

Our eyes lock on each other.

I completely don't care that we are in public, on display, or that everyone is looking at us because she is the only thing I care about. I don't care that Matt looks like I've just stolen his favourite toy, glaring up at us from behind his glass of beer. I don't care about anything other than her. And right now, she is the only person I want to see. Her face. And I don't want her to go another second thinking I don't love her with every inch of my being and then some.

"Duch." I place my other hand over the top of hers, pancaking it between both of mine. I anchor myself in those fluttering brown eyes. "I know you think I don't love you *for you*—"

She interjects with a pleading little voice, "Konnor, stop, I know—"

Pathetic desperation causes me to cut in. "No, I need to talk to you. I ju—"

"Konnor, *I know*," she says. "It's okay. I was going to come see you soon. I wanted to see you. I wanted to talk."

Oh, thank fuck!

"Duch, do you-" I clear my throat. "Do you wanna go for a long pointless walk with me?"

She smiles. "Yes."

I am so consumed by being with her again that I don't even remember leaving The Grill. But we are now strolling silently, hand-in-hand. We walk like we had weeks ago when we thought we were just strangers strangely drawn together.

Stopping, I turn to face her. She mimics me, giving me her undivided attention.

"Will you let me speak? I may ramble. I just have to say some things that have been on my mind for these past few weeks."

Her eyes smile at me. "The floor is yours, Mr Slater."

I inhale a big deep breath for courage. "I know you think that I don't love you for you, Duch! For the woman you have become. But you are *so* wrong. My love for you is goddamn pathological. I do love Liz, I do. I grew into half a man without her, thinking about her, and I love her more than my own life.

"But I love the person she has become too, just as much,

just as intensely. You have become an incredible woman. You're so talented. So funny. I love that you mock me and laugh at me when I get jealous. I love that you look at me like I look at you. I love the way you press your tongue between your teeth when you smile. I love how your giggle comes from your throat, and how when you laugh, your shoulders shake, like you can't stop even if you wanted to. I love the way you say, '*O...kay*' in a cute voice when I convince you to do something that makes you nervous ..."

Her lips tremble, and shiny tears run down her face as she begins to cry. Her chest rises and falls more rapidly, as does mine. And then she giggles through a silly splutter of tears.

That giggle, those tears of happiness. *I did that.*

"I love that you're happy with a hot dog over a five-star meal. I love that you're terrible at puns. I love that you check me out and don't try to hide it."

She gasps when I pull her into me. Her chest rests right where it ought to be —against mine.

"I love you, Duch. It's insane, but I *fucking* love you." I wipe a tear from her cheek and watch as she processes my words. "Don't cry."

"I just didn't want to be loved for her."

"You aren't. Give me a chance to show you."

She sighs into a smile. "*Okay*... You had me at cello."

Damn that sounds good to hear...

Those six words of hers smother the fire that's been burning inside me for the past two weeks and soothe me like nothing else could. Stealing a moment, I just look at-

"Are you going to kiss me already?" she interjects.

I laugh. "Woah, slow down girl. I mean, you're pretty, but, seriously, at least take me out for dinner first."

She glares at me, but her grin conveys her true feelings. I

can't help myself. I need to claim those lips. I caress the nape of her neck while I guide her towards my mouth. Brushing my lips gently along hers, I savour the moment. We both exhale on contact, releasing all our need. I part my mouth, running my tongue slowly along her lower lip and tasting the saltiness of her tears. When her lip twitches against my tongue, restraint becomes impossible. I need her. I need her now.

Her whole body goes slack when my arms tighten around her waist. Pulling her onto her tippy toes, I crush our lips together. My mouth kneads hers, moulding our lips together. Blesk moans and every part of me reacts.

I massage her tongue with mine, wanting to suck it, taste it. I kiss her with so much passion, as if without her lips I may die. She tastes as good as I thought she would. Nothing has ever felt this right, this good. Nothing ever will. Her lips were meant to be on mine.

My hands enjoy the feel of the delicate curves from her waist to her arse. I deepen our kiss, tilting my head and showing her the depth of my yearning. I trace the arc of her spine and feel her muscles spasm in response to my fingertips, quivering beneath my touch. My breath is lost somewhere in her mouth. She is stealing my air, my sanity, and any hope I had of surviving an existence without her. I'm in crazy, irrevocable, undeniable love.

twenty: deakon

Deakon

"WHAT DO YOU MEAN?" the boy asks the man who is hovering over his bed and looking at him with pity and concern. The boy doesn't want any of it.

"What do you mean?" the boy repeats, involuntarily caressing the soft sheets below him and blinking at the surrounding lights. It is too bright for him. The man pats the boy's shoulder, a long, firm pat that feels like it could leave a bruise. The boy can't remember the last time someone touched him there. Maybe no one ever has. The boy forces his eyes to bear the bright lights so he can look up at the older man. "Say it again."

The boy doesn't understand the words the man has been repeating to him. Or perhaps he refuses to, because that would mean believing them and that would mean they are true. And that would be completely unbearable. Unbearable for a boy who has endured four years of imprisonment. A new level of unbearable.

"I'm sorry. She's gone."

They said they would find her and keep her safe, the boy thinks to himself. *Protect her.* They used the word *protect.*

We will find her.

The boy repeats the words he heard in the woods, preferring them much more to the ones he is hearing now.

We will find her

"Liz fell. We did everything we could," the man says.

We did everything we could.

We did everything we could.

What does that mean?

What did they do?

What did they need to do?

Why didn't they ask me?

I could have told them.

She gets scared in the dark.

She falls on steps sometimes.

She is allergic to bee stings.

She is very bad at math.

She thinks there is a girl in her class who doesn't like her.

Have they asked that girl?

Why didn't they ask me?

I could have told them.

What did they need to do?

The boy feels sickness rack his body. Heat rises up his throat, but he forces himself to remain calm. He frowns up at the man for more answers.

"How many days has it been?"

The man breathes out loudly. "One day, Deakon."

The boy is too sad to talk now.

Liz.

"She's gone, Deakon. She has gone somewhere better."

Somewhere better?

Then she would be with me.

Or she would take me.

Why wouldn't she want to be with me?

I only want to be with her.

Somewhere better?

I don't understand.

The boy suddenly smiles. "She doesn't know where I am," he says, realisation brightening his eyes. "Tell her and then she'll come back."

The man shakes his head slowly. "No, Deakon, she won't be back because she's gone to heaven."

She wouldn't go anywhere without me.

"Where is heaven?"

The man slouches on a deep sigh. He blinks at the boy for a moment before turning to talk to someone behind him. The boy doesn't like this man. Or the other one.

"Where is heaven?" the boy yells, more panicked than he can ever remember being. "I need to know how to get there."

twenty-one: blesk

Blesk

Chapter Song
Joshua Radin —Someone Else's Life

I'VE NEVER HAD a kiss consume my whole body, smother my mind in relentless need, and coil its warmth around my soul like an entity apart. He holds me against him with a gentle dominance as he leads without hesitation, with a natural rhythm and yearning. His lips are the perfect mixture of soft and firm. His big strong hands move around my body possessively, obsessively.

Every kiss should be measured by this one!

But most of all, I feel safe. I feel safe in his arms and pressed to his lips. Somewhat of a new feeling for me.

After we break our kiss, he holds my hand and we walk together. It isn't until we are wandering past Adolf and into the elevator that I realise our destination is his apartment. I've been in a daze of bliss, my feet moving in pace with his, but not noting the direction.

When we enter his studio, an unwelcome shudder niggles at my belly. Konnor's expectations for the next step could definitely conflict with mine. I want to be with him. I always have. But now... I feel ready. I'm ready to tell him everything he deserves to know and suffer the consequences. The rest is up to him because I don't have the willpower to stay away from him any longer. If, once he's privy to everything, he still wants me, then I'll be the luckiest girl in the world and I won't ever walk away from him again.

But first, I need to tell him the truth, every dirty aspect of it. About my father, about me, and about what I did to him all those years ago. Then we can release the secrets and horrors of that life into the wind and be us, as we are now.

I glance around his apartment. It's missing a few things. This only furthers my sudden unease. Moving towards his bed, I notice how different everything feels.

"Where is your alarm clock?" I ask, staring at his bedside table.

"That alarm clock was a jackarse, so I broke it. Presenting me with your letter was the last straw." I tilt my head at him and smile. He shrugs. "It had plenty of warnings."

"It's an inanimate object, Konnor," I say with a chuckle.

"Oh, trust me, that didn't stop it from bossing me around every damn day. I did us both a favour. It didn't have very nice things to say about you either."

"And everything else?" I spin around and tilt my head at him, gesturing towards the bare room.

He takes a deep breath and lowers his chin, a flush of shame spreading across his cheeks. "Broke a few other things too, Duch. *Buuuuuut* I have a present for you." He wanders over to the walk-in closet. Swinging open the door, he squats slightly and reaches inside. Turning to grin at me mischievously, he pulls out a huge piece of canvas. Every part of me brightens, because I know exactly what it is.

The painting.

I jig in place like a little kid, waiting for its unveiling. Watching my expression intently, he brings it over and sits it on the kitchen bench. He pulls back the paper sheet and studies me while my eyes take it all in, rolling over every colour and shape. My breath catches in my throat and I press my fingers to my smile.

It's beautiful.

The figures are vaguely prominent, but they are still visible to anyone really looking. Each human stencil is distinguishable within a different colour: Drake is mostly purple, Elise is orange, Jaxon is primarily red, and Konnor and I are in the centre, barely coloured at all, just defined by outlines of red and pink. Like a heart. Our white silhouettes explode with these two colours, whereas the rest of the canvas is coated wholly. My heart aches because it is so ludicrously unambiguous that we are in love with each other right there, in that moment.

I'm unable to take my eyes off it, unable to comprehend how we could look so in love. In love *before* we knew we were Deakon and Liz, when we were *just* Konnor and Blesk. When we barely knew each other. Nevertheless, it is ridiculously clear that we were crazy about each other even then.

I swallow pasts the guilt I have about what I've just put him through.

"I... I love it."

Placing the painting flat on the kitchen bench, he grabs his phone and activates the stereo with it. Joshua Radin's voice plays through the speakers in a humble acoustic beauty. "Someone Else's Life" begins to play.

"I'm glad," he whispers. "I love it too."

I am feeling so much. Too much. He reaches for my elbow and stops me from ducking away. He envelops me in his arms, knowing exactly what I truly need —what I don't even know I need. I let out a small sigh when I feel his body against mine. His heartbeat is running rampant, like mine. He lowers his head, nestling it sweetly beside my cheek.

"I love you, Blesk," he says into my ear. His words hit me like an electric shock. This time, I know he really does. "I can't write or play the guitar, Duch, but this song reminds me of us." He feeds his fingers through mine and begins to dance with me, lowering his hand to the small of my back so he can lead.

"SING WHILE I DANCE, *Kon. Sing, and whistle.*"

"I wish I could dance with you Liz, like a walzz."

"It is called a waltz. With a T."

"Yeah, a waltz. But I would be in charge because I'm a boy."

"Na-ah! I'd be in charge! Watch me, watch me twirl. See ... Spin in your cage, spin like this. It's fun."

"You're a terrible dancer, Liz."

"You're a terrible singer, Kon."

HE HUMS the tune with a silly grin on his face and sings a few of the lyrics to me.

As I sniffle, I try to hide my glistening eyes, ashamed I'm tearing up again. I'm just so darn sick of crying all the time; however, if I had to choose between either never crying again or crying both these tears and the ones brought on by adversity, I would choose to cry so I could have moments like this. Wrestling with my attempts to hide my flushed face, he steals a kiss.

The wine has warmed my cheeks, and his unwavering attention warms every other part of me. He cradles me close to him, rocking, swaying and dancing. He moves with confidence. I giggle as he steals more kisses from me, from my neck, my jaw, my shoulders. "You're a terrible dancer," he whispers with a chortle.

My tongue pushes through the middle of my teeth as I smile up at him. "You're a terrible singer."

IT IS AFTER MIDNIGHT NOW. We are both a little drunk, lying on his bare mattress, facing each other as we've done before. We're sharing a pillow, and his emerald irises are only inches away, every freckle within them visible. He gazes at me, his eyes bouncing around my face, almost as if he's mapping my features to a grid in his mind.

"I've spent so many nights thinking about touching you." He sighs. "Thinking about touching more than your finger." He places his index finger tenderly on my shoulder and I shiver beneath it. The warmth from that one body part ignites my core. He traces a path slowly from my collarbone down to the crease in my elbow, along my forearm, and to the centre of my palm. His breathing deepens as he circles the patterns of my hand's inner centre, focusing on every etched line. His eyes are heavy as he gazes at me with that look —the one that carries so much emotional responsibility.

That look of love.

"I know this sounds weird, but I always dreamed of being

able to touch you. For four years I laid on that mattress in the dark and ran my index finger over my thumb — over and over, dreaming my thumb was you. I would imagine being able to heal your cheeks and your lips with my finger." As he speaks, uncertainty crosses his face.

"I remember seeing your bruises, Duchess." I stiffen and inhale sharply. I had many bruises and often.

"I wanted to touch them and soothe them, on your wrist and knees and chin... I thought that if I could touch them or kiss them, I could make them feel better. The stupid things kids think, hey?" He laughs. "Is that weird?"

I frown at him. "I would never think that was weird," I murmur, trying to settle the nervous twitch that always inundates me when my past life is discussed.

"I'm going to touch you now," he states, his voice husky and intense.

I sink deeper into the pillow. "Okay."

He lifts a finger to my neck, stroking the quickly accelerating pulse at the column of my throat. Every cell inside me can feel the heat from his fingertip as he trails a line across my skin. Tracing the outline of my chest, he strokes down until he's just above my nipple.

Oh, hell.

This is more intimate than anything else I've ever experienced. My heart goes into overdrive and starts beating against my ribcage.

Breathe, Blesk.

He searches my expression, narrowing his heavy-lidded eyes further. "Can I keep going?"

I give him a nervous nod. His finger rolls over my nipple. Both of us suck in a quick rush of air. But he doesn't hover there. Instead, he continues to stroke my torso, dipping down to my navel. His finger circles my skin, causing shivers to rush up my spine. He slides down further and all of a sudden, I flinch, causing his finger to retract from me.

"I'm so sorry." My voice squeaks. "I'm just not ready for ... *that*." Disappointment weighs my insides down like a lead boulder; this moment means so much to him.

I engulf my face in my palms, hoping that, somehow, I will miraculously slip away into oblivion. I can't see his face from behind my hands, but I'm positive he's frowning at me. His fingers feed through mine. Pulling them away, he reveals what I'm sure is a sheepish expression.

"What is this? Why are you hiding your face?" he asks. The pain in his voice cuts sharp to my core. "Did I do something you don't want me to do or make you feel uncomfortable, Duch?" His expression is tight, brows knitted together in confusion, eyes a muddle of emotions. He hasn't done anything wrong or presumptuous and doesn't deserve this ambiguity, but I don't want to discuss Erik. If history is anything to go by, then as soon as I trust a boy, conditions are invisibly attached.

He soothingly brushes the hair from my face. "I don't want anything from you. Ever. If you don't want to do it" – he lowers his head and shakes it back and forth– "then neither do I. *Fuck,* I should've known better. After everything you've been throu-"

Guilt floods his face. Rolling off the bed, he wanders over to the bathroom and walks inside. I hear a *thud.* My breathing shutters nervously in my chest as I climb to my feet and follow him. Gripping the basin, he stares at himself in the mirror, his face filled with loathing.

He turns to look at me, his irises dilated to the point of near blackness. "I *hate* what he did to you. It kills me."

My stomach knots up. "I just need time."

His jaw tightens. "Did I make you feel uncomfortable?"

He moves to my side, pulling me back to the bed and squatting in front of me. He places one shaky hand on my knee and the other on my shoulder while he peers up at me with those lovely green eyes. "I'm sorry, beautiful. I am *so* sorry. I never want to make you feel uncomfortable."

He hasn't done anything.

I grab his hand and look at it. The cuts on it have split open and are oozing blood again. He's still bruised and beaten from two weeks ago. Pulling his hand away, he hides it behind his back. "Duch, say something."

I release a long breath, but despite my attempts to stop them, tears filter out of my eyes. "I'm sorry, Kon—"

"No," he cuts in, shaking his head. "Don't ever apologise to me. My feelings for you are making me go damn right out of my mind. But I'll slow down. I'll do better."

I touch my finger to his mouth and hush him. He forces a crooked grin, but his eyes still appear sad. And then he kisses my finger, again and again until I move it away.

"You're so quick to blame yourself," I say. "This is my issue. I'm the one stuffing up, Konnor."

"No, Duch." He cups my cheek, peering up at me. "You have been through so much. It's my job to look after you now. Whatever that means, whatever I need to do, I'll learn. I'll do better."

God, he is so perfect.

Tell him the truth, tell him now!

"Konnor." I shake my head free of his hands. "I have something to tell you."

His expression stiffens. "Okay." His voice borders on panic. "I'm not liking that look in your eyes, so just say it."

He parts my thighs and moves to fill the gap between them, resting his arms on my legs. Gripping my waist, he peers up at me. "Say it. Just get it out."

Summoning all my courage and accepting he will probably never want to speak to me again, I dive in.

"The reason I struggle with Liz ..." I begin, looking everywhere except his face. My palms start to sweat, so I rub them on my dress. "With being her, is because my father wasn't the one who kept you locked up. He wasn't the one who had the key. He wasn't the one who..." The words get caught in my throat and I need to choke them out. "I had the key. I could have let you out. The reason you can't remember much wasn't because you were sick. You were never sick. I was drugging you."

My heart jumps into my throat and I wait. Silence.

Then the strangest thing happens.

A grin tugs at his cheeks.

I blink in astonishment, then blink again and again. He is smiling up at me with what looks like relief.

"Why are you smiling like that? I'm a monster," I say, radiating more duelling emotions than I ever thought possible. He chuckles, shaking his head slowly. My shoulders slump and I narrow my gaze at him, scrutinising his nonchalant attitude. "Did you hear what I said?" I almost growl.

"I already knew that, Duch."

My mouth goes slack. "You what?"

"Of course I knew," he states, rubbing my thighs with his hands affectionately. "Well, about the key. But you didn't have a choice. You were a little kid doing what you were told. You were just as innocent as me, Blesk. You didn't know any better."

I've been dreading this conversation, but he already knew. My brain is flipping, shuffling, trying to organise this new information. My guilt over this led to years of self-destructive behaviour. To all the self-hate, guilt, and anger that festered in me and coaxed me into...

And he already knew.

I gape at him. "Why did you keep taking the pills then? Every day when I gave them to you? Why didn't you refuse?"

"Because *you* gave them to me and I didn't want your father to hit you anymore."

"When you told Elise everything, you said you were sick though," I question, my voice breaking in confusion.

"Yeah, because I didn't want her to know. I don't want anyone to have a single negative thing to say about you," he admits.

My head feels dizzy. "Oh God, Konnor, that has been tormenting me my whole life. I killed her memory. I buried her because I blamed myself for doing that to you."

He reaches for my face again, stroking my cheek with the pad of his thumb, his soft emerald eyes boring into mine. "Well, now you can let it go, Duch. If I knew that that was what this was all about ... *Fuck,* I'm so relieved."

What that was about?

Heat radiates in my ears.

"No, Konnor, this is a huge deal!" I stand, pulling away from him and hugging myself tightly. "Huge! I tried to kill myse -" I halt halfway through the word, immediately regretting saying anything.

My breath stops.

His face.

Realisation.

He winces as if my words have the capability to cause him physical pain. My hand flies to cover my eyes, gripping the tension in my forehead and protecting my heart from the vision of that look. The silence isn't nice as it mingles with his heavy, angry breathes and my soft whimpers. Unable to see his expression, I imagine the worst. Heartbreak. But seeing I was so weak and yet, he was so strong. I now imagine fury.

I lower my hand and search his expression.

Gutted.

"No." He swallows hard. "Blesk, tell me that's not true."

My eyes drop to the floor.

"I was so young and not having you *hurt* all the time. What I did to you ..." I suck in a shaky breath. "The police told me that I couldn't live with that over my head, that people might blame me, that everyone would know I was the daughter of the man who stole the famous Deakon Nerrock. That it wasn't safe for me because of who you were. Your picture, your story was all over the news. For four years, I-" I try to steady my breathing. "I believed them. I believed that people would blame me because I blamed myself." Wiping my eyes with the back of my hand, I attempt to remove all the hot sticky tears flowing uncontrollably from them, but they're quickly replaced by more.

"And people *did* blame me, Konnor, they *did*. So how could I not blame myself? The night I helped you escape, after we split up, my father found me." My words come out between gasps now. "I tried to scream, but he beat me unconscious. The cops surrounded our house and arrested him. They found me locked in my father's wardrobe. It was terrifying. I didn't trust adults. I spent that night in the same hospital you were in."

"They told me you'd died," he murmurs, his voice detached.

"I did. Someone knew I was there. Someone blamed me for what happened to you. My first night in that hospital, a man came into my room and held a pillow over my head. I tried to fight him off, but I was only eight. I passed out and–" bile fills my throat. "I was legally dead for two minutes. They revived me, but the police said it would be safer for me to stay dead — so to speak. So they gave me a completely new identity and reported my death." A wave of nausea floods me. I begin to heave, gasping for air. Dropping to my knees, my palms hit the floor with a slap. My chest wheezes, aching with each rush of strained air. I focus on inhaling and exhaling small measured breaths so that I don't vomit.

Konnor follows me down and embraces me tightly. "Breathe, Duch."

When the memory of that night, the feeling of that pillow over my head, the feeling of that man's hand pressed firmly on the other side of it, fills me with terror, I cry out, "Someone wanted me *dead* for what I did to you, Konnor! I was only eight! I was only eight!" My body quakes violently within Konnor's strong arms.

"Stop talking, please, calm down," he begs. His voice bursts with emotion as he talks into my hair. The sorrow and pain surrounding us is dangerously palpable —a presence all their own, as if they are living, breathing things.

"NO! I need to get this all out now," I continue, speaking through sharp breaths. Choking and coughing out the words because I need them out, all of them. I want them out of my mind. I want them out of my life.

"The next year was like a nightmare. I was hollow. I was still her, but I wasn't. I was no one. I sliced my thigh open in the bathtub."

"Fuck, I don't wanna hear this, Blesk. Stop." He cries, tightening every muscle that is holding us both together. "This hurts. It hurts so bad to hear you talk like this."

I just keep talking as if the words are vomit that I need to expel. "I wanted to die. I was a terrible daughter who didn't know how to love my mum or dad." I gasp for air. "I put them through hell. I put *you* through hell. Erik found me bleeding out in the bathtub. I was dying all over again, and I wanted to this time. I just wanted the hurt to end, the guilt—"

"Please stop talking, please. I can't take it. Everything you've been through is breaking my *fucking* heart. I need a second. Please, just focus on breathing." He holds me to him, his hand wrapped around the back of my head, his fingers locked in my hair. As he rocks us back and forth, he chants quietly, "Just focus on breathing. Just focus on breathing. Just focus on breathing."

I press my wet cheek to the wall of his chest. "I hated myself. I hated myself, and I'm sorry. I am *so, so sorry,* Deakon. For being so weak. For giving up when you were so strong. I could—"

"*Shit!* Liz, fucking stop talking, I can't hear any more!" he shouts. He tightens his arms around me further, coming completely undone as he sobs into our embrace. Pain cuts through my core as his sounds become so fitful that I fear I may hear them every time I close my eyes. He's broken. I broke him.

twenty-two: blesk

Blesk

I CRINGE AT THE DAWN, my head throbbing, my eyes dry from dehydration. As I slowly come to, I spread my fingers across the sheets to discover Konnor's side of the bed is cold and empty. My chest tightens. I knew he would leave. I knew it would be too much for him to bear. Flapping at me from the bedside table is a letter.

Duchess,

I woke up when you were still asleep. I watched you sleep for a while, feeling like everything has gotten so fucked up. But don't worry, beautiful, I haven't left. I've just gone for a walk to clear my head. That was horrific. But...

it was good as well, Duch. It was good because we have no secrets now. We are finally in this together again.

To think you were in the same hospital as me when they told me you had died. I should have looked for you. I should have known you were alive. I should have felt it.

Whoever that man was who tried to kill you in the hospital, he was sick. You are not to blame for anything. I never, for one second, thought that. And I will make damn sure no one else ever will.

I will never understand why you did what you did. I will never be able to get those words out of my head, I will never be able to get that picture out my head. Everything inside me would have died with you that day had I known.

We need to finish this. We need to finish their story and try to gain some kind of closure. I know you want that. That is why you said goodbye to Liz. It was like a ritual... so you could move on. But it didn't give me closure. And us? It didn't finish our story. We have so many questions still unanswered... Why did your dad take me? Who tried to kill you that night in the hospital?

Now I know you aren't going to like this idea, which is why I'm writing it down. You can have some time to process it and then we can discuss it together, as a team, when I get back.

I think we should go visit your father in prison. I know you won't want to. God, do I know. But we need to. We need answers and he has them. He probably has all of them. Then, if you want, we can bury Deakon too. If that is what it takes to make sure you never feel that lost, that guilty, and that hopeless again, I will do that for you.

But I won't sit by and let you drown again, Duch, because I will be in that goddamn water with you. I will be there until I am so fucking weak from holding you up, that I will go down too. So I need to be proactive —we need to. And instead of me trying to take care of you all the time, let's spend the rest of our lives taking care of each other.

I love you, Duchess.
Xo Konnor

AS I READ, I clutch my heart. Although I don't want Liz to be a part of our lives, he does, and that means I have to come to terms with what happened. Konnor is right. Liz and Deakon have so much of their story left to finish before we can truly find closure.

My father doesn't know I'm alive. I don't know whether he was the one who orchestrated the attack on me at the hospital. The motives don't quite make sense. He had already been arrested and plead guilty by then anyway. Either way, he knows nothing about me now.

We will keep it that way.

It is time for me to be brave for Konnor. This is his story too. No more running. I'm so proud of the man he has become, a man so beautiful and so compassionate. My father has answers that Konnor deserves, and my running has been inadvertently keeping them from him. I will not be the reason he doesn't get them. With him by my side, I'm ready to step backwards in order to move forward.

twenty-three: konnor

Konnor

WHEN WE ARRIVE at Blesk's dorm, Elise starts probing for answers as we pack an overnight bag. She insists we take her along. After how emotionally drained I am from last night, I actually don't think it's a bad idea. Plus, I can't deny the little chick anything.

When we leave their dorm, I spot Jax waiting in his Prado. "Should probably take the Prado. Your beamer isn't comfortable at all," he says, leaning out of the window.

Well, apparently Jax is coming...

I grunt with minor annoyance. "Fine. But I'm driving."

Gardier Prison is a three-hour drive from campus. As I sit in the driver's seat, it's hard to shake the thought of what Blesk did to herself. I keep picturing her in that tub. It's damn near incapacitating. If she'd succeeded... I'd have never seen her again. It's an unbearable thought. I wish she knew —understood —that her body, her soul, every little thing that makes up a part of who she is, is so, so precious to me.

Jax clears his throat, interrupting my thoughts. "Everyone is always going on about Shakespeare! I get it, the dude was good, but seriously, in high school, all I ever heard about was *bloody* Shakespeare." He slams his boots down onto the dashboard.

"Shakespeare has coined more words than anyone else. He literally wrote ten percent of our vocabulary," Elise says.

"Yeah, it was easier back then," I reply. "Hardly anyone could afford education and the educated had a lot to be desired. We have more competition than Shakespeare ever did."

Jax scoffs. "He didn't write my dictionary!"

"What, the *Moron Dictionary*?" Elise cracks up.

"The Australian Dictionary, *Elise*," Jax states very matter-of-factly. "Where we add an 'O' to the end of certain words. Get it, kiddo?" Jax laughs as he knocks me with his elbow.

"Give us a *demo*?" I smirk.

"Haven't you already heard most of them, *Kono*?" Jax says, feeding chips into his greedy mouth.

"Dunno, Jaco, I wasn't really listening to your *convo*," I reply, shifting gear to the take the next corner.

"That is because you can't concentrate when you're sober. So let's stop at the *bottlo*. Everyone knows *Kono* is an *Alco*." Jax grins at me with a mouthful of crushed up chips.

Cheeky motherfucker!

I scowl at him, light-heartedly. *"Righto,* but we'll still need to stop at the *Servo* in the *arvo—"*

"Stop talking, you *deros*. You're making me *aggro*." Elise snickers, smacking both of our headrests from the backseat. Jax and I look at each other as we laugh.

Elise and Jax continue to verbally abuse each other—*or flirt.* I glance in the rear-view mirror and catch a glimpse of Blesk. Her cheek rests on Elise's shoulder. Her blonde hair spreads out around her. Her eyes are closed to the world and her headphones are in. With a relaxed expression on her face, she bobs her head slightly to an inaudible beat.

She looks like she's never had a bad experience in her life. She looks content. I haven't seen this look on her before. I peer back at the road. Then back at her again. Then back at the road.

What is she listening to? Whatever it is, it's my new favourite song. I need to be beside her. I pull over and slam on the brakes, jolting us to a standstill with more force than intended.

"What the hell?" Jax yells as the Prado comes to a complete stop.

I spin in my seat and look at Elise and Jax. "I can't concentrate. I need to sit next to Blesk... Elise, get up front." I crawl in the back.

Elise pushes her glasses up the bridge of her nose. "Fine, Jaxon, get ready to learn how to drive a stick properly."

"Whoa!" Jax stares at me and shrugs questioningly, mouthing, "What the?"

Elise jumps out and walks around the car.

I smirk at Jax and whisper, "I think she likes you." He tries to hide his flattered expression, but I catch it right as Elise climbs in the driver's seat.

I turn to see Blesk has woken from her music coma and is sitting up, observing us intently. She grins at me, her tongue coming out between her teeth.

I have to have it.

I lean in and suck her tongue into my mouth, pulling her

into me. I can feel the vibrations of her hum against my lips and chest as she melts against me.

Sliding my hand up into her hair, I deepen our kiss. I love every second her lips allow me the pleasure of their touch. I love their silky moistness, the moans that escape them, and the way her tongue massages mine. I just love absolutely everything about our kiss and everything about her.

As the car starts to move forward, we break our kiss so I can get my belt on. Motioning with my hand, I signal for her to take out one of her earplugs. She grins at me, tugging a plug from her ear.

"What are you listening to, Duch?" I ask.

"The Lumineers," she says, her smile and sparkling eyes wrenching my heart. She brushes my hair away from my ear and puts the loose earplug in it. She kisses my cheek, then rests her head on my shoulder without any further contemplation. Nestling into me, she relaxes. I wrap my arm around her and pull her as close as possible, kissing her forehead. I can hear the two miscreants bickering in the front seat, but Blesk doesn't seem to register them at all. Her expression is perfectly content, and now she is in my arms.

With that expression.

My heart is full.

All I want for her is peace... with me. She raises her leg and folds it over mine. She has never looked more beautiful than she does right now, bopping her head to the beat only we can hear, in her yoga pants, in her singlet, barefooted, and with no makeup on.

Her basic is every other girl's spectacular.

twenty-four: konnor

Konnor

I WOULD RATHER HAVE a holiday with Hitler than be here. I would rather be on the beach in the first scene of *Saving Private Ryan* than be here. I would rather be a blonde prostitute in *American Psycho* than be here. For some reason, it never occurred to me that I might have an adverse reaction to seeing a prison. To seeing a huge cage. To seeing a place without escape. To seeing captive humans.

The barbed wire, the layers of fences, the barred windows, and cold steep walls are my own personal *hell*. My whole body fights the urge to vomit as we pull into the visitor's parking bay. Then it happens so quickly. I feel every bloody cell rushing out, draining my cheeks, paling my face.

I completely stop breathing.

I have one feeling.

Only one.

Panic.

Fuck!

Jaxon and Elise twist back to look at me. I'm wide-eyed, frozen, blanched, unreachable. They're talking, but I can't hear them. Their mouths move, their faces distort, their heads tilt, but I can't hear anything. Panic has its claws around my throat, and I can't breathe, can't think. Everything around me moves slower than normal, slower than feasible. Then I hear something, and although it is muffled, I know I need to respond.

"Listen. Konnor. Listen. It's Blesk ..." Her voice trails off.

I turn to look at her and see that her mouth is moving, forming my name.

But I don't hear anything.

Like a damn tsunami, the air smashes back into me. I fly forward, gasping for oxygen. When I feel her sweet touch on my thigh, all of the sounds in the world suddenly get sucked straight into my head and I hear them all at once. They are yelling my name.

Fucking loud.

I grasp my ears, both hands covering my head.

"Fuck! Stop yelling!" I scream.

"Konnor, baby." Blesk places her palms on either side of my face and kisses my forehead. I force my hands away from my ears and down to my sides. I will the tension shredding my spine to yield, to subside. Her lips touch my cheek, soft and moist and loving. She kisses my chin. She kisses me with everything she has and everything she is feeling. They each convey a new meaning. That she understands, that she is petrified for me, and that she is here. She is living this nightmare vicariously through me. I shouldn't act like this.

Ridiculous, pathetic, emasculating.

Weak piece of shit...

Your girl needs you.

I don't want her to see me like this.

"Stop, don't touch me. I'm fine," I state curtly, trying to evade eye contact. I shrug her off, waving her hands from my face. I'm too in my head, too angry at myself. My rejection shocks her, but she doesn't surrender. Grabbing my cheeks with more force, she searches my expression empathetically. When she kisses my lips again, I cease avoiding her, defeated by her warmth. Her lips oppress every other erupting emotion. She pulls away and looks me dead in the eyes, offering me exactly what I need: acceptance, tolerance, understanding, and love. She knows what is happening. I need her. I need her more than anything.

She hushes me. "*Shhhh*, baby." She pulls me to her chest, rocking me against her until my heart slows.

Breathe, Konnor.

"I don't think I can move, Duch."

My voice sounds strange, like it isn't my own. "I'm trying to move my feet. I'm trying to, but they won't budge. I'm supposed to look after you and I can't even move right now. I can't go in there." I suck a sharp breath in, trying to regulate my heart's rhythm.

She strokes my hair. "We're looking after each other, remember? *We're looking after each other.*"

Jax grimaces. "What the hell is going on with you, dude?" he yells before jumping from the car and slamming the door behind him.

"Jax!" I call after him.

He turns to stare across the field that surrounds the penitentiary. Gripping the back of his head, he rubs his hands forward through his hair. I know it's unfair to ask him to continue watching all this drama unfold without some kind of explanation.

Fuck, I need a drink...

"Don't worry, I'll talk to him." Elise pats my arm. Swinging open the car door, she goes to Jax. Their conversation is inaudible from inside the Prado, but their body language is quite distinct. She places a tender hand on his back as they exchange words. His arms jolt around; his head shakes.

I look at Blesk. "You can't go in. This is a mistake, a *huge* mistake."

She sighs. "No, it isn't."

"Yes, it really is," I mutter.

"We need answers. I'm getting them."

Hell no!

"You're not going in there without me." I shake my head. "There's no way."

She smiles at me with big comforting eyes. "I can do this."

"You're kidding, right? That man beat you for years. He ruined your life. There is no way you are going in there alone."

Her expression tightens. "Konnor!"

"No, Duchess, not without me. It isn't open for negotiation."

She takes a strengthening breath. "I have to do this for you and for me. I can do this."

"Nope," I state, dismissing what she just said. "Not happening, just let it *go!*"

"Stop it. You said we would look after each other, but you don't believe I can hold up my end of the bargain. I need you to support me and let me do this. I can do this, Konnor. Why don't you believe I can?"

My chest deflates. "Duchess, you can do anything you want, anything you put your mind to. You are the *bravest* person I've ever met." I grin at her and exhale on a sigh. "Once upon a time, there was a little girl who stood up to her abusive father and helped her best friend escape the prison he was in for four years. You risked everything when you did that, and you did it completely alone. You faced him alone. I will be *damned* if you have to face him alone again."

She looks down at her feet, contemplating something, before looking back at me. "I will take Elise in with me."

When I look in her eyes, I still see Liz, that little girl. But she's right, she isn't that little girl anymore. She is a woman —an incredible woman, and sometimes my desperate need to protect her clouds that fact. I want to help her flourish, to gain strength within herself, and to love herself as much as I love her—because she is just so *unbelievably* lovable. All I want to do is protect her, it is all I've ever wanted to do, and I will. I will always be there to catch her should she fall, always and forever. But I need to support her and not shelter her...

I sigh again, exasperated. Working my jaw, I consider her proposal. She sits tall, with an edginess to her that looks incredibly hot. She needs to do this —with or without me. This is one of those times when she needs my support and not my protection, even though it scares the shit out of me. Because she is right...

She can do this.

I roll my eyes reluctantly. *"Fine,* Duchess, but you do not tell him anything, hear me? Nothing! If that means he doesn't give you any information, then fine. Don't mention your name, your university, anything, understand?"

"He thinks I'm dead," she says. "Remember?"

"Yeah, so he's gonna have questions." The more I talk, the sicker I feel. The more I contemplate the conversation, the more I hesitate.

"Konnor," she says, reaching out to stoke my cheek. "He won't be able to find me. I live in a different town. I live a different life with a different name. I will be fine. I'm going to tell him who I am. But give him nothing else."

I massage my temples. "Kiss me," I order. She leans in and presses her mouth to mine. As her tongue teases my lips, I fist her hair, pulling her in more deeply —desperately. I love her. *God,* do I love her. The thought of someone hurting her kills me. I pull away and stare at her. "Be careful."

A subtle and yet resolute smile crosses her face. "He can't hurt me in there."

I press my palm to her heart. "Here... He can hurt you in here."

Her face softens. "No, he can't. Not anymore."

I watch her walk with Elise through both layers of fencing, then through the sliding doors. Every step seems exaggerated. Every little glance over her shoulder seems like a goodbye, causing every muscle inside me to tense with the need to run after her even as my every thought goes to the darkest place it can find. I step outside the car and pace. I pace back and forth like an animal, like an animal in a cage. A big, human-holding cage.

Dammit!

My face tightens, molars clamping together as I make my way towards Jax. I start to slump down on the grass near his feet, but my legs suddenly buckle and I fall onto my back. I wince as the wind is knocked out of me.

He drops down beside me, and we both stare at the sky. I can feel my brows knit together so tightly that today will probably imprint permanent worry lines on my forehead. I've never been to a prison, never spoken to anyone who has. *Will the guards search her or Elise?* The thought alone makes my ears radiate with heat. *What if her dad tries to touch her?*

What if he lunges at her? I groan at the thought and rub my face roughly with both hands.

"Say something," I groan at Jax, wanting him to take my mind off the images in my head. "You *clearly* have something to say, so just fucking say it."

He scoffs. "Fine, I will. This isn't normal. This whole thing, you and her, the intensity of it. You have started doing this *awesome* new thing where you phase out, and it is just fucking magical. I mean, really, it's like you aren't even there anymore. It's really freaking me out, and yet, you won't tell me what's going on. It's fucked up and it's making you act like a psycho."

I entwine my fingers and cup the back of my head with my palms. "Maybe I was always a psycho. You just didn't know it."

He mimics my position. "I've known you for a while now and have never seen you act the way you have over the past month. You've known this girl for, like, what? Five seconds? And you worship her. Whenever she's around, you're in this weird daze, like you're not even Konnor anymore."

I grunt and turn my head to flash him a serious look. "You need to stop talking about Duch like that or we won't be coming back from this conversation."

"See, like that! It's irrational."

"It isn't fucking irrational. I just won't lay here and hear a bad word spoken about her, so cut it out."

He makes eye contact with me momentarily before turning back to the sky. "Listen, Konnor, the past month you have been acting crazy —missing practice, missing games, missing classes, missing fucking grad classes. You're gonna fail."

"*Oh, come on,*" I groan. "It has been *one* fucking month. Get over it."

"Yeah, it has been a month. One month of you acting like a complete lunatic," he says gruffly.

I roll my eyes. "I have known her a lot longer than you. I've known her for seventeen years."

"*Riiiiiiight.*" He drawls. "When you were children."

My jaw suddenly gets tight and I growl, "Don't say it like that! You have no idea what you're talking about."

He releases a sharp, exasperated breath. "Well, then tell me!"

"I can't," I snap.

"I like B. You know I do. She's a cool chick. But you two are crazy together. *Way, way* too intense. Too, I don't know … Just too much. I keep feeling like I need to watch out for shrapnel 'cause you're gonna explode at any moment."

He's so right. "Yeah, I feel like that too," I mumble.

"You know that isn't normal, right?" I notice in my peripheral vision that he has twisted to look at my side profile, attempting to gain more of my attention. Perhaps, even convince me with his severity. "That kind of intensity? You are meant to improve each other's lives, not derail them."

I frown at the sky and then turn to acknowledge him. "No, it isn't normal. It's *phenomenal!* Every goddamn part of it. Her hands, her lips, everything. And I'm totally okay with the intensity. I've been in love with her forever, since before I can remember anyone else, and I am not ashamed to say it. I don't care if I sound like a pussy. I just don't care. Her face has more familiarity, seems more like family, and has more connections to the word *home* than any other face on earth. We are working through things at the moment, Jax. Things will get better; it just isn't a quick fix."

He sighs sadly, his shoulders deflating from the effort. "I

don't understand, dude." He shakes his head. "I just don't get it."

I clear my throat. "Your mum or dad, your sister, their faces... They are the clearest things from your childhood, right? Your aunties, friends even? You have memories of them and of the things you did. You probably even have photos. *All* I have is her. Her memory, *our* memory, memories of the childhood we shared, just the two of us.

"We are one, bound together by circumstance. All I remember from before I was nine is *her*. There is nothing wrong with *us*; Konnor and Blesk are great. We always have been, even from the start. The issue is who we were when we were kids and what happened to us. We just need time to figure out how we can put our past and presents together."

Jaxon groans, frustrated. "*Please,* for *fuck's sake,* give me more than that, dude. That makes fuck-all sense. I'm worried about you."

"Okay, Jax! Okay! But not many people know this. My family knows what happened, obviously, because they adopted me, and Elise knows because Blesk wanted her to, but no one else. Not even Drake."

He scoffs. "Don't do me any fav—"

"I want to tell you."

And I do.

I proceed to tell him. *Everything.* I try not to watch his expression as I run through the events of the past seventeen years, but I can tell he is getting choked up.

He never makes a peep.

To my surprise, by the end of my story, I'm smiling. Because, even though I am on display, all of me, I'm also free. The sun flickers above me. The trees move in the wind and the grass is soft beneath my back.

After hearing my story again, in its entirety, I realise it's almost over. We are so close to truly moving on now. And I have Blesk, my Duchess.

I chew on the inside of my lip in contemplation. "There are a lot of things about me that are a result of that experience," I admit to Jaxon. "I play them off, of course, as personality idiosyncrasies, but they aren't... They're scars, some of which I'll *never* share with Duch. I don't need her feeling any more guilt.

"The first year after I got out, I got sick —a lot. I wasn't used to all the germs people carried, and I was pretty much always on some kind of antihistamines or antibiotics. My system was shot to hell. I never felt... *right*, ya know? Even though I knew the world was big, it still kinda scared me."

We both sigh and continue to blink at the sun overhead. Jax's expression is stiff and concerned, steadfast in his fight to not offer ubiquitous comfort, but obvious in his overwhelming need to.

"You'll laugh at this," I continue with a sheepish chuckle. "But, ah, I was shy once. If it wasn't for two boisterous sisters, I might have disappeared altogether. They forced me out of my shell and I mean literally *forced*." I laugh, reminiscing.

"When I had my first drink with Flick, it was like it enlightened me. With that in my system, I had courage. I was funny. Impenetrable. And... I felt closer to the boy in the basement. I was in a bit of a daze in that cell, mate. The drugs I'd been given warped the way I saw things." Hesitation changes my tone, dropping it to barely a choked whisper. "The thing I've never told anyone, *ever,* Cassidy, Flick or my shrink, is... I missed the basement. I missed it because it had become me. And it was where *we'd* shared a life. There, I got to be with her all the time, every day. And then I was alone, and it was scary. I was scared all the time...

"I slowly moved on. I started to cope without her and without the basement. And yet, the last few weeks, without Blesk... For the first time in several years... I missed the basement all over again."

Relieved that I've finally said it, I lay back on the grass and stare at the clouds, exhausted, but happy. Suddenly, a silhouette blocks my view. Blesk straddles me, one foot on either side of my waist, as she peers down at me. Lined in silver from the sun's beams, she looks like an angel. Relief floods me.

"Hey there, Mr Slater. Come here often?" she asks with a cheeky wiggle of her brows. I sit up and grab her knees, pulling her down onto my lap. Her incredible arse meets my thighs. I shuffle her against me, and her breath catches on impact with my body.

"Miss Bellamy, what's a girl like you doing outside a place like this?" I ask, purposely displaying both dimples when I grin.

Elise chuckles. "*Aww,* you two are hopeless!"

Jax scoffs and jumps to his feet. "*Fucksake,* have your menstrual cycles synced or something?" He wipes his eyes, hiding the emotions he's still trying to control.

"*Jealous,*" Blesk says in a singsong voice, beaming sweetly up at him.

"No," he states. "Because I find my balls and spine both necessary."

Elise chuckles. "They're cute."

"Kill me if I ever act like that," Jax mutters to Elise.

Completely ignoring them, I keep my eyes trained on Blesk's playful grin, which is creasing her cheeks and widening her lips. Her lips are so kissable right now. If Jax and Elise weren't here, my hands would be roaming her perfect body. I lean in to kiss her, but she pulls away teasingly and giggles. Tuting, I thread my hands under her backside and force her into me harder.

"Do you want that distinction, Miss Bellamy?"

"I thought all I had to do was show up?" she challenges, resting her forearms on my shoulders and running her delicate fingers through the back of my hair.

"That was before I knew your potential." I lean in again and wrap my mouth around her lower lip, sucking and tugging on it. She goes limp on my lap and moans into my mouth. Both of us momentarily lose ourselves in each other. In our kiss. In our moans. I sulk when she reluctantly pulls away from me, flashing a look at our company. I lick the remnants of her taste off my lips, hating how often we have to part.

Damn, she tastes good.

"So..." I say apprehensively. "Tell me how it went. Tell me everything."

She slides off my lap, and I immediately feel her absence all around me. I frown as she positions herself cross-legged beside me. Her face turns serious as she mentally prepares to have, what I know will be, one of the hardest conversations of our lives.

"Well, we had to sign in. I had to give them my full name, but they assured me he would only be given my first. I wasn't even sure if he'd see me. To him, I was a stranger. Anyway, after we were given our visitor badges, we had to wait for the sniffer dogs to check us.

"We waited for a while in what looked like a cafeteria. As the seconds passed, I started to get super nervous. When the door to the prison cell block opened, I physically flinched. Lots of mean looking guys walked out in green prison scrubs. And... I recognised him immediately. I wasn't sure if I would because I just couldn't picture him in my head at all. I'd tried many times, but his face was always blank. And yet, when I saw his icy-blue eyes, I knew it was him.

"He sat opposite me, smirking. I thought maybe I would feel something. Maybe I would remember I loved him once, that he loved me once, but I felt nothing.

"We sat in silence for at least five minutes, but I refused to be the first to break it. Then he rested his elbows on the table and leaned forward. He told me that I have my mother's eyes, and he called me Lizzy. He recognised me too.

"I asked him why he took you. He ignored my question and just said I was prettier than my mum. I asked the same question again. He scowled at me and signalled the guard. I thought he was just going to leave. When the guard approached, they spoke quietly together. He laughed with the guard, then said something about me being a 'knockout'. Then he stood up and walked away from me. He looked at me a few times and I thought maybe, just maybe, he wanted to remember what I look like. Like maybe he does care, in his own way."

"I wasn't sure if I was mad or disappointed or sad. I was sad for you. I'd failed you and it was all a waste of time. We had to wait for a few minutes before we could leave. Maybe five minutes later, when we were walking from the cafeteria, the guard my father had spoken to stopped us. My heart leaped into my throat. He asked me to hold my arms out and stand still. Then he ran his hands up and down my sides before putting something in my pocket. That was it. That was all that happened."

A half-smile curls her lips, but the creases between her brows reveal her true unease. Her hand goes behind her and she removes something from her back pocket. A piece of paper. She hands it to me. It's light, yet it should somehow be weighing down my palm with its significance.

I gesture to the inanimate object in my hand. "This is it? It seems inadequate, almost."

She shrugs. "I haven't read it, but please don't get your hopes up."

"Yeah, mate, for all you know, it says, 'Fuck you, have a nice day'," Jax says, looking down at us on the grass. Elise and Jax both watch me intently as I take a big breath and then unfold the note.

Lizzy
It is all yours. You've earned it.
Safety deposit box 101
45 South Side Street Moorup
2217
Daddy

"HE'S SUCH AN ARSEHOLE." I scrunch up the piece of paper in my hand, loathing it. "This is a joke." My knuckles turn white around the note. I'm never going to get any answers, and I was pathetic for thinking that maybe I would. I jump up and punch at the air, hating myself for hoping. "Fuck!"

"Slater, maybe there is actually something in that box?" Jax states.

"Nah, fuck it!" I shake my head fanatically, scowling at the world in general.

I hear her sweet sigh before she mutters, "Baby, we're going to Moorup to look in the box."

"You have to. I mean, if you don't, you'll always wonder," Elise says.

I snort. "No, we don't. That is exactly what he wants. For all we know, someone is going to meet us there to finish what they started in the hospital that day." As soon as the words pass my lips, I want to rip my own head off.

Blesk's face drops; I did that. I'm responsible for that sad look.

You're an arsehole, Konnor.

Elise's hand goes to her mouth. "Konnor!"

Blesk gasps. "Don't ever say stuff like that, Konnor! Oh my God." She bounces to her feet and walks towards the car, sniffling and wiping at her eyes.

"There could be some truth in it though," Jax calls out, watching Blesk walk away.

"Shit!" I growl and take my anger out on the grass, kicking it and stomping. Spinning, I jog after her, cursing my lack of tact.

Leaning against the car, she folds her arms across her chest, frowning and sulking at me as I approach. Cutest little pout. Cutest little sulk. Thank God I've never seen this face before because it renders my own will obsolete. I would do anything for this face. Placing both palms beside her head on the car, I force a smile and stare directly into her glistening chocolate-brown eyes.

"Duchess." My voice softens. "I'm sorry. I should never talk like that, and if you want to go, then we'll go."

She sniffs back a tear. Glancing down at her feet, she shuffles them in the dirt. "He wrote 'You earned it'," she whispers, her voice cracking with each word. "Like I've earned whatever prize he got for keeping you kidnapped, like I was his accomplice or something."

She peers up at me as a tear drops from the corner of her eye. It glides slowly down her cheek.

I wipe it away with the side of my finger. "He's an arsehole, Duch. He wants to hurt you. He probably knows you blame yourself."

"I know," she says sadly. "But it still makes me feel sick."

Sighing, I brush her hair back with my hand; her golden locks slip through my fingers like silk. I remind myself how lucky I am to have her, how lucky I am to touch her, and how incredibly lucky I am that every time I touch her, she moves into me, letting me know she wants me too. Nothing else matters.

"I love you, Duchess. You know that, right?" I say.

She nods. "I just ... I was hoping to feel some kind of family connection. Anything. He is the only person I know who shares the same blood as me," she mumbles, dropping her head back on the car.

"I'm your family." I pull her into my chest, hugging her, before peering over my shoulder and calling out, "Looks like we're going back to the District."

twenty - five: blesk

Blesk

AS WE ROLL over the Brussman Bridge, I'm overwhelmed by its grandeur and height. This city is thriving, rich in wealth and... in gossip. I can see the streets of Moorup from above, streets that appear akin to veins pulsing through this living city.

When we roll into the visitor parking lot at the Trans Moorup inter-district rail line, we devise a plan.

Elise and I stay in the car while Jaxon and Konnor go inside. They are going to get the lay of the land and then come back to see us before actually opening the locker. I highly doubt my father has managed to organise an ambush since speaking with me less than two hours ago. Nevertheless, we are all prickly with nervous tension. My fingers search for something, anything, to fidget with as we anxiously wait.

This train station has several floors; the inclined floors are for bus transportation and parking, and the lower floors are for trains. The locker could be on any level. Security at city stations of this size are usually second to none... or so I keep telling myself. The words from my father's letter keep flashing in my head. I feel like I've missed something.

It is all yours... You've earned it.

What is all mine? The information? Money? Again, it's always about me having to earn something. In my father's case, it was trust. In Erik's, love.

And now I'm thinking about how Erik could wake up at any moment. Will he press charges? Probably not. If he did, I'd be forced to tell everyone why this all happened in the first place...

Out of nowhere, the image of the ceiling in my parent's bathroom permeates my thoughts. It was the last thing I saw before Erik dragged me, senseless and numb, from the red pool. He literally saved my life that day. At only twelve years old, that must have been something worthy of a nightmare. His little sister, laying in a bloody tub. Unmoving.

I twist in my seat, peering back at Elise, words on the edge of my tongue.

"What are you thinking about, Wally? You have that little dimpled brow thing happening."

Trying to relax my face, I reply, "What dimpled brow thing?"

She chuckles and points at my profile. "That one!"

"Honestly? I was thinking about Erik."

Elise slumps into the upholstery and crosses her arms, tilting her head questioningly. "And?"

"He loves me. I'm not excusing what he did. No excuses, I swear. Just, I'd like to hear what he has to say."

She takes an exaggerated breath in and out. "It's hard to understand why anyone would put up with what you have, it really is. But then... Okay, so before I say this, please don't think I agree with you, because I *don't*. I don't think you should listen to anything he has to say. But I just want you to know I'm actively trying to understand your stance on this subject. So here I go.

"The first time I met you, I thought Erik was your boyfriend because of the way he looked at you. It was pretty clear he adored you. He watched you move; he watched your mouth when you spoke. Then, when you said he was your brother, I was like, *wow,* I wish I had a brother because he seriously loves you. I wish I had someone who adores me that much. Yes, I don't deny he loves you. But... what could he possible say?"

"I'm alive because of him."

"Yeah. One right doesn't make up for all the lefts," she states adamantly. "What about Konnor? Because seeing what he saw that day must have really messed with his head. We both know going down there destroyed him. I mean, look at him today! He couldn't even look at the prison. Which, mind you, is fair enough. I went crazy when I fractured both my legs and had spent eight weeks inside with my nanny. Imagine four years. I don't know how he isn't *more* stuffed up.

"But that day he went down there, chasing after your cries and saw what he saw... You can't ask Konnor to be okay with you being in the same room as Erik. Forgiving Erik, even a little, would break Konnor's heart."

Everything she says has me barely holding myself together because she's *so* right; I can't do that to Konnor.

Elise leans forward and touches my knee. "Stop, Wally. I know that look. Stop self-hating. There's too much going on in your head. You've faced some crazy hurdles today that most people couldn't even comprehend. I think you should trust Konnor enough to talk to him about it too because he's reasonable and has your best interests at heart. But you need to attempt to make decisions that consider his feelings too, because he will only think about yours. He needs some looking after as well. I worry about you, Wally, I do, but to be honest, I also know I don't need to because Konnor will love you and look out for you...if *you* let him."

I nod. "I'm going to love him and look out for him too."

She beams at me. "Good to hear because love you he does."

"Love him I do," I whisper, the words sounding so nice to actually hear out loud.

"Tell him you should," she mutters knowingly.

I jump when both car doors swing open. Konnor moves in behind the wheel and Jax slumps down behind me. The energy in the car shifts as they glance hesitantly at one another.

"What have you two done?" I ask, squinting at them.

"Nothing." Konnor chuckles evasively and flashes Jaxon a 'busted' kind of look. "We haven't done anything."

"Why are you both grinning at each other like that?" Elise probes.

"We just got some stuff for you," Jaxon says, pulling a Pez out from his back pocket and handing it to Elise. "I got you Daenerys Mother of Dragons, Pez style." His lips curve up to the side as Elise's eyes widen.

And I'm completely missing something...

She snatches it from him and holds it to her chest, exhaling slowly.

"Explain?" I query, my eyes shifting around the car. Elise sinks into her chair with the Pez clutched tightly to her heart, a big dopey smile stretching from ear to ear.

She melts into a sigh. "I told Jaxon and Konnor last time we went driving that I hadn't been on a real road trip before. They were horrified. Anyway, now apparently Pez is one of the major staples of a road trip. But Jaxon couldn't find any. I also told them about my two mums, who are both lawyers. Which, by the way, they seemed *awkwardly* eager to hear about," she teases.

I cock an eyebrow at Konnor. "Were they just?"

"I don't know what you are implying, Elise, but I object." Konnor laughs.

"Lawyer jokes." Jaxon guffaws, taking on a pose to obstruct an incoming hand or fist from Elise.

Elise hisses at them playfully. "Shut up, you two delinquents... *So* Jaxon and I had lunch a few days ago, and he dared to challenge my woman power—"

"Oh no, he didn't," Konnor cuts in. I crack up laughing as he twerks his finger and bobbles his head. His smile, his playfulness, his confidence —it is the most extraordinary thing I've ever seen, and I love it.

I love him, and I love the look in his eyes right now.

Jaxon snorts. "I didn't challenge your woman power or whatever you just said, *thank you.* I just said growing up without a masculine presence would have been hard. There is no wonder she is so... I dunno, little and quaint and shit."

"And shit!" Konnor mocks. Then we all laugh because Elise isn't the least bit quaint.

"He said, no wonder I was so fragile and girly. He said *fragile and girly.* I said, having only mothers has made me way fiercer than if I'd grown up with a father. Women are crazy protective and extremely resilient.

Women have been squashed for thousands of years and have only been given a real voice in the past fifty. I said, look at what we have accomplished in that time. I told him that he wouldn't want to see me mad because I am fiery."

I exhale with realisation. "*Ah,* and so he got you a Mother of Dragons Pez. Aw, that's kind of sweet."

She grins at me with a new look, a goofy, Elise-in-love look. "Yeah."

Konnor leans in and kisses my cheek before running his lips quickly across to my chin and then giving me a chaste peck on the mouth. He opens the car door and steps out, caution flashing in his eyes.

"Don't get upset okay? Just be happy," Konnor says. Leaning down beside the tyre, he winks at me as he fiddles around with something on the floor. When he rises, he's holding a white cardboard cake box in his hand. A pleased smile crosses his face. Climbing back into the car, he flashes a look at Jaxon, then puts the box into my eagerly outstretched hands.

"This is from Jax, Elise, and me. We know that you missed out on a lot of birthday cakes over the years and we wanted to rectify that. We got you twenty cupcakes, one for every birthday we missed. Because we didn't mean to miss them and we will never miss another one again."

"This is such a *Wallflower* moment," Elise says with a grin.

I stare at the box open-mouthed and wide-eyed. This moment, right now, is the happiest of my entire life; this moment, right now, rivals every happy moment anyone has ever experienced. This moment means more to me than I could ever express.

These people are my family.

I don't try to stop the tears because this type of crying I like. This kind makes every other tear worth crying.

"Thank you," I say. "Thank you so much."

"What flavour are the cupcakes?" Elise asks.

"All different, I think," Konnor says. "We got them from this little bakery in the station." I pass the cake box back to Elise, and she places it on the seat between her and Jaxon.

Konnor pulls me over the centre console and onto his lap, engulfing me in his arms as I lose a few of those awesome tears, those happy tears, those tears of joy.

"And now don't get mad, Duch, please." Konnor hands me an A4 yellow envelope. My face immediately crumbles as I squint down at it. I slide from his lap and back into the seat beside him, unease stirring my belly. He looks nervous, which makes *me* nervous. My fingers wrap around the envelope, and I fake a grin while searching his guilty face.

"Duch, we didn't go to the locker. We asked a security guard to go for us, and tipped him handsomely, might I add. He didn't seem too fazed at all. He returned with this. I know you are probably mad I didn't discuss it with you first, but I'm just relieved it is done. So... that's it."

"I'm not mad." I crinkle the envelope in my hand and hold it to my stomach, my breath quickening. The first part of accepting my new friends, my new family, is to trust them and their decisions. "I'm freaked out and I'm not happy you took a risk without discussing it with me first."

"We knew you'd say no, and we were there," Jaxon says, leaning forward onto his knees. "And the guy at the desk approached us, and it just felt like a natural thing to ask and organise. So we just did it without thinking."

"You buttered us up first with cakes and Pez," Elise says, still clutching her gift tightly.

"Yeah, we really did," Jaxon admits clumsily.

"Did it work?" Konnor asks, searching my wide-eyed expression with a tiny bit of unease.

I lick my lips, which are now ridiculously dry.

Clearing my throat, I say, "Yes, it worked."

"So what now?" Jaxon asks. "The anticipation is killing me."

As my eyes explore the envelope in my hand, I begin to feel sick. Part of me fears its contents, and part of me is excited to finally set it free. Konnor puts his hand on my knee and stares at me, his expression soft and knowing.

"Wanna blow it up?" Konnor asking jokingly.

"Or shred it to pieces?" Jaxon adds, laughing.

"Or spit on it?" Elise says.

"Gross, Elise. *Jeez* you always take things too far," Jaxon teases.

I grin at them because they seem to know exactly what to say.

Konnor cuts in before I can reply. "I think we should stay at my folks' place tonight. It's only thirty minutes away. We can go through the envelope there. What do you think?"

"That isn't fair on everyone else, Konnor," I point out, peering back at Elise and Jax questioningly.

"I'd planned on staying away until tomorrow anyway," Elise says with a shrug. "I love our adventures. We should do more of them."

Konnor grimaces and tilts his head to look at Elise, his brows drawn tightly together. "I don't want to get kidnapped again, Elise."

Elise's mouth goes slack. "*Oh God,* yes, sorry, of course." She squirms in her seat as her big apologetic eyes glance around at us. Konnor suddenly bursts out laughing, and I relax into a chuckle.

"Your face!" he states between sounds of amusement.

"Jerk, winding me up like that." Elise pouts, punching Konnor in the arm.

Jaxon chuckles. "Don't worry, Elise, Konnor isn't that sensitive. Yeah, I'm in, if everyone else is."

"Sorry, Elise," Konnor says, smiling at her. "You're so *preeetty.*"

She slumps back as she grumbles, "Sycophant." Folding her arms across her chest, she pretends to sulk.

Konnor turns his gaze back to me. "Duch? You wanna meet my family?"

My chest tightens. I must be pale because I can almost feel the blood drain from my cheeks. I blink at him and gulp down the strange, dry knot that has formed in my throat.

"Ummm, actually, that makes me a little nervous." I glance down at my feet. "Look at what I'm wearing." I gesture to my black yoga pants and plain wrinkled shirt. "Konnor, I'm not shallow, but you're important to me. I really want to look nice when I meet your family."

Stupid road-trip wrinkled shirt.

He cups my cheeks, smiling widely. His charming dimples gloriously melt my nerves away. "They will love you! Your standard is everyone else's deluxe."

"That is *so* true, Blesk," Jaxon states very seriously. "Except mine." He laughs. "Your standard is my poor."

"Shut up, Jaxon." Elise playfully nudges him with her elbow.

"She's gonna get a big head. I'm just keeping it real," Jaxon admits.

"What do you think?" Konnor asks me, anchoring me with his gaze and ignoring the banter in the backseat.

I sigh loudly. *"O...kay,"* I say in the little voice I know he loves. He exhales loudly and grins.

He knows I did it intentionally for him.

twenty-six: blesk

Blesk

THE SLATER FAMILY sure has money. After Konnor enters a code on the keypad, sliding gates at the foot of the driveway open. We drive past gardens rich in greenery before being greeted by a stunning water feature. Something about their property and house appears old-worldly, as if it's a part of a noble ancestry.

"Wow, you are kidding, right?" Elise says wondrously, her mouth agape. "You are *rich*! And not like, 'Yeah, I'm well off.' Like, *rich!*"

Konnor chuckles as he continues to navigate around the property. "Lucky, hey?"

"Wait till you try his mum's Long Island iced teas. They're epic," Jaxon says.

"Yeah but you won't be having more than two of those bad boys." Konnor laughs. "Or I'll be holding back your hair."

"You've been here before?" I ask Jaxon.

He unbuckles his belt and begins to collect the items from the back seat. "Yeah, a few times. They're good people, hard not to like."

"What do your parents do?" Elise inquires, staring out her window.

Konnor glances at her in the mirror. "A lot of stuff, really. They own some shares in some pretty affluent companies. They are partners in a few local businesses."

The fully rendered house has two storeys, beautifully separated by wrap-around balconies, a skillion roof, and double doors high enough to fit a giant through. Konnor drives the Prado past the house and to the rear, where an electric garage door opens. He pulls in alongside a pink Lexus, a red soft-top BMW convertible, a Rolls Royce, and two Harley Davidson motorbikes.

"Whose Harleys?" Elise asks.

"Guess?" Konnor says.

"Your dad's?" I say.

"Nope, my sisters'. Not even kidding. Flick can pull it off, but Cassidy looks ridiculous. She never really even learned to ride. But she always had to have what Flick had. And, well, no one can say no to Cassidy." He smiles at the bikes. "I'm kinda surprised my dad hasn't sold hers yet," he says as his smile grows, spreading across his face.

Suddenly a nervous flutter fills my stomach. If that is the reaction they can inspire in him from a mere thought, what will happen if they don't like me? I pull my tie from my wrist, then gather up my hair and fasten it into a high ponytail. Dropping the visor down, I check my eyes in the mirror, smooth out the top of my hair, and try to rub some colour back into my cheeks.

Konnor grabs my hands from my face. "Stop it, Duch. You

look like a goddess. Honestly, they are the most none judge-mental people in the world."

"Why do I find that hard to believe?" I murmur, glancing around at the array of brand-new vehicles.

"You're being silly." Konnor laughs.

"You are being a Wally!" Elise chimes in.

Konnor gets out of the driver's seat, walks around the front of the car, and opens my door.

He holds his hand out for me to take, smirking playfully. "Duchess."

I place my hand in his. "Kind sir."

Elise bounces from the car, and all four of us exit through the open garage roller door. There is a door in front of the Lexus that seems to enter directly into the house, but Konnor walks us back outside the way we drove in.

"Jax, you go in with Elise and show her around. I wanna take Duch somewhere," Konnor says.

"Alrighty, hop on, little girl." Jaxon squats and Elise bounces onto his back without a moment of hesitation.

"Call me little girl again and I will drop kick you," she states.

Konnor chuckles and waves them away before yelling out, "See you inside in a few!"

He entwines our fingers together and leads us towards an outbuilding about a hundred metres away. The property is lush; it appears there must be an elaborate team of care-takers to maintain it.

"Cassidy will probably be in her studio," he says, pointing towards the building in front of us. "Dad had that built for my sisters. They both needed somewhere for dance practice *away* from the house.

I peer wide-eyed at him. "He built them a whole studio?"

He nods. "Yeah, but it wasn't an impulsive decision.

Cassidy attends a formal ballet academy. She also teaches dance part-time. So this is really *her* studio. It wasn't a small expense, but she has to contribute some of the money she earns from teaching to general expenses like electricity and stuff. Dad isn't one to dish out if he doesn't feel it's a good investment."

I grin at him. "So are *you* a good investment too?"

Konnor splutters out a laugh. "Nope! I'm just an expense. But Cassidy, well, she'll be performing all over the world one day. She made a promise to stick at it, and she did. But believe me, it's pretty gruelling. Seriously brutal. I complain about university rugby, but the amount of blood, sweat, and tears she puts in every day makes *me* look like the princess."

"I love the way you talk about her. She's your little sister, so shouldn't she be annoying you and embarrassing you in front of all your friends and stealing your stuff?"

He beams at me. "*Oh,* don't you worry, she has done *all* that. Cheeky little pipsqueak."

My mouth drops open in response to the studio's grandeur; the exterior is nicer than the house Erik and I grew up in. It is a cream brick construction with a blue skillion roof and tinted windows. Decorated with an L-shaped couch in the far-left corner, a six-seater table and chairs, a built-in barbeque, and three egg wicker hanging chairs, the porch appears to be the entrance to a nice family home.

The music gets louder as we halt at the door, and I recognise the song playing immediately. It's "Riptide" by Vance Joy.

"This isn't ballet music," I say, arching an inquisitive brow at him.

Konnor rolls his eyes. "I'm a bit embarrassed to admit I know this, but she is probably freestyling... Like, um, warming up."

I crack up laughing when my manly rugby-playing boyfriend uses a word like *freestyling*. I just can't help myself and try to refrain from clutching my stomach as the laughter shoots through my abdomen. "You needed a brother, hey?" I manage.

"God, yeah, I *really* did."

When Konnor opens the studio door, we are overwhelmed by lights and music. Apart from a few doors, mirrors cover every inch of the walls and railing runs the full length of two of them. The ceiling has more downlights than necessary and a few strategically positioned spotlights.

Cassidy doesn't notice us. Konnor presses his finger to his lips and then points to her as she glides across the room, watching herself in the mirror. She's tiny. As she slides and bounces around with perfect precision, a huge smile stretches across her face. She is genuinely enjoying herself as she twirls around. She makes each movement look purposeful, elegant, and fun. Her strawberry-blonde hair, with wisps of red, is in a high ponytail and sways as she moves. She is wearing a pink leotard, tight black shorts that display her lean legs, and thigh-high white stockings. I can't help but smile at her because she looks incredibly beautiful and free-spirited.

Her eyes pop out when she sees our reflections in the mirror. Coming to a complete stop, she yells, "Konnor!"

Bolting over to us, she slams into him. He grunts on impact. He envelops her in his arms and arches his back to lift her off her feet. She squeals, leaning on him and kicking her legs off the ground. He places her back on the floor and bumps her playfully. They both share a grin.

He turns to me. "This is Blesk."

She waves. "Hi, welcome to the thunder dome." Grabbing hold of Konnor, she yells over the music, "Come dance with your sister." She beams at him and tugs at his hand, attempting to pull him further into the room. While she beckons Konnor over, I get a better view of her facial features. I know she is eighteen, but she looks much younger, with delicate freckles on her nose and cheeks.

He digs his heels in. "Pipsqueak, no."

She scoots backwards into the centre and waves her hands in a silly way, gesturing him over. "Come on, come on..."

He gazes at me, playfully exasperated. "*Seeee* what I have to deal with."

My cheeks ache from smiling at Cassidy while she bounces around and begs Konnor to dance with her. I shrug and grin at him.

"Come on, you're a beautiful dancer!" she yells over to him.

He shakes his head adamantly. "No, Cass."

"You owe me for missing my birthday!" Her words are only faintly audible over the music pulsing from the overhead speakers.

Konnor sighs, tilting his head back in defeat and rolling his eyes. "Thank God Jax isn't here!"

He walks over to her and takes her in his arms. She straightens her back as they formalise their stance in unison, sticking their noses up to the ceiling in a feigned snooty way. Chuckling together, they begin to waltz. Her movements are fluid, both weightless and feather-like. She shuffles her feet with ease as Konnor pretends to lead. Whipping her body around, she exaggerates each step. The young girl in his arms adores him so obviously, it makes me want to cry those awesome tears again.

He did learn to waltz.

They have done this many times before, that much is

clear. He pretends to be embarrassed when he flashes me a quick look, but he isn't, not even a little bit. As they move across the room effortlessly, I fall even more in love with him. Because he *is* a beautiful dancer, a beautiful brother, a beautiful boyfriend... and a beautiful person.

He is just so very beautiful.

twenty-seven: konnor

Konnor

AS THE WATER runs heavily down my head, soaking my hair and splashing onto the tiles below my feet, I find myself smiling. Downstairs, a few short metres away from where I'm standing, Cassidy, Elise, and the love of my life are all laughing and getting to know each other. Jax is already in the guest bedroom, having fallen into a food coma after his and Cassidy's stupid cupcake challenge.

Though everyone else had put their bets on Jax, I wasn't so naive as to discount Cass.

Jaxon 7: Cassidy 9.

Where does she put it? I just don't know, but we should have her tested. It's quite freakish.

I smile underneath the spray. I truly never thought this moment would come. My past and present really have collided today. Although I've forced this on Blesk, I knew she'd be welcomed with open arms. Cassidy loves everyone, sees the good in everyone. My parents are unrivalled in their tactful and tolerant natures. Everyone gets a chance and, more often than not, seconds and thirds. I should know.

Grabbing the soap, I begin to lather myself up and down. It doesn't feel any different being back here, in my room. It feels like nothing has changed.

When Blesk pries herself away from Cassidy's grip and joins me upstairs, the first thing I'm going to do is show her the window I used to jump out of every night just because I could. Although my room is on the second story, there is a lattice fencing on the outside of my wall that I can easily climb down. I run my hands up my face and through my hair, rubbing the suds through my scalp and then washing them out. My mind drifts to the envelope we've put off opening.

Is there actually closure awaiting us within or are we being played by a sick, twisted man as a part of his last hurrah? I just don't feel ready to open it. I have no idea what I'm going to see. I'm not sure I'm ready to know.

Pushing that aside, I think about my girl again. I love how quickly Duch and Cassidy have bonded, even though they couldn't be more different, physically and mentally. Cassidy had everything handed to her. Even though she is an awesome little soul, she never had to want for anything. While Blesk was neglected, abused, and deceived and yet, has come out the other end with an incomprehensible purity. Standing naked in the shower is not the best time to be thinking about her purity or... her in general. I breathe deeply as I stare down at my drumming cock, which is slowly gaining in density.

I wonder how much time I have.

On a deep exhale, I wrap my hand around my favourite appendage and start to jerk off. What does she look like naked? My shoulder and forehead meet the tiles as I begin to pant through the steam, drawing my hand up and down. What noise does she make when she comes? What would she look like on her knees, sitting below me right now, staring up at me while I pump into her throat?

Fuck.

I lean against the tiles harder. I stop tugging on my cock to enclose my fist tightly around the crown. Zaps of warning shoot through my abdomen, but I ignore them, liking the tightness. I groan. "Blesk." I grunt her name between pants. "Blesk." I rock my hips into my palm faster, wrap my hand tighter. "Blesk... Fuck." My mouth parts. Thinking about her...her breasts. Her sweet scent. I fuck my fist hard. My legs start to buckle. My bicep trembles and a long hiss passes my lips.

Then I hear footsteps in the hallway. *Fuck!*

Think about something else...

My mum. My dad. Grandma walking around the house naked.

A heavily obese man covered in jelly.

Yep, that did it.

Turning the water to cold, I breathe deeply and focus on regulating my heart rate. But when the door clicks open, I freeze. Blesk must have come up. The lapping of the water around my body interrupts the sound of her feet moving across the bedroom floor. My body responds to her proximity. My pulse speeds up again and my cock ignores the cold water. The door to the bathroom opens, lodging air in my throat.

"Konnor, do you mind if I brush my teeth?" I hear her ask so quietly her words are only faintly distinguishable.

Fuck, no, I don't mind!

"Yeah, Duch, come in!" I call out.

Moments pass, then seconds, but I don't hear water flushing through the tap or any other sound, for that matter. I frown and concentrate on her movements until I can't stand the suspense any longer. I pull the curtain back just enough to see her.

Oh. My. God.

My heart starts to drum in my cranium like a damn machine gun firing. She is standing completely naked in front of me, staring at me and breathing heavily. I pull the curtain back the whole way. Taking her all in, every part of me starts to race, my mind, my pulse. She gulps and forces a nervous smile. Her eyes rake me unabashedly. Hovering on my erection, she draws in a quick breath before returning her gaze to my face.

She moves towards me slowly—apprehensively. And *fuck me...* Her breasts sit heavy and full, nipples firm and the perfect shade of pink. Her skin is flawless. And that stomach —fuck—soft, flat, and perfect. My eyes drop and I'm suddenly on the edge of frenzy.

Fuck, she's magnificent.

Cleairng my throat, I quickly adjust the water temperature. "Duch, you—"

She cuts me off as she steps into the shower. "*Shhhh*, I want to."

"How much have you had to drink, baby?" I ask guardedly, taking a few small steps backwards so my hands can't grab her and pull her into me. I feel not unlike a crazed animal being backed into a corner.

"A few glasses of wine, Konnor. Stop pretending you're a gentleman, Konnor. I know you aren't like this with other girls."

My eyes scroll her body. The water splashing over my

shoulders makes contact with her chest, leaving beads trickling down her skin.

"Well, you aren't like other girls," I state.

She leans in and kisses me, sliding her tongue into my mouth and humming against my lips. I'm naked and she's in my arms —naked. My arms wrap around her tiny waist and pull her into me. As her skin rubs against mine, I grab at her with more need. She goes limp against me, giving me complete control to manoeuvre her around the shower. My cock twitches, pressed between our bodies. I want to go slow. I want to savour this, revel in it, but goddamn it if my hands don't want to be everywhere all at once.

I need more fucking hands.

I feed my fingers through Blesk's hair, forcing her lips harder against mine

I love you.

My lips trail their way desperately down her chin to my favourite part of her neck where her pulse throbs frantically, and then all over the delicate skin around her chest.

I love you.

My hands trace the perfect curve of her back, caressing her spine from the nape of her neck to her bum.

I love you.

I grip her spectacular arse cheek, sinking my fingers into her flesh, and grind her into my pelvis.

I love you.

I'm *so* ready. I'm painfully hard. My erection jerks around between us, contracting with want. She feels so *fucking* good.

She leans into my ear and purrs, "Is this what you want?"

God, yes.

"Only if you want it, Duch," I say against her skin, breathless already, like a damn rookie. I glide my hand forward from her arse to stroke her supple stomach until I am cupping her breast, squeezing it and groaning as I use my palm to stimulate her nipple. My pelvis rocks against her hip. Then I lose it, impatiently pushing her against the wall of the shower. Grabbing her leg, I wrap it around my back. She gasps. The water from the shower makes our bodies slide together effortlessly and warm. Rubbing myself against her, I kiss her more deeply, mashing our mouths. My hand feeds through the middle of our bodies, and I position the tip of my erection between her legs.

"Oh God, Duch, thank you, baby. Thank you for wanting me like this," I moan, feeling her wetness rub along the crown of my cock.

Her lips suddenly cease moving and I hear a small whimper escape them.

A good whimper, I think. I pull away to look into her eyes.

Where did all the air go? My heart stops.

She's... *crying*.

Fucking crying.

I frown. "What's going on?"

Her bottom lip trembles. Her eyes look everywhere except where they should —at me.

I think my heart just broke.

My hands drop from her as I take a wary step back. "What's going on, Blesk?"

She blinks through the water, beads getting stuck in her lashes and running down her cheeks.

Silence.

"Dammit, what's going on?" She stares at the white tiles beneath her feet, seemingly concentrating on breathing. "Duchess?" I beg again, my voice crackling, panicked.

I don't think I can breathe.

I grab her chin and try to make her look at me, but she purposely deflects my gaze.

"What have I done? Tell me and I will *never* do it again?"

After several painfully long seconds, she finally stares straight at me through empty, shallow pools. I blink and tilt my head, trying to analyse the void in front of me. All the love she showed me today is lost from her gaze.

She murmurs in a half-voice I barely recognise, "Don't *ever* thank me for that again."

"What?"

She strangles a sob. "Isn't this what you want? Isn't this how you treat women?"

"What?" I shake my head, lost in her words.

"How many of those other girls am I not like?" she whispers so damn sadly my insides contort.

"What?"

"Last week," she mumbles. "The week before that. How many girls am I not like?"

My stomach sinks.

Her broken little voice as it is right now, at this moment, our most intimate moment to date, will forever haunt me.

"Baby," I say, my tone edging on desperation. "We weren't together."

Her lip stiffens. "That isn't what I asked."

"Don't do this, Duch. Plea—"

"Just answer the question, Konnor!"

"Where are you hearing this from?"

"Tell me it isn't true. Tell me that the girl I met downstairs was lying to me. Tell me that Cassidy's friend, Faith, who just dropped by, was lying to me. That you didn't sleep with her and her friend Maggie last week—"

Fuck.

I brace myself on the tiles at my side, trying to keep my balance while my head spins.

Fucking Faith and her big mouth.

Her tears start to flow. I can practically taste them, feel them inside me, stinging. "Tell me that you didn't sleep with them and then make them leave the very next morning. Tell me you didn't treat them like whores. Tell me she's lying."

I stare at the water rushing through the drain because I don't know what else to do. "It isn't a lie."

She winces.

All the weight of every emotion smashes down on top of me, fracturing little pieces of my heart everywhere. I couldn't breathe without her last week. I couldn't think. That wasn't me. She must know that. The look in her eyes right now, I want it to stop because it is cutting me up.

"So?" she cries. Spluttering, she barely chokes her words out between whimpers. "Answer the question."

"We weren't together," I say again, my eyes deep with regret.

"So if I slept with lots of guys last week, that would be okay with you?"

No, it would destroy me.

Dammit.

My eyes shut as I try to wipe the image of her face right now from my mind, hoping that when I open them, she isn't still looking at me like that. They stay shut until I hear her moving, then they fly open and I grab her wrist. I'm desperate. She tugs away from me with a small whimper. Stepping out of the shower, she wraps a towel around her and leaves me standing here, motionless and completely wrecked. Those girls meant nothing to me, less than nothing. Yet, my sweet-hearted Duchess seems to find that the worst part. I've never felt self-loathing like I do right now.

Both my palms meet the tiles on either side of the faucet. I dip my head between them, focusing on breathing out my frustration. How am I going to fix this? There is no question, I have to. It *has* to be fixable. I breathe through the fall. She hasn't left my room, so that's a good sign. I would have heard her leave if she had.

Then it hits me: Faith may still be downstairs.

I jump out of the shower, quickly dry myself off, and wrap the towel around my waist. I cautiously enter the bedroom. Blesk is lying under the covers, her back to me. Even though we are fighting, even though she hates me right now, her beautiful body cocooned in my blankets, in my childhood bedroom, is a lovely sight. I am going to fix this. Within seconds, I have a pair of grey track-pants and a black tee-shirt on and am heading downstairs. They'll be drinking in the game room.

When I enter, Elise, Faith, and Cassidy are all laughing together around the pool table. Faith is leaning over it to take a shot at a far pocket. Her tits are pushed up tight in her white camisole; her hair drapes down her cheeks. She's a good-looking chick —ashy-blonde hair, pretty petite features, but she doesn't hold a torch to Blesk. Knowing she's caused Blesk unnecessary pain makes me wish she were a guy. A scowl contorts my face. My eyes narrow as I focus on her, and my fingers dig into my palms. Cassidy grins at me, but then her face crumbles when she sees my expression.

"What's up with you, big brother?" she asks suspiciously.

I pace towards Faith, who takes quick steps backwards. "What did you say?" I growl.

"Konnor! What are you doing?" Cassidy grabs my arm before I get too close to her friend.

"I didn't say anything!" Faith yells at me.

Waving Cassidy off, I lean towards Faith. "Don't lie to me. Why are you talking shit?"

"I'm not," she says. "I didn't lie about anything."

"What are you two talking about?" Cassidy cries, her voice sounding pained.

I back Faith into a corner. "You knew the score. You knew what it was. I told you I was in love with Blesk. You knew exactly how it was and wanted to hook up anyway."

"I know," she admits.

"So why are you acting like a woman scorned and talking shit to Duch?"

She smirks, her brow lifting. "Duch?"

I shake my head warningly. "Don't start."

"Konnor, slow down," Elise pleads from behind me.

I freeze in my tracks, flashing a quick apologetic look at Elise and Cassidy. Then I turn back to Faith.

Calm down.

Taking a big breath, I intentionally soften my gaze. "*Sorry,* I've been drinking for the past five hours. I'm sorry if I upset you last week." I shrug questioningly. "I must have, right? For you to go running your mouth."

Faith snickers. "Konnor, you're such an arsehole. You act all sweet and innocent, but you *use* people."

Oh my God! I throw my hands up. "You used me that night just as much as I used you," I growl, my jaw working uncomfortably beneath my skin.

"Okay, that's enough!" Cassidy states, stepping between Faith and me. "Faith, you should leave."

"Cassidy?" she whines, insulted.

"No!" she snaps. "He's my brother, and he was in a really bad place when we visited him. What did you do?"

"*Riiiight...* so I seduced him. Did Maggie also seduce

him?" she hisses, folding her arms defensively across her chest and leaning back on her heels.

"No, I didn't say that," Cassidy states adamantly. "I know what my brother is like. I'm not naive. But if you actually did say something to Blesk tonight, then that fricking sucks, Faith! Because we listened to him crying his eyes out about how much he loves her, so whatever happened between you two when I left is not *all* his fault. Don't make him the bad guy. You knew where his head was at."

Elise scowls at Faith before saying, "If a guy fucks a girl when she's drunk and sad, it's basically a criminal offense. I'd know. My mums love those cases." She raises a brow, knowing all too well my state of mind during that time of my life. I doubt I actually picked up any of those girls. I was way too fucked. "You took advantage."

And I feel like Charlie with my own team of angels.

Faith rolls her eyes. "Whatever. That's fucking stupid."

"No it isn't," Cassidy says.

Faith sneers. "What if he forced me, hey? He *was* drunk?"

"Are you fucking serious?" I yell, moving towards her more aggressively. "Are you fucking serious right now?"

Elise grabs my shoulders and halts me. I let her.

I wish Faith were a guy...

"Let me handle this, Konnor," Cassidy states. "Faith, get out!" She points towards the door. "I know Konnor wouldn't do that, so just get out because you are upsetting him and that's upsetting me. I barely ever get to see him, so please just go."

"Just gang up on me then."

"Konnor." I hear Duch's voice come from behind me.

We all turn and peer up at Blesk standing in the doorway, looking uncomfortable. She fidgets with her hands and scoots her feet. She is wrapped in my robe and I can't help but wonder what is underneath.

My pulse starts to thunder. I inhale a big breath and jog over to her. Taking her hand in mine, I kiss her knuckles. As my lips touch her skin, I peer up at her, silently pleading for forgiveness. For her to be okay. For us to be okay. For everything to go back to the way it was two hours ago.

She forces a smile. "Please just come to bed."

They are the best five words in the world to me right now. "Okay," I say definitively. "Elise, you know where your room is, right?"

Elise nods. "Yep. Wally, do you need me?"

Blesk shakes her head a few times. "No, no. I'm okay. I'll talk to you in the morning."

Placing my hand on the small of her back, I steer her up the stairway and into my bedroom. When I close the door behind us and lean my back against it, she turns to stare straight at me.

"I'm sorry," she mutters, wiping her sleepy eyes. "I had one too many glasses of wine and—"

"Stop," I interject. "Don't. Don't apologise to me. You're right. You were right. I acted like an arsehole while we were apart."

I move towards her. Placing my hands on her hips, I sink down into a squat to look her straight in the eyes. "But, baby, I'm monogamous. When you left that day, it destroyed me. I'd lost you once and I just couldn't cope with losing you again. Really, it *broke* me. I acted like an idiot. I treated people like crap. I slept with a few girls, baby, and I did treat them badly. I'm so, so sorry. But I *am* monogamous now, I swear. I'm yours. I was yours before I knew you, Duch." I dip my head when she starts to cry, trying to maintain eye contact with her. "There is only you.

There was only ever you. And if you ever realise you are too good for me, *which you are,* then there will *still* only ever be you."

As my hands gently rub her hips, her robe slides open. Peeking out from between it is a little, black silk nightgown that ends halfway up her thighs. Her wavy blonde hair streams down over her breasts. Shuffling nervously in place, she breathes in sharply.

Fuck me, she's stunning.

She swallows hard. "I got jealous."

My chest aches.

I exhale a long deep breath. "You *never* ever have to be jealous."

"But I don't get jealous," she whispers. "I never have."

A sad chuckle escapes me. "Yeah, it sucks, hey?"

She blinks at me, seemingly contemplating something. "How many girls?"

Ashamed by my lack of an actual number, I stare at the ground. "A few."

"Did you ..." She sniffles and shuffles her feet. "Did you care about any of them?"

"If I say yes, you'll hate me. If I say no, you'll hate me."

She grimaces. "Just say the truth."

I groan and rub my face roughly with my palms. "No. But you agree, we weren't together, right? We weren't together, so I didn't cheat on you, right?"

She gives me a sad little nod. "I know that in your head you weren't cheating on me. I know that."

"I would never *ever* cheat on you. I want one girl, just one. You," I state.

Her tears begin to fall harder down her cheeks. "She said she made love with you last week. She said the words *made love.* I just couldn't breathe when she said that."

I chuckle and shake my head slowly. "Duch, I don't know if I've ever 'made love'."

"I wasn't even really mad. I told you it was over, so you didn't owe me anything. But it still hurts so much. I can't imagine a worse feeling. It's sickening. I'm scared of this feeling. I'm so scared of wanting you this much." Panic fills her voice. "Or you wanting someone else. I can't even imagine you with anyone else. *God, please,* Konnor, if you don't want me, just—"

Gripping her tighter, I stare her dead in the eye. "Duch, I have only ever loved you. I will only ever love you."

The slightest glimpse of relief flashes through her expression. "Yes... but do you want just me?"

I wipe a tear from her cheek with my thumb. "Even when I was with them, I only thought of you. I only want you."

She sinks into my grip and releases a strained laugh. "I feel like I'm going crazy."

"Hey, join the club." I laugh. "You can be the deputy if you want, but I already got dibs on president."

She offers me a soft smile. "Konnor, I'm *so* crazy." She pauses, the words seemingly stuck in her throat. "I love you... I am so crazy in love with you."

The air thickens. My eyes start to water. My legs can no longer hold me straight.

My heart fucking flips.

She loves me.

I've waited a long time to hear her say that.

My hands cup her cheeks. "*Fuck,* Blesk," I say, barely holding myself together. "I love you. I love you so fucking much!"

I kiss her. I kiss her knowing that I love her and that she loves me.

Sliding the robe off her shoulders, I watch it fall to her feet.

Walking her backwards towards my bed, I shield her head when she hits the mattress, then crawl on top of her.

My arm tucks under her back as I position her on the bed so her hair is fanned across my pillow. I press my lips to hers. Her mouth moves lovingly on mine while her slender fingers gently hold my back. As small sighs of contentment escape her, I try to memorise those noises.

Shuffling my hand out from under her, I reluctantly pull my lips from hers, and position myself on my elbows, aligning our sight. The feel of her silky dress under me drives me out of my mind. I comb strands of her hair from her face as I gaze at her red lips and heavy-lidded eyes.

She loves me.

Leaning in, I press our foreheads together. "Can I kiss you more?"

She blinks at me, batting her lashes nervously. "You can do anything you want to me."

I think I speak for men everywhere when I say... *Best. Sentence. Ever.*

My lips find hers again, becoming needy. Desperate. I kiss her chin, licking a line down from her jaw to her neck and up again. As I trace the column of her throat, her pulse beats against my tongue.

She loves me.

Without thinking or over analysing, I remove my pants with one hand, shuffling them down to my ankles and off my feet. My shirt comes off next in one quick motion. I fling it across the room, hitting a lamp, which prompts a nervous giggle from Blesk. I stare down at her. She's smiling now and it's adorable.

My elbows take my weight as my bare chest presses

down on top of her tiny silky torso. When she parts her thighs for me to move between, my cock jerks with need. I want to be inside her so bad, and *my God,* I think she's going to let me. Her hands brush through my hair. A giggle escapes her. I nuzzle her neck, applying chaste kisses to every inch of skin I can reach.

She loves me.

Leaning on one arm, I use my free hand to caress and tease her outer thigh. She closes her eyes on a deep breath and presses her head back harder into the pillow. A little shiver rushes along her skin as I slide her dress up above her hips. I seek out the fabric of her knickers... but all I feel is smooth skin

My groin throbs, turning into a steel rod pressed between her legs.

God, she's going to let me.

An unwelcoming feeling floods my stomach, filling the pit of it with shame.

I don't want her to *let* me. I want her to *want* me. My hand stops at her hip. Her bare skin feels so soft and fucking beautiful, it pushes me to the edge of frenzy. But goddamn it, this moment is too important to fuck up. I can't feel like I did last time. If she starts crying again, it will destroy me.

"What's wrong?" she asks, sliding her hands up and down my back.

I sink my teeth into my bottom lip. Although my cock hates me and every other part of my being curses this decision, I roll onto my back beside her and will my pulse to steady.

"I can't," I state, trying to concentrate on the ceiling and nothing that is throbbing impulsively.

There is a moment of silence where neither one of us moves. It's a sad silence. Then she takes a loud breath in and sits up. Sliding her leg over my hip, she straddles me. Her hands stroke a path down my abdomen. My muscles pulse in response. Her pussy hovers only inches above my erection, naked and bare and hot.

Fuck, I won't be able to stop myself again.

Her nightgown hangs over the slopes of her breasts, but her impeccable nipples protrude through the material. My hands slide up her thighs, feeling the heat from her skin and the ridge of her hip bones beneath the silk. She gazes down at me with heavy eyes. My cock throbs at the view of her on top of me. That natural blonde hair, those perfect tits... This is my heaven.

Relaxed on the mattress, I stroke her stomach up to the curve where her plump breasts meet her fragile ribs. I trace each curve up and down through the silk of her dress.

"What are you doing, Duch?" I watch her expression sort through so many emotions.

"I want to do this," she whispers, breathing heavily.

"Why?" I ask, wanting to hear her tell me she loves me again.

"I want to make you happy...I don't want you to ever want to be with anyone else. You are so good to me. You've been the best friend a girl could ever have. You've been so patient with me, and I know I'm not easy to be around sometimes."

My heart sinks.

Given the look on her face, she sees it.

I sigh. "They are *all* the wrong reasons. I will never *ever* want to be with anyone else. But, baby, what are you thinking? You don't owe me anything for me being your best friend or for being patient or for loving you." I can't hide the disappointment in my voice. "I don't want you to do this because you want to make *me* happy. Your mere existence makes me happy. I want you to do this because it will make *you* happy. I want you to *want* to give yourself to me. I want to love you, Duch, touch you everywhere so you feel precious, worshipped."

She peers sheepishly down at me. Pressing her palms on my chest for support, she wriggles her naked thighs over my hips. Fuck. I feel an overwhelming need to bite my bottom lip, needing to suppress a groan.

"Konnor, I've only been with one person," she mutters.

Fury crosses my face. *"Erik..."*

She nods, looking almost ashamed. My face tightens as anger weighs my heart down, but my hands don't stop tracing her body in case this is the last memory I have of it. She could run at any moment. I'm memorising her bends with my fingertips, making a mould in my mind of what perfection should feel and look like. I want to make her feel good. I want her to *want* me. I want to love her completely with my mind and my body.

I want to touch her, feel her insides clutching around me. I want to fucking remove any memory of him inside her and replace it with me, fill her with me.

She gasps when I sit up. Twisting, I quickly roll her beneath me. I part her thighs with my hips and slide up along that silky black nightgown until my lips brush hers. My hand strokes her hair tenderly as I stare straight into her deep brown eyes.

"Duch, I want to make *you* feel good. Every part of you is so beautiful. I need you to know just how much I worship you, that your body is not an object to me, it's a *fucking* shrine. This will be about *me* making *you* feel good."

Her eyes flutter under me. She pauses for a few long moments. "I've never felt good doing this."

My jaw locks and I need a moment to process everything

she is saying and not saying. All I can think is that I want to make her feel good. I want her to enjoy this because right now, I understand why she has been so reluctant. She has been used, enjoyed, but never appreciated.

It has never been for her pleasure, only for his.

Calming breaths... Calming breaths...

"Baby," I whisper in her ear, "I love you. If you want me to stop, you just say it, and I will."

When she doesn't stop me, I crawl down her. My lips ever-so-slightly caress the silk of her dress. I nuzzle my way down her stomach, her navel, and the seam of her gown until my shoulders are between her naked thighs. My eyes stay glued on hers until her head falls back onto the pillow.

She pants loudly as I glance at her breasts. They look magnificent from here; their frantic motion up and down is crazy hot.

When I lower my gaze, I get snagged on a scar. A huge scar that runs down the inside of her left thigh. I wince, squeezing my eyes together.

I hate that scar.

I hate that I wasn't there to stop her, to pull her from the tub, to hold her when she cried. I breathe through the pain. When I'm finally able to open my eyes again, I lean in and kiss the scar that I hate so much. She whimpers. I kiss it again. And again. And again. And again.

"Never again," I say.

She sighs. "Never."

Threading my arms under her thighs, I position her legs over my shoulders and leisurely trace the contours of her torso. "Just say stop," I say again. "This is so *you* feel good, baby, because I worship you. When you're ready, Duchess, put your hands on the back of my head."

Gripping her hips, I pull her towards my mouth. She

moans. She is perfect. Every part of her is pink and soft and sweet. Lapping my tongue up her slit, I then latch onto her clit, mouthing it softly, allowing her to relax, to give in to the sensation. Her thighs tighten around my head. Silky smooth flesh rubs against the stubble on my jaw.

She tastes as perfect as she looks. My groans of pleasure fill the room as loudly as hers do. Rocking my hips into the mattress, I apply more pressure to that throbbing little coil. Her beautiful skin is warm and slick against my mouth.

"Konnor," she moans.

"Blesk," I gasp, rubbing my erection harder against the mattress. When her fingers grab my hair, I take it upon myself to up the stakes. Opening her up with my thumbs, I then push one inside her. She bucks below me slightly, squirming and panting my name. *My* fucking name.

I speak against her hot flesh. "Every part of you is so amazing."

The vibrations of her moans course through me, forcing more pressure to my erection. I seriously don't know how long I can hold out for. My cock is acting like a damn teenager. Her insides tighten around my thumb as I push in deeper. I can't wait to feel those smooth muscles kneading around my cock. I suck on her harder. Make love to her with my thumb faster. She writhers, panting and wriggling. She's so close. Her fingers tighten in my hair. Her walls squeeze me. Hips tilt up into me. She cries out, whimpering *my* name and God's.

Her thighs crush against my cheeks as she shudder. Silky liquid leaves her as I assault her with my tongue. I lap at her, loving her noises, her taste, her squirming. Love fucking her with my tongue through her orgasm until she sinks into the mattress.

"Oh God, Konnor," she breathes, raising her arm to cover her forehead.

A grin tugs at my mouth. "Yeah, I know, right?"

She slaps my arm as I crawl up her body and settle between her legs. I peer down at her. Her face is flushed and the most adorable grin plays on her lips. "Was that nice, baby? Do I get permission to do that again sometime?"

She giggles, her cheeks glistening and pink. "Yep. Permission granted."

I cock a brow at her. "I get a high distinction then?"

She smirks. "Well, I didn't set the bar very high—"

"Cheeky little thing," I say, attacking her delicate ribs with my fingers. She giggles and squirms beneath me, her pelvis rolling over my erection. Groaning, my fingers stop. "Fuck, I'm so hard baby. I want you. Do you want me?"

She sucks a quick breath in and slowly nods. "Yes."

"I'll go slow, okay?" I swallow hard, crazy nervous to finally be inside her, to finally feel her. "I want you to go on top, Duch. I want you to be in control. I think it's important." Darting her eyes away, she lowers her head. "Hey"– I tilt her chin up– "don't be shy."

"I've never..." Her brows tighten. "I've never done that. I wouldn't know what to do. Oh God, this is *so* embarrassing to say."

"Don't be silly. I like that I can share firsts with you. Never be embarrassed about that. You go on top. I'll still do everything, okay?"

She nods.

I reach for my wallet on the bedside table and pull out a condom. "Do you want me to wear one?"

"I'm on the pill."

Enough said. I throw the condom to the floor. Rolling over, I pull her on top of me. Gripping her dress, I yank it over her head. My heart thrashes against my ribcage. Her naked skin glistens with remnants of her arousal. Her mouth parts as she breathes through her nerves. Without her dress on, I can see her whole extraordinary body open to me. My cock is so hard it aches.

"I want you so bad. You're so fucking beautiful."

She leans forwards and presses her lips to mine, sliding her tongue slowly and lovingly inside my mouth.

"I love you," I say against her lips. "So much." Ending our kiss, I look between our bodies and wrap my hand around my aching erection. I position myself in between her beautiful folds, grip her hips, and slowly lower her down on top of me.

The relief is almost blinding.

Each inch forces a hiss from my mouth as I feel her stretch around me, see her shudder and pant, and hear her moan. "Oh God, Blesk, you feel so good. I love you. I love you so much." I gaze into her eyes. "Are you here with me?"

"Yes," she breathes. Her lips latch onto mine. We kiss and pant in rhythm with her rolling hips. "I love you, Konnor." She gasps. Sweat builds up between our bodies. Her breasts slide along my chest. I pump my pelvis up into her, needing to be deeper, needing to be closer. Holding her at the root of my cock, I cup one of her breasts. Breaking our kiss, I wrap my mouth around her nipple and suck. As she trembles around me, she starts to move on her own, slipping up and down my length.

"Oh, fuck, baby, yes, like that," I growl against her flesh. Groans rumble up my throat and vibrate against her nipple, hardening it further on my tongue.

"Konnor," she moans again as her arse slaps against my thighs. That sound... *that fucking sound.* I release her nipple with a pop. Cupping her cheeks, I thrust my tongue inside her mouth, swallowing all her sounds of pleasure. They are mine. All those sounds. Groaning long and low, I pick up pace. I'm inside Blesk. Her scent is all over me; mine is all over her. She is finally fucking mine. I want to go slow. But I can't. How can I? I'm glad she's on top or I'd be animalistic by now.

"Tell me it feels good," I gasp against her mouth. "Please. I need to hear you say it."

"Feels so good, Konnor," she moans, closing her eyes shut.

She tightens around me. Her breathing becomes even more laboured as she begins slamming down on me. Harder. Faster. Her hips quake.

"Oh God, Konnor," she cries out as she climaxes.

"Fuck," I hiss, sinking my fingers into her hips — so close to coming. I drag her up and down my cock as she loses momentum to her own orgasm. I am right there. My balls tighten. My abdomen surges with fire. A wave of heat rushes up my thighs, the sensation too much, too intense. I grunt, slam her down on me, and come deep inside her, groaning and growling with each burst. As my vision fades momentarily with pleasure, all I see is stars flickering.

"*Fuck,* that was the most intense orgasm of my life!" I pant.

Collapsing on top of me, she buries her head in my chest and hugs my torso. I envelop her with my arms and close my eyes, feeling myself drifting off almost immediately.

What a day.

She loves me. I want to be hers. I want more than anything for her to be mine. A small hum leaves my lips as my arms tighten around her lax body. I love feeling her heart beating against my torso. She didn't stop me this time. She didn't stop me from loving her.

THE NEXT MORNING comes out of nowhere because I barely remember falling asleep. My eyes flicker open, and the smile that eludes my face is ridiculous and wonderful all at once. With Blesk curled up like a cat on my chest, her feet tangled with mine and her breath warming my skin, I am the epitome of content.

Sex is great. In fact, it is irrefutably one of my all-time favourite pastimes, and I think many people would agree. Sex with Blesk though... *Fuck me.* Epic. Extraordinary. Phenomenal. Mind-blowing. We fit together like a damn glove. She is perfect to roll around in bed with. Actually, 'perfect' is an insufficient word to describe being inside her. Yet, I doubt any other would suffice.

Her breathing evens with consciousness. When she wriggles against me, I press my lips to her forehead. "Morning. How did you sleep?"

"*Really, really* good." She hums as she wipes her tired eyes. Rolling off me, she stretches her arms and arches her back. She yawns before resting her cheek down on my chest and nuzzling my neck.

"You must have been so *exhausted*," I say smugly.

"You?" she asks sweetly, ignoring my hubris. She smiles up at me with sleepy brown eyes that seem even more beautiful this morning.

"Oh, yeah, it was okay, I suppose," I tease, looking away and feigning nonchalance. "I've had better."

She sticks her tongue out between her teeth, grinning up at me. "Meanie."

I place my hand over hers, feeding our fingers together and watching with strange satisfaction as they become one unit.

"What? Me?" I tease. "Surely not. I'm a delight to be around. Or under. Or on top of."

"If you do say so yourself?" She laughs, rubbing her nose along my jaw.

"Oh?" I taunt, looking mockingly confused. "Didn't hear you complaining last night. Heard you screaming. Heard you pray to God a lot and I didn't even know you were religious."

She slaps me playfully on the chest with our combined hands. "You're so up yourself."

"Actually, I was up *you*, sweetheart."

Her mouth drops open. "Konnor..."

I cringe a little. "Sorry, Duch, too far?"

"Yes," she whispers, smiling through a slight grimace.

"Okay, can I take it back?" I say in my cutest voice.

She raises her nose to the air. "Nope," she says through a sweet smile

"Well, can I kiss you then?" I ask, releasing her hand and scooting down until we're face to face. Cupping her cheeks, I press my lips to hers firmly and with passion.

Her lips stretch wider as she mutters, "No," into my mouth.

I part her lips with mine and talk against them. "Just try to stop me."

She laughs, swiping her tongue along mine. "Don't talk with your mouth full." She arches her back and presses her pelvis into me.

I pull away from our kiss. "Don't make that sound. And don't do that with your hips or you'll wake him up."

"Good morning," she purrs, stroking her fingers down my stomach and to my pelvis.

My brows shoot to my hairline. "Wow. You just spoke to my cock. Can you get any hotter right now?"

She giggles and that noise echoes between my thighs,

stimulating my standard morning tendencies even further. "That giggle was for him too, wasn't it? He seems to think so."

Her eyes sparkle as she smiles at me. "Maybe I like him more than you."

"You know what? I'm actually okay with that." Laughing, I press myself against her a little harder.

We spend hours lying in bed, sharing a pillow and kissing with our legs tangled together. Last night was perfect and so was this morning. I wish I could screenshot this, the feeling of her against me, the smell of her, and that lusty, alluring expression on her face.

This moment is the deluxe version of perfect.

twenty - eight: blesk

Blesk

AS SOON AS Konnor leaves for his morning run, his absence is palpable. Although my skin still tingles from his touch, I can't help but miss him. While I am cuddled up within the warmth of his sheets and am gloriously inundated with his scent, my mind starts to sort through the previous day's events. My love for Konnor has clearly progressed over the past few days into something as uniquely beautiful as it is petrifying.

My inability yesterday to subdue the sickening feeling that clawed at my stomach when I heard about Konnor's array of blonde conquests is unacceptable. I should be able to control those emotions. Even more so, my actions in response to them. Konnor didn't deserve that. But... my mind can't help but scroll through scenarios of him with other girls. Courting them, flirting with them, strategically showing them his dimples. Each one of them would have been beautiful and much more sexually experienced than me.

So if this is what jealousy feels like, I don't like it.

Konnor has always made me feel beautiful —with every word he speaks to me, with every use of his pet name for me, with the intensity in his eyes. And yet, I have never felt more beautiful than I did last night when he drew pleasure from my body. *God*, and when he was giving me pleasure... The things he did with his tongue smashed down all my barriers. For the first time in my life I wanted someone... I wanted to be touched.

Previously, sex had been a methodical exchange of services. Erik's love, compassion, understanding, and protection, for my body. In contrast, Konnor uses this act as a way to share himself, his vulnerabilities. He reveals his soul. Tenderness. True nature. With Konnor, every part of me ignites under his fingertips. Every feather-like caress of his tongue stimulates my pulse. When he's inside me, nothing can cause me torment. My past disappears and I'm entirely present.

In the present with him.

It was explosive, and I want to do it again and again. I want him to be mine. Which is why I can't seem to shake the thought of him being that vulnerable with another girl.

The thought of his lips against Faith's neck, of him whispering in her ear how good she feels, makes me sick to my stomach. My mind involuntarily flashes with images of them together, her slim body pressed below his strong athletic physique. Did he cuddle her after? Did he stroke her hair? Kiss her with the same amount of passion as he did with me?

Get over it, Blesk.

He wants you.

Pulling my phone out from under my pillow, I unlock it and check my messages.

Elise: You okay after last night, Wally?

I text back, knowing her phone is permanently connected to her hand.

Blesk: Yes, I overreacted. Did you sleep well?

Elise: OMG so well, this bed is amazeballs. That Faith chick was baiting you on purpose don't worry about her. You know K only has eyes for u.

Blesk: Guess what?

Elise: The suspense is killin me.

Blesk: Guesssss...

Elise: You're really a man.

Blesk: Close but no... I had sex with Konnor last night...

Elise: How is that close? And OMG! Yay! How was it? I want all the details!

Blesk: Later... I'll draw you a picture.

Elise: Thank God, because you know I'm more of a visual learner.

Konnor comes through the door abruptly, wiping sweat from his brow and wearing nothing but long shorts that display his muscular legs. As he breathes heavily, his chest pulses with exertion and his sculptured abdomen trembles with fatigue.

Konnor's face drops when he sees my expression. "What's up, Duch? You have that face on."

"How come everyone can read my face? What face?" I ask, pulling the covers up to hide everything except my eyes.

He chuckles and sits on the edge of the bed. "The I'm-thinking-too-much-and-not-just-enjoying-the-moment face." His fingers find the edge of the covers and pulls them down below my neck. "Tell Konnor what you're thinking?"

I giggle. "You sound like Elise when you talk like that."

"She taught me everything I know." He laughs. "Now spill it."

I giggle playfully. "Nope, don't wanna."

He narrows his eyes. Still gripping the edge of the blanket, he pulls it down further. Slowly, leisurely, he exposes a little bit more of my bare skin beneath. My pulse gallops in my throat. Yearning fills his hooded eyes as he watches the covers fall below my breasts. The cold air licks at my flesh. He moistens his lips before leaning down and wrapping them around one of my nipples, sucking on it gently. As his groan reverberates through me, my body opens and melts into a hum.

He flicks my nipple with his tongue slowly at first and then a little faster. The heat from his breath blankets me. Unintentional moans escape my mouth as I fist his hair. Arching into him, I want him closer, want him everywhere. His hand runs up my stomach and squeezes my other breast.

He purrs as his tongue circles my sensitive flesh. He slowly moves his lips towards my collar bone, applying soft delicate kisses until his mouth is mashed with mine.

"I love you," he whispers against my lips. "I love your

tits." He kisses me again. "I love your skin and the way you smell." He sucks on my lower lip. "The way you taste." And then he kisses me deeper, his tongue lashing inside my mouth.

"I love you, Konnor," I reply between his kisses.

"Fuck, Duch." He tears himself away from my lips. "You don't know what hearing that means to me." His forehead presses to mine and his eyes fix tightly shut. The weight of my admission is evident in his posture and laboured breaths. This is it. This is how it should feel to be loved by someone. Every day, more and more ghosts attack us, but we execute them as a team, banishing them back to the past where they belong.

Is there anything we can't overcome now?

"I love you, Konnor," I say again. "I love you." He whimpers and then follows that sound with a hungry and loving kiss. His lips spiral me into a puddle of longing. Tingles rush down to my toes, and my arms fly around his neck, pulling him closer. I sink into our embrace. That manly scent, that longing touch, his groans, and the warmth of his body send my system into a spin.

Reluctantly pulling his lips from mine, he peers down at me. "Now tell me what you were thinking about when I walked in."

I puff out a big breath, tilting my head at him. "Okay, I was thinking about last night."

"What part, cutie?" he asks while tickling my waist.

"About whether you ..." I trail off. "Well, it isn't the same for me. You know that being with you, in that way, is beautiful. You're beautiful." A sweet smile plays on his lips. "It felt like we were connected." He cocks a brow at me, smiling suggestively. I roll my eyes at his smutty mind. "And not *just* literally." He snickers cheekily. Contentment makes him mischievous, but it looks fantastic on him. "Konnor, seriously, I want to know whether it's different for you. Is being with me different than when you are with other girls?"

His brows knit as he leans in closer, the sincerity in his eyes undeniable. "Yes. God, yes. A hundred times yes, Duch. Nothing has ever felt like that. Nothing has even come close."

"How is it different?" I ask timidly.

He exhales. His eyes dart around as he contemplates his answer. I shouldn't have asked. It was a silly thing to ask. He finally rests his line of sight back on me.

"Every time I was with a girl, there was always something missing. There was a hole —emptiness. No matter how much I tried to fill it, it only grew. As if the more I tried to fill it, the clearer the inadequacies of what I was trying to fill it with became." He clears his throat.

"What I'm trying to say is, every girl I've been inside, every girl I've touched, has only made not having you in my life more obvious. Yesterday was the first time I've ever wanted to whisper, 'You're mine' in a girl's ear. That was the first time I've ever wanted to whisper, 'I'm yours' and 'We belong to each other.' That's the first time I've ever made love, Duchess. Being with you feels like every part of me is full, finally. Nothing else feels that good, nothing ever will."

I love that answer...

I love Konnor.

And I am his.

And he's mine.

SITTING with Konnor on the porch, eating his signature waffles-with-cheese concoction, which, despite my initial reluctance, are actually delicious, gives me blissful insight into what a forever with him could look like: a big house surrounded by gardens. We would spend the weekends leisurely on the veranda, where Konnor would read the paper while I watch the kids as they run around on the grass... *Wow.* That thought came out of nowhere.

Still, I like the image in my mind.

Elise and Jax walk across the lawn with tennis rackets in their hands, waving at us. I'm not used to this kind of life. Peace. A gentle life. The sun shines through the trees, flickering us with its beams, as we sit around the table.

Konnor sits facing the landscaped garden descending the deck in front of us, with his ankle rested on his knee and his arms relaxed up on the shoulders of the chair. He's wearing a V-neck green tee-shirt that enhances his emerald eyes and a pair of black loose-fitting track-pants. His hair is messy in the most scrumptious way. He looks sexy, comfortable, and at home. As I watch him, he appears to be the master of his destiny. He is powerful for the first time. There are no shackles on this boy. No restraints.

Then a noise startles him, and he turns to look at the French doors behind us.

"Dad." Bounding up, Konnor envelops the older man in his embrace. They both beam and pat each other on the back.

"Son, are you going to officially introduce me to your lovely friend?" Ben asks.

Konnor releases him and turns towards me. "This is Blesk. She's—" He pauses and then smiles. "My girl."

"Blesk, it's a pleasure," Ben says. Turning back to his son, he adds, "Now, what are you doing here? Not that I'm not pleased to see you."

Everything about Ben is genuine, like his affection towards his family and his old-school manners. Pulling a chair out, Ben shuffles in beside us, making himself comfortable.

Despite Ben's strong figure and youthful physique, the kind wrinkles that form around his eyes divulge his true age. He has salt-and-pepper hair, is freshly shaven, and has the same hazel-coloured eyes as Cassidy.

Picking up Konnor's fork, he begins to tuck into the waffles on his son's plate. "I've missed your cheese waffles."

Konnor laughs. "They're killer, hey?"

Shovelling in a mouthful of the maple and salty cheese creation, Ben looks at me. "What did you think of them?"

I chuckle and cross my legs under the table. "Well, they are actually really nice, but it still seems weird."

"Yeah, well-" Konnor pauses and looks at me. "An old friend of mine used to put sweetcorn in with mac-and-cheese, so there is just something about the sweet and salty infusion of flavours that I really like. It reminds me of her."

My mouth drops open. My hand flies to my lips, smothering a small gasp.

He remembers.

"I didn't know that," Ben says. "I always thought it was just a happy mistake and that you were trying to sabotage breakfast."

Konnor's eyes twinkle as he feigns a scoff. "Come on, that doesn't sound like something I would do." Ben takes a sip of his son's orange juice. "Don't lie to the poor girl. Konnor was always trying to prank us growing up."

"Was he really?" I say intrigued, arching a questioning brow at Konnor. He smiles. It is strange hearing about his life from someone I don't know as I was the only one in it for so long. I am new to his family, to this life. And yet, not new at all.

Ben nods, bumping Konnor with his elbow. "Yep. He went around dying everything green for a week—"

"Oh, she doesn't need to hear this," Konnor interjects.

"Hush, son, your old man is telling a story. I woke up one morning with green hair and my work shirt was green." He laughs. "Even the damn tap water was green."

Konnor leans back in his seat, looking almost impressed. "I got me some mad skills."

I giggle. "How old were you?"

"Twelve," Ben says.

I've missed so much. Never again. "How did you make the tap water green?" I ask.

Konnor looks delightfully smug. "Well, Duchess, I'm so glad you asked. I put green jelly crystals in the faucet under the washer."

"I remember that!" a voice says from behind us. Cassidy appears and sits on her dad's knee. "What up, Daddy-o?" she says, kissing him on the cheek. Ben noticeably brightens with Cassidy in his arms and he gives her an affectionate little squeeze.

"You're too old to sit on Dad's lap, Cassidy," Konnor states, pinching her trim little stomach teasingly.

She sticks her tongue out, crinkles her nose, and feigns a bratty tone. "Daaaaad, Konnor's hitting me."

Ben grimaces at Konnor. "Now, now, Konnor, let me keep my little girl for a while longer. God knows I lost Flicker as soon she came out of the womb."

Konnor sighs and shakes his head at his little sister. "Such a bloody princess." He turns to face Ben. "Where is Flick? Cassidy just said she was away for the weekend."

"Isn't she with her new lady love?" Ben asks Cassidy.

Cassidy steals a piece of waffle and talks with her mouth

full. "Yeah, but I don't know where. Probably in Connolly somewhere."

Konnor shrugs at Cassidy, narrowing his eyes. "Who? Why Connolly? Who's she seeing?"

Cassidy chews the food in her mouth and then swallows, looking apprehensive. "You don't wanna know."

Konnor glares at her. "Who, Cassidy?

"Stacey Grange."

Ohhh, that's why he won't approve.

"I know Stacey," I say, trying not to appear completely idle. "She was friends with Erik for a while. She went to Connolly High."

Konnor's expression hardens, looking anything but impressed. "Great. So she's been hanging out with that crowd."

Ben chuckles at his son's reaction. "Don't worry, Konnor. The boys know to behave here. They've grown up a lot since you left to study."

"Are you talking about The Butcher Boys?" I ask, although I know the answer. Stacey Grange is a family friend of the Butchers. And it's a well-known fact that Stacey is off-limits romantically, apparently until now.

Cassidy peers at me questioningly. "You know them?"

Yes.

"Not really." I wave indifferently. "But doesn't everyone in the District know *of* The Butcher Boys?" I offer Konnor an apologetic smile because I know his adverse inclinations towards Max Butcher, especially after the rugby party a few weeks ago.

Konnor scoffs. "Yeah, alright. I'll have a chat with Flick when I see her next, but you stay clear of them. Please, Cassidy. They are just bad news."

"Yes, big brother." Cassidy rolls her eyes dismissively before standing up and wandering back inside the house.

"Glad you're back, son, so you can do some of the fatherly duties for me." Ben chuckles, looking proud. "It makes my life easier when you're around to watch the girls."

"I hate those guys," Konnor grumbles, folding his arms across his chest. He looks adorable when he pouts. I want to sit on his lap and smooth the lines forming between his brows. His protective nature appears to bleed out into all aspects of his life. He will make a wonderful father.

And there's that thought again...

Slow down, Blesk.

My phone vibrates with an incoming call. Konnor's eyebrows furrow as he stares questioningly at me. He mouths, "Who is it?"

The word 'Dad' flashes at me from the display, causing a strange flutter to shift through my abdomen. I stand and nod politely at Ben and Konnor before walking around the corner of the house and out of earshot.

Placing the handset to my cheek, I answer. "Dad." I lean on a pillar and hug my stomach with my free arm, staring out at Cassidy's studio.

"Kitten, how are you?" His voice echoes through the speaker.

"Why is it so echo-y?" I ask, plugging my other ear and focusing on the sounds coming through the line.

"I'm at the hospital," he says. Then I hear the beeps and hums in the background.

My pulse drums in my veins.

"Erik is awake, kitten. He's been asking for you. You're the only person he wants to see," he continues.

I am paralysed by an array of emotions —something akin

to relief laced with fear. My mouth won't respond to my mind's instructions.

Say something.

No words are forming.

"Did you hear me? I said Erik's awake," my dad repeats.

I gulp as silently as I can. "Is he okay?" My voice comes out almost strangled.

A huge relieved breath gushes through the phone. "Yes, kitten, he is. Though his short-term memory is vague, the doctor said it'll probably return. But at this stage, he doesn't remember much about the day of the assault."

Convenient.

"Does he look tall?" I ask because it's the first thing that comes to mind.

"What do you mean?" he asks, sounding concerned. "Kitten, where are you? I'll come get you."

My eyes start to well up and my lungs contract in my chest, making my breathing strained and my head dizzy.

I jump and clutch my heart when someone touches my waist. I fly around wide-eyed, to find Konnor with his hands held up in clear view, his face riveted in shock.

"Whoa, Duch." He grimaces. "What the fuck's going on?"

My face tightens as I try to stop the tears pooling in my eyes from escaping.

He ducks his head to stare me straight in the eyes. "What's going on?"

My dad's voice comes through the phone, which is now at my side. "Kitten? Blesk?"

Konnor looks down at the phone and then back at my face, drawing his brows together. Disapprovingly, he grabs it. Although I gasp when he snatches it from me, I don't try to stop him. He ends the call, then holds down the lock key until the display blackens.

Konnor pulls me into his arms, kisses my temple, and rests his cheek on my forehead. "Who was that?"

I wrap my arms around his waist, scrunch his shirt behind his back, and nuzzle his chest. His gorgeous scent makes my body melt into him on an exhale.

"That ... was my ... dad," I stammer. "Erik's awake."

I'm not sure why I'm tearing up. I'm not sure why my hands are shaking. I'm not sure why I'm equally happy and sad. "Please don't be mad at me, Konnor, please don't. But I want my brother back. I feel like I've lost him. He might as well have died because I can't see him. I can't talk to him. I feel like I'm in mourning." I peer up at his face. My chest tightens when I see how wrecked this conversation is making him. He stares straight ahead. His eyes narrow as his jaw muscles dance beneath his skin.

"Konnor, you're my best friend, but I just need to try and organise all these feelings. Baby, I'm so sorry if this hurts you." His scowl remains unwavering, trained on something in the distance. He combs my hair and keeps me tightly pressed against him, very tightly. With his heart beating ferociously against my ear, I can barely hear anything else. "Baby?"

His eyes drop down to acknowledge me, but his head stays rigidly stationary. "Duch?"

"Don't be mad," I plead.

Don't cry, Blesk.

He shakes his head just once and scoffs slightly. "I'm not mad. I can't shake this feeling, Duch, that's all. Just ignore me, say what you need to say, and we'll work through it." His tone is chillingly apathetic.

He's lying. He's mad.

I rest my cheek back against his chest, partly because I don't want to see his wounded face a second longer and partly because I want to inhale him, knowing it will help soothe the knot in my stomach.

"What do I do?" I ask defeatedly. "What do you want me to do?"

He takes a violent breath in and then slowly exhales. "I want you to be happy."

"Konnor, what do you want me to do?"

He flinches. "I hate him. The thought of him makes me feel crazy."

"I know, I know. So what should I do?"

"What does he want?" His voice sounds clipped, hoarse, and cold.

"My dad says he doesn't remember much," I admit. "But his memories may come back."

"So what, you just forgive him and pretend it never happened? Is that what you're thinking? Please tell me that's *not* what you're fucking thinking."

I shudder at his tone. "It isn't that black and white, Konnor. How do I explain to my dad why I don't want to see his son? His only living blood relative?"

"Oh, I don't know," he hisses, sarcasm lacing his words. "Maybe, just maybe, tell him he's a *fucking rapist!*"

My breath is knocked from me.

I nearly choke over his words and tone. He drops his arms to his sides and pumps his fists so hard his shoulders quake. Despite his rigid stance, I squeeze him tighter and stroke his back soothingly. His body is frighteningly taut, muscles rippling beneath my fingers as I attempt to calm him.

"Should I?" I ask. "Is that what I should do? Honestly?"

He grabs my shoulders and holds me at arm's length so he can search my expression. "I'm sorry, Duch. But look at me. I'm seething. But I love you. *Sooo fucking* much. If you want me to..." His eyes turn to slits as his voice falters. "Fuck,

I don't even know what you want." He releases my shoulders and feeds his fingers through his hair, scuffing it back and forth aggressively. "What do you want?" He groans. "What do you want from me here?"

I don't know.

"I think I need to see him," I whisper, hating the words and the feeling they evoke. "And then I'll know when I look in his eyes. I'll know."

His cheek muscles contract as he grinds his teeth together. He stares at me like I'm completely crazy. "A few seconds ago, when I touched you, you jumped. You were scared." He shakes his head. "And that isn't a normal reaction when your boyfriend touches you, Duch, *especially* when he spent a good half of last night *inside you!*" He yells the last two words. Still shaking his head, he says, "You shouldn't see him. You shouldn't be in the same room with him." I hardly notice Elise and Jaxon as they jog, bright-eyed, up the steps towards us. I glance at Elise just as her expression crumples.

I turn back to Konnor as a sob escapes me. "Come with me?"

His face distorts as if I've just slapped him. "Are you fucking *crazy?* I would strangle him with his own IV line, Duch." He grimaces and waves his hand towards Elise. "Take Elise. Fuck, I gotta go for a walk. This is such bullshit."

My mouth drops open, but before I can reply, he saunters across the property. "Konnor!" I yell out to him, desperation clutching at my voice.

"Konnor!" Elise echoes.

Jaxon jogs after him, shouting, "Slater, slow down!"

Elise walks slowly over to me. Leaning against the wall at my side, she watches me as I grip the pillar and squeeze it tightly. He hates me. I can't make everyone happy. I can't make anyone happy. I can't make my dad happy. My brother.

The love of my life. I am at a loss. For the briefest of moments, we had a glimpse at a peaceful life together, but 'life' keeps throwing obstacles at us.

"Wally, I'm going to take a leap here and say that that was about Erik," Elise whispers.

"What gave it away?" I snivel, trying to suppress all the boiling emotions. Sniffling, I wipe my eyes and look out over the perfect garden to avoid looking directly at her.

Elise moves to stand in front of me. "The, and I quote, 'I will strangle him with his own IV' bit. That part *really* gave it away."

I release the pole and look straight at her. "I'm sorry. I know what I said last time we spoke, but Erik is awake and I just got all messed up. I have to see him. I need to look him in the eyes and see if he is still my brother."

She nods, dubious. "Okay, let's do it then."

"Really?" I say with desperate hopefulness. I don't want to go alone.

"Yes, of course." She sighs. "If that's what you want to do, then I'm here to support you."

twenty-nine: konnor

Konnor

SHE HUMS SWEETLY. Rolling her shoulder to her cheek, she grins and squirms beneath the sheets. Her face is soft, *pleasured* even. As her body arches and feminine sounds of bliss escape her mouth, I move towards her and sit to the side of my bed. I can tell she's dreaming. I hope it's about me.

Fuck, yes.

My breathing quickens with hers. I shuffle my weight along the bed.

Fuck.

My hand goes to her cheek. She moves into it, applying tender pressure to my palm. I lick my lips in preparation to kiss her.

She smiles. "*Mmmm.*" She moans. "*Erik.*"

My eyes fly open and I jerk upwards.

IT DESTROYS me that whenever I close my eyes, I see him. His body grinding against hers, her dress hiked up around her waist, her underwear tangled at her ankles. Smudges of mascara line her teary eyes and there is remnants of paint in her hair. His greedy claws grasp her thighs as he presses himself into her.

What I don't see is me.

When I close my eyes, I don't see me under her, stroking her skin or rubbing her cheeks and staring into her eyes to make sure she is right there with me. I don't feel her clenching around me as I move in and out of her or see the way her lips look when she says, "I love you."

Yeah, I don't see that.

When you give someone everything, when you offer them everything you are, heart, body, mind, and soul, sometimes you end up an empty shell, like there is nothing left of you because that other person fucking took it all.

So I'm pretty intoxicated; other than the liquor burning my throat and the drumming in my cranium, I don't feel much.

I almost killed a person. I tried to kill my friend, as much of a friend as he could be with what little we have in common.

I stare up at Jax from the grassy patch I've been sitting and snoozing on for a while. "So, could I have done something different?" As I speak with my hands, the liquor in my glass sloshes around. The bourbon splashes onto my shirt. "Oh, crap," I complain, wiping it with my hand.

"Yeah, mate, that isn't going to work. That stain can just join the others," Jax says, exasperated.

"Could I? Because she *loves* him, and I could go to jail for what I did, so I just don't know anymore," I say, then laugh hysterically. Because it is so funny. Seriously. What a riot. I lie back on the grass. The condensation seeps through my shirt, making me feel not unlike I'm in a pool. I think I like it.

Jax sits on a fold-out chair beside me, nursing his glass and frowning at the horizon.

"So there you go, Jax," I slur. "Erik's been keepin' this secret from us. You jus rape a girl for a *goo* four years and then she'll eventually fall in love with you."

"Shut up, man," he groans, not making eye contact with me.

"Fuck you!" I growl.

"Slater, you're my bud. Okay? You're one of the best. Maybe, just maybe, you deserve better than this."

I sit up abruptly. "Seriously? Fuck off. She's my girl. I could never deserve better than her."

"I don't mean you deserve better than her." He exhales loudly. "Just better than this. Look, I love B, but you guys need to, like, mellow or something. Man, girls claw each other's eyes out to be with you, and you just so happen to also be a really decent bloke. A much better bloke than Erik. All I'm saying, and doing a crap job of it, is look after yourself too."

"I love her," I say very matter-of-factly.

"Yeah, I know you do. And she loves you," he states emphatically.

I scoff and splutter my drink out.

Does she love Erik?

He has been her everything, lived in her house, held her while watching scary movies. He's been in her room. Been in her bed. Been inside her! I groan as these thoughts pass through my mind, bringing with them more unwelcome images.

When the police told me that Liz was in heaven, I believed them despite the concept of the word *heaven* being foreign. I didn't even try to find her.

When the police declare someone's death, then they are dead. If only I'd followed my gut. If only I'd searched for her. Then maybe I could have been what she needed. Maybe I could have stopped her from slicing her thigh open. Could have stopped him from touching her. Could have loved her every day of her life preceding this one and everyday hereafter.

I wince and hug my stomach. "Do you think she loves him?"

Jax exhales loud enough for me to hear. "I don't know."

OVER THE NEXT FIVE HOURS, I manage to drink my weight in alcohol despite Jax's best efforts to moderate me. I've passed out twice.

When I hear the friction of the Prado's tyres on the pavement and that familiar low howling that accompanies the outer gate closing, I immediately regret my current physical and mental state. Blesk is in that car. She's been to see Erik. I feel sick.

Thankfully, my father and Cassidy have more productive things to do at 2:00 p.m. on a Sunday than witness my impending emotional breakdown.

The car pulls up and parks in the drop off circle. I pretend to swing casually on the wicker chair at the house's entrance. But my expression is too firm. My molars grind together within my caged jaw. Between my heaving chest, my fisting hands, and my neck which is begging me to crack it, I can't possibly concentrate on suppressing my aggravated expression.

Fuck, look at her dress...

I want to snap out of this mood. I want to because she is getting out of the car, wearing that sundress with her legs exposed and her golden hair over each shoulder. But of course, I had to use my personal choice of crutch and now I'm fucking wasted. I want her to see me smiling and charming.

I hate Erik.

Elise jumps out and meets Blesk by the passenger door, cuddles her, whispers in her ear, and then walks with her hand-in-hand towards me.

So I'm the fucking enemy? Blesk needs an escort to approach me because I can't be trusted or my reaction could be unpredictable? I stand, make the briefest of eye contact with Blesk, and strut through the doors. My feet take me away from her as fast as possible, not because I'm mad at her, but because I actually *can't* trust myself. I *am* unpredictable right now. Damn Elise for knowing that. I want more than anything to hold Blesk, to smell her.

I freeze.

Go to sleep, Konnor.

You're fucking dirt-drunk.

I still in the hallway, listening for the front door to click closed and their feet to shuffle towards me. I spin around and look at her. Her big, brown Bambi eyes blink hesitantly at me. I want to hold her in my arms, feel our hearts beating together. I want to kiss and lick and taste her to remind her who I am.

Elise releases her hand and walks up the staircase quietly. Bowing her head, Blesk walks straight into me. My arms sweep open seconds before I realise she's moving into my embrace. Then she's gripping me tightly, fisting my shirt behind my back and panting into my chest, expelling every ounce of emotional strength she holds. Blesk begins to sob as I wrap my arms around her shoulders and head, enclosing her within me.

"Konnor," she sniffles. When I hear that sweet voice, my arms tighten further around her, twitching with the need to protect her and clutching with the need to keep her. Lowering my head, I nuzzle her golden hair and breathe in her perfect scent.

Fuck, I'm an idiot.

"God." I find her upper arms and clasp them with my fingers before pushing her away so I can study her face. My shoulders drop when I see it, when I see her sad little face.

"Baby, fuck." I shake my head, not wanting to ask the question as I'm already anticipating my revulsion to the answer. I work up the courage to say it. "What happened?" She leans back into me, and I can feel her nails on my back through the fabric of my shirt.

Sniffling and tilting her head just enough to talk, she murmurs, "I love you, Konnor. I hope you know that."

Something in me breaks. I feel my insides twist. "What happened?" I repeat, monotone.

She isn't saying goodbye, Konnor.

She isn't.

Her eyes drop. "Let's sit down."

Fuck.

I won't survive losing her.

Again...

What is it?

He's convinced her to tell the cops?

She's leaving me for him?

Defeat and self-loathing crawl into my veins, wheeling and dealing irrationality.

Taking my hand, she drags me along behind her as she enters the living room and sits down on the couch. She motions for me to sit, then crosses her impeccable thighs over each other and entwines her fingers around one knee.

She leans forward as I half-stumble towards the couch opposite her.

She blinks at me. "How much have you had to drink?"

I scoff, rubbing my forehead and temple with my fingers therapeutically. "Not enough for this talk, Duch." A strained chuckle escapes me.

I drop down onto the cushions and fold my arms over my chest defensively, defending my soon-to-be broken heart. Desperation sits heavily in my bones, weighing me down.

She flutters her lashes at me. "You look mad."

Shrugging, I say, "Mm, not mad."

Her eyebrows rise practically to her hairline. "Okay, that was convincing."

"Sorry," I say sarcastically.

Stop it, Konnor. Drunk dickhead.

"Do you really want to know what happened?" she asks, brushing a strand of hair away from her cheek and tucking it behind her ear. Her eyes are so full of sadness.

"Yup, shoot," I state, feigning nonchalance.

She reluctantly begins to talk. "Let me finish everything before you react, okay?" She takes a deep breath. "When I got to the hospital with Elise, we got some coffee from the vending machine and had a chat because I was nervous. I don't want you to think this was easy for me because it wasn't. It was horrible and I felt sick the whole time. When I approached his room and heard his voice, everything inside me froze, then recoiled. I wanted to turn and run away. I didn't want to be there. I heard the same two sentences over and over again in my head: 'I'm the only person who has been inside you, right? I need to make you feel this again'."

My molars slam together. "Stop." I fly up, thrusting my hands through my hair, before kicking my dad's ottoman over. "Did he fucking say that shit to you?"

"Sorry, Konnor. I'm just trying to tell you how I felt," she says, peering up at me as I pace the living room.

I grimace. "Can you save me those kinda fuckin' deets, Duch?"

"Yes, sorry. Sorry." She shakes her head as if she should have known not to say that.

The thought of him saying those thing to her coils hatred around my very existence.

Slumping back onto the sofa, I try to moderate my angry breathing. "Continue."

"I went into the room. When he saw me, I could tell immediately that he remembered everything he did. He sat up straight away and the look in his eyes killed me. He knows, Konnor. The shame and guilt were so obvious. I moved to sit beside him, shuffling awkwardly and avoiding his eyes. He reached out and touched my hand. My heart jumped into my throat. When I retracted my hand, he winced. We must have sat in silence for at least twenty minutes."

"Where was Elise?" I ask rigidly.

"Watching from the doorway. We sat without talking for ages. He could barely open his mouth due to the wiring. Then he spoke. His voice was gravelly and strained and not him. He said, 'Is there anything I can say that will bring you back to me?' I shook my head. He said, 'Are you with *him* now?' I sighed, and it felt really good to answer. I said, 'Yes.' When I said, '*Yes*'... I was smiling. He said, 'I promise I'll do anything to earn back your trust, anything. Just name it.' I started to cry and said, 'Promise?' He said, 'Yes, anything. I promise, Bebe.' So, I said, 'Don't call me, don't try to see me, and if you do see me, walk the other way.' Then I left."

My heart throbs in my chest, contracting with relief. "So you're not leaving me then?" I keep my eyes anchored on the unmoving ground because focusing on her features is too difficult.

I need to lie down.

She moves in beside me and puts her hand on my knee. "Did you really think that that was a possibility?"

I gulp and turn my attention to her, dazed and sheepish. "After the way I acted? Yes, Duch, I did."

She kisses my cheek. "Leaving you will never be a possibility."

BLESK SITS with her back flush against my headboard as I lay curled half-conscious in a drunken foetal position between her thighs on the mattress. I spoon her leg. Her loving caresses satiate my senses. She gently brushes my hair from my face. My eyes are shut, but my mind is taking in this moment's perfection.

The deluxe version of perfect.

I'm going to feel like shit for the rest of the day... and most of tomorrow.

Why does she put up with this?

Why does she put up with me?

She's wearing a dress. A tiny white sundress, and it's driving me crazy. Her fingers continue to comb my hair and cheeks, tickling my neck and shoulders. Her thigh makes for a supreme pillow.

My hands tighten around her knee before running up her thigh. One feeds under her backside while the other ends up between her legs. A small surprised gasp escapes her. I bite my lip, groaning when I feel the heat between her legs. My thumb rubs her through her knickers, circling and kneading. She hums. I stare up at her and watch as my fingers make her come completely undone —eyes closed, breathing deeply, arching into my palm.

Grabbing her thighs, I drag her down the bed until her head hits the mattress. A gorgeous little whimper breaks her lips and her eyes widen with excitement.

Make that sound again.

I lie down between her legs, using my hips to encourage her thighs to part further. My breathing becomes laboured, strained and fast.

I want to be inside her —now.

My hand caresses her neck, goes up to her cheek, and into her hair. My other hand moves down to unbutton my jeans and release some of the pressure caused by my swelling erection. I shuffle my pants down and kick them off the bed. She peers up with those nervous big brown eyes, wanting me to take her. I can tell.

Be gentle with her.

"Blesk," I almost plead.

Her fingers stroke the contours of my back. "Konnor, make love to me."

At the words, I let out a long groan. My cock pulses, beating against my stomach.

My breath hurdles out of me. "Ask me again."

She smiles. "Make love to me," she purrs.

Best. Sentence. Ever.

When I feel her thighs tighen around my hips, I grind

against her, moaning deeply at the base of my throat. "Ask him," I tease, peering down between our bodies.

She giggles and looks down at my cock. "Make love to me," she says playfully.

I touch the delicate decorations on her dress. "He wants to know if we can keep this pretty thing on."

She smiles. "Yes."

Making a quick job of kneeling and yanking her knickers off, I hear myself almost grunting with need. She responds immediately, arching to help me pull them from her ankles with ease.

Moving back up, I nuzzle her neck, claiming that soft skin with my mouth. She moans as I reach down to grip her spectacular arse. Slowly, I push inside her.

———

AFTER WORKING off my alcohol on top of Blesk, taking a long hot shower, and downing two Panadol, I actually feel half-human again.

"We need to look in that envelope, Konnor," she states as I walk out of the bathroom.

"Or we could just have sex again?" I suggest, nodding.

She talks through an adorable grin. "At some point we have to drive back to campus."

"Or we could just take the year off and stay in bed."

"Seriously, Konnor."

"I am being serious," I say, walking over to her and grabbing her perfect arse cheeks. I pull her into me, kneading her slightly against my groin. "Do I feel like I'm joking?"

She rests her forearms on my shoulder and peers up at me, tickling my neck with her long fingernails. I grin down at her. I love the way her nails feel running through my hair.

Goose bumps lace every inch of my skin. I shiver and keep rubbing her back, kneading her bum into my cock and feeling her shapely figure beneath my fingers.

My God, she does things to me.

She allows me the pleasure of putting my hands on her most prized possession, her most personal aspect of living. When I kiss her neck, I can feel her heartbeat vibrating through her artery. I can taste her skin and sweat when I lick her. She allows me this honour. I will never take it for granted. I will never stop touching her. For as long as she lets me, my hands will be on her.

She arches her neck up and raises her brows at me, her expression displaying a level of severity I don't often see on her.

I roll my eyes. "Okay, Duch, let's open the envelope."

WHILE SHE SITS on the floor below me, perusing and analysing various documents, I actively ignore them. And fail. Bank statements. Photos. News articles from when I was taken. A deed to Knight Estate. A collection of paper-based trophies that arsehole kept. I have no interest in them.

Or do I?

This is probably my innate self-preservation technique brought about by this potentially life-changing situation. All I'm focusing on is her mouth and the way she licks her finger before she turns each page. Part of me is praying there is a lack of revealing information in amongst that pile. I'm happy. There is nothing in there that could improve my life. I have everything I need right here... licking her finger.

Sitting up, I say. "My biological mother died, as you probably know. She'd died a few years after I was taken. My biological father thought it'd would be best if I got a fresh start. He didn't want me to go through life experiencing nothing but pity and having people treat me as if I was broken or damaged. So he never came to collect me. Instead, he put me up for adoption." I exhale loudly and admit, "At least that's what they told me."

"You've never met him... Never wanted to?"

"Nope."

"Why? Did the adoption upset you?" she asks with an exact level of pity that makes my biological dad's decision justifiable.

"No. I had very little memory of him anyway, same with my bio-mum, so a clean slate seemed fine. To be honest, from the moment I got free, the only person I wanted to see, the only person I wanted to be with, was you."

Reaching out, she rubs my knee. "Tabula rasa."

I blink at her questioningly before chuckling. "Harry Potter spell?"

She giggles. "It's Latin. It means 'scraped tablet', but usually gets translated into 'blank slate'. I guess we both received a *tabula rasa*, in a way. I feel our personal circumstances are more akin to the 'scraped tablet' translation though. I mean, it wasn't blank, it was scraped."

"Such a smart cookie, Duch. Maybe that'll be my first tat." I laugh.

She glares at me. "Don't you dare mark that beautiful skin."

I slap my knee theatrically before saying, "Oh man, but all the other kids'll tease me."

Rolling her eyes and ignoring my comment, she picks up an old candid image and taps on a young woman. "Who is this? She has your eyes, Konnor."

I blink at it for a while, strangely apathetic. "I have hers. That's my bio-mum when she was in high school."

She offers me a smile. "She's beautiful, Konnor."

I nod but remain aloof. "I suppose she was."

"Do you know these other people?" she asks, running her finger over their faces.

I stare at it for a while. "That's Dad, Ben. I don't recognise the others. They all went to school together."

She lifts a blonde brow. "Coincidence?"

I shrug, dubious. "It's the District, Duch. Everyone knows everyone. There are like four degrees of separation here."

"Less, I suppose, when they were growing up," she says, flicking through pages, seemingly unimpressed with the spread on the floor in front of her. Her brows tighten and her shoulders drop on a sigh. "This is just useless stuff, all articles we could have found online." She stays seated and squashes her nose up at me, pouting. "Did Ben ever tell you why he adopted you?"

Nodding, I shuffle back along the mattress and cross my legs in front of me.

"Yes, my bio-mum and Ben were close in high school, so when the cops found me, he did everything in his power to get me. He knew my story, and I think he loved my bio mum. I think he loved her a lot. He wanted to make sure my future would be better than my past. I guess he didn't want to leave it up to chance. He has always been quite forthright with me about it."

She tilts her head at me. "What makes you say he loved your bio-mum?"

I shrug and chew on the inside of my mouth, contemplating. "Sometimes he looks at me with this weird expression. Then he sighs and tells me how much I look like her. I don't really know, it's just a feeling I get. Like I should be comforting him or something. It's hard to explain."

"It's plain to see he loves you, Konnor. You're his son in every way but blood. My parents always wanted a girl, and apparently, when my mum saw me, she fell in love with me. What's your adoptive mum like?"

"You'll meet her soon. You can decide for yourself."

"Come on, Konnor," she pleads, peering up at me with those big doe eyes.

"Okay, Duch. We are doing some touchy-feely stuff, hey? Not really the touchy-feely stuff I had in mind, but I'll oblige." I chuckle. "Well... Mum is awesome. She's a little like Cassidy. A bit eccentric. A little weird. She —" My words get caught dead in my larynx when something catches my eye. The air seems to thicken.

Jumping off the bed, I reach for a bank statement with a $5,100,000 deposit listed on it. "That's a hefty transaction," I murmur under my breath. I check the sender's account: Lumad LTD.

My breath catches.

Why do I recognise that account?

I glance at the name displayed on the top of the sheet: Donavon Knight. I check the date of the deposit: August 22, 1999. Blesk follows my line of sight and then glances between the statement and my tight expression. My brain is in overdrive, calculating. I can feel my face harden, my brows draw together.

"What is it?" she asks, looking anxious.

I shake my head because what I'm looking at must be a typo.

"What is it, Konnor?" she says again, her voice hiking up and down with nerves.

I motion with my hand. "Give me that news article, the one from when I went missing."

She picks it up and hands it to me. I check the date. August 22, 1999. My fingers feel numb as they hold this weightless document, which seems impossibly heavy. I jump up and grab my phone, dialling so fast that I type the wrong number twice. "Dammit!" I grunt, smacking the phone on the wall because it feels good to do so. I begin to type again, then wait for the tone to drop.

"Adolf!" I say through the handset. "Konnor Slater."

"Mr Slater, is everything alright? How can I be of service?"

"I need you to go into my apartment. Go into the top drawer of my bedside table and take a photo of the invoice in there with your phone. Then send it to me." I clutch the phone so tightly that my palms start to lose all colour and sensitivity.

There is an uncomfortable pause.

"Sir, what's this about?" he enquires, his tone wary.

"Adolf, I'm sorry to ask this of you, but I need you to do this. I'm in Brussman and I won't be home 'til later tonight. I need to see that invoice."

He clears his throat. "Of course, sir. I will go up right now."

"Thank you." I hang up rather abruptly. I turn to look at Blesk, whose face is ashen with worry.

"Konnor?" she says while on the brink of tears.

"Give me one second, Duch. I'll explain everything in a second, okay?"

I walk out of the room and down the staircase. Walking straight to the bar, I pour myself a much-needed bourbon. My hands shake wildly, chinking the ice around the glass. I take a sip. It really doesn't suffice, so I throw the whole thing back.

I pour myself another.

I wait.

And then my phone buzzes in my pocket. Without considering the possible ramifications of the information I'm about to discover, I open the phone and view the new multimedia message from Adolf.

My body turns to stone when I see the document that confirms my fears.

It's all a lie.

Everything I believed in. Everything I built for myself on this foundation of family —Cassidy, Flick, Ben, Renee, the Slater family... it's all a lie. I run up the staircase two steps at a time.

"Duch! This account." I rush through the door and sit beside her on the floor. "This account, Lumad LTD, it's the same account that paid my tuition this year. It's the same account that I saw on a sponsorship invoice for the new sporting precinct. Adolf just sent me a picture of it. It's the same account. It's the same *fucking* account, Duch!" My voice is panicked, the words hurtling from my mouth too fast to allow for adequate air intake.

She exhales in a rush. "Okay. Slow down. What does that mean?"

"The same person who transferred Donavon Knight over $5,000,000 on August 22, 1999 —the same day I was taken —also paid my tuition this year."

"What are you saying?"

"Ben and Renee Slater paid your father to take me."

thirty: deakon

Deakon

"DEAKON? My name is Ben Slater. I'm a friend. Do you mind if I sit with you?"

A gentle-looking man approaches and stands by the boy's side, a half-smile tight on his lips.

The boy has gotten more attention than ever before. The people at the hospital are always checking him, testing him, and putting him in machines that beep and clank. They stab him with needles, take blood from him, and add fluids. They are helping.

Go away, the boy thinks to himself.

The boy gave up on caring and hoping a few days ago. But unlike before, he now knows when the days pass because he stares at the ticking hand as it slowly circles the clock face.

Just go away.

One of the men yesterday, when the big hand was on the two and the little on the five, called him *hostile*. He doesn't even know what that means.

He just wants to be left alone. There is this weight in his belly that won't go away, and he feels full and nauseated and yet empty at the same time. The boy scowls.

They said they'd protect her.

Turning his stare to the window, he watches the outside world. The same world he is both desperate and terrified to see. He loves looking at the sky. He hasn't stopped since the nurse opened the window when the big hand was on the ten and the little was on the seven.

The man takes a seat on the visitor's chair and shuffles to make himself comfortable. The boy has watched that spot for days. It's always been empty —until now.

"You have very green eyes, Deakon," the man says, then coughs awkwardly. "You know what, Deakon? I'm not sure what you remember, but if you want to talk... If you want to talk about it, well, you can talk to me. It's what I do." He chuckles and the boy flashes a quick look at him. "I have two little girls. They both talk my ears off. I'm an excellent listener."

The man waits patiently while the boy scowls at the sky, his little face cold, his thoughts wrestling with one another, wanting company, but hating the kind he has recently received. *Adults lie,* he thought to himself. *They are all liars.*

The man starts to talk again. "The nurse told me that you haven't spoken to anyone since yesterday. Is that true?" He waits for an answer but knows he won't receive one. "Well that's okay. Like I said, I have two little girls that do plenty of talking. Felicity is only a few years older than you; she is eleven. Cassidy is only five and she's here today. Would you like to meet her?"

The man watches the boy's face intently. The boy tries hard not to look intrigued by his offer.

I would like to meet them.

Kids don't lie.

Even when it's hard.

Even when it hurts.

The boy's eyes move to the man, no longer keeping his interest a secret. Liz was four when he met her. He can count to five, so he understands that is nearly half his age. He misses her. The boy nods, just once.

The man smiles. "Okay, but first, can you do me a favour? Cassidy is still very little; she needs someone to look after her. Do you think that while I go grab a coffee, you could watch over her?"

A flutter of excitement fills his chest. The allure of importance causes him to nod again, but he still doesn't smile.

The older man, who the boy doesn't hate as much as the others, stands and says, "I will get her."

Once the man is outside, the boy jolts up to peer through the open doorway. A few short moments pass before the man walks back in, tailed by a small blonde girl.

The boy sucks a quick breath in.

She is smaller than Liz.

Blonde hair like Liz.

I like her.

The girl grins, showing her gapped teeth, bright and white. Her cheeks are rosy and full of character. The boy's eyes widen when she rushes over to him, crawls onto his bed, and wriggles over to his side. Curling her knees up, she rests her head on the pillow they now share.

The boy stares at her hazel eyes, which are filled with laughter and courage and confidence. He wishes he'd seen that look on Liz. The girl's knee presses against the boy's, and he wants to move away, but doesn't. The girl giggles.

The boy turns to look at the man. He tilts his head when he notices the man staring back with a strange expression. That is when the boy realises he is smiling. He is smiling at the little girl.

"I've always wanted a brava," the little girl says.

I like her.

thirty-one: blesk

Blesk

THERE HAVE BEEN DEFINING moments with Konnor that will stay with me forever, despite the blessing and curse of time and how it can conveniently dwindle significant memories from my mind. I definitely won't forget the chilling expression on his face when he said, "Ben and Renee Slater paid your father to take me."

He's seething. His cheek muscles dance under his skin as he rushes up the staircase towards his dad's room. His fists pump at his side. His whole back is almost out-of-worldly rigid. As his feet take him as fast as possible to the top floor, the thundering of his heels is inundating.

I chase after him. "Konnor, wait!"

I feel like I'm going to break from his pain. His whole world is crumbling... again. I barely notice how much I'm crying or how wet my face is as I follow him to the top floor.

He swings open a door, walks straight up to a wide-eyed, startled Ben, and slams the bank statement down onto his desk.

"Fucking explain that!" he growls lividly.

What happens if Ben did pay off my father? Shouldn't we be calling the police, preparing for some kind of retaliation to the truth being unveiled?

Ben stands. "Son, what is going on here?"

"Don't fucking call me 'son'." Sneering, Konnor flings his arms around. "Why have you been lying to me?"

Ben looks at my alarmed face and then back at Konnor, who seems to have grown taller somehow, his anger manifesting itself into his physical presence.

"Explain!" Konnor yells, pointing at the statement. He starts to pace, unable to keep still. He prowls the room, scowling at Ben as if he were prey. Every little noise, every little creak from the air escaping the wood beneath his feet, every little flap from the document seems to be heightened. He is on the edge of a complete mental breakdown. His eyes are barely slits. I have never seen him look less like himself.

I soften my stance. "Konnor, ple—"

He spins to face me. Clutching my shoulders, he stares down at me. "Duch, if you need to leave, leave now... there is nothing left to restrain me." The broken boy looking back at me chips at a piece of my heart. He releases me and turns back to his dad. "Answers, now!"

My heart races.

Ben pulls his glasses up his nose, looking fretful and disorientated. He takes his eyes off Konnor and peers down at the statement that is now in his hands. He mouths silently while he reads until something transforms his face.

Realisation?

Devastation?

Perhaps both...

He closes his eyes and grips the paper, crinkling and ripping the parts enclosed in his fist. As his knuckles turn white, he groans under his breath. "Nerrock."

The negative energy pouring off Konnor is tangible. Ben's eyes fly open and find me, caution flashing within them. He doesn't know my involvement in all of this. More than likely, he has been keeping this secret from everyone. For how long?

"Blesk, you shouldn't be here for this," he states curtly.

Every part of me but one wants to run, to flee like I always do. But my heart and love for Konnor keeps me rooted to the spot.

Konnor jolts towards Ben warningly, pointing at his chest. "Don't talk to her. Don't you dare even look at her. She stays as long as she wants!"

He glowers at Konnor. "You want her to know everything then?"

"She knows more than you do!" Konnor hisses.

Ben's eyes dart hesitantly between us. "Fine. Everyone sit and I'll explain."

Konnor huffs. "You don't get to make demands now. Tell me why you have been lying to me. Tell me what that means." Konnor motions towards the document laying on the expensive jarrah office desk.

Someone puts their hand on my back, causing me to jump. I cover my face. Everything is so intense right now, making me fear for everyone involved. I feel like, at any moment, I may need to rush over and pry Konnor off his own father.

The person behind me wraps their arms around my shoulders protectively. Peering down, I notice blonde hair on the man's forearms, confirming it's Jaxon. Although, I already assumed it was.

"Everything okay in here?" I hear Jaxon ask sternly. "Should I take Blesk away?"

Konnor turns towards us. "No, Jax, she should stay. I want her to stay." He looks at me, or rather, the person wearing Konnor's face looks at me. "Do you want to stay?"

I want to suck it up.

Be strong for Konnor.

I nod. "Yes."

"Mind if I stay?" Jaxon asks, taking a seat and positioning himself in a manner that presents his question as more of a statement.

If things get out of control, I know I can count on Jaxon to step in. He pulls me down onto his lap and holds me there as I cry quietly. Konnor eyeballs us momentarily and then nods.

Jaxon strokes my shoulders with both hands, subtly trying to soothe me. "You okay, B?"

"Yeah, it just hurts seeing Konnor so lost," I murmur. "Where's Elise?"

"She sent me up to check on you," he whispers in my hair. "She doesn't want to intrude." Konnor eyes us while we covertly talk to each other.

Ben rubs his hands together. Placing both palms on the desk in front of him, he stabilises himself. "Konnor, what do you remember about why Dustin Nerrock gave you up for adoption?" he asks cautiously.

Konnor scoffs and scowls as he turns to look at Ben. "I have a better idea. Why don't you just talk. Tell me what I know or what I don't." There is not even a glimpse of warmth in Konnor's voice or eyes. I hear someone suck a sharp breath in behind me. Konnor's face crumbles when he turns and sees who it is.

"What's going on?" Cassidy asks from the doorway. "Why are you yelling at each other?"

Konnor walks up to his sister. "You should leave, Cass."

Ben stands and quickly approaches his daughter, causing Konnor to noticeably stiffen.

"Cassidy, sweetheart, this is Konnor's business," Ben presses. "It isn't something you need to be involved in."

As her narrowed eyes focus on Ben, a lethal expression transforms her face. "If it's his business, then it's mine."

"Sweetheart, it's—" Ben begins.

"No," she snaps. "I'm not leaving until I know why my two favourite people are yelling at each other." She turns back to meet Ben's anxious face. The severity in her eyes is not to be ignored. Ben nods and then moves back to his desk, almost falling onto his chair. He looks like a man whose whole world has just permanently shifted off its axis. He looks the epitome of destroyed.

Cassidy crosses her arms and leans on the door frame, challenging Konnor to object with her uncompromising stare.

Konnor tilts his head. I see the slightest smile creep onto his face. "Fine, Cassidy."

Ben clears his throat, and we all acknowledge that as an attempt to gain our attention.

"So you don't want me to ask questions, Konnor. That's fine. But then I can't distinguish what information you have, and so I'm going to just lay it all on the table, and between the two of us we can sift through the pieces and hopefully come out with a puzzle that looks like a picture. I went to school with your mother, Madeline. I'm yet to meet a woman who could summon the kind of infatuation that woman could. She was wild and intriguing and sharp as a razor, with the biggest green eyes and a strange mind. But she was also very insecure and often troubled. She thought too much, and that always led her to the horizon, looking for something more." He looks down at his desk, moving the paper under his fingers.

"She married Nerrock not long after high school. They had a son." Ben's brows furrow. "They looked beautiful together and their son was picture perfect. It wasn't until later that these rumours started to circulate. You all know what the District is like with gossip. Well, the rumour was that Deakon Nerrock ..." His voice falters and he peers over at Konnor. "That *you* weren't Dustin's son.

"Now, Dustin's family has a lot of money. They are one of the founders of the District and are deeply rooted in Catholicism. Adultery was completely reprehensible. People loved the rumour. I mean, Dustin and Madeline were political celebrities and the envy of everyone. Their love, life, and every moment was caught on camera and plastered all over the District. Which made what had happened even more impressive. Because, Christ, the whole world had been watching them. And yet, this had happened right under everyone's noses. You were taken. Missing."

Konnor leans against the wall. The aggression has left him. Without the adrenaline that made him a giant, he is now rendered to a shell. He takes a fist and places his other hand on top of it, cracking his knuckles. I don't know how to help him.

But I can try...

I wander over and slouch against the wall beside him. Tilting my head, I look at his sad profile. He turns to me and I see *defeat*.

Ben continues, "I'd be lying if I said I liked Dustin, but I never thought he'd go so far as to have a child kidnapped. I thought he might, well ... I worried about your mother's safety, but not yours. You were just a child. Who would hurt a child? Especially not you, the golden child of the District."

He shakes his head. "I hadn't realised how far he'd gone until now."

My chest flutters, feeling lighter than it should. Ben looks distressed, and his face twists with anguish before he speaks again. "I don't know for sure, Konnor. I have no proof. But if this statement is true, then someone paid that man to take you."

A small gasp escapes Cassidy.

"And I know in my heart that it wasn't Madeline, so that leaves ... Well, it's Dustin and Madeline's account."

"That's bullshit, such bullshit. Money came from that fucking account for my tuition! How's that possible? Answer that question!" Konnor presses his forehead against the wall and groans. "I saw it, Ben," he says to the plasterboard. "The invoice was clearly made out to the university for my tuition."

"Konnor, your mother had handed the rights to that account over to me a few weeks before she died. She'd said it was for you and you alone if you were ever found or ever returned. That money would have gone to Dustin's other children, his future children, and she knew she didn't have much time left. So I have been using the funds for your tuition and for anything else I see fit. We didn't need the money, of course, but it was important to Madeline that it go to you."

"You loved her," Konnor states, turning towards us and fixing his emerald eyes on us all. He presses our shoulders together before whispering to me, "I just need to feel you next to me."

I lean more of my body weight on him.

Ben peers at Cassidy hesitantly. "I love your mum, Cassidy, but, yes, Konnor, Madeline was my *first* love."

Konnor considers this information for several seconds,

hope flashing in his eyes. "Okay, so are you my dad? I mean are you my *biological dad?*"

Disappointment washes over Ben's face as he regretfully shakes his head. "No, Konnor. I wish I was. You're my son, but you're not my blood. I'm sorry. I don't know who is. She never told me."

That fleeting sparkle leaves Konnor's face and he breathes out. "So you two had planned my adoption? Before they even found me? That's such crap."

Cassidy shakes her head adamantly. "That makes *zero* sense. This sounds like fricking B.S, Dad. When kids go missing and they aren't found for *four fricking years*, don't people just, kind of-" She looks around apologetically. "Assume they're dead?"

"Madeline had never given up hope, not for a second. I don't know if she'd suspected foul play because she never told me. We very rarely spoke, Konnor. We never discussed the adoption. I received a letter in the mail one day, and it just said that I was entrusted to make sure you'd receive the money if you were found or that it went to her charity if you weren't." His eyes drop to the desk. An unmistakable sadness flashes across his face. "It was from a lawyer. She hadn't even sent it herself."

Then the look is gone, and he's back to staring at Konnor.

"I'm not sure if you have heard about this, but Madeline started a charity for you. Nerrock Missing and Beyond. It is for lost children and their families. This is *your* legacy, Konnor. If you were never found. If you were just... *gone.* All the money would have been donated in your name. That was Madeline's wish. Well, that was what the letter said."

"You never tried to talk to her?" Konnor presses. "Face to face?"

"Of course I did," he states curtly.

I don't like his tone, but given the circumstances, I understand it.

Ben sighs. "I was completely disconnected from her. No one would let me speak to her."

"Did she know?" Konnor asks. "Did she know Dustin had something to do with my disappearance?"

Ben holds his hands up calmingly. "Slow down. Firstly, we don't know he did for sure. We are just speculating here and only because you came in here, guns blazing. But since we are, I can admit it crossed my mind. It was very peculiar that months after the rumours of your legitimacy as a Nerrock began, you went missing."

Konnor huffs disapprovingly. "She stayed with him anyway?"

"Even if she did suspect him, you don't divorce people like Dustin Nerrock. It's too... dangerous," Ben states, his tone strangely evasive.

I watch Cassidy as she absorbs this information. I get the feeling she won't take kindly to their dad lying to Konnor. Or lying to her. Our eyes meet momentarily. Then hers bounce back to Ben. I can't read her.

Konnor shrugs. "I don't understand."

Ben clasps his hands behind his head. The leather of the chair creaks beneath his shifting body. "I know you don't." He sighs. "Because I have worked very hard to keep you kids out of that world. The District's streets are run by The Families. The whole structure is corrupt. They are just dangerous company to keep, and even more so to marry into."

Jaxon's eyes widen. "So, what, like the mob?"

"Something like that," Ben admits cautiously.

"And Nerrock is involved?" I ask, glancing between Konnor and Ben.

"Well, he would deny it," Ben confirms. "They are just business men, Blesk."

Konnor takes a few methodical steps closer to Ben. His tone drops as he says, "Are you involved with them?"

Ben looks offended. "God, no!"

My breath catches. "Is my... I mean, the man who took Konnor, was he involved?" I ask, not really considering my question before the words escape my lips.

Breathe in and out.

"I don't know, Blesk," Ben replies, looking around the room and trying to reassure us with his calm expression.

"Whoa, this is a bit intense. Konnor, you're a mafia kid," Jaxon says in an almost naive awe.

"No, I'm not! I'm a Slater," Konnor states forcefully.

Cassidy steps forward and looks at their father, avoiding Konnor's eyes. "Is Butcher one of them?" she asks.

"Cassidy, why?" Konnor grumbles. "Why would it matter?"

Dodging Konnor's glare, she says, "Just wondering. Flick hangs out with them a lot now."

Konnor moves towards her until she has to arch her neck to catch his line of sight. "You're lying," he states, looking her straight in the eye. "Why do you care about The Butcher Boys? Why is that name even coming up?" Konnor's voice raises ever so slightly.

"They are our friends, Konnor. That's all," she assures.

His brows dart up. "Oh, so now they're *our* friends? Not just Flick's friends anymore?"

What's happening here?

"Konnor," I say, touching his hand, trying to pacify him.

"Son, what is your qualm with them?" Ben asks. "Do you know something I don't?"

His face tightens. "Don't like them, that's all. I don't want Cassidy hanging out with them."

Cassidy scoffs in frustration. "Well, I guess it's a good thing I'm not five anymore and can do what I fricking like."

"Cassidy, calm down," Ben states. "Your brother just worries."

"Great, now I have a restriction on friends."

"You're acting like a brat, Cassidy," Konnor snaps.

"I'm acting like an eighteen-year-old girl who is being interrogated by her brother because she has *boys* who are friends. Can you be more of a cliché? I bet you wish I were gay like Flick."

"Not boys, Cassidy. *Butcher* boys," Konnor states with disdain.

"We are digressing," Ben states. "These aren't conversations we should be having. Nor are they necessary. Luca Butcher's sons are not the issue here, and you're not in any kind of danger."

I peer at Konnor. His eyes bounce quickly to me and I can see the same thought in his eyes.

Then who tried to kill me in the hospital?

"This should go without saying," Ben continues, "but this is Konnor's business. None of this can leave this room." Ben darts his eyes between us, finally singling out Konnor. "Konnor, if you want to make arrangements to discuss this further with other parties, then you can, but it should be discussed here, with me first. I can't stress this enough. Everything I've done, all the truths I've withheld, have been for you. Promise me you won't go ruffling feathers. Okay?"

Konnor slowly nods. "Does Nerrock know? Does he know where I am?"

"Yes, of course," Ben says. "He knows who you are,

Konnor, and where you are. But you're not in any danger. It's over. You're mine. Trust me."

My stomach twists up. "How can you be so sure?"

"Trust me," he repeats.

Please, God, let him be telling the truth.

Ben rises to his feet and walks over to his son. "Do you? Do you trust me?" He places his hand on Konnor's shoulder and squeezes tenderly.

Squinting and tight-lipped, Konnor stares at his dad's hand. The wheels churn in his head; the seconds that pass are long and torturous for everyone, especially Ben.

Creases line Konnor's forehead as his brows lift and he exhales a strengthening breath. "I trust you, Dad."

My shoulders loosen and a smile plays on my face. If Konnor trusts him, then I do too.

The weight of their conversation sits heavily on Konnor's shoulders. He's about ready to collapse. I search Konnor's drained expression and there is something new in it. He's finished. With this conversation. With searching for answers. I think, he's content being a Slater. Happy, even. It was the possibility of losing that identity —another identity —that was simply unbearable for him.

Konnor, Jaxon and I leave Ben and Cassidy alone in the office and make our way downstairs. Jaxon retires quietly to his room. No words are exchanged between us because they are simply redundant at this point.

We crawl into his bed.

Facing each other, we fall asleep.

thirty-two: blesk

"I inhale courage and exhale fear."

Blesk

AFTER WE EAT breakfast on the veranda, we all decide it's time to leave the District and head back to campus. We spend the next four hours in the car, the streets of the District passing us by, and the darkness of what had happened there is left behind. The clean air that hits us when we leave the city is not only physically relieving, but emotionally too.

I feel lighter. Free. I'm not alone anymore. Konnor and I share this story and this life together. We may never uncover the truth about who tried to kill me in the hospital, but we have a support system around us now and I'm okay with leaving the darkness... in the dark. I know what we really need is peace and comfort in our togetherness.

No more searching.

Questioning.

Digging.

Elise smiles back at me from the front seat while Jaxon drives. Konnor reaches out and entwines our fingers, pulling them onto his lap. Gazing down at our hands, our fingers thread together, I feel a sense of unbelievable belonging. His palm is warm against mine. I lift my index finger up and his somehow meets mine. We press them together, accepting our past and promising each other a future.

He is both Deakon and Konnor.

I am both Liz and Blesk.

And we have already faced the hardest thing of all —*us*.

thirty-three: liz

Liz

SHE CAN HEAR PEOPLE SPEAKING. Even though she can't see their faces, she can tell they are concerned. The quiver in their voices, deep tones, and intermittent words reach her through her slumber. She is exhausted. The girl could sleep for a year and still feel the need for more. This is the first time she has allowed herself to become vulnerable and just...finally... relax. She feels safe. Safer than she may have ever felt before. She knows he is here with her, in this same hospital. She knows he is fine. The girl listens to footsteps approach and feels movement at her side. The mattress sinks. A warm hand touches hers. A gentle, feminine voice speaks.

"Oh, you've been through something haven't you, little girl?" The woman sighs softly. "I want you to know that you're safe now and that you can wake up. I know you're tired and hurting, but we need to know you're okay. Please, little one, it's time to wake up."

The hand moves to her forehead. The girl shivers beneath its tender caress. She wants to sleep for longer despite the pleading tone coming from the lady on her bed.

The girl wonders why she must wake up. She doesn't have anymore chores left to do or the boy to look after anymore. Can't she just sleep now?

She vaguely recalls the past five hours. She knows they escaped. The police had found him first. She knows because she watched from behind a tree as he panicked in their grasps.

Then her world went dark.

The next thing she remembers is the policeman scooping her up off the floor in her father's cupboard. She remembers the officer cradling her in his arms and how he held her with protective confidence. She remembers him laying her down and covering her up with a blanket.

She remembers the noise of the hospital and the feel of her bed moving under lights.

That is all she remembers.

Now she just wants to sleep next to the unfamiliar gentleness of this stranger.

"Okay, sweety, you sleep. I will be here when you wake up. You're such a brave girl, do you know that? You are safe now. We promise you're safe now. I hid your unicorn under your pillow for when you wake up."

My unicorn.

The mattress lifts as the woman moves. Then her footsteps disappear into the distance. The girl swallows hard. She doesn't usually mind being alone. She just really liked the warmth of that stranger.

She doesn't open her eyes yet, simply lies there in silence.

Footsteps approach her —faster, deeper, heavier steps.

"Get it over with," she hears a gruff voice say.

It all happens so quickly. A body is beside her. A pillow is pressed against her face. It is soft. Then it isn't. It is hard and unforgiving.

I can't breathe.

She tries to moan. Her eyes open, widen, but she only sees white cotton. Her hands fly up to scratch at the pressure. When that does nothing to relive it, she considers giving up. It's easier...

Something stops her from doing that: fear, adrenaline, anger ...

Kon.

She reaches behind her head and pulls out her unicorn. Slashing the air with it, she uses all her strength to fend off the pressure.

But she is too little, too weak.

The same voice snaps, "Hurry up!"

Relentlessly, she swings, gasping and groaning as she blinks puddles into the fabric over her eyes. She hits something, making it grunt. Pressure builds behind the pillow. She loses energy. Her arms fall, weightless.

And then there's no air.

THE END

epilogue

Blesk

"SO IT SAYS five to seven days, baby," I say, sitting on Konnor's bed with my legs crossed in front of me. He paces the room, a hand on either hip, his head shaking slowing with unease.

His brows weave. "What if I get aggressive and upset you?"

"I'll call Jaxon or Adolf," I confirm with an adamant nod. He's worried he may act out and ruin what we have, potentially changing my perspective of him. I'm not worried. My faith in his strength of character is completely irrevocable and infinite. I know it will be hard. I also know he can do it.

Konnor releases some anxiety by rubbing his palms down his face. "Yeah, but will you think different of me?"

"Konnor, nothing in this world would make me prouder

of you," I confess, watching his internal debate with sympathy.

He moves over to sit beside me and places his hand attentively on my naked thigh. "What if—"

"Stop what if-ing! You can do this," I state emphatically. "You can do anything."

He searches my expression, exhaling long and loudly. "Fine," he nods. "Read it to me again."

I read from my iPhone. "Stage one is anxiety, nausea, and abdominal pains."

He groans. "Can't wait for that magic."

"Stage two is high blood pressure, increased body temperature, and unusual heart rate."

"Yay!" he mocks.

I giggle and talk through a smile. "And stage three is hallucinations, fever, and agitation."

"Okay... well, we know I would do just about anything for you." His eyes roll over my face lovingly. "Scrap that. I would do anything for you."

I lean in and press my lips to his, humming through our quick chaste kiss. "All you have to do is show up and I'll be impressed. What we are doing now is for *you.*"

He beams at me, displaying those undeniable dimples. "I'm in."

I grin up at him, filled to the brim with pride. "I have all sorts of beverages in the fridge, as well as lollies, chocolate, and lots of greasy food for Justin."

His face tightens. "Who the fuck is Justin?"

I giggle. "Just-in case."

"Your puns are adorable. I thought I was about to have to kill some guy named Justin," he teases, walking over to the sink. His shoulders sag on a sigh as he unscrews the cap of the first bottle of bourbon. We both watch the rich brown liquid that has been Konnor's comfort for nearly half of his life, get poured down the drain. "Detox, here I come."

our thing - book one & two

Have you read Max and Cassidy's story?

Blurb:

Cassidy Slater wants two things in life.

The first is to be the youngest leading ballerina in her academy.
She will need unwavering dedication. No time for men.
Unfortunately, her heart didn't get the memo, because her second
secret want... is *Max Butcher*.

Max Butcher's scowl is notorious.

He has a dark intimidating presence, hinting at a life lived hard and fierce. He is the heir to an underground empire, and a man of few words, but his actions cut straight to the point.

To him, Cassidy is a silly little girl.

But one he can't keep his hands off.

Forced together, Cassidy will learn fast what it means to be wanted by a man like Max Butcher. And his world is going to intoxicate her. The ruthless bastards that he calls family—The Family—will want to use her, tutu and all.

But she is his now.

It's an eye for an eye where he comes from, and he's willing to blind the whole damn lot of them.

For her, he'll start a damn war.

Get book

the district - origin story

Jimmy Storm—1979
Controllare le strade; control della citta
(Control the streets; control the city.)

MY FATHER WAS a *ladder-man* in the late 1940s. In the old country—Sicily. He was the boy the Family trusted with their money, for he was the one with the clearest vantage point. The expression *ladder-man* had come about back in the early gambling days when young men would stand on ladders on the casino gaming floors, watching and waiting for misconduct.

My father was the most trusted and feared man in Sicily —a complete oxymoron, I know. But it all depended on who was doing the trusting and who was doing the fearing.

The Family paid him ninety lira an hour, which was good money back then, and so of course, the crooks of the club— the ones on the gaming floor pocketing chips, counting cards, and winning too much of the Family's money—found death quickly. There was very little chance for rebuttal once my father had them in his sights. He was an adolescent then and rather engrossed in the power bestowed upon him, as would any young man be with the strength of many at his beck and call.

Things were irrevocably simpler back then. If there was a misdemeanour, it was handled quickly, quietly, and strictly; very few people lived to talk about it. Which is how it should be.

According to gossip, my grandfather was a 'likable type' and had no knowledge of his son's activities. Luckily for us, my grandfather had died when my father was sixteen, leaving him without any relations. *Luckily?* Yes, because there is little I can learn from a 'likable type' of man.

After three years of being the boy up the ladder on the most notorious gaming floors in Sicily, my father became an orphan. And an orphan he was for exactly two days before the Family picked him up and officially made him their own. They bought my father. They owned him then. It wasn't until then that he really understood what he'd signed up for.

He had married the mob.

When you marry the mob, as when you marry a woman, you are contractually, spiritually, legally, and emotionally bound to them. The key difference being, there is no such thing as divorcees—only widowers. That is where it all had started—humble beginnings and a life of servitude to the Family.

When I was a young man, my ego was larger than Achilles', rivalling my father's in every way. It would be fair to say I flexed my muscles every chance I could—at the boys at school, at the people on the sidewalk offering me less than obedient glances... at everyone. I was a *sfacciato* little shit, and partly because of that cheekiness, I learned to thrive on the sensation people's submission gave me. I'd usually be hard as a rock beneath my trousers in the midst of a power play.

I am Jimmy Storm, son of Paul Storm, and my name is legendary. Storm is not our real name, of course. My father named himself when he became a made-man.

Half of Sicily owed the Family money, which meant we owned half of Sicily and her people. We managed people with ease, for their lives were worthless to us and priceless to them. I grew up around the cruellest, slyest, dirtiest bastards in the country and they set the benchmark for my behaviour as an adolescent; they were my idols.

When I turned twenty-seven, my *zu* Norris and I left Sicily, taking with us blessings and funds from the Family, with our sights set on a new place of profit. We flew to an area of Australia renowned for its wealthy residents—a secluded section on the coast consisting of four towns: Brussman, Connolly, Stormy River, and Moorup. I recently learnt of an Australian idiom for this kind of unmonitored and isolated area—'Bandit Country'.

I was out to prove myself at any cost.

Which brings me to today, and the reason I have my shoes pressed to a man's trachea.

"I am *Jimmy Storm!*" I state. The rubber of my heel presses very slowly on his windpipe, and when he tries to buck away, I know I have found the *puntu debole*. He tries desperately to claw at my foot, attempting to relieve some pressure. He can't, but that doesn't save my shoe from getting covered in fingerprints, and *that* is just so inconvenient.

My *zu* and I have been in this miserable part of the world for three god forsaken weeks and have found nothing short of disorganised, disrespectful, and inferior versions of la Cosa Nostra. The young man whose trachea I'm currently crushing is Dustin Nerrock, and he is 'the name' about these parts. A slightly hostile *parràmune* has taken place and I am simply establishing my dominance.

We'd met under casual terms, but this disrespectful man forgot his manners along the way. I've been told, 'What the Australian male lacks in brains, he makes up for in brawn' and I truly hope so. Since being here, we have found a lack of connections, a lack of muscle due to scope—all of Sicily is smaller than this area of Western Australia—and far too many new legalities to... manipulate without consultants to advise us. Despite my indelicate means of conversing, the end game is to get Dustin Nerrock and a few other big-name families in this area to work with us.

For us...

Dustin's father died last year, leaving him with businesses scattered throughout the area, but with no idea on how to utilise them. Money and dominance are the game. The man under my shoe has more money than sense, an ego that rivals my own, and a name people know. And soon, here, people will know mine.

"Do you have any idea who-" Dustin chokes, struggling to force words out while my boot is pressed to his throat.

Pity...

"*Oh scusari,*" I say, feigning concern. "Did you say something?" His face looks so feeble; I want to crush it 'til it goes away. Men who bow are ants, small and helpless, but infinitely useful when put to work. I've been told my temper is an issue. Apparently, it is obvious when I'm irate; I speak a mongrel version of Italian, Sicilian, and English, and my accent seems to thicken... *Personally, I don't hear it...*

"*Madonna Mia,* are you going to cry like a *paparédda,*

Dustin. You're the man about these parts. Stand up!" I yell, and then press my heel further into his jugular... so he can't. *"Alzarsi!* Stand up!" He can't. I won't let him, and the whole idea of that makes my dick twitch.

I find myself tiring of his weak attempts to fight me off. I remove my shoe from his neck, allowing him to gasp and drag some much-needed air into his lungs. And he does, sucking like a man possessed. His palms meet the pavement under the dimly lit street lights and I take a few steps back to allow him room to stand. His pushes off his hands and climbs to his feet, a scowl firmly set on his face. Dustin all but growls at me and then spits blood to the side, his body shuddering slightly while he regains air and stability.

I mock, "Are you okay, *paparédda?"*

"You're in deep shit," he hisses, coughing at the pavement.

The bitterness in the air is tangible, an entity apart. It is time to switch the play and lead the conversation in a more mutually beneficial direction. I've humiliated him, and now I shall woo him.

"Let's talk like gentlemen, Dustin," I begin, removing a handkerchief from my pocket and offering it to him as he coughs and clears his throat. "Please oblige me?" I wave the folded white material in front of him, a feigned gesture of a truce.

He takes it and uses it to wipe away the little pieces of gravel pressed to his cheek. "Talk..."

"Perhaps we can start again. *Se?"* This is my favourite part of conversing—switching the play, manipulating the conversation. "You know who I am now, and I know who you are. You also know what I do, *se?"*

He stares at me, his brows drawn together, his eyes narrowed. "Yes."

"Well," I say, clapping my hands and grinning widely at him. "That's an excellent start. May I recommend we take this little *parramune* to a more appropriate place? I know an establishment not too far from here... Will you join me for a drink? Put this *little* and unfortunate indiscretion behind us..."

IT DIDN'T TAKE LONG for me to gain Dustin Nerrock's favour. In fact, it took less time than I'd imagined. The man is hungry, power hungry. I recognise it in him. It is indeed a trait we share. After three hours with Dustin, I'm even more convinced that this area holds infinite possibilities. To start with, there is a high crime rate, which, of course, is a huge benefit to my cause as protection comes at a cost. There are strictly governed gun laws, which, of course, means demand, and I am happy to supply. There is a vast class division, which means two things: an opportunity to clean up the riffraff at a cost, and addicts—I love addicts.

My father once told me to never choose a side, but to rather find out their motivation(s) and make them beholden to you. 'Control the streets; control the city.' I share this philosophy with Dustin. The final and most tantalising piece of information is that this country is bursting at the seams with minerals and is far too big to secure thoroughly. There is gold, diamonds, and unsealed access roads.

"I have never met a rich man I didn't like," I declare, clinking Dustin's glass with mine.

A grin stretches across his face. The grin of a man whose eyes are suffused in dollar signs. "Well, that said, there are others we need in on this..."

"Yes." I raise the glass to my lips and the smoky whiskey

fumes float deliciously up my nostrils. "A man who my *Capo* told me about. *Big* pull in the old country." I use my hands to talk. My Sicilian mannerisms are hardwired. "*Big* pull. But he seems quite the enigma. I could not track him down. He has recently married some beauty queen from England and is probably just... How do you Australians say it? *Fucking* and *fucking*. No time for business when there is pussy. *Se?*" We both laugh and I play the game of equals; that is what I want him to believe. "So this man," I continue, "he is a half-Sicilian, half-Australian, mongrel. *But* the Family... They seem to love him. The name I was given was Paul Lucchese."

Dustin's gaze narrows, his amused expression slipping. "I know who you're talking about...We can't trust that bastard." And I'm immediately intrigued...

"He is very important to the Family." I feign a sigh, but I'm eager to meet the man who has inspired such a reaction. I have never liked 'likable people'; it is the unlikable ones I prefer. They have attitude and spirit. They make excellent soldiers.

Dustin seems to study my expression. "He will never agree."

"He will. I assure you—" My attention is redirected to a clearly inebriated character as he swipes a collection of glasses off the bar; the sound of them smashing rudely invades my senses. I tilt my head and watch from our booth as he begins to yell and threaten the bartender.

Well, this is a pity.

I was having such a peaceful drink, and I have my favourite shirt on. The inebriated man's grasp of the English language shocks me, and it makes me wonder whether it was his mother or father who has failed him so profoundly; perhaps both.

"Listen, 'ere," he starts, pointing a shaky finger at the bartender. "I ain't sellin' nufin. I'm just 'ere for a drink."

Interesting...

I shuffle from my seat and excuse myself politely. After walking slowly over to the man at the bar, I lean beside him and smile.

"Wah you want?" He lowers his voice. "I ain't sell nufin'." His mouth opens and expels words only vaguely fathomable. It is a damn pity about this shirt.

"Scusa." I motion across to my table. "I was drinking over there with a very important colleague of mine and you're making it rather hard to concentrate. May I suggest finding a different establishment, *se?"*

It has been a long time since a man dared strike me, and it is apparent why over the course of the next few seconds. He stumbles backwards and then jolts forward, throwing his fist into my face. The smell of his breath knocks me harder than his knuckles do. My cheek burns for a short moment.

I shrug apologetically to the wide-eyed bartender and jab the bastard beside me twice in the throat. *Jab. Jab.* His knees meet the floor with a thud. My knee rises to connect with his chin. *Crack.* A guttural groan curdles up his throat. My knee rises again. Another groan. The back of my hand collides with his cheek. How *irrispettoso.* I can't stand disrespect in any form. As I stare down at his swaying body, I notice a small stain on my shirt.

"*Madonna Mia. Fare le corna a qualcuno,*" I hiss at him. "Look what you did."

DUSTIN'S brawn most definitely comes in handy as we relocate my new friend to a more private locale—an old building Dustin inherited. He doesn't look quite as lively laying bound on the cold concrete floor. Although, my dick does like the bindings...

I can already tell that after this exchange, I'll be in dire need of a lady's company.

"Will you drag Mr...?" I stare questioningly at our bound captive.

"Get fucked ..." He chokes on his own words.

"Very well, will you drag Mr Get Fucked so he is sitting against that wall just there, *se?*" I smile calmly in my new partner's direction, pointing at the rear brick wall. "Thank you, Dustin."

This disused warehouse would make an excellent abattoir; perhaps I will recommend a new business endeavour to Dustin. I ponder this as I remove a few items from my bag and set them down on the wooden workbench behind me: a blade, a bottle of aqua, and a Luna Stick. Pouring a small amount of water onto my shirt, I gently wipe at the stain. The chill from the liquid sends shivers down my spine.

"Such a pity," I mutter to myself. When I tilt my head to watch Dustin manoeuvre our intoxicated captive to a more suitable position, I feel serenity wash over me. These are the moments where I truly shine. In the grit. When others usually waver, I am at my most contained. Perhaps, it also has to do with my new partner's eager and obedient behaviour; after all, I did nearly squash his throat into the pavement a mere few hours ago. A sly grin draws my lips out. Who said money can't buy happiness? Money can purchase the most loyal of comrades, and fear has no limit. Empires have been built on the foundations of both.

"I am Jimmy Storm. You know me?" I query, though I know the answer.

"No," our barely coherent friend snaps, pulling away from Dustin's grip.

"Well, this is Dustin Nerrock. You know him?" I ask, once again knowing the response. Our inebriated friend glances up at Dustin and nods, appearing to exhibit a suitable level of unease. "Well, now you know me too. Jimmy. Storm. I would like to know who you work for."

"I'm not fucki—"

"*A-ta-ta-ta.*" I wave my finger at his rude interruption. "Before you say no, we found ten grams of heroin on you. Now, don't lie to Jimmy. Tell me who in this town supplies you...And then I will give you an offer you can't refuse."

"I'm neva snitchin'. He'd fuckin' kill me."

"I see." I sigh and turn to my assortment of items. "I respect that." As I pick up the switch knife and feel the cold metal in my palm, I run my finger over the blade, the rigid edge grating my pad. The excitement of what's to follow forces blood directly to my groin and I find myself in a state of impatience, eager to show Dustin how I assure success.

I spin on my heels and walk directly to my captive. I lean down. The blade slices through his flesh like a zipper parting fabric. The knife ruptures the nerves within. The deed is done. His eyes widen and his hand grips his left wrist. Blood trickles through his fingers and drips onto the concrete.

"Shit," he cries. "Wha tha fuck? You said you respected tha."

"I do, very much," I state adamantly. "I hope you live. Loyalty is my favourite virtue."

"*Christ,*" Dustin mutters from behind me. *Yes,* this is how we interrogate in *my* Family.

"You will die from exsanguination within ten minutes." I squat at the man's side and grin, watching his face pale and his head bobble on his neck as nausea floods him. I have seen this look many times. "I am a spiritual man. You would not know, but I am a Catholic. And I could swear to Mother *Maria*..." I stare at him as he struggles to hold his head up, narrowing my eyes to better study his. "I could swear you can see death take a man. The seconds just before... in his eyes... you see death enter him."

Something akin to a whimper splutters from his throat and panicked tears burst from the corners of his shallow eyes. This poor underprivileged street rat will not be missed and without any evidence, his disappearance will be stamped as drug related. Which, in a way, it is. "Now, tell me where I can find your boss and I will help you live."

"What? How?" Dustin asks me.

I laugh from deep within my abdomen; I just can't help it. "I told you, I'm a spiritual man."

My weeping captive tries to speak, "He is... he owns..."

"Can you feel that chill?" I ask him, moving so close my lips brush the shell of his ear. "*He* is near, my friend."

"He owns Le Feir. The bakery." He passes out, seven minutes before closing time. The smell of his blood, metallic and tangy, hits my nose. It pools around his outstretched legs, creating small glistening puddles. *Yes,* I think to myself, *this warehouse would make an excellent abattoir.*

Deciding to keep my word, I stand and walk briskly over to the workbench, retrieve the Luna Caustic nitrate stick— one of my favourite tools. While I roll up my sleeves and wet the stick's tip, I think about what a real shame it is that my captive won't be conscious to feel the burn. I hear it is quite a unique sensation. My dick is throbbing like a stubbed toe below my zipper as I approach my captive and squat by his side. I begin to cauterise his slit wrist. The blood makes it rather difficult, however, not impossible, and I've had plenty of practise. "So young Dustin," I call over my shoulder, my eyes unwavering as I work. "We will pay Mr Le Feir a visit tomorrow, make a deal. We don't want any product besides ours hitting these streets. This is now our *quartier,* our *District.* Why is this?"

"Control the streets, control the city," he replies, his nerves stammering through his voice. A chuckle escapes me. I think I may have scared my new partner; how quaint. It appears Dustin Nerrock doesn't get his hands dirty; he must be a proficient delegator. But as my father once told me, 'It is the dirt that makes the man appreciate the sparkle'.

"More importantly than Mr Fier," I say, "is organising a meeting with the man my *Capo* spoke about...You know him. Where will we find him?"

I hear Dustin release an exaggerated breath. "He doesn't go by Paul Lucchese anymore. His name is Luca Butcher and he lives in Connolly."

nicci who?

I'm an Australian chick writing real love stories for dark souls.
Stalk me.
Meet other Butcher Boy lovers on Facebook. Join Harris's Harem of Dark Romance Lovers
Stalk us.

Don't like Facebook?
Join my newsletter

facebook.com/authornicciharris
amazon.com/author/nicciharris
bookbub.com/authors/nicci-harris
goodreads.com/nicciharris
instagram.com/author.nicciharris

Printed in Great Britain
by Amazon

49819371R00229